Praise for Diane

Lorna Mott Comes Home

"The divine Diane Johnson's latest propulsive novel . . . [is] a layered yet airy confection. . . . Johnson is a master plotter. . . . [An] entertaining story that is hard to put down." —*Air Mail*

"Inspired. . . . *Lorna Mott Comes Home* is a dishy drama with crystalline sentences . . . delicious." —*Shelf Awareness*

"Johnson has perfected the comedy of manners. . . . Her latest novel allows Johnson to play to her strengths." —Berkeleyside

"Johnson returns with undimmed joie de vivre to the delicious Francophile vein she mined so successfully in her National Book Award finalist *Le Divorce*. . . . Everything one looks forward to in Johnson's books is delivered in abundance here: nimble plotting, witty narration, edifying juxtaposition of French and American cultures. . . . Johnson shows us why she's been compared to writers like Henry James, Jane Austen, and Voltaire." —*Kirkus Reviews* (starred review)

"Delightfully absurd. . . . Incisive. . . . Johnson gently but deftly skewers everyone as they scheme for financial gain and languorously search for meaning and happiness." —*Booklist*

"Johnson makes a welcome return to her wheelhouse in this propulsive domestic dramedy of manners. . . . [Her] usual razor-sharp prose and astute observations are on full display. . . . Provocative . . . poignant. . . . [Johnson's] fans are in for a treat." —*Publishers Weekly* (starred review)

DIANE JOHNSON

Lorna Mott Comes Home

Diane Johnson is a bestselling author and three-time finalist for the National Book Award. She lives in Paris and San Francisco.

Lorna Mott Comes Home

LORNA MOTT COMES HOME

A Novel

Diane Johnson

VINTAGE BOOKS
A DIVISION OF PENGUIN RANDOM HOUSE LLC
NEW YORK

FIRST VINTAGE BOOKS EDITION 2022

The Library of Congress has cataloged the Knopf edition as follows:
Name: Johnson, Diane, author.
Title: Lorna Mott comes home : a novel / Diane Johnson.
Description: First edition. | New York : Alfred A. Knopf, 2021.
Identifiers: LCCN 2020013976 (print) | LCCN 2020013977 (ebook)
Classification: LCC PS3560.O3746 L67 2021 (print) | LCC PS3560.O3746 (ebook) |
DDC 813/.54—dc23
LC record available at https://lccn.loc.gov/2020013976
LC ebook record available at https://lccn.loc.gov/2020013977

Vintage Books Trade Paperback ISBN: 978-0-525-56265-8
eBook ISBN: 978-0-525-52109-9

Book design by Soonyoung Kwon

vintagebooks.com

Printed in the United States of America
10 9 8 7 6 5 4 3 2 1

To the memory of John Murray

Lorna Mott Comes Home

1

Sometimes the metaphorical significance of a random event startles with its application to your life.

Lorna Mott was thinking this when she asked Monsieur Jasse to stop his taxi so she could walk a little way along the road above the graveyard of Pont-les-Puits. The whole village was talking this morning about how, in the darkness during last night's heavy rains, the cemetery had dislodged itself and with the stealth of a nocturnal predator slid five hundred meters downhill, where the astonished citizens this morning had discovered a huge, sticky hillock of treacherous clay, burst coffins, broken stones, corpses, and bones. Only the oldest gravestones remained standing with unseeing dignity above the sacrilegious chaos.

It was Lorna's last day in Pont-les-Puits, and she would leave with this ominous sight in mind as a kind of cautionary reminder of consequences unforeseen. Her departure—escape, as she was thinking of it now—was both impulsive and planned. Once she was safely on the train to Lyon, she could admit that subconsciously she had been planning awhile for a future in California without her husband, Armand-Loup.

They needed some time apart, and things she'd been doing could be construed as unconscious strategies to accomplish this, for instance recently publishing her collected art lectures and accepting a lecture appearance in Bakersfield, California, where she was headed now.

Bakersfield was hardly at the level of places she'd lectured before her marriage, but going there was a toe in the water of her return to professional life. She had been thrilled with the invitation, out of the blue, from Bakersfield, and it had been the impetus she had needed to take up her professional life again, revive, expand. These were gestures toward autonomy, surely, even if she hadn't thought of them that way.

In these her middle years, as people called the late fifties, early sixties, she was too old to cry about leaving. Armand-Loup was her second husband; she had been through marital difficulties before—why did she feel so near to a well of sobs as she neared the station? There are times you feel you've made a mess of your life, that was the sum of it, the harder to bear when you think of yourself as a basically competent person, even an accomplished one. Two failed marriages, and so late in the day, argued the opposite: incompetence. But, she told herself, marriage does not define your life.

The first to discover the upended condition of the cemetery had been children crossing through it on their way to school. They had burst into the classrooms with excited descriptions: "*Squelettes!* Skeletons! Bones sticking up, I saw teeth . . ." Skeptical teachers had gone to look for themselves, then alerted the mayor and members of the city council. The children had not exaggerated: dozens if not hundreds of graves stirred together in the muddy batter as if at the last trumpet; the righteous and sinners alike had burst their tombs. Among the villagers who came along to look, though most were revolted, horrified, some believed it to be a sign of the truth of the Resurrection. Or maybe a curse on the village. The mayor and several members of the village council of Pont-les-Puits, a village in the French Drôme Provençale, were meeting to discuss which and what to do.

The two events—grisly mudslide and Lorna Dumas's departure— tended afterward to become linked in people's minds in a cause-and-effect way and became part of the mythology of the village. Lorna Mott Dumas throwing suitcases into a taxi and driving off, Monsieur Dumas just standing there bemused while other citizens started looking for the bones of their ancestors.

·   ·   ·

Monsieur Armand-Loup Dumas (not descended from the writer) was one of the council members summoned to discuss the cemetery problem. Some younger citizens of Pont-les-Puits might have dismissed him as a raddled, amiable old raconteur who hung around the bar-buffet in Hôtel La Périchole, but he was reputed to have once been a noted museum curator; he had views on most things and, occasionally, useful knowledge. You could see he had been handsome, but now he was also stout, and his curly black hair had receded and was gray at the sides.

It was to Monsieur Dumas people turned now. No one discounted his opinions—he had published a book on the philosopher Jürgen Habermas and other members of the Frankfurt School—though his anecdotes were sometimes doubted because of the name-dropping: How could someone from Pont-les-Puits have met Catherine Deneuve or Archbishop Tutu?

People had liked his American wife, Madame Lorna Dumas, the small, pretty, high-strung woman who had publicly left that morning. Everyone had seen trouble coming; in the last few months, their house had abruptly been leased to an English family and was also for sale, and Monsieur Dumas was negotiating pleasant temporary rooms over the boulangerie. Some said that before this final fracas, young Madame Trebon, wife of the baker, had been seen delivering brioches to Monsieur Dumas in the late afternoons when Madame Lorna was out. Next to the voluptuous Madame Trebon, Madame Lorna looked like a slightly desiccated sprite, seeming young until you looked more closely; then you thought, Young for her age.

Lorna and Armand-Loup had been married twenty years. It was unclear when during the preceding months her recent frequent absences, away doing her lectures, had become the status quo, but something in her manner made everybody predict that this time she wouldn't be back, and who could blame her? Everyone liked Monsieur Dumas, but he was a notorious *tombeur*—that is, skirt chaser, often with inexplicable success.

·   ·   ·

The problem facing the village council was how to clean up the mess in the cemetery while respecting the distress of people whose loved ones, in whatever state of putrefaction or petrification, now lay entangled and anonymous in literally a potter's field of the same clay the village used for making its famous sauceboats. Among the exhumed bodies in the cemetery were several whose disorderly reappearance might get noticed in the newspapers. These were Saint Brigitte Fauxbois, whose grave, according to local legend, sometimes manifested an aura of light, generally in summer; Russell Woods, the noted American painter, whose posthumous enormous prices at auction were making him a household name in the U.S.; and Roland Bussy de Larimont, a former mayor from a prominent local family.

"Woods, the American painter," Monsieur Dumas reminded the other members of the council, "the old fellow always up there daubing—hundreds of views of the church in the changing light? Alone, forgotten when he died, except by Lorna. He and my wife were good friends—the two Americans in town. She's an art historian, you remember. She thought highly of his work."

The names of dozens of others would have to be divined from the cemetery records, which would take time, but these were the few the council could remember off the tops of their heads. They foresaw that DNA expertise would be required, and other expensive technical assistance that in former days people would not have expected. Where they had the names of families whose loved ones or ancestors were likely among the jumble of bones, they would assume that such people, once contacted, would be responsible for picking up an appropriate proportion of the cost.

In the train, Lorna knew from experience, her spirits would rise, they always did, but right now she felt like she had forgotten something in the oven and would eventually have to deal with a charred, smelly mess, the remains of a fragrant, delicious concoction she'd slaved over. For a moment she felt failed, depressed, sad, slightly panicked, daunted by the practical problems she was facing, of supporting herself, reviving a career almost dormant for twenty years, and explaining to her adult children her second marriage wreck. Where had twenty years gone? What had she been doing all that time? Visiting the sick, volunteering at the village library, giving art lectures to the American cooking groups that came to Pont-les-Puits for courses in mushroom picking or knife skills. Paltry pastimes. She had been happy, though.

People generally would have said that Lorna Mott was the epitome of a successful woman: lovely offspring, grandchildren, health, a French husband, a delightful house, and an independent career involving travel and public appearances—public appearances requiring expensive clothes (or clothes that appeared expensive)—an uncomplicated, sociable nature, and an intellectual life. She would say this herself, she was always grateful for her luck, except for now, perhaps heading to a second divorce—she was not going to think that far ahead—which she knew officially counted against your happiness score. And, of course, not so young anymore. Of a certain age. Or, face it, a bit older than the French meant when they spoke of *une femme d'un certain âge*.

Her plan was to take the train to Clermont-Ferrand, then the TGV to Lyon, and, from there, Air France to New York. She'd recover in New York for a couple of days, network a little, and get in touch with the publisher of her book in hopes of lining up some readings or publicity. From New York she'd contact her children—but how to tell them why she was there? Lorna had three children with her previous husband, Randall Mott: Peggy, Curt, and Hams. They probably had no suspicion of her difficulties.

Then to San Francisco, her hometown, soon to be her home base again, then overnight to Bakersfield to give her lecture. She had some cash in dollars in her purse, and her credit cards, and a small bank account in the U.S., where she had been stashing fees and royalties, unconsciously preparing her escape.

The French village of Pont-les-Puits had been her home for twenty years, or, rather, eighteen: when she and Armand-Loup first married they lived in Paris, and he was still at the Musée d'Orsay. But she'd loved Armand-Loup's ancestral village and was happy to move there when he retired to write his book on post-Impressionism in the delicate period before Abstractionism set in. Guidebooks said of Pont-les-Puits that it was "favorably situated at a convenient driving distance from the sea, benefiting from a mild and healthful climate." It had the usual number of historical monuments, including Roman ruins, a tower from the thirteenth century, a doorway—the Portail de Fernande—from the fourteenth; ritual Jewish *bains;* the summer châteaux of les évêques de Die; chapels; fountains; and walls and so on. Now tears did come to her eyes as she glimpsed the shadowy ramparts of the château of the counts receding from the train window. Her dreams receding into the mists of the disappearing view.

Lorna loved Pont-les-Puits, even though by some standards it was a slightly run-down little backwater. In its heyday, the manufacture of a certain local form of earthenware double sauceboat, adapted to skimming fat from the gravy (a *puitière*), had brought prosperity, but recently its use had fallen off, and the town's young people had left for business schools or jobs as au pair girls and tutors of French in Scandinavia, where they propagated on their uncritical patrons the rough local accent, with its heavily rolled *r*'s so derided by Parisians.

The future held some promise for Pont even so—there was now a growing group of British expatriates drawn to the cheap and potentially charming run-down real estate. They in turn expanded the prosperity of the village by bringing an enthusiastic group of American cookery writers who didn't speak French, and also chefs enamored of a species of local onion, the *Allium tanisium*, related to the Japanese allium. Now there were numberless cooking residencies and classes, sometimes combined with French conversation tutorials, to the great delight of the people who kept the inns and restaurants. Lorna occasionally was asked to give an art lecture about the local monuments to the American foodies who subscribed so expensively to these courses. She was always glad to do it, and in that way kept her hand in. She was especially good on certain nineteenth-century neglected painters like Meissonier and Fantin-Latour, and she hoped to help her painter friend, the late Russell Woods, get his proper place in art history.

How could she leave this beloved place? But she had to, unless Armand-Loup would really change his ways. There was also the tragedy of having to sell their house, the sense of a beautiful idyll—twenty years long—over, finished, done. But on the upside, in California she could be of help to her grown children, and, really, it would be nice to be in America again. She had a rosy view of it. No matter where you are, you don't stop being American.

On the train, she stole another look at the words she'd downloaded from the French consulate website:

It should be noted that a spouse who leaves the family domicile without a court authorization may be deemed under French law to have committed a "fault" giving rise to significant financial consequences. Thus a spouse should avoid doing so until it has been possible to consult with French counsel.

Tant pis—too bad, so much for that—she was doing it. And now it was time to think of the future. She would prove, to herself if to no one else, that you can make a new life at any age.

As she was climbing into the train, Armand-Loup telephoned her cell and said in a cold voice, *"Chérie, tu as oublié ton argenterie."* She'd left the sterling silverware she'd taken with her from California when she married him and moved to France. He must have realized she might not be coming back for a while.

Tant pis.

2

We must be prepared for things turning out differently than we expect.

In the plane to New York, she had a plump, permanent-waved, chatty seatmate who pried things out of her, for instance that she had grandchildren. Lorna loved her grandchildren but didn't think of herself as a "granny," which was how the woman next to her put it. "I'm a granny," she said. "How about you? How old are yours?" Lorna had to think: it changed all the time. Julie must be about twenty, twenty-one, and Curt's twins, what, four? She didn't inquire about the ages of this other woman's grandchildren and, though she wasn't in denial, did wonder if her own age and grandmotherhood would detract or add to her authority as an art critic. For a man, it would add, or be irrelevant; for a woman, she didn't know.

"Where are you from?" persisted the irritating seatmate. "Were you on vacation?"

"Originally San Francisco," Lorna said, "but I've been living overseas." She had learned over the years to say "overseas," like a military wife, instead of "I live abroad" or "I live in Europe," which could seem elitist or excite the suspicion you were CIA.

"Are you happy there?"

Lorna thought it an odd, unanswerable question, and rather nosy, too. What would most people say? Yes, when they really weren't, or no, though they were? Did people even know? Happiness was like one of those floaters in your eye that you can never focus on, intangible and fleeting. But she knew she was happy at the idea of wonderful America, its big mountains and expansive generosity—happy to be going there, to be home again permanently after all these years away.

In the twenty years she'd lived in France, Lorna had often been to America, to San Francisco to visit her children or, in the first years, to New York or Massachusetts or even South Dakota to give lectures, keeping her professional life going. Then her lecture engagements had begun to taper off, almost without her noticing. So, today, it wasn't exactly culture shock, arriving in New York, it was the new finality of her plan to stay that made her appreciate pleasant American things— the cheery man in customs who said "Welcome home" to people in the U.S.-citizen passport line; drinking fountains; the smiling face of the handsome new president, Obama, on posters in the reception hall.

She felt a surge of sentimental patriotism, of oneness with her native land. America was more suited to her temperament than the exigent rectitude of formal, hidebound France. She was home; maybe she'd been homesick these twenty years. Missing the open faces, enchiladas, Japanese cars.

She would postpone the unwelcome task of giving the news of her whereabouts to the children and facing their questions. But she did call Margaret, Peggy, her oldest child, who lived in Ukiah, California, and was recently divorced from her husband, Dick Willover, a man whom both Lorna and Ran (Randall Mott, Peggy's father) had been crazy about at first. *Tant pis.* Lorna predicted Peggy would be the most understanding. She telephoned her from the hotel.

"Peg, it's Mother. Are you there?"

"Mom! Where are you?"

"I'm in New York, honey." How to explain? "I'm on my way to San Francisco, then Bakersfield, where I give a lecture. I should be there by Wednesday. I'll explain it all in the fullness of time."

"Are you coming here? Is Armand-Loup with you?"

"No. Peg—I'll be staying in San Francisco awhile. Armand and I are taking some time off. Don't mention it to Hams or . . ."

Predictably, Peggy remonstrated. "Time off? Are you leaving him? That's terrible, Mother. Are you sure? Have you seen a counselor? What's the matter?"

"Please, Peg. I've analyzed my situation. With all its dismaying ramifications . . ." She spoke in a light tone. She herself would have to understand better before she could explain.

"I suppose you have," Peggy conceded. There were a number of negative ramifications Lorna was only now seeing. For instance, how much detail about all this was she really going to go into with the children? She had not been feeling that she needed to explain to them about her return, but now she was obliged to recognize that she was uncomfortable telling them her main reason for leaving Armand-Loup.

It was his wild infidelity. Infidelity at their age was embarrassing, maybe even comic, because at their age—the children probably thought—you were supposed to be not only beyond caring but beyond doing anything much, and way beyond enduring the rituals and incurring the expense of illicit sexual capers, in Armand-Loup's case the escalating expense of wooing demanding, ever-younger young women.

She had been surprised by his infidelity. She knew the reputation of French husbands, but she had believed it was overstated, Frenchmen being more or less like other men, with normal physical capacities and the normal wish to avoid trouble. Besides, she had thought that she and Armand-Loup got along very well in that department of life. She also knew that French wives would, or would have in the past, turned a blind eye, or exacted some domestic price in private, to compensate for the dinners, the flowers, the concerts, and the weekends spent with *poules de luxe*. Lorna begrudged both the time and the expense of Armand-Loup's adventures. And in his case, the costs had risen with his weight, and he was now rather plump—he who had been such a beauty, and a fantastic skier. Now the girlfriends were younger, plainer, and more expensive, especially a couple of expensive medical events involving these young women. With their cost, eventually, had come the need to sell the house, though this exigency was disguised even in their private conversations as sensible downsizing.

And though she understood that he was trying to fend off age, *bon,* as a result of his betrayals she had become less and less motivated to throw herself into her assigned duties as helpmeet—why would you want to slave for a man who was weekending with some chick in Marseilles? And there were larger cultural issues: whatever she did, in their village, she'd always be the awkward American woman, never quite right, said to once have had some career in America, but never, ever getting the cheeses straight. All was failure.

And yet—and yet wasn't there more to it? A more positive force had also prompted her to leave. Her own sense of adventure? Of not wanting to feel that life was just reaction to fate, or to the infidelity of someone else? Was it wanting to have a new life while there was still time? Was she having a midlife crisis in an interesting way? Okay, too late to become an opera singer or a congresswoman, she still looked forward to the new chapter.

Twenty years ago she had gone off with such glee with her hot French husband, leaving the children to their adult lives: the newly married Peggy with her baby, Curt and Hams in college. Over the twenty years, all of her kids—Peggy, Curt, Hammond—and in time their spouses and kids had loved their holidays and summers in France, in her postcard-perfect stone farmhouse, *mas,* in Pont-les-Puits. They loved to loll in the sun of its courtyard, hike the pretty mountain paths, and feast on the special foie gras and fragrant chèvres of the region. She had had little reason ever to come back to America.

How much did a grown-up like herself need to reveal to her adult children anyhow? Did she owe them explanations? Had the balance already tipped on the dependence scale toward her being more dependent on them than they on her? She didn't think so, but maybe they thought so.

She was unwilling to struggle with the matter of her official story for too long and thrust it from her mind, giving Peggy the cheerful version: grown apart, missing America, never really at home in France, lonesome for you children, also the grandchildren, wanting back into her intellectual life while she still had her wits about her . . . Armand-Loup, she explained, was selling the charming village house. There had been no question of her staying in the house at the time of the separation discussions, as it had been his to begin with, and his to sell, as he was now trying to do, very reluctantly.

At moments when her positive spin collapsed, she knew that coming back to the U.S. was a question of supporting herself, and she painfully foresaw that her career, however well she could manage to reestablish it, would with age inevitably wind down, along with the enthusiasm she felt now for writing new material, doing research, and keeping up with art historiography.

Now, sitting in a hotel in New York City, she was overtaken again by other negatives of what she was facing—the hurly-burly of the lecture tour, of mediocre library venues in Bakersfield or Fresno, even fears about her physical stamina; she'd been so tired last night, and she wasn't a tired person. What if she was coming down with something, the onset of some condition appropriate to her age that she would henceforth have to think about? People her age got diabetes, they got arthritis; they had to allow for their health, had to carry an embarrassing doughnut cushion with them, or an oxygen bottle, or excuse themselves to take medicine, or sneak pills into their mouths at table with that furtive sidelong look.

And yet, wasn't America the better place, where opportunity beckoned at any age, and people were not so conscious as the French of what other people thought? *Ça ne se fait pas,* said the French. That isn't done. In America, you could do it.

3

Thinking of others spares you thinking of yourself.

Apart from her own personal life, Lorna had another reason for coming back to America: her children. Though they were adults, they seemed to need her in practical ways that their father apparently ignored. Lorna's children with Randall Mott, in order, were Peggy, the oldest at forty-four; Curt, the older son, forty-one; the younger son, Hammond, called Hams, thirty-eight. All were in Northern California—well, Curt at this moment was in Southeast Asia somewhere.

Lorna reviewed her worries for each of them. They had the normal problems of adult life—the oldest, the divorced Peggy, was poor and in debt; the younger son, Hams, also, to a lesser extent, because he lived on the fringe anyway, sort of an ex-hippie; and there was Curt, her most promising child, who had been on the cusp of launching a start-up, already crowdsource funded and ready to go, when he had a serious bicycle accident with unforeseen consequences. Lorna could not be free of fears for any of them—first of all for Curt, of course, and then for the others, and then for the grandchildren, new hostages to fortune who continued to arrive, like the baby Hams's wife, Misty, was expecting. She was sure they all needed her. She was also aware that she must not interfere with their lives or give the slightest sign of being bossy.

The recently divorced Peggy Willover lived in a little house in Ukiah, California, where she kept herself going with various craft enterprises, like personalized dog collars, thus contributing to her daughter Julie's college expenses, and bought nothing for herself. She had a little venture in Internet commerce, buying bargain items, especially handbags, on eBay, fixing them up, and reselling them to RealSteal or private customers. She also made earrings to sell at craft fairs, sold cheese and jam made in her backyard shed, and worked in the local library. By nature optimistic like her mother, she nonetheless, when she really thought about her situation—early forties, alone, and stone poor—could get fits of despair. She was aware that her mother, Lorna (the well-known art historian Lorna Mott Dumas!), was probably hard up, too—men had been difficult for both of them. Peggy sometimes thought that Lorna hadn't prepared her correctly for a world with men in it. Peggy had tried to tell her own daughter Julie (age twenty) certain realities while avoiding cynicism or bitterness, and so far Julie had been so free of man troubles, Peggy had started to worry the other way.

"Don't you know any boys, honey?"

"Mother! The boys"—Ukiah High School, UC Berkeley—"are revolting here."

"I can't believe there isn't one nice one at least."

"Not even one, always pawing you, or else ignoring you."

If Peggy worried about Julie, Lorna in turn worried about divorced Peggy's own nunlike and low-paid—rather dreary, in fact, to Lorna's view—humdrum days beset with financial problems, Julie's expensive schooling, for example, and Peggy's increasingly old-maidish way of worrying about small things like the garage-door opener being broken. Peggy's ex, Dick Willover, was no help with any of this.

"If you moved to San Francisco, there'd be art and music at least," Lorna prompted Peggy.

"Mother, it isn't that easy. Anyway, art and music are not what I need."

. . .

Curtis Mott, second child of Randall and Lorna Mott, had always been the star of the family, at school, in college, and in his professional life. Happily married, with a thriving software enterprise, young twins, and a beautiful house—all was going well until almost a year ago, when he had suffered a near-fatal bicycle accident and for a while seemed to be destined to die young, the fabled doom of such golden boys. But he hadn't died.

For nearly five months, he had lain in a coma, occasionally appearing to wake or stir. Lorna, who had flown to his side, had regretfully gone back and forth from Pont-les-Puits, asking for constant updates in between. There had been despair, or moments of hope, once when he had sat up and said "Donna!" before lapsing back into his former unseeing state; and some then began to believe he would recover.

Some did not. His pessimistic wife, Donna, had once said—no one could believe she could say such a thing—"Do we need to discuss, um, whether this goes on forever?" Was she talking about the plug? The others had gasped at her cold realism. Donna was not their favorite, but this was beyond imagination. No one else had even thought of pulling the plug—there was no question of anything besides waiting. What was in her heart, really? Arrangements were made to put him in a facility where people would manipulate his limbs to maintain his muscle mass and monitor his breathing. Luckily he hadn't terminated his hedge-fund day job, so his workplace insurance had paid most of the stupefying costs.

There had been enough good signs in the situation of Curt Mott, beginning with the fact that he was alive, to stanch the fears that Lorna had reserved for him since his childhood. Her sturdy daughter Peggy had never worried her, the younger boy, Hams, was Hams, no altering that; but Curt, the firstborn son, had had such a penchant for danger, and such bad luck, and, as she imagined, frail health, though outwardly the picture of wellness, and had so much promise that anxiety was almost her automatic response when she heard his name, even without his serious case of measles (had she forgotten to get him vaccinated?), his first bicycle accident (was he too young to have had that bicycle?), his fall off the rings in gym class, breaking his arm, his getting lost at camp, and much more. The long grim weeks of his coma had thus in a way been no surprise, his awakening a joyful exception to her expectations, his vanishing right in line with her fears. But he was alive.

Then, something strange, breathlessly imparted to Lorna by Donna on the phone to France: Curt had woken miraculously from his coma and, after a few days of regaining strength, announced a spiritual quest that required him to go to a jungle somewhere in Southeast Asia, inaccessible by Skype or FaceTime. A few days out of his sickbed, frail and diminished though he was, he bought an airline ticket and began his packing to go to Thailand, giving the impression that he had spent his coma months gestating like a larva some elaborate plan that drew him away. If she didn't come right now, Lorna would just miss him.

The family believed that his bicycle accident had damaged his brain some way, obliterated the site that controlled ethical behavior and probability and affections, making it possible for him to go off, without concern for his wife and small children. His twins were boys aged four. His wife Donna, fanatically attentive during his illness, had actually despaired and had begun building a new life, rather surreptitiously out of consideration for his parents and siblings. She did endless yoga classes and video-coached sessions on her stationary bike, in case she met someone. She studied the want ads from Silicon Valley start-ups, even those known to be hostile to women. His waking up surprised her more than anyone.

At first, with globalization, Curt's trip to Thailand could seem almost normal, business related. But he hadn't returned. Donna claimed to get the odd postcard from time to time, but never Skype, FaceTime, or an email address. He had closed his email account, there were no credit card charges that might give a clue to where he was, he never called, but he did considerately reassure them by sending postcards with blurry, unreadable postmarks, and these usually said things were going well. Donna's priest (Donna, his wife, from an Italian family, was Catholic) counseled patience, while Donna, in despair, tried to wrestle with the problems of a huge mortgage and the lively four-year-olds.

That was Curt. After Curt, it was her second son, Hams, whom Lorna worried about most among her children; Peggy, after all, was balanced and resourceful. How glad she would be to see Hams. Despite his rumpled, bag-person aspect, she had an especially soft spot for him, saw into his inner sensitive self, his unexploited musical ability, remembered the tears that came to his eyes as a child whenever they read something sad aloud, "King of the Golden River," wasn't it? Or the Oscar Wilde story about the statue who gave up its jeweled eyes and ended in pigeon shit?

Hams had married a woman, aptly named Misty, who had flirted with Scientology, but now they were both in a Brazilian religion that Lorna gathered had something to do with sacrificing goats and enabled you to fix your vacuum cleaner with beams radiating from your hand. Peggy had seen Misty do it.

Misty and Hams were expecting a baby, their first. Misty, though she'd done graduate study in psychology, worked in a dry cleaner's. Lorna had always found Misty a little scary, with her several piercings and hair dyed a startling red not found in nature, a look widespread in their East Bay set. Lorna also found it hard to imagine someone with those nose rings and studded eyebrows pushing a baby stroller, but knew she was old-fashioned, and that Misty was at bottom a normal middle-class girl. She also knew Misty and Hams would need help with the baby and asked herself how she could help when the time came.

After Peggy, she telephoned Hams. Not home. However much she loved him, she was slightly relieved not to get him on the phone, as Hams always had some problem to discuss that was usually expensive and beyond her means to help, especially now, with life on a shoestring. Though helping him, and her other children, was her principal resolve.

4

Who was it who said, "Brighten the corner where you are?"
Lorna's daughter, Peggy Willover, sitting in her patio in Ukiah, had been engaged in trying to help Mother's book along when she got Lorna's call. She had had a sense that things hadn't been going well in Pont-les-Puits, so she wasn't entirely surprised at Lorna's news now from New York. After her divorce from Father, nearly twenty-five years ago, Mother had enacted the fantasies of freedom and glamour her children themselves were too busy to fulfill, and shortly, very unwisely from a career point of view, Mother had married a Frenchman. It had seemed that her future would be French, and the horizons of the family had expanded in the delightful direction of soirées and *cassoulets,* though the children had worried that Lorna might be becoming Eurotrash, the sly suggestion put forth by their father, Lorna's first husband, Ran.

Once installed in France, till now Lorna had given the family no warning signs of trouble, but had lived in domestic harmony in a remote village in southeastern France, welcoming them in vacation periods and whenever they could come. Now the downsides of her return rained on Peggy like a shower of arrows: Mother without a husband at her age, nor money—was it a health problem? What really was the matter?

She and Lorna talked a bit longer, and then Peggy went back to what she'd been doing with a renewed sense of its importance. She had been writing on Amazon, under various names, reviews of Mother's recently published book: *Painters Despised*. The first review began "I heard one of Lorna Mott Dumas's wonderful lectures a few years ago, and it changed my life. It turned me into an art lover and an art history buff! She's a fantastic scholar. I'm thrilled that her talks are now being printed as a book."

"Having loved Mrs. Dumas's lectures since I heard them once in Baltimore, I rejoice to have a print copy, especially her essay about the small Redon landscapes, and also her work on the neglected painter Ernest Meissonier . . ."

She'd already forwarded that one to a friend, Nellie L. Brown, to sign and send from Los Angeles, in case Amazon could somehow tell if all the reviews were coming from the same computer or the same city. Could they? She cranked out a few more paragraphs, planning to forward a third letter to her brother's wife Donna to send from San Francisco.

Privately, she had always been afraid her mother's lectures might be light and superficial. She didn't herself feel competent to judge, but she found embarrassing the stagy English voice, well-rehearsed poise, and theatrical gestures with which Lorna delivered them, on the podium so unlike the real-life woman and far from motherly, a transformation that unsettled Peggy even at her age. Onstage, Mother's voice acquired an unfamiliar resonance, and her gestures had a practiced confidence, as if, were you to stop her and she had to start over, they would come out exactly the same each time, same flutter of the hand by her left ear accompanying certain phrases, evolving to a dramatic, emphatic finger-pointing at the audience, a gesture possibly learned from watching You-Tube videos of the historic British prime minister Margaret Thatcher. Peggy and her siblings had seen Lorna watching Mrs. Thatcher on tape over and over, a scene of the Iron Lady confronting a coal-mining official, and they were pretty sure this is where the voice and gestures came from.

Peggy didn't tell her mother she was writing these reviews, because Lorna would definitely forbid it, even though she wouldn't be displeased. A related scruple kept Peggy from checking to see whether her reviews had ever been posted by Amazon; she just flung them out spontaneously like broadcast seeds, hoping one would flourish in the vast Internet topsoil and start some crop of virus in behalf of Lorna's book. They all, the whole family, badly needed money, they seemed hopeless about this commodity, and Peggy, she knew herself, was among the worst. Well, their father didn't need money, of course, married as he was to a Silicon Valley millionairess.

Now to the *Weekly Standard*'s art critic, in the guise of Lorna herself:

> *"Sir, I am not confident enough to imagine you have heard of my work, but I'm encouraged to send you this copy of my recently published lectures by your continuing defense of painters that I too have championed, Meissonier among them—perhaps you will like my observations about the realism of his equestrian painting, nothing finer since Bonheur, and so much better than the more admired Stubbs, if one can compare French and English painters . . ."*

She went on a little in this vein, borderline plagiarizing from a Victorian novel she was reading and from her mother's own text. Here she signed her mother's name and just hoped Mother would never find out. She began another: "Dear Mr. Silvers . . ." She signed this review with her own name, Margaret M. Willover, but omitted spelling out her maiden name, Mott, so that the connection with her mother wouldn't be too obvious. She didn't want to deceive, exactly—Amazon could easily look up the *M* in Margaret M. Willover. She thought it unlikely that Mother would find out about any of these efforts on her behalf. Lorna claimed to scorn social media, as was probably true for many in her demographic, though in Peggy's view, if Lorna was coming back on the career track, she really ought to apply herself and master some Facebook skills.

To look at, Mother didn't seem as though she belonged to an older, Facebook-challenged generation: she was slender, unlined, and lively, with pretty, tasteful, auburn–light brown hair and skirts of a fashionable length. Peggy couldn't help but have the sudden, culpably material realization that one consequence of Mother's unexpected rupture with her French husband was that she would no longer be able to pass along some of her terrific Paris clothes to the taller Peggy, who had to let down the hems on ones that she planned to wear herself, but the rest she sold on a website, the RealSteal, where she conducted her little Internet business, and did well with French designer clothes. "Givenchy jacket, navy blue, size 36, only worn twice."

She was sorry to think that now that wardrobe perk was probably gone.

Her reviews finished, Peggy sat a bit longer on her patio, thinking about Mother's Paris clothes. Peggy never bought herself clothes. She lived frugally in her little house in Ukiah and had nothing but worries, the newest of which was something she'd signed yesterday, almost immediately knowing she shouldn't have: a loan application; it sounded like a miracle the way the man had explained it. He'd come to the door, like a hobo, which ought to have been a warning sign, but she'd viewed it as a godsend, given her troubles with house payments, Julie's tuition, one or two personal bills for craft equipment she expected eventually would pay for itself but was meantime nearly five thousand dollars, and trouble with just day-to-day life.

"We look up people recently divorced," he said. "We figure they could usually use some help. Our aim is to help people."

Sure it was. She saw it now. Who believes in disinterested philanthropy? Now that it was probably too late, the thing was signed, harnessing her to an unbelievable, extortionate interest rate, foreclosure if she defaulted, clauses that seemed to have written themselves onto the pages after it was signed. She had tried so hard to avoid depending on her father or, rather, her father's rich wife, but maybe she'd have to ask them for a lawyer or something.

The money situation with Father was complicated—he didn't mind helping Peggy and her siblings, but out of pride they avoided asking for help. For one thing, they didn't want his rich wife Amy to think they were hopeless, even if they were.

She'd gone back to hemming batik scarves, with her cell phone beside her, and was surprised to get another long-distance call, this time from France, from the American Consular Services in Marseille, asking for her mother. Peggy explained that Lorna was not there but was expected in a day or two.

"*J'appelle au sujet* of the American painter Russell Woods." The person on the other end explained in franglais that Woods, whose posthumous fame was one of those art market phenomena—his work going from nothing to the hundreds of thousands in value—had originally been buried at the expense of the *ville de* Pont-les-Puits, and as the practical woman secretary of the *conseil,* Madame Barbara Levier, who served as mayor and financial officer of the village and was also the pharmacist, had seen a chance to recoup some of their investment, now that they had understood that Woods was somehow the property of, was connected to, Madame Dumas, the other American in town.

Madame Levier had got Lorna's address c/o Peggy from Monsieur Dumas and had begun preparing the papers detailing what Lorna would be obliged to pay to rescue Woods's bones, with the expense of identifying them once they had the DNA of his relatives. She understood that Madame Dumas was not a blood relative, no use in that quarter, but she might know of some relative, someone's cheek to swab, whom they had not been able to find at the time of Woods's death. In the meantime, *faute de mieux,* Madame Lorna Dumas had been designated next of kin for legal purposes, and Monsieur Dumas had given them an address he thought might work for her, and her phone number chez Madame Willover. Armand-Loup had also given them Peggy's email, mentioning that, as his soon-to-be-former wife Lorna was okay with email but always forgot to charge her cell phone, they might be better off emailing. Instead, Madame Levier, hoping to avoid the pitfalls of English both written and spoken, had enlisted the cooperation of the cultural attaché in Aix en Provence.

"When we are told about the death of an American in our consular district," said the consular voice in a heavy, French, Inspector Clouseau accent, causing Peggy at first to suspect some kind of prank, "vee get in touch wiz zee next of kin of the deceased, vee contact zat person by telephone immediately. Only now it isn't so urgent, *parce que la personne* has been dead for four years. But there are several important things that the next of kin must do in conjunction with the SCS unit that were never done for Monsieur Woods and thus must be done now before he can be reburied. Technically it is as if he were never buried, if you see . . ."

"But my mother is not next of kin to anyone called Russell Woods," Peggy protested.

"*Si, si,* we have her name."

"Can I have my mother call you?"

"*Oui, bien sûr,* without delay," said the consular official. "His bones may be identified at any time, and then all haste to do the proper burial. After the DNA analysis, which could take some time . . ."

Peggy found this conversation confusing, but carefully wrote down the string of phone numbers and promised to leave a message for Lorna, if and when her mother next got in touch.

5

There is no ego more fragile than that of a newly published author.
Before leaving for California, Lorna spent another day in New York, stopping in at Rudolph Lang Cie Art Publications to sign some copies of her book, *Painters Despised*. These were not visible in the window with their other newly issued titles, so, pink with diffidence, she asked a salesperson if they had it. "It just came out, and I thought I could sign some copies."

They were startled to see her; they had trouble dissimulating the fact that the copies were still in the storeroom, even though the publication was recent. "Probably ran out," they said mendaciously. "So nice to see you, Mrs. Dumas. I expect they are in the stockroom, ready to be shipped. Reorders."

In the stockroom, a few boxes were found. Lorna was full of chagrin about having overestimated the degree Rudolph Lang Cie Art Publications would be glad to see her, was ashamed to have embarrassed them, was embarrassed herself to have thought her book mattered at all: she understood that nowadays the public lecture was a bit out of fashion, what with videos and the Internet, and she had found, when she began rather furtively to weigh getting back into circulation, that people had changed; they were jaded by PowerPoint, and preferred YouTube's blotchy, primitive nineteenth-century film footage of women in big hats at garden parties and bearded old Impressionists in undershirts darting jerkily in and out of the frames. Was the essay, with the lecture, a doomed form? Should she try to find a better publisher? It was all a blow to her newly reestablished but fragile self-esteem.

Things would be more welcoming in California. As her plane neared San Francisco, Lorna's thoughts left the problems of publishing to fasten on the new set of concerns generated by her personal situation and the reunion with her children, toward whom she felt a normal amount of guilt. Though they were all functioning adults, Lorna couldn't rid herself of the belief that, without her career, her children would all starve, not literally, obviously, but they had expensive, adult problems—mortgages, medical costs, private-school tuition for their children—and she had always tried to help but felt she should have done more because their father did so little.

Helping them financially had been her mission for years, until their father had married the mega-rich princess and, she had assumed, would also help them. Her fears were rendered a little *amères* with the idea of her ex-husband Ran's smug prosperity or, to look at it frankly, huge wealth. Her fears returned when she saw that he was stingy about helping his children with her because he had this new family—new wife and new child, who must be about fifteen now.

His new wife was Amy Hawkins, who in her twenties had invested cleverly with some techie friends in Silicon Valley and rather improbably amassed a fortune of millions. With it, she had gone to France to study civilization, something she felt she'd missed out on by focusing too much on the computer screen. She was now over fifty, with a husband—the impressive, cultivated Randall Mott—a child, and many amenities of life, and she had the grace to enjoy and appreciate them. Lorna had never seen her and privately thought that Amy, if not Ran, could be a little more generous to Ran's children with Lorna.

These thoughts became more immediate as her plane made its approach to San Francisco, sank gracefully to the runway, and barreled along past the salt ponds and parked jets to the gate. Luckily she had a place to go, an apartment her old friend Pam Linden was lending her while she looked for a long-term place. All at once she felt less optimism than before. Or, reassurance mixed with defeat, for coming back to where you started is not what you plan when you start out. When you were much younger. To reinforce this feeling of rootless destitution, the airline had lost her bags between Paris and New York and had promised to send them around when they were found. But lost bags were not enough to reduce her pleasure to see the San Francisco Bay, the pinkish sky and rosy salt ponds.

She took a taxi from the airport, noting the changes to the San Francisco skyline, changed even since her last visit to sit at Curt's bedside, maybe ten months ago? Skyscrapers seemed to sprout like beans, overnight. The sight of her native city, like the face of a loved one, despite an unexplained shabbiness she hadn't noted before, induced a deeply reassuring return of confidence. San Francisco always looked both familiar and unfamiliar because the light was changeable, and a skyscraper or two had always been added to the panorama.

Lorna had grown up in San Francisco, but with living all those years in France, her visits to California to see her children and other family members, and of course during Curt's illness, were not enough to keep her current on the changes to the skyline. Now she was too tired to feel culture shock, or the ambiguous pleasure of being back in her native city; she had only a sense of disorientation, and a surprising, vestigial ability to cope with American transportation, getting herself from New York home to San Francisco and in a few days to Bakersfield. Of course it would be wonderful to see her children, despite their various situations.

As she passed through the city, her heart warmed with joy, despite things she hadn't remembered—a few shops newly shuttered, peeling paint, men lying here and there on street corners as she passed. This could not be normal. Of course the nation had just gone through a financial crash; she shouldn't forget that. She told herself, it was wonderful to be in America, and especially California, which was not like other places, there was nothing like it, though it was hard to say this was a positive; the San Francisco weather was very similar to London's, and the hills made it unwalkable for many, and it had nowhere near the abundant museums and theatrical events of even the smallest European city. At least she knew where she was, and what to expect, or rather what not to expect—trouble—here safely outside the zones of international conflict and important media events, where all disputes were local and real-estate related.

It was twilight when Lorna's taxi pulled up to her friend Pam's apartment building. Following the instructions Pam had sent her, she collected the key from a wary-looking doorman, who noticed her lack of luggage. She let herself into Pam's flat, a place that Pam, her friend since grade school, had claimed not to need for a couple of months, Pam recovering from a knee replacement down in Ojai with her daughter. Since Lorna had nothing to unpack, she just plunked herself down in a chair by the window and tried to calm herself by looking at the expansive and beautifully nuanced pink and gray San Francisco landscape of buildings, bridges, the cobweb of mist over the Bay, details that were the glory of this view from the top of Russian Hill, in an otherwise nondescript building, though it had doormen.

Inside, her friend's apartment had the brave but losing look familiar among Lorna's contemporaries, of belonging to a downsizing person of a grandmotherly age and former affluence: too much furniture, too many books and family photos, some art objects crammed in, everything slightly faded or dated, as if long shut up for some archaeological reason. She looked around. She peered into the bedroom closet, where Pam had considerately pushed her own clothes to one end to leave some hanger space for Lorna. Pam's shoes—too big for petite Lorna—looked forlorn on their tidy rack. She could get along here very well and hoped to God her friend would stay away awhile longer. The apartment's musty, uninhabited smell would soon dissipate, as would the old-clothes, thrift-store odor of the closet, a scent of sachet mingled with the oxidizing smell of an older person.

She'd have to go out for provisions, there was likely nothing in the fridge; nobody had been here for months. Lorna had lived like this in borrowed apartments before, on tours, and had a basic kit she knew it would be necessary to lay in of coffee and tea, a bottle of Chardonnay, a loaf of bread, butter and jam, milk, apples, and corned beef hash, things that always tided you over. She didn't know if there was a convenience store in the neighborhood, but the doormen would know.

Screaming sirens now drew her attention back to the window and a developing scene ten stories below, distant figures moving up Jones Street, and two dozen motorcycle police, blue lights flashing in the twilight, the screaming of their sirens filling the resonant canyon formed by the walls of this building and its counterpart on the other corner, where the imposing escort was just pulling up. A curious detail: on either side of the doorway of that building stood men wearing black top hats, red tights, and red-skirted minidresses with white ruffs and crimson stockings, the costume worn in travelogues about England. They were carrying pikes, as if to skewer anyone trying to go in.

The pikemen stood at attention as several other men alighted from a Lincoln Town Car and walked toward the door, two of them a respectful distance behind the third. It was easy to conclude that this was a dignitary going to visit the former governor who lived in the penthouse of this ritzier building catty-corner across the street. An English dignitary, she inferred from the Beefeater costumes, which looked ridiculous in San Francisco, but maybe it was a film shoot. Wasn't there a hotel downtown that had those costumed doormen?

Ridiculous or not, the scene touched Lorna unexpectedly. Though she'd lived abroad for two decades, she still understood and shared the internationalist aspirations of her native city, its hope to be more than just an exceptionally beautiful and remote, hilly little port town yearning for significance. Here it was, trying its hospitable best to make an Englishman feel at home. She found rather sweet the idea of hiring people in costume to make some dignitary feel at home, though it was embarrassing, too. Mostly, she was beyond feeling embarrassment for any form of naïve San Francisco provincialism—she'd made enough gaffes in her French life not to sympathize instead with the anxious protocol official who had thought this up.

Who could warrant such effort? Surely it couldn't be Prince Charles? From her perch, it was impossible to tell; it could have been Prince Charles who walked quickly into the building without glancing at the

Beefeaters. But what would he be doing in San Francisco? She pulled herself away from the window, then turned back at the rising sound of a crowd, and chanting, the oompah of a tuba. A little scrum of new people was streaming into the intersection of Jones and Green, waving placards she couldn't read from here. Now they were milling around, and the policemen were letting them. Never mind, she found a market basket in Pam's rudimentary kitchen, put on her jacket, and got the elevator down, happy to be back in California, in a meaningful world of politics after her years in an insignificant, though peaceful, French backwater.

6

They say there is no such thing as coincidence, but we have all had coincidences.

As she set out for provisions, in the street, much to her surprise, Lorna spied there among the protesters, or whatever they were, milling around at the corner, someone who looked like her own granddaughter, Julie Willover, her daughter Peggy's girl, noticeable for her strident beauty and queenly presence. Julie was hoisting a placard that said CARRY THE RAINBOW. Julie must be twenty by now, with the flowing, caramel-blonde locks girls all wore, and, in her case, black-lashed blue eyes widened in surprise. Did they spy their grandmother? Yes, Lorna saw Julie see her. Had Julie seen Lorna see Julie?

Lorna felt a wave of jet-lagged fatigue sweep over her; she had the distinct feeling of having been caught in some petty crime, having to face sociability when she just wanted to creep into Pam's, eat a little supper, and crash. Instead, here came Julie, and of course Lorna's heart swelled despite itself with grandmotherly pleasure at her embrace.

"Grandma! What are you doing here?"

"Julie dear! How amazing. Staying in a friend's place; I'm here to give a lecture, well, in Bakersfield. I was just going out to buy some eggs and whatnot. I came literally a half hour ago." She'd explain further to Julie when she felt stronger.

"Can I help you? Let me go to the store for you."

"No, thank you though, you have your picketing. What is it for?"

"The Circle of Faith. We're supporting an important British politician working with Rainbow, the Circle of Faith's outreach program. It's about cultural diversity. The Circle meets in that building, where he went in."

"I'm hoping your mother will be coming down here tomorrow," Lorna said. "We'll all meet. Will she know where I can find you?" Lorna for now planning to say goodbye, put her head down, and scurry along Green Street toward where she thought there might be a 7-Eleven. She knew it was unnatural for a grandmother to evade her grandchild, but she couldn't face other people just yet, and Julie's energy exhausted her just to feel it, she who normally had plenty of energy of her own. But Julie had seized the market basket and trotted at her side toward the Fog Corner Convenience Store.

And in the convenience store—horrors—there was another person she knew, and hadn't seen for forty years, and couldn't avoid: there was Philip Train, now the Reverend—maybe even Very Reverend—Phil Train, standing at the counter. Philip Train had been at Stanford in their undergraduate years many decades before, a popular campus figure and a friend. She'd heard he was a successful cleric now, and he was indeed wearing a turned collar and black jacket, and had an efficient close haircut, gray and crisp, like a football coach's.

For an instant, she thought of turning and creeping out without saying anything. She recognized him—would he recognize her? Or had she aged so much as to be no longer recognizable as herself? She had a moment of self-consciousness about her looks but banished it: she was a nice-looking woman of a certain age, hair a lighter color now, of course, than when she was twenty, like everyone who had altered their natural hair color, which meant, in France, everyone.

It was not a pleasure to see him, because, as with seeing Julie, this collusion of coincidence defying her wish to be unnoticed seemed to portend an intention on the part of fate or San Francisco to resist her wishes; yet it was also strangely gratifying to be in a place where you might run into people who knew you.

From the slightly furtive expression that had crossed his features for a second when he saw her, she thought he might have the same mixed feelings, or maybe had been buying cigarettes. If so, he had hastily annulled them. The cathedral, she remembered, would be just nearby. He recognized her immediately, just as she had recognized him, as if no decades had intervened and there was nothing strange about them both being in a Russian Hill convenience store.

With the practiced sociability of the cloth, he engaged her directly: "Lorna Morgan! My dear old friend!" They exclaimed about the interval—forty years? Nearly fifty? She introduced Julie, who then tactfully absented herself among the shelves, picking up the eggs, a packet of bacon, the coffee.

Asked about herself, Lorna found herself as they stood there telling him more than he must have wanted to know about her lecture plans and her new book. She knew she was nattering on, but she felt anxious to defend herself as a person of some professional seriousness and was rather wounded that he hadn't heard of her, though she didn't expect it, either. Her account of herself had been honed by the interview she had given over the phone for *Publishers Weekly* when her book came out, not that she was so famous, but in the art history world she had a certain stature, as she had to keep reminding herself.

". . . and now that my lectures have come out as a book, I'm on the road, book touring for a few weeks, and, finally, after all these years, am back home. For the moment, I'm staying at Pam Linden's apartment up the street—that is, Pam's away. I've stupidly leased my house in France . . ." Of course it was more complicated than that.

"I live in France most of the time. Or did. In Pont-les-Puits, in the south, I'm married to a Frenchman . . . I'm ostensibly an expert on the tapestries of Angers . . ." The clerk, who had been listening, moved off to do something else.

"Didn't you marry Ran Mott?" Phil remembered her first husband.

"Yes, well, a lifetime ago," she agreed. "Randall Mott. I still use the name Mott professionally, along with Dumas, my married name now. Lorna Mott Dumas." Morgan her maiden name. "Lorna Morgan is long gone."

Phil Train didn't contribute anything about his own life during the intervening years, the convention being, she supposed, that a clergy-man's life had been too upright and uneventful to bear recounting. Long ago at Stanford, he dated a girl in her dorm, Cerise Boatwright, she remembered, and he'd been a notorious binge drinker, an Alpha Delt. The Somewhat Reverend Train.

Lorna was not in touch with her first husband, Ran Mott, father of her three children, formerly a dermatologist, now morphed into the admired, exemplary philanthropist Randall Mott, who during their marriage had been abusive and drunk. After their divorce, he'd dried out, shaved, and wooed his now wife—Amy Hawkins, a girl-woman—who'd made a fortune in Silicon Valley. Looking at this upstanding, attractive man, people they knew tended to blame his former problems on his unhappy marriage to Lorna Mott, and blamed Lorna herself for being career minded, restless, arty, and not much of a housekeeper.

A few years after his marriage to Amy Hawkins, Ran Mott had given up his dermatology practice and now did God knew what, managed Amy's money probably, and took her to charity openings. Amy was no doubt perfectly nice, but Lorna did feel an occasional pang at the caprices of Fortune who had landed Ran so firmly on his feet, when she, hardworking, serious, and not getting any younger, hadn't a home of her own or a bean to her name, plus the cares engendered by their three adult children, whom Ran had more or less washed his hands of. She explained to Phil Train about her second husband, Armand-Loup, and all those years in France, and about her recent reentry.

"You must come give one of your lectures to our Altar Forum, they have a cultural series. How pleased they would be! There's a lot of interest in art in the Bay Area."

Though he meant to be welcoming, these words struck Lorna with much more force than their actual significance; they brought back the maddening things she'd experienced as a young art historian when she'd first begun to lecture. Because she was female and married, people had expected her to give her lectures for free and pay her own way. Their assumptions had been that a woman should be thrilled to be lecturing at all, would not expect a fee, and would donate her time and expertise (such as it was) to worthy community groups.

The same assumptions lurked behind this invitation now, nothing had changed. She would like to tell Phil Train she had lectured at the Louvre in Paris, at the Doria Pamphili in Rome, at the Whitney Museum in New York—but these would mean nothing to him. She didn't mention her forthcoming trip to Bakersfield. She saw how it was going to be—she would be drawn back into the West Coast, small-time, amateur world, and she had no alternative, and no energy to transcend it. Coming back to San Francisco, she was finished.

As she and Julie walked home to Pam's apartment, aspects of her life she didn't go into with Phil Train came rushing into her mind, deepening the sudden onset of partially jet-lagged gloom. Thinking about what she had described to him, she was almost resentful that her anonymous arrival today for a stay potentially restful and not engulfed in memories and family problems had been assaulted in the first half hour by not one but two representatives of real-world responsibility and duty, a grandchild and someone who had known her in college. Now thoughts could not be kept back, pushed in like paparazzi or bill collectors.

Normally Lorna was not introspective. After the storms and sobs of her first marriage, she had realized there was no point to it. You just got on with things. But now she felt her heart speed up at recollections of the general mistakes of her life: one divorce and probably another in the offing; her present shaky finances; her daughter Peggy's financial problems and the imminent foreclosure of Peggy's house; the ongoing problems of her son Curt, his wife Donna's possible need to sell their house; the amount of the note Lorna had signed on Curt's behalf; her own trouble concentrating on her work, the reentry problems, the humiliation of hustling for lectures and trying to find new subjects, the pathetic fees you got for the occasional book review . . .

All these cares tumbled through her mind during the simple five-minute walk from Fog Corner to the intersection of Green and Jones, no one problem formulated clearly, just a general sense of having botched her life, with opportunities for fixing it getting more limited the older she grew—all this reflection brought on by the simple expression of interest from a clergyman doing his job of appearing interested.

His face had clouded with sympathy with the word "divorce." And how odd that the Very Reverend Train remembered her long-ago marriage to Randall Mott. And she had always found it odd that old divorces were assumed to be wounds, life failures, and scars on the psyche; she had loved that divorce and never thought about it now, all these years later. She should have reassured Phil Train she didn't feel it now, she was preoccupied with her new divorce. She sometimes wondered if she'd recognize Randall Mott on the street.

Yet, though they had been divorced for more than twenty years, Ran was still a presence in her life as a permanent source of resentment, in that via his dot-com millionaire second wife he could have assumed a lot of the continuing costs of their three now middle-aged children if he wanted to. But he didn't. She hadn't seen him in decades and could almost have forgotten their personal relationship except for this abiding, pointed lack of help. Her ex-husband Ran's new wife (not new, at least fifteen years or more, guessing their child was fifteen)—his wife Amy had hundreds of millions and was generous with them, but his pride, a spurious emotion masking genuine malice, wouldn't let him ask her for anything. Ran had said, "I'm not asking Amy for money for those children," as if they weren't his children but only Lorna's. As if his pride was more important than the children's life needs.

When it came to Ran, Lorna had mostly guarded herself from bitterness and judgment—she generally accepted the idea of karma—but serenity wasn't easy. Here was another thought—memory—to be squelched, of him saying: "I'm not paying Peggy's mortgage, she's a grown woman," though he'd put it more rudely than that.

She thought of all this now as she and Julie retraced their steps. The protesters had vanished; the Lincoln Town Car still stood in the intersection, with several motorcycle police, but the costumed Beefeaters were no longer there. Julie had rolled her banner on its stick and carried it like a cane.

Julie was taller than her mother Peggy, and towered over Lorna. She had something of her father Dick Willover through the eyes, though Julie's were large and blue where his were brown. Her hair was dark golden and she had always carefully washed it with Lite N Brite to keep it from darkening, according to Peggy's instructions, which had in turn come from Lorna. Lorna thought of this now, how pretty Julie was, and could she help her?

"Grandma, are you here for a while? How long are you staying?" They would see each other soon, Julie was sure, embracing her outside Lorna's building.

How long *was* she staying? She by now with reason mistrusted the idea of permanence as a cynical hoax: the metaphor for real life was earthquake, and unwittingly, she was back in the right place for one.

7

We mustn't expect to have our hopes fulfilled immediately. If ever. When her grandmother had gone inside, Julia Willover walked down to North Beach, disappointed that Grandma Lorna hadn't invited her up, or asked about her life; but she understood that Lorna, whom Julie hadn't seen in two years, must be tired, had just arrived from Europe. Still, it would be so easy to have shown her the material for the Greek studies program she was hoping to sign up for through her major at UC Berkeley, explain costs and what a great opportunity it was. She also hoped that Grandma Lorna would be interested in donating to the inspiring and virtuous Circle of Faith they had been rallying in support of just now on Russian Hill, hosting a visionary British politician, their sponsor.

Julie was the only child of Lorna's only daughter, Peggy, and Peggy's ex-husband, Dick Willover, a rather Ran-like man, in Lorna's view; she thought him, though attractive, assertive and cheap. They do say that girls marry their fathers, at least the first time, and in Dick Willover, Peggy had done that, maybe even a slightly worse version—in Lorna's view. Lorna and Ran had loved Dick at first.

Julie was finishing her sophomore year at Berkeley, majoring in Peace and Conflict Studies (PACS). ("Fuck-all knows what that might be," Dick had protested, when asked to pay for Julie's college, "let her do something practical and then I'll cough up.") Peggy's divorce settlement had not required him to do so.

Dick Willover, an avid tennis player, spent a part of almost every day at the Cal Club and would hang around the bar after his game, picking up stock tips, or just yakking, hail-fellow-well-met. His coming out had not affected his habits or social life in any way, though he had left Peggy for a man seven or eight years before, someone he was no longer with. There was a certain amount of suspense in the family about which was his natural inclination, which the aberration, as he hadn't taken up with anyone else of either gender since breaking up with Tommy. Peggy had been devastated by what seemed to her as a rejection not only of her person but of her whole sex. She was only now beginning to feel some return of confidence in herself as a woman. Julie had accepted her parents' divorce as part of the times.

Dick was an architect, the author of the reliably selling guidebook *Bridges of the World.* He was also a devout Episcopalian—perhaps explaining Julie's bent toward the Circle of Faith, some gene-driven inclination toward spirituality or good works. He was known for his good works and goodwill, except toward Peggy. The court had not insisted he give her any money, and he didn't, figuring that since she got the house in Ukiah, that was enough. He also didn't give money to his daughter Julie, except intermittently, though there had been a court order about child support in force till she was eighteen and he had complied with that.

Julie Willover's beauty and resolve had been apparent from the time she was a toddler—she was now twenty. One of her earliest resolves had been to get out of Ukiah, California, where she was raised, but till now she had only made it as far as Berkeley, California, and Berkeley was not far enough; hence this plan to go to Greece.

Julie lived with three roommates in a house they rented together in the Richmond District, and she commuted by BART to the Berkeley campus for her classes, which took an hour each way. She'd managed to work her schedule so she only had to do the trip three times a week, and the other days she worked part-time at Macy's. She hoped to be kept on in some temp capacity or other throughout the summer, and had been interviewed for the billing office. She knew she was spread a little thin when her grades had dipped in the winter semester, but she needed the money, so what was the alternative?

Her hapless (in Julie's view) mother Peggy would have liked to help with the Greek project, but couldn't see why Julie needed to go all that way away, and had hoped that she would major in something practical, be a veterinarian, for example, or an athlete; in childhood she'd been wonderful at track. Peggy, as mothers will, had at times indulged a vision of Julie breasting the tape at the Olympics, then harvesting endorsements, being photographed, then moving into modeling or film. It was not even that unrealistic, except that Julie felt no inclination for sports, or animals for that matter, and was strangely indifferent to her own looks, having been gawky as a child, the self-image that remained with her.

Julie happened to have her brochure from UC about studying in Greece. She'd been showing it at the Circle of Faith. She tucked it into Lorna's market basket:

We will be choosing students who are creative, adventurous, and turned on to life. You have to be self-motivated, self-aware, poised, and someone who can forget Self in the service of others. And, yes, grades count too.

That was Julie to a T. The cost was forty-two hundred dollars for the semester, not including airfare, but including expeditions and side trips, board and room. Could Lorna help?

Dear Grandma Lorna, this is the program I told you about.
xoxo Julie

8

Hope springs eternal and is sometimes justified.

Julie's grandfather, Lorna's first husband, Randall Mott, had remarried. He and Amy Hawkins, the second wife, a much younger woman who had made a fortune in the dot-com world, lived in the woodsy community of Woodside, down the peninsula, nearer to Palo Alto than to San Francisco, on three acres, in an ivy-covered house older than those that most other dot-com millionaires were given to building themselves, but with a patina of comfort and charm that came only with the decades-old planting, and a purposeful indifference to fashion, with gables, outbuildings, vines. There was a tennis court, a pool fenced in against deer and other animals and toddlers, a stable, and a gabled quadruple garage with a second story and a weather vane atop a little cupola. To the basic house, several rooms had been added in an ell when Ran and Amy's child, Gilda, was born, for the nanny, for Gilda's nursery, and a playroom.

Gilda Mott, Ran and Amy's daughter, a lovely girl of fifteen, had been born a few months after their marriage and was their only child. Gilda had met but barely knew Papa's first family, and longed to know them, and loved them from afar, that is, from Woodside, where she, Papa, and Mama lived, thirty miles from San Francisco, in a suburb of lofty trees and the rustic, horsey air of privilege, the scent of pine and oak, large houses discreetly invisible through the landscaping and pool fences.

Gilda had much to regret—her name, Gilda, pronounced "Zheelda," a whim of her father's, mad for Verdi at the time of her birth; her only-child status; and above all her birth defects: she had been diagnosed at the age of seven with childhood diabetes and was obliged to wear a little machine to monitor her blood sugar continuously, an embarrassment every time she felt the gentle buzz against her hip and had to step into the girls' bathroom to prick her finger; and she often had to go to the hospital—a lot more often than other people.

Mostly she bore these afflictions with patience, the result of a sweet nature, but sometimes she felt a fiery bubble of resentful tears gather in her chest, with a pressure almost intolerable till it burst and trickled away under the impress of reality: there was nothing she could do. Sometimes she fantasized about letting insulin go wild in her bloodstream so she would lose consciousness and not have to deal with any of it and maybe not wake up.

Also, by a strange collusion of genes that neither of her normally pigmented parents had been aware of having, she was nearly an albino. Though it gave her very beautiful silvery hair, it also gave her pale eyes with a lashless look—she had experimented with mascara, but it was not allowed at her school—the inability to sit in the sun, and an unearthly walking-dead pallor that made people stare. "Like a vampire," she said of herself. She had read up on this condition, too—oculocutaneous albinism—and was reassured to learn that unlike diabetes it wouldn't shorten her life.

She attended a well-regarded Episcopal girls' school, Saint Waltraud's, that did a good job of shielding her from the realities the public schools might have exposed her to, like getting called a freak. Her parents adored her and tried to protect her from every harsh prospect, though she didn't especially want to be protected. She had read that the life expectancy of childhood diabetics was not very long, but she kept from her parents that she'd ever come upon such a crushing fact, and she tried not to dwell on it herself. She felt alive. Her mother donated heavily to the Children's Diabetes Foundation and other diabetes-focused charities in the expectation that something would be discovered in time. Gilda expected so too, and hoped so; for it to be otherwise would spoil everything.

Though he no longer practiced, her father Randall Mott kept up with his medical field. He hadn't been sorry to close his office for the practice of dermatology—dermatology had begun to bore him long since ("If it's wet, dry it out; if it's dry, moisturize"), and he saw his present role as being more important in the long run, steering his and Amy's funds toward the right causes, especially medical ones where his expertise counted. And especially toward subspecialty research bearing on diabetes, the horrendous affliction suffered by his child with Amy—his most beloved child by far. The three with Lorna, settled into their more or less unattractive early-middle-aged lives, he had loved with equal ardor when they were little, he supposed, but he couldn't remember that phase exactly, and the joys of child-rearing, raising that batch, had been compromised by constant friction with Lorna.

Now he seldom saw them. This was mostly for reasons of geography—Hams in Oakland, across the Bay Bridge, traffic impossibly stop-and-go most of the time; Peggy in Ukiah, obliged to drive through Santa Rosa, also impossibly jammed, also stop-and-go most of the time. And though of course ready to help them if asked, he didn't feel very involved in their lives. An exception was during Curt's coma, which brought out both the doctor and concerned parent in him.

Ran and Amy kept an office/apartment in San Francisco near the Embarcadero, not a medical office but for business or meeting friends up in the city, or where he and Amy could stay over when they went to the opera or a movie. Amy had an office in Menlo Park, too, where she ran her affairs, mostly managing the money she'd amassed investing in early tech start-ups; Ran began each day by driving to San Francisco from Woodside (after the commute hours), reading the papers, then catching up on selected medical periodicals that he subscribed to by mail or online, idly reviewing the general articles in the *New England Journal of Medicine* and then developments in his specialty of dermatology.

Ran loved the Woodside house where he lived with Amy and Gilda—it was his love for it that made him force himself to go up to the city and read medical journals every workday, for fear of sinking into the condition he was actually drawn to, that of idle, older house-husband of younger rich woman. He needed to elude the pull of this enviable and comfortable state, and the interesting details of Amy's life, which he tried not to meddle in; she was fully busy with her Silicon Valley–related, mysterious concerns. With his wife so much younger, he needed not to feel old; he played tennis and jogged; and when his gout kicked up, he explained it as a tennis injury.

In a few days, Amy and Ran were to sponsor a fund-raising affair, a dinner to be held after the opera, where half the money, ten thousand dollars a plate, was to go to the opera itself, and half to the Children's Diabetes Foundation. There was no shortage of people to attend at that price, and the high price ensured that it would have some social cachet. Now that the dot-com generation was beginning to take an interest in civic issues and culture, these fund-raising things were always oversubscribed. Both California senators would be there, and many rich people in San Francisco, the glamorous woman attorney general, and possibly the great diva Anna Katrova Miller, if she wasn't too tired after her performance (in *La Wally*).

It was known by many that the Motts had a seriously diabetic child, though not known whether she was old enough to attend the dinner. Amy herself had no social ambitions, and—Ran admitted to himself—few social graces, and was an unusually forthright person, like many of her Silicon Valley friends. But she valued culture: though Amy Hawkins Mott came out of the dot-com milieu and had kept her many friends there, she had also spent a year or two in France when she was younger and had brought back a certain impatience with the local scale of things, thought the California and Colorado ski areas almost too small to bother with, and took the family to Chamonix in the winters.

One recent morning Ran had made the drive to San Francisco, fixed his coffee, finished the medical journals, and was just reading the item in the *Chronicle* about the slipping cemetery of the French village of Pont-les-Puits, an amusing story in itself, featuring, especially, the bones of some saint and of Russell Woods, the painter. The name of the town caught his eye because of his first wife Lorna living there. His view of her had softened over the years; now he understood that during their marriage she had been struggling for her identity—Amy had explained to him about female identity crises. She had no rancor toward the unfortunate Lorna.

"There she was, stuck at home," she had sympathetically diagnosed Lorna's plight in retrospect. "She was overqualified, frustrated. All those little children, no one to help her . . ." Amy, much younger, had been saved by Silicon Valley, but was well versed in the psychology of the benighted times before women like herself could have interesting professional lives. In Ran's view, Lorna had been a bitch for sure, and a terrible mother, but even there, with the passage of time and the comforts of affluence, his former rancor had diminished. He didn't follow her doings and was unaware of her domestic problems, and had assumed she was still over in France, married to the Frenchman.

Then his granddaughter Julie turned up unexpectedly at his office—Peggy's daughter, Julie, a nice girl with get-up-and-go whom he was able to steer toward a job. Julie caught him by surprise—he was really not much in touch with his daughter Peggy or her family, though he and Peggy spoke from time to time and he saw her ex-husband Dick Willover at the Cal Club and in summer at the Bohemian Grove. Julie was in college, busy with her life, and Amy hadn't shown much interest in her, though Amy doted on Curt's little twins, Marcus and Manuel, and sent them educational gifts, Legos and such.

Now Julie, Peggy's only child, was here, a pretty, cheerful-looking girl, who must be a junior in college by now. Taller than her mother—gets that from Dick—with the blondish long hair girls wore now, very pink cheeks, and quite well filled out. A strong girl, he thought.

"I really hope I'm not disturbing you, Grandpa Ran."

"We don't see enough of you, Julie, tell me what brings you."

She'd been a little reluctant to approach her grandfather; she didn't know him very well. Certainly her mother was afraid of him, or maybe mad at him, and they didn't see him often. Peggy and her brothers were all kind of estranged. They felt friendly toward each other, as nearly as Julie could tell, but lived too far from one another in the sprawling Bay

Area. Toward their father, some resentment that he wasn't more helpful; but she got up her nerve. No one in the family needed to know she'd seen him. He'd been perfectly nice, welcoming even.

She had been much younger the last time she saw him, and then he had seemed old, but now, from the perspective of being older herself, she was surprised at his youthful looks—she wasn't so sure about the golf shirt and khakis. Probably she'd last seen him when she was about seventeen or eighteen, and probably everyone had looked old to her then, but now at twenty she could see he was a nice-looking man, his hair wasn't even that gray, he looked physically strong and fit, tan like a jogger, only the least little paunch, or not even—not like a grandfather—but she hoped he felt grandfatherly.

During the interview with Grandpa Ran, Julie mentioned that she hoped her grandmother Lorna would be helping with her study funds, implying that her grandfather would not want to be outdone.

"Grandma Lorna hasn't told me yet how much she can spare, but I can prepare a budget to show you both, with all the figures. Airfare, extras." Suggesting he would want to equal Lorna in generosity. She added that Grandma Lorna was newly returned from France.

Ran found this kind of blackmail easy to resist. He proposed Julie could earn some money helping the caterers with the opera dinner he and Amy were giving.

"Okay, great, I'm happy to do that." She wrote down the details. "Will I wear a uniform? I guess they'll tell me." Her enthusiasm reassured him about her sincerity and willingness to work. She was as pretty as her mother Peggy had been at that age, possibly even prettier.

"I have no idea what caterers pay, but I'm sure it'll help," her grandfather said firmly. "No need to account to me. I'm sure Lorna will appreciate some numbers though," as though Lorna were the Shylock of grandmothers, mean and exacting. This scared Julie a little, since she didn't really know Grandma Lorna very well, either.

9

W hich is worse, to meddle or withdraw?

Ran Mott, seeing Julie, had not been able to suppress a little feeling of family-related guilt. Earlier that morning he had had a disquieting interview with a former associate of his son Curt's, who gave his name as Harvey Avon. Avon turned out to be a slight man in his thirties, beginning to bald, wearing jeans and boots and a black T-shirt, the uniform of the tech world. Avon, not bothering with much in the way of introduction, said he was an investor in one of Curt's start-ups—a system of software-controlled hydroponics, growing things in water without soil, soil which would be in short supply sooner than we think. Avon had an interest in seeing through things Curt had started.

"I should tell you I know nothing about Curt's affairs," Ran warned Avon. What had happened to Curt was heartbreaking enough, though he didn't say it to this stranger, without the pain of probing in more detail into his life and businesses, to discover either that a great mind had been wasted, or that his son had been a fool, neither something he wanted to know. He'd also been infected with some of Amy's rich-person wariness about approaches from strangers.

Harvey Avon spread his hands to express how little Ran's ignorance mattered. They were used to people not understanding the details of their software innovations, and investors had to depend on their track record, which, if he did say so, was brilliant, especially when Curt had had it in hand. Curt's accident had left them all in a bad place, bad, bad, bad, but it was great that he was recovering in—Thailand, was it?

"No one is quite sure. His wife gets the odd postcard."

"I hope she realizes she's a partner, she'll be liable for the money he took out."

"I'm sure he's left things in good order," Ran said, not sure at all.

Thinking about Curt made Ran think guiltily of the last time he'd seen Curt's wife Donna, right about the time Curt had woken up. He'd gone as usual to Curt's care facility, on Q Street below Parnassus, and parked along the driveway where Donna's car had pulled in. The driveway was reserved for clients—God knew where the staff attendants were expected to put their cars. Sometimes it was still possible to park around there, one of the few parkable areas left in town. This care facility had at one time been a residential duplex, now converted, with handrails, sterilizers, and ramps, faintly smelling of benzene, rubbing alcohol, and pee.

During the coma, the ritual was to peek into Curt's room, stand in the doorway for a few minutes, as if staring at him would make him stir, until discomfort—pain—overtook you, and you gently closed the door. He had learned to let emotion take him instead of trying to come up with cheerful, bullshit thoughts about the probable prognosis. Ran had schooled himself to tamp down the anguish he always first felt seeing his son like this, prompting recollections of Curt as a little boy getting them up at night for drinks of water or to dispel his fear of wolves under the bed.

His daughter-in-law had usually been sitting reading in the living room–cum–waiting room and would get up dutifully to be pecked on the cheek. He remembered once noticing she looked unusually attractive—he didn't usually think about her looks—and wondered if something was improving in her life. Peggy and Lorna, and perhaps others, had always believed that Curt would one day wake up. Ran, a more pessimistic and also better-informed person, at that point didn't, but didn't really know. Donna reverted to pieties about God's will. When he had gone to sit at Curt's bedside, twice a week at least—perhaps less often as time wore on—there would be Donna sitting there. He remembered the last time he'd seen her.

"The nurse told me he opened his eyes last night. She didn't see it happen, it was on the night report. The doctor is coming, which is why I've stayed."

Her fidelity had given him a better impression of her than he'd once had, revising his less-than-enthusiastic welcome of their marriage. At first he hadn't liked her, found her insipid, short, and vague, not that pretty, even if she had been homecoming queen when she was at U. Delaware, the main thing anyone ever said about her. As always, he found her too passive and quiet now, kind of permanently stunned-seeming, though she did have a trim little figure. Some bloom of duski-ness shone under her skin—Italian grandparents, she had said, but he thought maybe Hispanic, or a Southern octoroon thing wouldn't have surprised him.

Donna and Curt had met in some tech environment where they both worked, but she left off work as soon as they were married—she was pregnant already. She'd quickly produced two small twin boys, Marcus and Manuel. How strange it was, this onslaught of twins in the world, an in-vitro-fertilization phenomenon but surely not in this case. What a good mother Donna seemed to be, the twins always immac-ulate in matching little denim jackets and hats, always with skinned knees, like real boys.

Ran knew she had money problems, with huge mortgage payments, the absurd school fees for the twins—whom he thought of as Romulus and Remus—God knew what other expenses. Donna's problems inter-ested Amy, who liked her—they had the tech world in common.

Since Curt's escape to Thailand, Donna had hung on the cusp of belief, tipping toward the side of mistrust, anger, despair, and she could see that her father-in-law Ran was tipping, too, toward the same idea that Curt didn't mean to come back at all, sticking her with maxed-out credit cards, small children, nursery-school tuition of more than fifteen hundred a month and that's just for the morning, three-days-a-week-only program, so she couldn't go back to work, and the jumbo mortgage with staggering payments, which Curt had said not to worry about. And now the bottoming out of the housing market meant she couldn't sell if she had to. She was sick with worry, which Ran could well understand.

And now this man Avon seemed to be saying that Curt had also borrowed $1,750,000—nearly $2 million—against his share of the company Curt, with Avon and two others, had started, with capital they in turn had borrowed from the Bank of America two years ago. That is, Curt had taken this money out of the company—in what form? And used it for—what? They couldn't find it; notes were due at the B of A.

"Did he ever mention what he did with it?"

"I have no idea," Ran said, stunned and mistrustful. "His mortgage, maybe?" Ran was a professional man, a physician, ergo no business-man, didn't know much about Curt's world, and found Avon mysteri-ous and slightly off-color, too slick.

Ran had been disappointed, ever so slightly, in Curt's career, had certainly never mentioned his hopes that Curt would have gone to medical school, at Stanford like him, or at least UCSF. Instead, Curt had got an MBA at the Wharton School, whatever that was, doubtless due to the baleful influence of Lorna, who had been more at home than he on the East Coast because of her lecture venues. Like Lorna, Ran was born in California and went to Stanford; though she had wandered off far into the great world, they were both Californians all through— that is to say, optimistic most of the time.

"I'm not sure I can get hold of Curt," Ran told Avon. "You've prob-ably tried yourself. We don't hear from him."

"He'll have to come out of this Fu Manchu phase eventually. I guess he's living high on the hog over there?"

"I've wondered about his finances," Ran said, truly enough.

Donna was in his thoughts also because he had heard recently from his wife Amy that she planned to do something especially hand-some for the absent Curt and the abandoned Donna by paying off the enormous mortgage they had unwisely incurred before Curt's accident, when he had been on his way to doing well, and which was now in danger of being foreclosed. People were losing their houses across the nation, something about rot in the bond market, or—nobody knew why. Maybe Amy understood it. Ran had counseled against her paying off Curt's giant mortgage on general principles, for the moment.

"It's underwater as it is," Amy said. "These high-end properties are liabilities. I suppose things will recover, but at the moment . . ."

"That's a lot of money," he mildly observed, knowing full well the mortgage was more than three million dollars. Would this protect Donna from Harvey Avon or just give her an asset he could sue to acquire? He said nothing.

"They can pay me back when they sell someday," Amy said. "When things get back to normal. It makes no sense to just let the bank have the house and lose all that equity. Nor to keep paying the loan for that matter. Even if it is underwater. It probably is, but the value will come back. The interest alone would come to more than a million by the end of the term."

Ran thought, uncharacteristically, about his other children and their problems that money could help mitigate. Well, Hams and Peggy—Curt apparently went off with some money. He would like to have said "What about the others?" but had a rule never to bring up his Lorna children to Amy, especially their limitations, as she was touchy about them. He believed she saw them as incompetent and retarded. It was just a look she had, with a tiny shake of the head when she heard of yet another of their screwups. Unfairly healthy when their own child had heavy afflictions. Ran didn't ever push or promise on their behalf, but gave limited help when he remembered. Mostly, the problems of his Lorna children could be construed as their own doing, stemming from lack of application or the wrong spouses, but the problems of Curt and Donna lay with fate, were not their fault, were deserving of her pity and help.

"No good deed goes unpunished," he warned her.

10

Someone will always say "I told you so."

Lorna spent a restless, jet-lagged night in Pam's unfamiliar, once expensively upholstered bed, decorated in the distant past in a very pretty Colefax and Fowler print, the fabric now faded and shredded around the bottom, the work of some former or absent cat. Despite not sleeping well—unused to the urban sirens wailing all night at the foot of Russian Hill and through North Beach—Lorna, taking stock, could see already that she hadn't thought through a number of other potential problems she might be facing: whether to drive, where to live, would anyone ever ask her to dinner? She'd been focused on her lectures and her professional reentry, but there was much more to reestablishing yourself in your old social life, too. Eventually, she'd have to face the DMV. Which restaurant to invite the children to tonight?

She felt herself repaired the next morning, and braced to call the other children to announce her return, make dates with them, hear the news, offer support and sympathy. She was now ashamed of her selfish evasions of the night before. She would call her granddaughter Julie first. She bounded to the shower, found something of Pam's to put on, dried her hair. What joy that her thoughtful hostess had arranged for the *San Francisco Chronicle* to be tucked under the door, or else had forgotten to cancel it: reading the paper postponed the interface with reality.

But she found she had only the most passing interest in the local news. It hadn't changed for twenty years—bickering among the supervisors, shootings, the same calendar of events, the same events and even the same sponsors. She scanned the social columns without success for the names of Amy Hawkins Mott and Randall Mott.

When she went into the tiny kitchen and opened the cupboards looking for a plate and a cup, a feeling rose again of displacement and defeat, Pam's can of stale Folgers coffee a rebuke. Some people didn't move on to Nespresso pods, didn't throw out jars of spices years old, slept in faded beds. Some people came back where they started, but the worse for wear.

From New York she had spoken to Peggy and emailed Hams and Donna that she was coming back to America, without explaining why. She had not felt that she needed to explain (never apologize, never explain). But she had been rather startled when not one of them expressed any surprise, as if it were foredoomed for a grown woman with grown children who'd been so unwise as to flit off to France in middle age with a French husband. They had also seemed to find it normal that a person living abroad would eventually come back to California. California was like France in that if you began there, you always came back. Their adolescent disapproval when she'd left made it more painful now to acknowledge they'd been right.

At about ten, Lorna confronted checking in with them, though she was still uncertain how to explain her return to America except as a career move, not a defeat. A feeling of maternal excitement, jolted by having seen her granddaughter Julie the night she arrived, intensified, prompted her to gather them all for dinner that night.

She began by telephoning Peggy, who had already heard the story, and who knew she must be in San Francisco by now. But questions were postponed when Peggy told her at once about the strange phone call from France about the catastrophe that had befallen the cemetery. At first Lorna laughed merrily, remembering the tumbled graves and imagining the civic consternation. Also very funny that the village of Pont-les-Puits thought she was related to Russ Woods.

"If I were his heir, that would be one thing," she said, laughing. "Wouldn't that be nice?"

"They spoke of billing and charges, Mother," Peggy said. "I think you better make it clear that you aren't."

She and Peggy spoke a bit longer, about Peggy's life, Lorna ready with maternal advice. In Lorna's view, Peggy's problems were more existential than practical: in a rut, stuck somewhere in her forties, without money or profession, she needed to find direction. Luckily she had inner calm, or was it just a slightly bovine nature? As her mother, Lorna could propose some sensible mitigating measures: a better haircut, refinancing, taking a class, losing ten pounds, joining something—that commonplace stratagem for meeting people. Lorna might urge her to get a job—something that would put her out into the dynamic world, instead of devoting herself to making stained-glass wind chimes to sell at a loss.

After her worries about Peggy, her reflex worries about Hams prompted her to call him and Misty next, to propose dinner, a restaurant of their choice, since she didn't know the restaurants anymore. Could they suggest a restaurant nearby? In France she would have roasted a big leg of lamb in the medieval fireplace of Armand's—their—former house, but she didn't feel she could organize groceries and cook in Pam's little kitchen.

Hams and Misty, who lived penuriously in Oakland, had nothing to suggest in the way of San Francisco places to eat, nor did Julie, who had a night class, so after they hung up, Lorna walked around and reserved at a little restaurant on Polk Street. It didn't seem very grand— she'd hoped for a little more festive splash. She suspected that the ease with which she was able to get in meant it wasn't chic, possibly not good, but it was within walking distance, so she hoped for the best. People had told her you had to book weeks in advance for good San Francisco restaurants now, they were always crowded with adolescent vegan dot-com millionaires drinking fabulous vintage wines. Would Hams and Misty think she was taking them to a down-market restaurant? Or maybe it was a fashionably plain restaurant? Would Donna scorn it, she who was probably used to better, living as she did in splendor in Pacific Heights? Where were the good restaurants now?

After talking to Peggy and Hams, instead of mustering all her force to call Curt's wife Donna, whom they all found difficult, Lorna called the realtor Ursula Aymes. When she had last lived in San Francisco, after her divorce from Ran, Lorna had found a house to rent with the help of Ursula, an agent at Tubb-Brandish, the highly successful real-estate company. Before she spoke to the children tonight, it would be prudent to have a strategy about where she'd be living.

Ursula was a glamorous Middle European woman, perhaps Czech, always newly divorced from some senior insurance executive or clubman. She had hair tastefully blonde and wore wonderful jackets that could be Chanel, came to galas in Oscar de la Renta, and exuded an air of sandalwood and something else, her personal scent: Was it Fracas? She specialized in understanding what sort of property people like herself, and like Lorna—people of taste—would want; she had considerable cachet, an enviable client list, and all those ex-husbands judiciously chosen from the list; and though none of her marriages had worked out, she always stayed on good terms with husbands, escrow officers, and banks, and even with clients initially disgruntled.

"Just a pied-à-terre, I won't be here too much." Lorna mentioned a reduced budget, but she didn't reveal to Ursula just how reduced. She wasn't sure herself what things were going to cost. They agreed that Ursula would pick her up at two that afternoon for an initial look around.

At two, Lorna went down in the elevator and waited outside the building. Ursula Aymes pulled up in her Mercedes, late model but not ostentatiously brand-new, the de rigueur car for San Francisco real-estate ladies, an inevitable badge or requirement of success in the property market—although male agents sometimes drove BMW convertibles or even Jaguars.

Mrs. Aymes found Lorna overdressed in a beautiful dress of Pam's and heels. "Ought to make a solvent impression on landlords," Lorna explained. As they were old acquaintances, Ursula got out to embrace

Lorna. Her eyes flicked over Lorna's bag, which was impeccably French, like her *tailleur.* They embraced. "Lorna, you look marvelous." Ursula also looked marvelous.

As they set off, Lorna began to explain what she needed: small pied-à-terre, she'd be on the road a lot, only wanted somewhere for her clothes and books. Two bedrooms would be nice, so she'd have a study that could double as a guest room, so grandchildren could stay over. Quiet, if you please, and not in the fog belt; Telegraph or Russian Hill okay, or Nob in a pinch. Or around the Presidio but not on the ocean side . . . Parking, of course . . .

"Lorna!" Ursula seemed to be laughing. "What are you smoking, as the kids all say? Your eyes will open." Ursula's slight European accent—what was it?—enhanced her quality of astute reliability when it might easily have been the opposite, suggesting foreignness and deals.

Lorna had been used to thinking it was the French who lived in crowded little spaces—not in Pont-les-Puits, of course, but certainly in Paris—now she saw it was true in San Francisco, too. The new-built places down by the baseball park had mean little bedrooms and kitchen islands jutting into the living rooms, a feature the French referred to as *cuisines américaines,* which Lorna had always maintained didn't exist in America. Larger old Victorian conversions were dark, bicycles impeding the passages; dour modern buildings had been shochorned in between them, homeless people in pop-up tents outside.

At the end of three hours, Lorna was overwhelmed with despair, and Ursula had plainly tired of their futile excursion. She mendaciously pleaded another appointment, but promised to keep Lorna in mind if something should come up. "There's always something out there," Ursula said in her professionally reassuring voice, but Lorna recognized the lie. "Maybe you should look in Oakland," Ursula added. "Or even Richmond."

Another thing she said, Lorna would remember later: "I suppose you're getting an American divorce? I hear French judges are hard on Americans, especially the wife. A client of mine—well, you know her, Denise Hope . . ."

"Ah . . . divorcing," Lorna said. "I'll have to decide . . ."

Here was a new concern; she hadn't troubled about the details of a divorce—she and Armand-Loup had agreed about him selling his house, and how she wouldn't ask for support forever. If they did divorce—by *consentement mutuel*, they didn't want expensive acrimony. Now she saw she needed advice on this point—support—she was at sea: Where, France or America, was the best place to get a separation including some financial help? She understood that alimony was now a thing of the past, but her generation was used to it, and had not prepared themselves for self-sufficiency. Perhaps judges allowed for age-related deficiencies. She maybe hadn't internalized the new realities, but she still needed a little money, just for a while, to get her on her feet.

11

A love of art is as universal as admiration of fame.

In France, in Pont-les-Puits, the *bibliothèque,* which occupied part of the city hall—the *mairie*—had an exhibition space in which it was planning to hold a display of articles related to the painter Russell Woods, now that he had turned into someone so posthumously famous. He had left his brushes and painting gear in the hotel where he'd lived year in, year out, along with a paint-bespattered windbreaker, a straw hat, some letters and papers; and these would form the basis of a permanent exhibition, the way in other places Van Gogh's notebooks were shown, or matchbooks Picasso had doodled on.

These artifacts had come to Mayor Barbara Levier's notice when they had to open Woods's boxes looking for something with his DNA on it. Like Madame Grogue, his landlady, who had packed up his stuff after his death, Barbara was not comfortable reading English, so had given no more than a glance at the letters, looking for return addresses or an address book, which could be a source of next-of-kin information. Eventually, English-speaking art experts would come to read Woods's letters, she supposed, though they hadn't at the time of poor Monsieur Woods's death.

She'd been overjoyed to find an envelope addressed to Lorna Dumas, since Madame Dumas was someone they all knew and could get in touch with. Woods had directed this letter to Lorna's former French address but had never sent it, its contents a program from an art show in Toulouse. Madame the Mayor planned to forward it now, supposing Monsieur Dumas would have Lorna's current address. Maybe Lorna would appreciate having a communication from beyond the grave from her old friend Woods, with whom she'd spent a fair amount of time, two Anglophones both interested in art, who found themselves to be the two Americans in a small French town.

Madame Levier knew Lorna Dumas, the American wife of the respected Monsieur Armand-Loup Dumas. There had been these American wives around town before, although Monsieur Dumas's earlier two wives had been French. It was too strong to say Madame Levier hated Lorna, but she never liked any of these American wives of French husbands, trying to be more French than the French, inevitably with plenty of money, swanning around being stupid about the simplest things, and they were *souillons,* slobs, in their jeans like tourists. The cookery Americans who flocked to the village were all right, reverent and cooperative, eager to learn, but the American wives were apt to have a certain triumphalist air—whether to have captured a prize, that is to say, a Frenchman, or proud to have escaped from their own terrible, racist country with its daily lynchings and gunfights, and who could blame them? Their efforts to speak French were pathetic, especially if they'd studied it and prided themselves, because then they thought they knew French and tried slang. The junior-year-abroad types were the worst. To be fair, Madame Dumas gave herself no airs about her French. Madame Levier didn't like Lorna, but she would have to keep trying to call her, as they needed her in the matter of Monsieur Woods's bones.

12

Family feeling is important if sometimes misplaced.

For Mother's dinner, poor Peggy Willover had to drive one hundred fourteen miles down U.S. 101, mostly four-lane, to San Francisco from Ukiah to the north, but once in the city, or, as San Franciscans called it, the City, she'd stay over and sleep on Mother's sofa, and she could drive Mother the following day to the airport to get her plane to Bakersfield. Peggy was a little spooked; it seemed to her as she pulled out of her garage that she'd seen the loan shark parked across the street. Had he been planning to accost her about starting her payments? Had he been thinking of renewing his hint that if she slept with him, things might go better with her attempt to annul the thing she had unwisely signed? She had thought of a better way out of her contract—she would just not accept the money she'd theoretically borrowed. Then there could be no interest owed, though she'd probably still have some payoff penalty or fees. She'd tell the bank not to accept any automatic deposits in case he tried to force her to accept the money. Could he compel her to take it? Would he sue her?

Apart from her house worries, she was looking forward to seeing her mother; it had been nearly a year since Lorna's last visit. Talking to her friends, Peggy had come to realize that, as mothers went, Lorna, though seemingly defective in motherliness, at least had an interesting life, unlike her own. It would be nice to have her in America for a change. Peggy planned to help with the task of apartment hunting, and otherwise to make herself useful if she could, suspecting it was a tough time for Lorna, she was going through something.

She brought a few letters that had come for Lorna, including, it looked like, one from the French city of Pont-les-Puits, the same people who kept telephoning. Peggy was about fed up with fielding calls from the people in France, who had a tendency to forget the time difference and dial when they got to their offices in the morning, midnight in California. She had taken to putting Lorna's phone number on her own answering machine and turning off the ring when she went to bed. The result when she listened to her messages in the morning gave her some sense of the turn Lorna's life there had taken—here were the mayor, *agents immobilières,* and the cemetery people about Russell Woods's DNA. The speakers all had parody French accents when they spoke English: "Zees ees Barbara Levier, Pohn-lay-Pwee." Once, Mother's husband, Armand-Loup, in his somewhat-British-sounding English, left a brisk message related to a house sale. Poor Mother. Not surprising that she didn't want to talk about it all. Still, Peggy did wonder what had gone wrong between them. Lorna had been vague, things just not working out, the usual.

Another of the messages for Lorna had been from Peggy's sister-in-law, Curt's wife Donna, gasping strangely, promising "news" when they saw each other, which gave Peggy a stab of elation, for it could only mean good news about Curt, though this was followed by a chill of dread of bad news of some kind. Donna, who had a knack for saying the wrong thing, had a few days earlier planted a new fear in Peggy: about Lorna's coming home, Donna had said, "Oh, I hope she's okay. People like to get nearer their children when, you know, they get sick or older."

"I haven't heard she's sick."

"Didn't her father have early dementia?"

"Mother is fine," Peggy said, hoping that was true.

"What about the husband?"

"I don't know," Peggy had to admit.

"Women have midlife crises, too, you know. Not just men."

Peggy was as usual bemused by her mother and became more than a little worried about what Lorna's sudden return might portend. When Lorna was safely somewhere else, Peggy and her siblings were reassured that their mother was fine; with her return, the usual considerations people had to face regarding aging parents reared up: Midlife crisis? Or was Lorna ill? Was she getting—odd? Would she get odd in the future? As the daughter, Peggy knew all the care would fall to her, whenever it reared. At least if their father got odd, his rich wife could deal with it.

She would be appointed the caregiver on account of the banality of her life. Nothing better to do. Dad and his rich wife, Curt and his nearly fatal injury, poor hippie Hams struggling in Oakland—his life was not banal, and he got fun out of his music and being a chef, Peggy imagined. Hers was the only boring life in the family; she knew that but didn't know how to fix it, or if she even wanted to. She was pretty happy, but knew she'd be happier if she had the energy to do one or more of the things people were always advising—take a dance class or life drawing, join a church group, volunteer for orphans. It was that she felt she took up too much space at a dance class, say—was too tall or too shy—something. Mother, whenever in the country, was always telling her to tint her hair, which was the color that used to be called dishwater blonde. In her heart, she admired her brother Curt for disappearing.

She wondered what news Donna had for Lorna. Curt's family didn't really like Donna—a short MBA from the world of biotech: brittle, overinterested in money, East Coast, but without the possible advantages of East Coast–ness, like a nice island in Maine, or a woodsy camp somewhere with antler chandeliers. Donna was from Delaware—she had an MBA from the school in Philadelphia Curt had seen fit to go to, who knew why, and he'd come back with this degree and a bride, her. Donna was pretty, but not that pretty—that is, not pretty enough to explain Curt's going to the trouble of importing her to California, and flouting all kinds of unexamined assumptions about a suitable wife. Brown eyes, too, the only brown eyes in the family—until now, their twins, Marcus and Manuel. It had flitted across the family's mind that Donna could be Jewish, those brown eyes and dark hair . . . not that that would be anything against her, far from it, "We could use a genetic upgrade," Peggy had approved. Or Donna could be Hispanic, despite her maiden name Donofrio. Her exotic origins could explain why her reactions were not always in sync with what the rest of them would likely think.

Donna was a good mother—the twins were cute—but she was overprotective. You could just see the food allergies and tantrums coming on. From the way Donna scoured the floors and—surely apocryphal detail—washed the clothesline; they believed this although no one had clotheslines in Pacific Heights, there was an ordinance. Misty had eventually reminded them it was the prime minister of Israel's wife, not Donna, who supposedly washed the clotheslines.

But Dad's wife, stepmother Amy, liked Donna, presumably because they both came from the tech world and shared a vocabulary of bytes and binaries. She and Amy had long talks about at-home start-ups Donna could create, and an idea Donna had for a product-testing website, though anything she might have got going after the birth of the twins was on hold now because of Curt. Though the others didn't really like her, they were sorry for her not having some real family in the area, some natural constituency that would mitigate her slightly tense tactlessness. They also thought she was bossy and that she whined.

"She's like someone who suffers from an orphan disease," Peggy once said. "Wanting all the labs to work on her case only." They did admire her poise and courage during Curt's coma, given the threat of Curt's probable death and the consequence, omnipresent and incapable of being mitigated, of foreclosure and ruin. So enormous was Donna and Curt's mortgage—so beyond any hope given his condition, problem, whatever they were to call it—the only way to live with her situation was to talk about it a lot, with her sister-in-law Peggy, with Hams (she did not get on with Misty), and presumably with her own family, though no one had ever met any of them, in faraway Delaware. The Mott siblings indulged her but considered her a whiner.

About a year before Curt's accident, and before the bottom dropped out of the housing market, Curt and Donna had bought a house in Pacific Heights, at Jackson and Spruce, paying too much, as everybody had to do then to get any house at all, and they considered themselves unbelievably blessed to find this one, so exactly what they wanted, with enough bedrooms for their growing family, and enough pretensions to reassure his start-up investors, and a curious resemblance, purely coin-cidental, to their mother's house—Armand-Loup's house—in France; that is, in a French farmhouse style with the giant fireplace in the kitchen, beams, floors of polished terra-cotta, parquet in some rooms, the quintessence of *Architectural Digest* comfort and charm. Curt and Donna were not candid when it came to disclosing the price except to say they'd gone a little crazy but values would catch up. Mrs. Aymes, their real-estate broker, had advised them to make the stretch. "Even if you have to scrimp a little more now, eventually it will seem like a bar-gain, this is practically a law of economics," Ursula had assured them.

"It *is* a law of economics," Curt had said to Donna, "Ponzi's Law if there's a crash." Little had they thought of the kind of crash he would soon experience. Their mortgage payments were more than eighteen thousand dollars a month.

Since Curt's accident, Donna knew—was constantly being told—she should sell, but at first she couldn't give up the belief that Curt was going to wake up soon, and what would it be like to tell him his house was gone and they were homeless, living somewhere like Pacifica or Daly City, and would have to start over? She knew that happened—the news was always showing foreclosed people. The newscasters reported in voices of unctuous sympathy that barely concealed their scorn for people who had overreached or allowed life to treat them badly. People who were living in their cars.

13

So many things are begun or settled over family dinners.

Arriving at Lorna's friend's apartment, Peggy braved the faint sneer of the doorman, who took her ancient Subaru off to be parked out of sight, and went up to the tenth floor. Lorna embraced her. Her mother was looking well and no older, Peggy noticed with relief, though it crossed her mind that Mother's hair color, tinted a very French brownish-reddish gold, a color seldom seen in America, would be hard to duplicate here. Hams and Misty also turned up at Lorna's (Pam's) apartment, soon after Peggy got there.

Lorna found her daughter-in-law Misty as scary looking as ever, with metal rings hanging out of her eyebrows, and now thinner than Lorna had remembered. With the clarity of vision that lasts only a few minutes when you arrive somewhere, before familiarity distorts the reality, Lorna could see her children clearly. She found Peggy no thinner and as badly dressed as ever, and not disguising the gray that was starting—early, it seemed to Lorna—and Hams was suddenly a middle-aged man. She saw he'd put on weight and had the coarsened skin of adulthood and a not-unpleasant male smell.

Lorna's heart stirred with motherly concern. What would these people do without her, someday? They'd be fine, of course; she had deserted them once already by going off to France, and they'd been fine.

Ambivalence, the most insupportable of states, tore at her, too complicated to be borne. She was grateful that Hams was happy enough, but
in the past, their meetings were always tense and involved him asking
for things she couldn't provide, chiefly money and, once, her car, or,
when she had the house in France, that she welcome droves of his wandering hippie friends or appear at meetings of the New Age organiza-
tions they tended to join and abandon. She blamed herself for his easy,
morally fragile, sponging mentality; she feared it was the legacy of her
going those few times to EST or those Big Sur spas back in the sixties,
before the children were born.

That had been her ski-bunny phase, but things were so different
then. Her own children had never had ski-bunny phases, had moved
directly from college into a sort of attenuated form of semi-adult life,
except for Hams, who remained stuck in the seventies. Just as the Vic-
torians must have been shocked by the bawdy free-love ways of their
parents' generation of eighteenth-century freethinkers, so Curt, Hams,
and Peggy would have been shocked if they knew some of the things
their mother and her friends had been up to, before her marriage to
their father, of course, and a little bit after it. It was the times. Now no
one looking at the polished, soignée art lecturer would imagine a raffish past.

When Lorna gave them a glass of sherry out of Pam's drinks cupboard (remember to replace), Misty refused in reproachful tones, adding, "After all, I might be pregnant."

"But that's wonderful! What great news!" Lorna had a moment of
compunction. Would Hams be an adequate father? "In France, they
think a glass of wine is okay," Lorna said. "Here not, I gather." She'd
forgotten the sanctimonious health preoccupations of Americans,
which the French derided but ended up emulating.

"Fetal alcohol syndrome," Hams explained, as if France, in its ignorance, was rife with it. Would Hams and Misty think of their baby as
"the fetus"? Lorna was dismayed to see that Misty seemed to think she
would poison her own grandchild, "fetus."

"Centuries of mothers have been drinking a glass of wine," Lorna
persisted. "Maybe in the first few weeks . . ." Her brain whirred. Had
she damaged her children's brains with alcohol? Been a good-enough

mother to Hams, that he should turn out to be this shabby person married to a dry-cleaner employee? No, of course she hadn't been a good mother, she'd been too preoccupied, all those years when his infant soul was yearning for attention and direction . . . She had mostly learned to manage these floods of remorse that could so suddenly course through her. Her friends all agreed that remorse was a normal, natural part of being a parent and even a grandparent; but peer support could only go so far to assuage it.

As they had put on their coats, needed in the June San Francisco chill, to walk down to the restaurant, Lorna had a moment to glance at the letters Peggy had brought. One from a legal office in Toulouse. She took a quick peek: Armand-Loup had filed some official paper in France, mentioning desertion.

They walked down Green Street to the Point d'Honeur restaurant. From Jones and Green, in one direction they could see the Bay Bridge ignite its festoons of lights; the city lay in the other; pink infused the sky. Where was it more beautiful than here? Lorna remembered that one of the Hearsts used to live in the brick house there, and the Vietnamese nail salon was no longer where it used to be.

Donna was already waiting at the restaurant, standing by the bar, not drinking anything. She looked younger than Lorna remembered, and she'd learned to dress more elegantly than when she and Curt were first married, less like a girl in the Hispanic soaps, back then all gold crosses on chains and low-cut pink blouses, now a Pacific Heights matron in Ralph Lauren. She looked happy. When they had sat down, she began to tell them something she said they would find amazing.

"I have this incredible news." Lorna's pulse quickened with the expectation that she'd heard from Curt.

"Hello, I'm Honeur Chu, your chef," interrupted a young Asian woman in a toque and apron, coming up to the table. "Is everything all right? Would you like to order? The salmon tonight . . ." Everyone studied the menus, and there were some questions about the dishes.

"I'm having the hundred-garlic chicken." Hams began discussing it with the chef and a waiter, who'd appeared next to her. Hams had cooked this dish at home and wondered about her methods. Lorna now took in the vaguely fusion nature of the decor, watery dragons woven into the brocade wallpaper, and smart wooden screens. She looked down at the prices. Oh thank God, not a cheap Chinese restaurant. She'd intended to splurge, to take them somewhere expensive, and it was.

"The salmon? Is it farmed?" Donna asked.

"No, no! Line caught," Honeur assured her. "Bio."

"Ah, okay," Donna said. "I'll have that to start."

Lorna noted that Donna chose lobster, the most expensive dish, for her main course. She had instructed Peggy, when she first began to date, never to order the most expensive thing if someone else was paying, but apparently Donna had not been told this.

"Any word from Curt?" Peggy asked Donna.

"Not directly since last week, but a friend of his called and he'd heard from him, something about their business. A postcard, just like he sends us. But just let me tell you what's happened . . ."

"Do we know what his business is?" Lorna asked. "It's been kind of a mystery to me. In Thailand? It sounds so much like illegal drugs or arms smuggling, not exactly the mild-mannered financial planner." She was joking, of course. But it did sound like drugs or arms, Curt's being in Thailand.

"It sounds to me like a gay lifestyle change," said Hams. "That's why people go to Thailand—for the boys." He smiled to show he, too, was kidding, remembering Donna never got jokes. If it was a joke.

Predictably, she objected. "There's nothing gay about Curt."

"It's so nice to be here with the rest of you," Lorna said, meaning to head off discussion of Curt's sexuality or incipient felonies, let alone of her own reasons for being here. "It's wonderful. I'm so happy to be back, though sorry about Armand-Loup and all of that. Americans are just meant to live in America, I'm afraid."

"Doomed to live in America," said Peggy gloomily. "You won't find it like it was when you left. People evicted from their houses, living in the streets."

"The rents, I agree," Lorna said. "I saw some apartments with Ursula Aymes this afternoon. I was stupefied." But none of them pressed her further about the reasons for her return. Was their incuriosity out of delicacy? She was their mother, after all; they didn't like to pry, were aware of the shadow of defeat that was implied in her ending up where she began. She could read in their faces that they saw her return as defeat and didn't understand that she saw it as a new beginning, a flower unfolding.

"This is the salt-and-pepper fried squid," Hams said as the dish arrived. "I hope it's good. I ordered it for the table." His take-charge manner suggested he had stepped into Curt's role.

"I've been dreaming of spicy food," Lorna said. "In France you just don't often get it. The French don't like things spicy."

"What did you miss the most there?" Misty asked.

"Enchiladas." A discussion ensued about food you would miss when exiled to another land. Lorna stuck to enchiladas, but the others specified hamburgers, too, as if hamburgers didn't exist in France. Lorna found herself defending French hamburgers. "Though they do put a fried egg on them," she admitted.

"I have this incredible news," Donna broke in. They continued to head off her soliloquy. It was bound to be more whining.

"My dears," Lorna began, struggling to express her stab of happiness to be among her children, in a normal American restaurant that was nonetheless very nice, even French people would admit. Even Armand-Loup, that is. Most French people were enthusiastic about America, but he tended to condescend; but even he would admit this was a nice restaurant. Yes, she was so happy to be here with her handsome family—Hams a bit scruffy, but Misty not even looking that odd, with her piercings merely colorful in the indefinable chic of an expensive San Francisco restaurant. She had lovely eyelashes. Donna not as irritating as Peggy and the others claimed. She looked rosy and excited—could she be pregnant? What was the time frame? No, couldn't be, Curt had been gone too long.

"How are the twins? I can't wait to see them," Lorna said. "I'm just so happy to see you all, and I feel I'm going to slide right back into San Francisco life as if I'd never been away. Contentedly."

"Please!" cried Donna. "This is important!" Realizing it could be about Curt, they put down their chopsticks and listened.

Donna took an audible breath and in an unusually loud voice said, "Amy is paying off our mortgage."

Startled into silence by her shout, they all waited for clarification. Donna and Curt's huge mortgage had been much discussed by the others behind Donna's back, and they all knew it was a jumbo. But what was she talking about? Lorna felt a chill up her spine, as if the ice fairy had touched it. She was sure the fairy touched Hams and Misty, too, the chill of something unnatural stealing into the room and poisoning the food.

"Amy called me two days ago. She decided to pay off our mortgage. Is just paying it off, just like that," Donna explained, her voice muffled with emotion. "Just when I really couldn't make the next payment, all was lost—about to be lost—this month. Things were really dire. Frankly, I faced imminent foreclosure this month. I'd talked to the bank and nothing could be done, they were so horrible, and then suddenly, Monday, out of the blue, Amy calls and tells me.

"All she said was, 'Please don't say anything about this. You can pay me back when you sell it someday.' I have a feeling she doesn't want anyone to know about her good actions. She asked for the mortgage papers and deeds and all that. She said she thought in our situation the best thing was to just pay it off, and I could pay her back when I sold someday. And I hadn't discussed it with them, not at all. She said, 'These adjustable mortgages are going to rise to the stratosphere, I have such a bad feeling about what's going on.'

"Now the bank is totally obsequious—when I went in with the papers they couldn't do enough about asking me to sit down and bringing me coffee." She went on about this miracle, her emotions, how it had unfolded, how thrilling it had been to walk into the bank and say, Well, about my mortgage, since you've been such pigs I've decided just to pay it off. To say, in effect, shove it, though she hadn't used those very words.

Donna didn't name the sum, but the others could figure it out. Peggy followed real-estate prices, and there'd been much family discussion when Curt and Donna had first bought their palace, for which Peggy had privately calculated that they must have paid around three and a half million. This meant a mortgage of at least three million dollars! Now Peggy's mental calculator speeded up. She wasn't sure how much repayment would come to with the payoff penalty, but she guessed it had to be more than three, perhaps three and a half, or in that ballpark, that their stepmother Amy was coughing up for Donna. Why? What estate financial planning move did this reflect, what will rewritten? What strategy of trusts, annuities? What did it mean for the rest of them?

A second of silence suggested that questions and complications were occurring to each of them, except Donna, who went on rapturously describing her own reactions, her joy, her hope that Curt, wherever he was, would hear that they'd been saved from financial ruin.

Finally speech came to the others. "But that's incredible! How wonderful! How amazing!" They all expressed their joy, their astonishment at Amy's generosity; no one admitted to the strange uneasiness, the sense of swallowing something that could grow inside you, like a tapeworm, the tapeworm of selfish hope or maybe of jealousy. Three million dollars for Donna. Nothing, so far as anyone knew, for the rest of them, at least until now, but there was a niggle of hope, not to be jinxed by articulating it, that Amy was systematically planning to help all of them, at the behest of their father, and that she would turn her and Ran's attention to each of them in turn. Peggy's own foreclosure problem. Julie's tuition. Hams and Misty's impending new baby and their living in a slum.

Peggy could not have described her own complicated emotion, but was able to exclaim "Donna, that's incredible!" with the others. Her second (not her first) reaction was genuine gladness that the dark threat of foreclosure had been removed from Donna and Curt's future. Threatened in the same way, she was conscious of how millions of other people all across the country were facing foreclosure because of the cupidity of unknown people swindling them. Not her—she'd made her own mess, she was beginning to see.

Her third reaction, which began to seep slowly into her thoughts for the rest of the dinner, was a mix of curiosity—why was Amy bailing Donna out?—and envy, since she herself was in need of rescue, and the hope that Amy intended something of the kind in her own case.

"I never heard of anything like this—this generosity. I know it's your father's doing, getting her to do it. Paid it off! Just like that!" Donna went on and on. Amy, her stepmother-in-law, who had never even been around to see Curt during his period of coma, as far as Donna knew, but she didn't say this for fear of seeming critical of Amy, now in her view a goddess.

"Of course Ran likes me. We often saw each other at Curt's bedside," she said.

This passed without comment. "When does this happen?" Hams asked. The transaction was in process, it was less straightforward than just mailing a check, she'd had to gather up deeds and papers and give them to Amy, she hadn't been sure where the papers were, whether everything was there . . . Trips to the safe deposit, questions for Mrs. Aymes, who'd drawn up the purchase agreement.

"But it's wonderful! How generous!" Hams and Misty exclaimed in the same vein. Lorna was thinking: Wonderful, but what about Peggy, what about Hams? And she was envious that Ran was able to help the children when she herself could do so little.

"I'm sure she is doing it because Ran asked her to, he was always there by Curt's bedside . . . ," Donna began, as if echoing Lorna's thoughts. She broke off, probably realizing it sounded like reproach, since Lorna had been in Europe all this time and, pleading the pain of it, had seldom come back to look down on his inert form; almost as bad as Amy.

"Isn't it several million dollars?" Lorna asked. Lorna was of the generation of women that grasped mortgages and finance perfectly well but were expected not to display too much understanding; but this was family.

"It's three million," Donna admitted. "A bit more." She didn't go on to say that even three million dollars hadn't got her off the hook entirely. She was facing a number of bills Curt had run up—for clothes he needed for his new business situation, whatever it was, but also his sexy BMW, and even his bicycle, the one that was wrecked, had turned out not to be paid for, or not entirely. Who could have thought that a bicycle could cost more than ten thousand dollars? His beautiful jackets, his cleanly folded slacks hanging forlornly in his closet. He'd wear them someday, of course, but had lost an awful lot of weight during his coma. You probably couldn't sell used men's clothing. Curt's personal bills came to more than forty thousand dollars and more seemed to come in daily.

She weighed whether to tell his mother and siblings about the bicycle, the suits. "I still have to come up with this month's payment myself, but that's the last one." She had been afraid to talk to anyone about still needing money for these extra bills, especially Curt's father and stepfather, for fear they'd think she was asking for more money yet. Curt's mother? She must be getting a chunk from the Frenchman, and remained a possible source; but hitting up Ran and Amy again was of course out of the question. She weighed whether to call Ran to tell him she'd had another postcard from Curt, it looked like from Laos.

Donna pushed on, her mind racing with concerns about how much to say: she hadn't known quite how to process the joy she felt, the feeling of exoneration and justification. Was it a reward for her goodness in the face of Curt's difficulties? Her instinct, not usually reliable, served her this time to tone it down when talking to her in-laws about her good fortune. She was insanely grateful for having her mortgage paid, a brilliant break, but she continued to experience a frisson of terror whenever she thought of what had been averted.

She certainly didn't mention that, on the day Amy told her of her good fortune, she had indulged herself, while the kids were at nursery school, by going to Union Square, to Saks Fifth Avenue, even using the valet parker, and buying a purse that cost nearly three thousand dollars. Just this once. By no means the most expensive bag Saks had, which gave her a feeling of thrift. She had decided not to carry it tonight to the dinner with Curt's family.

"Ran's wife has a lot of money," Lorna said. "She might as well use it to allay human suffering." Silence struck again. Perhaps they had detected the note of irony in her tone.

"Now, Mother, tell us what about you, what are you doing here?" Hams asked after a bit, like a hostess anxious to cover an awkward moment. "What's happening with Armand-Loup, all of that? Are you coming back to the States permanently?"

Honeur came with another platter of salt-and-pepper fried squid, so delicious they all fell to eating in silence. Three million dollars for Donna; the sum hung in the air. They had ginger clams and wok-fried chicken and "long green vegetable." Lorna reveled in pleasure after all those years of no Chinese food. "The French just don't have a feeling for Chinese food, but it's not their fault, there just aren't that many Chinese restaurants. They do have Vietnamese, toned down."

After all the dishes, as they opened their fortune cookies, Lorna was again swept over with a rather unearned, she knew, but welcome feeling of gratitude that she was safely here among her children and they, in their turn, seemed okay, and she herself was still alive, not yet struck with some fatal disease or dementia, inevitable as these were, probably soon, and that for now her troubles were behind her or, rather, overseas where they couldn't blight this precious time with these loved ones, minus Curt, and, truth to tell, probably a pleasanter dinner without him, since he tended to be overbearing and tyrannize his siblings, and even herself.

" 'Expect good news,' " Donna said, waving the tiny strip of waxy paper.

" 'Windstorms,' " Lorna's cookie said.

14

We have to let go of our grievances, as we all know, but there's something we like about them.

On the BART train on the way over, Misty and Hams had replayed their usual fight. Despite her fierce looks and eyebrow rings, the pregnancy had animated Misty's desire for a nest, her bourgeois sense of the precariousness of her life with Hams, its drabness and sleazy position on the edge; specifically she felt their need for a better income—a future— and fueled her resentments about Hams's lack of get-up-and-go and what she imagined was the immense affluence of everyone in his family but them, and now including Donna, but especially Hams's half sister, Gilda, his father's child with the mega-rich woman Hams's father was married to. There Misty was right; Gilda was a golden girl. Misty saw that their share of Ran's attention was less than Gilda got, and she tended to blame Hams for not being nicer or closer to his father, for acceding to their rather distant relationship.

She wanted to move and buy a house. "I just don't fucking want to bring up our child in this neighborhood," Misty said, maybe for the hundredth time. Gunshots had rung out at their corner and they were two blocks away from a crack house, which everyone knew was a crack house. There had been one neighborhood meeting; someone had been delegated to find out who the owner was and report him, or threaten him, but nothing had been done. Hams's father Ran had suggested Hams and Misty get a dog, and Hams still remembered the scorn in Misty's expression.

"No one is lending in this market in this neighborhood," Hams explained to Misty also for the hundredth time. "We would never get a loan." He hoped they might get a loan down the line, as Misty was steadily employed; they might go into the bank together, impress them as a couple, but she'd have to take out her nose stud for the interview, and he was not about to irritate her by suggesting that. Only a week ago, he had been thinking of phoning Lorna, who ought to be in New York. Asking her for a little cash, a hundred would help with some immediate expenses. They had no hope of buying a house, but a few small treats might cheer Misty up. And he could put in some extra hours at Craig's Cycles. Craig, Hams's oldest friend from elementary school, was sort of a bicycle fence, a business the two of them had begun in junior high school. Bicycles came from somewhere, and Craig stripped, filed, painted, and resold them. All these years, no one had ever bothered or busted them. The business was all Craig's now, but Hams pitched in from time to time, though these days Craig only paid him by the hour.

"You need to ask your parents. Your mother helped Peggy, I happen to know, and she probably helped Curt. Your father helped, too, probably, but they never do anything for us."

"You've got parents," said Hams. Misty laughed in derision. Her parents, elderly pensioners, had been high-school teachers, had never saved a penny, and lived in Watsonville in a double-wide.

"You'll take this seriously when we have the baby."

"I take it seriously now, I just don't see any way."

After dinner, riding back to Berkeley in the BART train, Misty turned on Hams in another rage, or a continuation of their fight coming over. In the face of Donna's news, he'd said nothing to his mother about the probability that their unborn child would die in the crossfire of random bullets flying on their Oakland street, and Misty didn't mention that Hams worked at least two jobs, while the horrible Donna had nothing to do but drive her bratty twins to their posh nursery school and live mortgage-free in her multimillion-dollar château in Pacific Heights.

"Wasn't there something about Martha and Mary in the Bible?" said Hams in his mild way. "Where the poor, modest one was the beloved?"

Misty stared indignantly at his callous, uncharacteristic use of biblical allusion. "Yes, the decorative, idle one was the one who got everything," she said. "Just like in life."

However downscale their lifestyle now, Misty and Hams had, in common with all bourgeois American children, in contrast to those who had been brought up poor, a belief in the intrinsic fairness of things, above all within their own families, and that life would work out. Hams said, "I think it's likely Amy is planning to help each of us. She wouldn't do one of us without the other. Donna's problems are just the most imminent." This might be wishful thinking; they had yet to hear from their rich stepmother Amy on any subject whatever, though Ran, Hams's dad, checked in from time to time. They had been disappointed in another way at dinner; they had hoped to borrow some money from Hams's mother, and instead had gathered she had no money at all.

15

What is the opposite of Schadenfreude?

When they had embraced and said good night to Hams, Misty, and Donna, Peggy and Lorna walked back up the hill from the restaurant to Lorna's digs at Jones and Green. Peggy was especially eager to talk to her mother about the startling development, Amy's more than generous help to Donna: Did Lorna think money would be forthcoming for the rest of them? Conscious of a vast understatement, she said, "Donna's windfall. That's amazing! Do you think there will be something for the rest of us?"

"I have no idea. I don't know the woman, remember," Lorna said. She had never laid eyes on Amy, and it had been years, in fact twenty-four years, since she'd laid eyes on her ex-husband Randall. Hearing about the three million dollars, she was conscious of her own ambivalence, glad for Donna and Curt, of course, but sorry and a little resentful that she could not be helpful to them herself. Glad for them, but not without other apprehensions, perhaps superstitious: good would not come of unearned windfalls. She hadn't recognized that she had such a puritanical streak, but she felt this. They discussed Ran's probable agency in steering Amy's money toward Curt and Donna, but neither had much expectation for the others.

"Ask your father about it," Lorna added.

Though it was only 10:00 p.m., Lorna felt her jet lag and turned in. Peggy tucked up on the sofa with an extra blanket and pillows and lay wakefully into the night. In the bedroom, at 4:00 a.m., the predictable waking hour of the jet-lagged, Lorna's eyes flew open, too, a swell of apprehension in her bosom that Ran was sowing mischief, as he always had done, by favoring Curt, by urging his rich wife to favor Curt with this one-sided largesse—to the tune of three million dollars—with nothing for his other children, nothing for poor little granddaughter Julie hoping to study in Greece, for example.

Rage took her. She recognized a familiar cast to this rage; it was the rage at Ran she had felt when they were married, its power presenting itself undiminished. Rage had lurked here more than two decades. She shouldn't have come back within range of it. Mistake, mistake.

In the morning, things looked brighter, as they always do. They were sitting over their coffee when Peggy's cell rang. It was Misty. Misty and Peggy didn't often talk but were friendly and often saw eye to eye on things Hams was against. Hams's siblings wondered what anyone could have seen in him and were grateful to Misty for straightening him out, up to the point he was straightened out. In Peggy's view, Misty was weird herself, and apparently that's what it took, someone pierced and tattooed, evidence of a psychic fragility that brought out his manly need to protect her, or whatever the psychodynamic was. She liked Misty despite these manifestations, believing a normal middle-class girl lurked behind the tattoos. Misty was calling to exult.

"Three million!" Wonderful Amy! Could salvation for each of them be far behind?

"It's true, you know, that money doesn't bring happiness," Lorna said to Peggy later. "That truism."

"How do you know, Mother?"

"I had enough when I was married to Armand. Not money money, but you know. Is your father happy with his rich wife?"

"I think so. They live simply."

"If simplicity is a prerequisite, we should all be happy."

"We are, aren't we?" Peggy said.

"Are you, Peg?"

"Except for my mortgage worries, and it's a little lonesome without Julie anymore, but I'm active . . . Activity is the secret to happiness, don't you think? Creativity."

"I do think that," Lorna agreed. "Though I never thought about it so directly. I think you can only spot happiness obliquely if you think about it at all."

Over coffee, Peggy and Lorna discussed another problem, that Lorna would need somewhere to live. They devised a house-hunting program. Lorna hoped that by looking with just Peggy, without the upscale Ursula Aymes, they'd have better luck. They would look online and in the paper, owner-to-renter directly, a better strategy. The soul-killing compromises required of a person house hunting had begun to chill her before they had even planned their itinerary or made their phone calls.

The want-ad pages were smoothed out on the table, sparkling with promise. "I'd like to stay in this neighborhood," she said.

"Your budget, Mom—we should look out on the Avenues."

"So foggy, it's so cold out there," cried Lorna. "I'd rather do with less space." Each site she'd regarded on Zillow was worse than the last: shrunken, pathetic rooms, grudging small windows looking onto seedy decks, neglected plants, exigence, improvidence, the futile optimism with which, in each for-rent photo of a repellent sofa, a misjudged decorative pillow in a cheerful color blocked the sight of a stain. Just from the photos she could smell the smell of other people's stuff in the old floorboards, and the closets. She couldn't help but think of the beautiful French farmhouse that was hers no longer, with its delicious odors of wax and flowers.

That house, in Pont-les-Puits, built in the late seventeenth century and added to auspiciously in the nineteenth, had belonged to Armand-Loup when they married and was thus, by being something he brought to the marriage, something he was entitled to keep, even if he was callously selling it. The pain of this one thing had made Lorna hesitate about a divorce, such was her love for the house, so entirely had she felt it to be her own, the house of her soul, an emotion she had never felt for the San Francisco family house on Lake Street where she and Ran and the children had lived all those years. Looking into the vast Pont-les-Puits fireplaces, where a whole sheep could roast, she had imagined Capetian noblemen, musketeers, English soldiers hunting down poor Jeanne d'Arc . . .

In California there was no one to imagine except the wicked mission friars who had enslaved the Native Americans, or the Zodiac killer more recently, or a madman with an assault weapon in the supermarket. She was sure her imaginative engagement with French history had immeasurably enriched her lectures, and here no one cared to hear them.

"Mother, are you sure you're doing the right thing?" Peggy asked yet again. Peggy had often fleetingly regretted divorcing Dick Willover and would like to warn her mother to think carefully, though when she really considered it, she knew in her own case she had done the right thing. Dick had snarled abusively at Julie and was in the process of coming out, something none of them had ever suspected but which had put him under a strain that fueled his constant anger. Peggy often asked herself whether, if he hadn't been so ill natured, maybe she could have lived with him being bi. It would be better than her present penury.

"Right thing?"

"What went wrong, if you don't mind telling me? In France, with the Frog Prince?" The children had never taken to Armand-Loup. Lorna had supposed they wouldn't have taken to any second husband. The circumstances of your own conception—happening so far before your birth—can be borne, but remarriage too pointedly reaffirms that your mother is still in the thrall of Eros, and they had found it slightly disgusting. Every book about how to tell the children about divorce had explained that they would.

Lorna couldn't bring herself to go into details. "Oh, village life came to seem so far from art, so far from real life," she said vaguely. "So far from America, though I never thought I would feel such a thing." She was certainly not going to tell them about finding someone's underpants in the glove compartment of their Peugeot. And what she had said was partly true, she loved being back in the art world, or thought she was going to love it, with no anxieties about culinary faux pas or the need to struggle with cooking the wild boar and pheasant brought in by Armand-Loup's hunter friends.

"That doesn't seem like much of a reason, if you don't mind me saying so. That charming village, the wonderful house. At your age. Can't you just work it out to spend more time over here? Without breaking everything up? It's not so great here, either, remember. My house isn't worth what we paid for it. You've seen the homeless all around." Letting people sleep outside was not the way she remembered San Francisco.

"Oh, honey, I've got my life in hand, it's yours I worry about," Lorna said, not quite truthfully but with some reason. Her heart did wrench to see Peggy looking so frumpy and distracted. Some money could help her so much. Should she suggest Peggy lighten her hair or at least get some streaks to blend with the onset of gray? Of course Peggy had earlier driven a hundred miles on 101, stop-and-go through Petaluma and Santa Rosa, a very tiring drive, no one would look her best. Peggy had not let herself go, exactly, and Lorna knew her life didn't require the latest haircut, stylish clothes, or uncomfortable high heels such as she, the more petite Lorna, had sworn to wear as part of her renaissance.

She restrained an impulse to suggest that Peggy could lose a pound and have better-fitting jeans. Lorna was not, not, an interfering mom, but Peggy, basically a good-looking woman of forty-four years, when she should be at beauty's prime, could use some sympathetic counsel. Nonetheless, Lorna held her tongue. She herself had suffered the exacting standards of Frenchwomen, and understood that Peggy was a struggling Ukiah single mother with no need to go out wearing lipstick and scarves. She tried to think of what she could do for Peggy—but what could she do for any of them until she got some lecture engagements?

16

However daunted, we can almost all of us rise to an occasion.

Next morning, when Peggy dropped her at Southwest Airlines for the flight to Bakersfield to give her lecture there, Lorna felt her professional persona assert itself. She was an art historian who had a certain reputation as an interesting lecturer, or had had in the early nineties, more than twenty years before. Back then she was known for bringing her subjects to life with an animated and perceptive way of talking about the visual arts, and with wonderful slides. Now the public lecture was a bit out of fashion, what with videos and the Internet, and she had found, when she began rather furtively to weigh getting back into circulation, that people's taste had changed. Armand, when they discussed it, had cynically said it was owing to the lack of public transportation in America; people were reluctant to hunt for parking places after dinner. The lecture as a performance art was more suited to village life, where people could stroll to hear it, then gather in the pub.

On the plane, she reread and mentally timed her lecture. Lorna had not learned her speaking style from tapes of Mrs. Thatcher in the eighties—not entirely—she had also spent a lot of time as a young woman in the early seventies hanging around the fascinating gurus of the mind-expansion movement, had seen Werner Erhard, had even once had a date with Timothy Leary, an attractive guy in those days, though married. Those were good public speakers. She had never understood what had saved her—vanity or timidity—from the dangers and silliness of their far-out subjects, given that she'd been kind of drawn to the ideas of expanding consciousness and visual representations of mental states—this in turn leading to her doctoral dissertation on the French Symbolist painters of the 1890s, especially focusing on Odilon Redon. What a busy time! She wondered, looking back on her virtuous stamina in those days, with young children and a husband, Ran—Randall Mott—whom she had been at the same time trying to leave. How had she done it all?

She'd have to work up anew the lingo of art historiography: Art Talk had changed so much since she was in graduate school, and now involved understanding semiotics, and dropping a few words like "disruption" and "signifiers" into her lectures. Some of her audience, Lorna was sure, actually wanted instruction for their own self-improvement, to learn about how to see a painting, really to see; but she suspected such people were rare. Most people just wanted to hear stories, and get a few clues as to what to say the next time they were called upon to comment on a painting, say when visiting a museum with a friend. No, she wouldn't mind giving it all up except for the need for the wherewithal to help poor Peggy and buy Hams a house and pay someone to find Curt—and now even for herself, the only one who truly had no money and had stupidly left the family silverware behind in France.

Lorna wasn't used to having financial problems. She hadn't ever been rich, but she'd always been solvent—when growing up, and then during her marriages to solvent husbands—first, doctor Ran and now rentier Armand-Loup. She felt there was something soul degrading and personally culpable about having money problems, though she didn't feel degraded in her own case, because she wasn't giving in to caring one way or another. If she had to live in a hole, she would. She began to understand the proudly poor in nineteenth-century novels, in Dickens, for example, or Trollope, proud ladies furtively mending their stockings.

But the things she saw around her on the San Francisco streets or read about in the paper suggested a new kind of poverty, unfamiliar even, among people who had been solvent and now had been undone by harsh structural events—their stores closing or losing their jobs. She had never followed economics closely, but now discussions could not be avoided of the falling house prices, iffy, perilous banks making unwise loans, people losing their homes. With her savings, she had bought some certificates of deposit—surely the government would not let them fail? But they paid a pitiful amount of interest.

For herself, she knew that leaving Armand-Loup meant she would have to get serious about her lecture schedule and raise her fees. The prospect of a plunge into work was what had firmed up her resolve to leave him and the unhappiness and tension in their lives. But what if there was no work? Her savings wouldn't last forever. And she had only now begun to understand how inadequate they were.

Now she was on the plane to San Francisco again. New York, San Francisco, Bakersfield, the lecture, overnight in the Bakersfield Days Inn and another airplane. It was hard to imagine that only six days ago she'd been in Pont-les-Puits, leaving Armand-Loup, alive with an inner sense of being on the brink of an important return to her essential self. Now she saw that getting back onto the circuit was going to take time, judging from the sparse attendance at her first lecture appearance, in Bakersfield.

Something about it had not been a success, and she would have to think about what that was. She hadn't been sure the topic would be right for Bakersfield: medieval tapestries. The medieval Apocalypse Tapestries of Angers, France. The Angers tapestries had been new to her until a year ago, when she saw them for the first time, and instantly had known they would become her new passionate subject, beside Symbolism and Dada. She attacked them with missionary zeal, had made them her own, and had worked up a fascinating lecture with beautiful slides. She needed to try it out, and Bakersfield had been the first audience to hear it.

Unloved, nearly unknown in America, the Angers tapestries were mighty and transcendent works of art, yet it seemed they were almost ignored in the scholarly world: more than eighty huge tapestries based on the Book of Revelation, devised by a powerful medieval imagination, informed by faith, woven by the unknown fingers of probably

Flemish believers, and with a romantic history of being lost, hidden, forgotten through the centuries. There was the apostle John, the author of the biblical Book of Revelation; there were Jesus, the devil, Mary, the Whore of Babylon, the Beast, and God himself—each more picturesque than the other, woven in sumptuous greens and pinks and blues, emblazoned with stars, towers, and raging waves. Her photographic slides, taken by experts with special lights and permission to briefly illuminate the panels, were in fact clearer and easier to see than the actual tapestries, which, too fragile to be exposed to daylight, were exhibited in almost total darkness, counting on the human eye to adjust in the vast, windowless space of a medieval dungeon adapted to contain them. The slides brought out the enchanting iconography imagined by that fourteenth-century genius in what must have been closer to its original transcendent beauty.

The Bakersfield audience had been polite and receptive, but somehow, during the question period, things had fallen apart. When she had referred to a numerical figure in one of the tapestries, a man had stood up, waited for the microphone to be passed to him, then shouted "Six-six-six is the mark of the Beast."

" 'Six-six-six' refers to Nero," Lorna began. She had tried to explain that the people of Saint John's era, afraid to mention their Roman oppressors by name, had employed euphemisms like "Beast." But, ignoring her completely, somebody immediately shouted down the original speaker, saying the Beast was Satan, as everybody knew, and moreover the Beast was nigh.

"We are in the Last Days," he whispered into the portable microphone.

"We are not," from someone else. Bakersfield was likely to be inundated, and soon. No, it would not. Destroyed by storms. No, drought. She found herself in the midst of a sectarian quarrel which engaged more and more members of the audience, people flinging esoteric biblical trivia instead of, as she had imagined they would, questions about the practical problems of getting to Angers, France, or which were her favorite restaurants in Paris.

She felt chastened not to have imagined that people who would come to an art lecture could be not art lovers but religious fundamentalists. They seemed to have been drawn by the word "Apocalypse" in the title of her talk. She was asked her view of the Apocrypha. She was asked if she had considered that she herself might be one of the two witnesses, returning as predicted . . . She was asked if she had found Jesus. Lorna was jolted to realize again that, except for nearly annual visits to her children in the years they didn't visit her in France, she had been gone from America for twenty years. Maybe America was everywhere like this now, boiling with piety. She had never thought of America as a society driven by faith, not anymore, anyhow; in France, fiercely Catholic in name, people didn't actually seem to go to church. But here they claimed to go to church.

Driving her to the Bakersfield airport, the lecture agent pronounced himself very well satisfied that her talk had been so relevant, so involving, and was sure to get good press coverage. Each note of praise had baffled her more; not one person had asked what it was like living in France.

"I'll email about setting up a date for Fresno," he had assured her.

17

The quotidian is the enemy of the ideal.

In the days that followed, Lorna occupied herself anew with seeing apartments—feeling it to be a futile exercise—making inquiries about lawyers, going twice to take the adorable grandsons Marcus and Manuel to the park, though these strenuous tots left her exhausted, and writing to lecture agents and university faculties to announce her availability.

When it came to calling her old friends, something strangely kept her back—reluctance to explain what she was doing here after twenty years, the thinnish sound of her explanation, the lack of conviction in her own voice, though she felt determined and strong. The two divorces, or almost.

She'd just wait awhile till she got settled, and got some jobs. She did confide in Pam, still down in Ojai, over the phone, where at least you didn't need to see the sympathetic pucker of your friend's lips, the little crease between her eyebrows. No one leaves a husband after so many years unless it was a misery the whole time, not her case. She'd had a lot of fun with Armand-Loup.

At the urging of Ursula Aymes, who seemed to have taken an interest in her case even without the hope of a rental commission, let alone a house sale, she made an appointment with a downtown divorce lawyer Ursula thought would be capable of dealing with any international complications. She hadn't heard anything more from Armand-Loup on the subject, but feared that French jurisprudence was operating in her absence, to her disadvantage.

As for being in San Francisco, it appeared that wherever she found to live would require several thousand dollars in deposit, first and last months' rent, and expenses to set it up with furniture, pots and pans. She'd expected that, of course, but it would still be a hit. How odd that she and all her children were facing crises about real estate—Misty and Hams wanting to buy in a better neighborhood, Peggy needing a loan to make her payments, not Curt and Donna anymore, but only recently out of the woods. She thought with a pang of her rich ex-husband Ran. She also thought with a pang almost as deep, or, actually, deeper, of her French house with its fourteen-foot ceilings and carven doors, and *poutres apparentes* that had been painted over the centuries with the names of artisans or residents, names faded now but decipherable, some of the same names of families who still lived in Pont-les-Puits. She loved the idea of tradition, continuation; she hated the idea of the teardowns you saw in California.

The only stirrings from Pont-les-Puits in recent days had been from the persistent mayor, Barbara Levier. Her *équipe* had not definitively identified the bones of Russell Woods, but they had some positive IDs for others, and the cost was running around fifteen hundred euros per case—it would be so civic minded of Lorna to advance the money she was going to have to pay down the line anyway.

"*Mais,* Barbara," Lorna would remonstrate, "*Je ne suis pas concerné par les* bones of poor Russell." People had been so forgiving about her franglais twenty years ago, she still occasionally invoked it, though she knew French perfectly well, except for forgetting, just now, the word for "bones."

Pont-les-Puits was implacable. Lorna was sure Armand-Loup was pulling the strings of this harassment; she could hear him laughing. Though she was also sure she would never really have to pay fifteen hundred euros for the bones of an unrelated acquaintance, she found the idea infuriating, when she so wanted to put Pont-les-Puits out of her mind.

She kept her best mind on the tapestries of Angers and finding another lecture venue. She hadn't heard from the promised contact in Fresno and, anyhow, Fresno . . . Had she not lectured at the Louvre, at the Doria Pamphili? She dutifully wrote and emailed places she'd given her lectures on Redon and Meissonier in the past. The past. How do you remind people of your existence? How do you reassure them you are still active, informed, plugged in? Was "plugged in" the expression? It came to her in French: *branché, au courant.* Not over the hill.

One positive bit of news, Barbara Levier told her; Mr. Dumas, good at reading English, volunteered to read the stuff in Mr. Woods's boxes, and there had found an unsent letter to Lorna asking her to make sure his pictures went to the right people. He mentioned several wrong people by name, and some institutions that apparently had scorned him. Perhaps, poor man, he'd had an intimation of approaching death. Madame Levier would send Lorna a copy.

Lorna said she'd be happy to do whatever, but doubted she could do anything now that Woods was a magnet for dealers and collectors. The discussion of poor Russell's reinterment had awakened Lorna's grief at his death, and above all the need to think about death. Generally, her attitude had always been that it was too soon to think about this depressing subject; she would do it later. But Russell's death, only seventy-one when he died, had dramatized its inevitability, the unwelcome pertinence of its iconography, the relevance of Montaigne and the other philosophers who seemed to go on about it. She wished Russell were alive, and she would help where she could to do things in his memory; but she didn't have the extra money to rescue his bones.

In Pont-les-Puits, work had proceeded on cleaning up the graveyard. The scattered tombstones had tentatively been set up following the plot map from the cemetery office, and bones had been gathered with reference to the coffins found nearest them and packaged for the DNA technicians, each package with a skull on top, all of them removed to the market hall and arrayed on the long table there, like party favors at a Halloween dinner. A Cambodian DNA team, cheaper than the Yugoslavs, had been hired but wasn't expected for a month, though a representative had flown in to supervise the collecting, which was done by the regular guardian—Monsieur Flores—who dug the recent graves and tended the shrubbery.

The enormous heap of bones was still drying and being sorted on large tables assembled inside the covered Pont-les-Puits market building. Attention was paid to where they had been discovered and to the basic facts of anatomy—that is, two legs to one rib cage, only twenty-four ribs to a person, only one skull, and so on. Where bits of clothing had remained, these were meticulously packaged into little cushions on which the skull was rested. Clothing, at least in the case of the most recent interments, was more recognizable than old bones; some more recent graves had yielded horrible apparitions of familiar faces now half mouldered away.

Not everyone could bear to look at what was going on. The mayor, Madame Levier, had gone to the cemetery once, had felt faint, and after that sent her deputy, Monsieur Blostin. She had never gone inside the market hall. Some people had been neither to the site nor the hall, but there were a few who were obsessively drawn to these places, ostensibly out of concern for the remains of loved ones and ancestors. It was one of these obsessives, Mademoiselle Berthaut, coming by the market hall after dark, though not late, say about nine, who saw gentle light emanating from one of the packets on the long table. She stared through the windows but couldn't really tell which packet, which skull; too bad because they could have safely assumed that the glowing one was Saint Brigitte. Madame Levier appointed a committee to take turns checking nightly to see if this radiance happened again. At a meeting, it was decided that to obviate the need for continuous surveillance, the hours between nine and eleven each night would be optimum, and someone was appointed to investigate installing some light-activated video-recording equipment.

18

Even the smallest gold-rush California town prides itself on its opera house, sure symptom of the culturally correct.

The San Francisco opera house arises amid parking lots and reconstruction zones in the Civic Center of the city, facing the golden dome of the city hall, itself resembling similar structures in Rome and Paris, shining in the occasional sunshine like the Institut de France or even Saint Peter's in Rome, though of course smaller. It was in the vaulted lobby of the opera house that Randall and Amy Hawkins Mott were tonight hosting their dinner to benefit the Children's Diabetes Foundation.

There is an adequate dining room in the *sous-sol* of the opera house, but because that is where people reserved and ate their dinners ordinarily, Amy had thought it wasn't grand enough for something as expensive as this benefit after the opera; theirs was to be held in the exalted marble lobby imposingly full of echoes and architectural references to both Palladio and Erté. Tonight the performance had ended, and the caterers commenced their installations, skillfully whipping in with tables and chairs even as the audience was leaving. Amy had authorized them to spare no expense on the flowers, to humanize the vast scale of the room, whose columns now sprouted great festoons of picturesque weeds, lilies, and gladioli. At the right moment, a forest fire of candles would spring to light as if by a signal from above. Amy and Ran had seen to the placement themselves, setting the little name cards and favors at each plate, helped by Amy's personal assistant, Carla.

In San Francisco, the younger dot-com billionaires cooperated only occasionally with the old guard represented by the ancient grandes dames and established San Francisco business fortunes derived from blue jeans and Pinot Noir; only on rare occasions did the younger Silicon Valley people notice or deign to support the needy and virtuous civic institutions like the opera and symphony that made San Francisco worth living in. God knew what other causes interested the younger rich; but little by little, like milk through muslin, drip by drip, once in a while one of them dripped through or oozed into the cultural life of the city—that is, the opera, the symphony, and the art museum, especially the photography department.

Par for her age group, Amy Hawkins (Mott) had supported photography but had been slow to take an interest in the opera, now at least to the extent of hosting this dinner at the opera house. Her main interest remained the General Hospital where they had once saved Gilda's life when she was a toddler, before the diagnosis of diabetes, when it had seemed that her mysterious illnesses might kill her.

The dinner was well subscribed by the generous community, including two of the older Establishment ladies whose money came from land grants and iconic clothing brands and was usually spent on wine growing, Picassos, and Pollocks. Over there was Joanne Drill— who wouldn't have known a byte from a megabyte but ponied up for operas and the art museum. Marian Whistler was a reliable donor to anything with singing. As the subscription had filled up so quickly, Amy had wondered if they should have increased the donation price, to allow people to pay more. Now Ran Mott and Amy Hawkins, he in black tie and she in floating Givenchy chiffon, shivering a bit in the June chill, greeted the benefactors and personally showed them to the various tables.

Ran and Amy had taken three tables themselves—one, at the side near the stairs, was for Gilda and several of her friends and other children of Amy and Ran's friends, the young people. Ran thought Gilda, dressed up like this and permitted to wear mascara for the occasion, looked eerily, palely, ethereally lovely and much older than fifteen, like a child playing dress-up. Her beauty was gratifying, as, looking so pretty, she was spared the malice with which people seemed often to remark that such and such daughter of a Silicon Valley billionaire had not been saved by her parents' money from being ugly as a pug. Gilda was silver and ivory.

The female waitpeople, including his granddaughter Julie, Ran saw, had been made to wear a sort of French-maid costume reminiscent of old-fashioned porn—white blouses and frilly little white aprons over short black skirts. Was this the caterer's idea or Amy's? Julie exuded radiant confidence as she swooped around with her tray, collecting empty glasses and discarded toothpicks from the hors d'oeuvres. He smiled encouragingly, approvingly, at her and planned to point her out to Amy; Ran tried to think whether his wife Amy and his grand-daughter Julie had actually ever met, beyond at a reception he and Amy had given after their marriage, a private ceremony with a few family members just before Gilda was born. Julie would have been only four or five. Back then they had weighed the tactfulness of entertaining the family with Amy so visibly pregnant, but after all, it was the modern world, especially for Amy's generation. People hadn't needed to come if they disapproved, but they all came.

As he watched, Julie approached Amy, who was talking to Babe Miller and Fuffy Stevens and a couple of the other elderly great ladies of San Francisco, and took away their empty glasses and replaced them with filled ones, apparently without stirring recognition by either Julie or Amy. Not that Amy had anything against Julie, or any of his children or grandchildren, but she was sensitive about the problems so unfairly loaded on their own child, poor little Gilda, while Ran's other children were nothing if not robust, except Curt after his accident.

Feeling self-conscious in her French-maid apron and cap, Julie scanned the room. Beside Grandpa Ran there was Step-Grandma Amy—that must be her, urging people to sit down. There was no mistaking which one was Gilda. Aunt Gilda! Julie spotted her right off, the silvery hair, pretty child's face, tinted glasses, and general shrinking puniness. Her mother and her siblings from the first batch referred to her as "the Princess." Terrible dress of blue knitted lace, exactly what a mother would make you wear.

Julie had always thought it unfair—violently unfair—that her fifteen-year-old half aunt, her mother Peggy's much-younger half sister, Gilda, had money for the asking, private schools, huge allowance, probably everything she wanted, though since she didn't know Gilda, she had no notion of what she would want. Julie's objections were philosophical as well as personal; she was all for the redistribution of wealth. She resented on her mother's behalf that Peggy's talented craft efforts—belts and earrings, candles, personalized shop signs—were so poorly rewarded; many were her projects, small was the recompense for honest handiwork, while out of sight was the recompense for the invisible profits of money managers and Internet and tech profiteers like her grandfather's wife, Amy.

Of course Julie wouldn't trade places with Gilda, but still, she couldn't help but wonder what it would be like to just ask for something and get it. A horse! A two-hundred-dollar pair of jeans! What kinds of things would Gilda ask for? Julie examined her heart for signs of envy and, thinking of Gilda's well-known poor health, exonerated her own character: she would not trade places with Gilda. When she got a chance, she took some glasses of Coke and orange juice to Gilda's table, and identified herself. A couple of fat younger boys sat at Gilda's table, typical rich kids in blue blazers.

"Hi, Gilda, you don't remember me, I'm Julie, my mom is Peggy— your half sister! I'm helping here tonight . . ."

"Julie! Hi!" The girl spoke so promptly, Julie realized Gilda had seen her already. Gilda explained to her friends about how this older girl was her niece, and they all laughed at the vagaries of chronology. Julie noted how accurately Gilda was aware of their relationship and knew how it had all come about, and how pleased she was to speak of their connection.

"You should come up to the city and hang out with me one of these days," Julie suggested. She hovered only a second longer, then went off with her tray.

Gilda hoped to do that; Gilda thought Julie the most powerful and beautiful girl in existence. Gilda was aware that a mysterious *non-dit* discouraged any discussion of Papa's first family; her friends assured her this was par for the course, their parents almost all had been married to someone they weren't encouraged to mention and had regrettable step-cousins or stepsiblings or whatever. She could see there was a faint family resemblance between herself and Julie, but Julie looked as if golden sunlight had been poured over a colorless Gilda prototype and warmed it till it grew and glowed and came to life.

Julie was conscious of her own ambivalence about the wealth and privilege the gala represented. Her own situation on the fringe, within spitting distance of fortune in her own family, via Grandpa Randall, qualified her views just a little, tainted them, some might say. She was made aware of the taint via her interface with the Circle of Faith, which represented moral values. But she also respected Silicon Valley, and regretted she was so lame with computers, an anomaly in her age group that held her back. Maybe that was why she was here in a waitress costume, doomed to waitress jobs or being a gym teacher. On the positive side, she was entitled to enjoy knowing both sides of her mother's family—her rich grandfather and her worldly grandmother the lecturer—without inheriting any of the rancor that they reputedly felt for each other.

She considered herself as not taking sides. She was positioned like a spy to report on this fancy party to her mother and her mother's siblings who might be interested but were of course not invited, though she suspected that the suave and handsome Uncle Curt might have been, and maybe her own mom if she'd been in town, but Uncle Hams never or his wife, Misty—joke.

Julie, while fascinated with her aunt Gilda, also couldn't help but notice the most handsome young man she had ever seen, sitting at the children's table there with Gilda and other young fashionables, maybe a bit drunk. This was Ian Aymes, son of the real-estate doyenne Ursula Aymes and her good-looking though transient second husband, Pud Aymes. Pud Aymes, now living in Argentina, had seen to it that Ian had been sent to a good eastern prep school and Brown, though he'd dropped out in his junior year and was at present doing some makeup courses at Mountain View with the hope, probably vain, of transferring to Stanford. He was twenty, too old for Gilda, who anyway thought of him as too stuck-up. In fact, he was a pleasant young man and, though he had no interest in fifteen-year-old girls, was good-naturedly decorating by his presence the kiddie table of Gilda and her friends at the request of his mother, who was friends with Gilda's parents. He actually liked Gilda and, despite the difference in their ages, had been made to go to her lavish birthday parties every year for years, and she had always spoken to him, among the mob of other kids of assorted ages whose parents were friends of her parents; and she always remembered to ask after his Dinky car collection, dear to him when he was much younger, which he still had.

Julie actually had to keep herself from looking at Ian Aymes, he induced such a strange feeling in her of self-consciousness, tongue-tiedness, awkwardness, even misery; this reaction was totally strange, even dangerous when you were carrying a tray.

Gilda had the same feeling, or worse—being only fifteen—or different, since she'd known Ian her whole life and had only now begun to see him this funny way, as if he were hot, the quality she and her friends would discuss later.

19

Girl talk.

At the opera gala, Julie had invited her young aunt Gilda to come up to San Francisco one day for a sort of girls' day, to get acquainted, and this was the day, Saturday three weeks later. Ran gave the outing his blessing, was pleased to think of Gilda getting to know his granddaughter, liked that there could be a connection between these two halves of his life, even if Amy wasn't interested or perhaps actually disliked the idea of his preexistence, his children with Lorna, their twenty years on Lake Street.

Gilda, excited about it, explained to Julie that her mom had a personal assistant, Carla, who would drive her up from Woodside and back, a trip of forty-five minutes or more each way depending on traffic. Julie laid out the program: they'd have lunch and see an exhibit of some sacred Chinese rocks at the Asian Art Museum, and go to Macy's if they had time. Gilda looked forward to it, but was apprehensive about not having anything to talk about to the older girl, of seeming too square and silent or, always at the back of her mind, having to deal with some diabetes thing that would make her late, or embarrassed, or a nuisance to others.

The first awkwardness came over paying for lunch, in the Asian Art restaurant. Julie saw that, as she was the older girl, it was up to her to pay. It was Gilda who could afford it, but Gilda probably wasn't used to paying—probably had never paid for anything. Feeling both resentful and self-consciously good, Julie reached for the check, $29.40, and hoped Gilda would mention this goodness to her parents. Gilda hadn't eaten anything to speak of, had not had dessert or a soft drink. Probably she was a food-fussy, a strike against her, Julie thought.

"Carla gave me some money for this," Gilda said, bringing out some tens fastened in a jumbo paper clip, and plunked it down with the bill.

"If you don't want to go to Macy's, we could go to my meeting," Julie said with relief. "I'm in a group that helps kids in Africa, and the meetings are sort of interesting, usually there's a speaker who tells about certain places or experiences. Today there's going to be a former slave." Gilda had no philanthropic impulses to speak of, though they were encouraged at Saint Waltraud's; but she liked the idea of meeting someone who was once a slave.

"Can you call Carla to take us?" Julie wondered, thinking of how wonderful it must be to have someone at your beck and call—like a slave.

"Actually, never mind, we have time to walk." They ended by walking as far as Union and Van Ness, and then taking a bus for the uphill climb to Jones Street. Julie pointed out the building where her grandmother was staying. "But I guess she's no relation of yours actually." Gilda knew who she was talking about—had learned about Lorna when googling her father, a long time ago.

"My dad's first wife," Gilda said with perfect aplomb. "She's a well-known lecturer." They paused a few moments in hopes Lorna might come out of her building, but she didn't.

Julie was gratified by the disinterested and sincere welcome the other members of Circle of Faith gave Gilda even if she was only fifteen and they had no idea about her money. Most of the Circle were in their forties, but some were Julie's age. Julie had got on to them when still in high school, looking for an extracurricular activity that would look good on her college applications along with her high SATs, and she continued to attend meetings because, though she had yet to see an African child, how often would you meet a statesman or a former slave?

The former slave, the speaker today, was from Eritrea, tall and black, thin as a spear, speaking a graceful English. He explained that like many of those sharing his lot he'd been sold by his family to an Arab when he was eight. By good fortune, he had escaped and gone to Harvard, and now went around telling his story. Julie, though riveted, couldn't help but feel a stab of envy at his good luck in getting to go to Harvard.

"By the grace of Allah, peace be with him," said the slave, "I have been given this mission, to talk to blessed people like yourselves." When the collection basket came around, Julie noticed that Gilda put in the rest of her whole wad of tens, paper clip and all.

As they stood outside waiting for Carla, Gilda suddenly asked Julie, "Have you ever done it with anyone?" Julie supposed Gilda meant sexual intercourse. She had, in high school, but didn't feel like discussing it with a spoiled fifteen-year-old heiress.

"Why?" Julie asked.

"I did it with Ian Aymes when he took me home from the gala. I mean, we got to fooling around, and you know . . . I was surprised, that's all. It was sort of 'oops,' and over with pretty fast. I didn't get the impression of the kind of thing you read about, the thrill. I know the circumstances weren't ideal, in the car in our driveway. Well, back behind the garages, no one could see. So," Gilda said, "I think I'm pregnant. Well, I am pregnant, I did the test kit."

Julie took a second or two to absorb this stunning confidence, and object: "But that's impossible."

"No," said Gilda. "It was my first time! What are the odds of that?"

What are the odds of that? Julie wondered. She thought of Tess of the d'Urbervilles, Hester Prynne—in novels it was 100 percent. "What are you going to do? Did you tell your parents?"

"He was totally upset that he let it go so far. I told him it was as much my fault as his. I suppose it was more his fault, he's older. But I did sort of persist."

"That's the boy at your table at the gala?"

"Yes, Ian. I've known him my whole life. He apologized, he was horrified, he didn't mean to. It was mostly all over my thigh."

"Have you told your parents?"

"No. I know they'll be mad, but they'll support me."

The word "support" to Julie invoked finances and loans, but Gilda was probably talking about emotional support. "This is terrible," she said. "They will be upset. You're only fifteen. You can't have a baby."

"No, I know," Gilda said. "But I would sort of like to. I could still finish school. It's not like my parents wouldn't help me."

"What a terrible idea," said Julie firmly. The practicalities came to her with great clarity.

"I know. I was only thinking about it. I don't think I'll tell my parents, they'll freak out. I was hoping you'd help me."

Julie had admired Gilda's marble skin and statuelike pallor, which suggested unmoving composure. She divined, suddenly, that part of Gilda's preternatural poise was a function of this pallor, which gave her the aspect of being cast in alabaster. Beneath the child's poise she could now detect earnest emotion, though maybe not panic. Money spared you panic. Money gave you serenity—the confidence that nothing was going to let you down, even in a spot like this.

Julie thought about the fact that Gilda's parents were her own grandfather and his wife and found herself wondering, when it came to a grandfather and his wife, where her duty lay, with another girl or with the parents? She could take Gilda to the doctor or a clinic, and her parents wouldn't have to know. But some states had laws that clinics had to tell the parents. Julie thought that was terrible, outrageous. What was the law in California? What was the moral course here?

"Let me think," she said. Her loyalty lay with a fellow female, she quickly decided, even if the girl was her aunt. "We'll go to a clinic. I'll take you," she said. Just then Carla pulled up for Gilda in a Chevy Tahoe. "Don't worry," Julie said. "I'll call you tonight. We'll think what to do."

When Gilda had been driven away, Julie kept going over the options, the possibilities, feeling it was up to her, since Gilda was plainly too young to understand her own plight. She thought of those programs where high-school girls—even in junior high, maybe—were made to carry around a sack full of sand for a month in order to experience the realities of pregnancy. If you went through with it, the realities were: (1) You had a baby and forever after had to take care of it, giving up all options for your future. (2) You gave it away but always wondered about it; eventually it got in touch and you didn't like each other, or you did. (3) You kept it, and your rich parents got a nanny for it so you could finish your education—clearly the best option.

Julie was glad she herself didn't have to decide. If it had happened to her, what would she have done? What would her parents have made her do? The solemn, universal, eternal nature of the grave choices women had to make weighed on her the whole afternoon and gave her bad dreams that night, though she couldn't remember them.

As far as Julie could see, over the following week whenever she talked to Gilda, Gilda hadn't come close to thinking about what she should do. She had a term paper on Chaucer, she had a soccer match—she was the striker.

"Are you going to tell your parents?" Julie asked several times.

"I guess I'll have to," Gilda said.

"Are you going to tell—ah—the boy?"

"Ian? I suppose so. It's his child." Gilda sounded taken with the drama of that dignified formulation: "his child." Gilda was also taken with other imaginings along the lines of stories she'd read—pro-life elements storming Planned Parenthood to keep her from going in the door there, a congresswoman involved; herself being sent on some excuse to a clinic in the South of France until it was over; death while cringing on a slab at Stonehenge; Ian's mother kidnapping the baby—the possibilities were nearly endless, though she knew she couldn't begin to imagine them clearly until she did tell her parents and Ian himself, or maybe she didn't really need to tell him.

That decision was foreclosed, though, when she did tell him, almost inadvertently, when he called to ask about that specific issue. "Is everything all right? You know."

She did know what he must be talking about, since he had never had occasion to call her in her whole life, and she couldn't very well tell him everything was all right.

"Not really," she said, in a low voice, feeling herself being overheard even if she was safely in her room. "I went to the drugstore."

"Oh my God," Ian groaned. There was a long silence, while what she was probably saying sank in. "That's awful. I'm so sorry." His good instincts and good upbringing told him it was important to respond with sensitivity here. Other implications would occur to him momentarily: Would she need money? Would his mother pay? It was an awkward conversation, to say the least, and he felt afterward, as Julie had, that Gilda wasn't really tracking this development. Of course she was only fifteen. A cold chill shuddered his frame: Was he now a sex offender? He'd heard of people who were unjustly assigned to this category because their partner—their victim—was under sixteen. You had to register; people were warned if you came to live near them. He saw his life shredded before him. Meantime, what should he do, in the simple social sense: What to say to Gilda this minute?

"I can't talk here," he said. "Should I meet you somewhere?"

Gilda didn't really want to meet, it would be so embarrassing, and she had homework. "I can't today," she said. "I'll call you tomorrow, or you call me. This is a good time, after school."

"Okay," Ian said, slightly bewildered at her attitude. "Gilda, you have to tell your parents. Can't you tell your dad at least? At least he's a doctor, he'll know what you should do."

"I guess."

"Really! You can't drag this out too long." Even he knew that. An afterthought occurred to him. "Do you feel okay?"

"I just feel normal," she said.

Who is more temperamentally optimistic than a realtor? Ursula Aymes was almost certain she had a buyer for the Curt Mott house, an eager Asian client who, in enumerating his wishes, needs, and bottom lines, exactly described the French Provincial recently bought by Curt Mott and his wife Donna, before Mott's accident and now strange absence from the scene. What was more, and despite the recent drop in housing prices, Ursula was pretty certain she could get practically double the price the Motts had paid, there was now such price confusion, and, thanks to her, they'd got such a good deal on it only last year. They had paid three million six; now she knew she could get six—if she could get the listing.

There were some hitches. For one thing, there'd been some acrimony at the closing; there always was. The termites had come in higher than expected; the furnace vents proved to be wrapped with asbestos; the seller husband had tried to stiff her on a portion of the commission. Curt Mott, citing the loan costs, had also tried to chisel a lower finder's fee and make her pay for removing the asbestos because she hadn't made the seller disclose it. These normal disagreements were survivable, usually. Usually the clients' happiness with their new homes effaced the stress of buying, and all that went with it, softened the recollections, warmed the new homeowners with gratitude. How often had she been invited to glowing dinners at the new digs of people who had been barely speaking to her at the end of escrow.

She could approach Donna Mott about this clever move, but it would be better to talk to the husband, Curt, who didn't seem to be around. If a certain rumor were true, that Curt Mott had skipped to Shanghai with some business funds—naturally she would not be bringing that up—Donna Mott might be in embarrassing circumstances, bankwise, and might grab at the chance to sell. She thought of speaking to Curt's mother, Lorna, whom she knew, though her failure to find Lorna an apartment might make it awkward. She might even speak to Ran Mott, who probably advised his son. Ursula had access to Ran because she'd had a date or two with him, between his marriages, and they had stayed friends these past more than twenty years. Ran would see the wisdom of Curt grabbing this chance to make a brilliant profit. The young Motts could easily find somewhere just as nice to live, she'd help them with that, and—two commissions!

Well, Ursula would just give Donna a ring to find out how they were liking the house. And in fact Ursula was of three minds about the Curt Mott house: sell it; buy it herself and flip it, since she had a buyer; or live in it herself for a while, as it was an excellent house, the best in that few blocks of Pacific Heights. She could then sell her present house, and also help Donna Mott to a sizable profit, everyone happy.

As it happened, Donna had also been thinking that she could sell. She knew she'd been good throughout the trying days of Curt's illness: uncomplaining, compliant, faithful, in the face of her instincts to leave California. But the iron had entered her soul. She would happily leave these people—her ostensible relatives the Motts—and get back to familiar territory in the eastern part of the U.S., God's territory and a better place to raise kids. She missed her own raffish, jolly Italian family.

This feeling had undergone some revision, since, thanks to Amy's generosity, her gorgeous house would now be free and clear, and Amy's vote of confidence gave Donna confidence in turn that she was more deserving than she herself had thought or at least must seem worthy to the Motts and to the rest of the world. But basically she'd still like to sell the house, repay Amy, make a profit after capital gains, and buy something very, very nice in, say, Connecticut, where things, though elegant, were cheaper? She indulged herself in daydreams of this nature. Maybe she could clear a million, even two, maybe even enough to live in New York City in a small, luxurious apartment, maybe around Sutton Place; she probably didn't have enough for the Village.

20

There is no gossip like family gossip.

Soon after the dinner at Honeur's, Misty, Hams, Donna, and Peggy had exchanged their impressions of their mother's emotional and physical state of health, her practical situation, and whether anyone had an idea of how to be of help to her. They loved their mother, if only because she hadn't been around enough to irritate them the way that many of their friends seemed to complain about their own mothers—such, at least, was Hams's observation. But not being around had also been their complaint about her when they were younger.

One issue in particular divided them: whether to reveal to Dad—Ran Mott—in his palace in Woodside, that Mother was back in town in a modest, precarious place on Russian Hill. With Lorna off to France after their divorce, the problem had never arisen before, if it was to be a problem, of the two of them living in the same town, running into each other in the Cal-Mart or at Louise Davies after the symphony. There was some difference of opinion about what to do.

Misty, speaking for herself and Hams, thought they certainly should tell Ran; in case Lorna got sick or destitute, his advice would be important. Peggy was more sensitive than the others to Mother's slightly abject, poor-but-genteel comedown from being the wife of an important French playboy in an elegant, twee French village. She also resented on Mother's behalf the difference in the conditions of her two parents, Ran so rich, Mother so poor, though she thought of herself as loyal to both. Not that Ran paid much attention to her or any of her siblings in the Lorna batch. Finally they decided that probably Dad should be warned.

Lorna had known that coming back to California would involve culture shocks of various intensities. Food would not be one of them— you could eat sumptuously in San Francisco. Between Whole Foods, Real Food, and various specialty grocery stores, the food situation was very positive, not that she was a foodie—if anything the opposite, trau- matized by all the expertise and trouble people went to in Pont-les-Puits and San Francisco both. But she could put on a convincing dinner and got to thinking she ought to do this, ought to begin having old friends over, just a few at a time in Pam's small dining space. She delayed doing it, hoping to find an apartment soon, with a proper dining room; but it was on her mind.

And she'd need a car, that was evident. She'd tried the bus a time or two, something she willingly did in Europe, but bus riding felt strange here, felt more foreign, and you had to wait longer for the thing to come. On bus 45, the one she had to take downtown, everyone spoke Chinese. Cantonese? You were surrounded by conversations you couldn't eavesdrop on, which made the stop-and-go progress of the bus through San Francisco traffic seem very slow, though it gave to the experience a pleasing sense of the exotic, as if you were in Hong Kong or Guangzhou.

She'd gone downtown, among other reasons to visit the lawyer Ursula Aymes had suggested, someone who supposedly knew interna- tional divorce law and could tell her about her situation. The woman, Casey Schwartz, Esq., was nice, but the office secretary, showing Lorna where to wait, had called her "dear." "Sit right here, dear, and Miss Schwartz will come find you." Once, in France, someone, jostling her on the bus, said, *"Excusez-moi, ma petite dame."* These people meant to be polite and welcoming, no doubt, both of them, yet these epithets piqued Lorna. Should she get a facial treatment? Was it time to see how much silver might have crept in under the hair color she had used for so long? She knew she should scorn these anxieties; she had more resources of training and reputation than most women and should be above anxiety about age. She ought to be thinking about the iconography of the Beast in the Book of Revelation.

She wondered if anyone called Ursula Aymes or Pam Linden "dear"? Dear. *Ma petite dame.* Of course, Ursula was tall. Which night was it she had a sort of sexy dream and awoke wondering if she'd ever sleep with anyone again? Had the dream—she couldn't remember it—featured Armand-Loup?

Armand-Loup and Lorna had met in San Francisco when he had come to curate a Nicolas de Staël exhibit at the San Francisco Museum of Modern Art in 1988. Lorna, prominent local art historian and lecturer, had naturally been invited to the opening. It was love practically at first sight; they had exchanged telephone numbers, had lunch two days later, things had moved very fast. Looking back on it now, Lorna could no longer capture the emotions, the excitement, the euphoria, except to remember it had happened, more than twenty years before. What had she looked like then? Armand-Loup had been slender and dashing.

Casey Schwartz, Esq., had explained to Lorna the procedure for separating or divorcing in California a person who was away in France: you sent them a letter to start it off, and the long arm of California would take it from there if there was evidence that Armand-Loup was in agreement. Lorna was not sure that Armand-Loup was, really; though he may have already filed some sort of papers in France, she suspected he would just as soon go on being married, if only for cover. Would he make trouble over being divorced in California? Lorna was confused about the California/France options, and no one, including Casey Schwartz, Esq., seemed to know much about international rules. If they had been married in California, all would be simple, things divided down the middle. But they had been married in Paris at the *mairie* of the first arrondissement, standing in the imposing Gothic *salle de mariage.* The mayor had worn a festive, official tricolor sash and medals to pronounce the solemn words. Had there been strains of *Lohengrin* or Haydn?

Armand-Loup had kept some of his San Francisco friendships and connections and therefore knew whom to call for news of what Lorna might be up to in respect to their situation. It got back to her that one or two people she knew had got calls from him. Was he also behind the continuing series of harassments, as she thought of them, from Pont-les-Puits about the damned graveyard in France and the idea that she had some responsibility for her friend Russell's bones? It was horrible, emotionally speaking, to think of poor Russ's bones, and she certainly didn't have the fifteen hundred euros it was looking like it would cost to do whatever it was to them.

The latest ploy by the Pont city fathers was a claim that she was the legal executor of his estate, nonexistent except for three or four canvases left at his lodging. They'd found a note in his handwriting, they said. They even insisted—"demanded" an ambiguous word in French that could just mean "ask"—they had demanded she come back and have a look, which was out of the question; Armand-Loup, in his bitterness, had probably even changed the locks.

The late Russell Woods had regularly sent his paintings back to his native town of Cedar Rapids, Iowa, where his old friend Dave Carlson had a little gallery and some connections in Chicago. It was in Chicago the Woodses had first been remarked, then sought after, now bartered at places like Basel Miami in the high six figures, soon probably to be seven. Dave Carlson still had several in reserve, not yet on the market, and had tried to find out if any had been left behind in Pont-les-Puits. It was thus, through the vagaries of the art market, they had learned in Pont that there was a current demand for Woods's work, and they had been pleased to realize that the commune owned outright the one that hung in the *mairie,* presented by Woods himself, and possibly some of the others, owed in payment to local merchants. His paintings inevitably depicted the church, a Gothic church with pre-Baroque elements that captured a play of light and shadow irresistible to a painter, a texture of gargoyle shadows and silhouettes of angelic wings, and the statues of the oxen that had reputedly hauled the builders' stones, with names carved beneath them. No one knew if these names referred to the stonemasons or the oxen themselves.

There were also the three or four paintings—depending on how you counted the one that appeared unfinished—left in the Hôtel La

Périchole where Woods had made his home. As he'd been a little slow with the rent, and died owing Madame Lafournier more than three hundred euros, she had no compunction about putting them aside pending the ultimate resolution of his affairs. Woods had been dead more than four years, but estate resolution took a while, and his works got more valuable with time. Could Madame Dumas be of help?

In San Francisco, Lorna invited her various children to lunch one by one, wanting to hear more about their particular circumstances, give counsel, financial support if it was modest—very modest—and generally put herself back into their lives if possible. She'd been too long away. With Peggy, she immediately discovered that these conversations would have a way of turning back on herself:

"Mother, how long can you stay in Pam Linden's apartment exactly?"

"Mother, won't you need a car? We could look for something 'secondhand,' they say that's always the sensible thing, a new car loses its value the minute you drive it off the lot."

"I know, Peg, I'll certainly be looking for a used car of some kind."

"Do you hear from Armand-Loup?"

"Are you filing for an actual divorce?" And so it went with Peggy, with Hams—actually also with Misty, who seemed to speak for both herself and Hams, a good sign they were getting along—and even with Donna, though Donna was mostly the exception, as she had little interest in Lorna's doings and contented herself with saying the things Curt probably would have said if he'd been there, about renting versus selling, and hybrid versus gasoline.

Since Lorna didn't know the answer to any of the questions her children put to her, she always equivocated. Her mind was more on reestablishing herself professionally, and this wasn't going terribly well. She'd sent out friendly letters by way of reminding art department chairmen and museum directors she was once again in America, available and enthusiastic about her new subject, the medieval tapestries of Angers. Several program directors at the various universities and museums she'd written to didn't respond at all, or hadn't yet responded. Those who had were friendly but strapped for cash, or had already hardened their lecture schedules for the coming year but promised to keep in touch.

It crossed her mind to take Phil Train up on his offer of the (unpaid) Altar Forum as a venue to give a lecture; speaking there might have some word-of-mouth legs with influential women in the audience and would help her by honing some of the details of the talk itself. For the moment, pride impeded this move, but she could foresee she'd weaken. She'd wait another week for some better responses from somewhere, for instance the lecture agent about—was it Modesto?

The lunch with Donna was a bit of a chore. Apart from her maternal concerns, Donna had no small talk and an invincibly literal mind, which Lorna had been slow to diagnose. When Donna said, "My bedspreads are green," Lorna's mind would flit to the environmental implications of bedspreads, or newness, as in "greenhorns," before understanding that the only responses were to say How lovely or What color are the curtains? Should Lorna have said, My bedspreads are white? But then what?

Thus they had little to talk about except Marcus and Manuel, who had been disruptive at nursery school and were threatened with expulsion. "They say Marcus bit a boy."

"They miss their father," Lorna diagnosed. "Small children are affected by absence. Boys especially." She regretted saying this, in case it sounded as if she were blaming Donna. She was sure Donna was doing her best, and it wasn't her fault Curt was so strangely absent.

"Oh no, they don't really notice," Donna said.

Hams requested a second lunch with his mother, without Misty, for a day he happened to be in San Francisco—crossing the Bay between Berkeley and the city nearly as significant a journey in people's minds as, say, Calais to Dover, requiring reflection and resolution before trying it, though it was only twelve miles of jammed bridge, metering lights, the anxiety of choosing one of the eighteen lanes and getting it wrong. From France, Lorna had thought of the Bay and lovely bridges as positive attributes of San Francisco, but now she saw them as features of the punishing commutes exasperated people were forced into daily, a means of separating families, like herself from Hams and Misty.

For lunch with Hams, Lorna bought a quiche on Polk Street and fixed a tuna salad. They sat in Pam's little dining room.

"How long are you going to be able to stay here, Mom?" he asked.

"I may have found something right near here," Lorna said. She gave him the details of an apartment Ursula Aymes had just shown her. Nothing was settled, but she could see he was reassured.

"Way to go!"

"What brings you over here today, dear?"

"Well, I wanted to see you. Misty wasn't feeling too well or she would've come."

"I'm sorry to miss her."

"I think if we could move, she'd be a lot better. It's getting to be an obsession with her. I was wondering . . ."

"You know I don't have a bean," Lorna said sternly. Hams looked hurt.

"It isn't that. I was wondering if you thought I should approach Dad? If they can give Curt three million dollars, it seems like it's worth asking." Hams was known to have said he would never see his father again, so enraged was he over Ran's vague disapproval of his general existence, or so he felt; but everything changes.

"Really, Hams, I have no idea. Your father might as well be someone I never met. Would I know him on the street? Anyway, it's his wife who has the money, I assume." She understood Hams's resentment, the imbalance of fortune, the sense of having misplayed one's hand, not that she had any regrets for herself.

"Sometimes I think Misty thinks she married the wrong brother," Hams said. It leapt to Lorna's mind that Misty might well think that, Hams not much of an earner, but of course she stifled the thought. It depended on your values. Hams was still in his thirties—he might yet take fire, his music or in the chef world. And so nice-looking, robust and manly—was he her favorite after all? She advised him to try his father, what could it hurt?

Hams had begun to agree that Misty was right and they should move. Something disturbing had happened. It was a night Hams had his chef gig at Chili Pride, and Misty, feeling uncomfortable with morning sickness, couldn't face a bowl of chili, so though she usually had dinner with Hams at the restaurant, tonight had stayed home. Sitting in the kitchen, she was surprised to see Sarah, her colleague at the cleaners, a druggy, taciturn woman of about thirty, at her back door, though the gate to the backyard had been shut, maybe locked, since her bike had been stolen out of it a few weeks before.

"Hi, Sarah, how surprising!" Through the screen door.

"Can I come in? This is Scott." With her was a spindly youth in T-shirt and jeans, carrying a briefcase. Misty didn't like strangers, but could think of no objection, since she knew Sarah and worked with her. "We were near here. Scott has to do something. We'll only be ten minutes."

"Sure, can I get you some . . . there's some Sprite . . ."

"Scott has to do something is all, and we were nearby. We can just stay in the kitchen."

"What? This is . . ." Misty had a bad feeling, but she knew Sarah and, as there was nothing to explain the apparently harmless but furtive apparition, she opened the screen door and they came in. "There's some Sprite, and fizzy water and stuff."

"We're okay," Sarah said. Scott had opened his briefcase and was pulling out a rubber tube, pipette, spoon, matches. Works. All too clear to Misty some kind of drug works.

"You can't do that here, absolutely not," Misty said.

"We'll just stay here in the kitchen."

"You can't do anything here," Misty said. The uneasy feeling in her stomach grew, confusing the already distended and rumbling stir of the baby in there.

Needles. "Get out of here, Sarah," Misty said.

"Don't worry, we will," Sarah said. "Scott isn't feeling good, he needs to do this." But Scott was wrapping a rubber tube around Sarah's own pale, thin, pocked arm. Misty began to feel queasy and went into her living room to sit down. Strangers in her kitchen shooting up. She smelled the wave of heat from a match lit in the kitchen. Please get them out of here. Her vulnerability crushed her; why didn't she get up and say, Sarah get out of here? Why had she opened the door? Why was she scared? It was this neighborhood, this house, they had to get away.

She tiptoed to the kitchen door and peeked in. Sarah was injecting something into a vein in her arm below the loosened rubber tourniquet. She looked at Misty looking.

"It's only speed," she said. Misty began to feel faint. Blood left her head; the scene grew pale. She looked away. In junior high school, she had fainted in first aid class at the diagram of a puncture wound in the handbook. You put your head between your knees until the wave of fainting goes away and the blood comes back. She did this.

When Hams came home later, Misty was apparently asleep, on the sofa, on her side, her head between her drawn-up knees. No one was around, but someone had been there; there were ashes in a jar lid on the kitchen table. He had to wake her to hear the story. She had fainted and somehow slid into sleep. After he heard it, he resolved to speak to his father. He realized it was more than three years since he'd seen him or spoken to him except to tell him about Misty's pregnancy.

He didn't tell Lorna this story about the crack visitors.

21

Sometimes the handwriting of Providence is hard to read.

At her lunch with Lorna, Donna didn't mention her plan to sell the house she had so providentially been given. Obtuse as she could sometimes be, even she could see the Mott family, especially Amy, was going to take it amiss, as a form of ingratitude. Maybe affronting them would be worth it if she could realize a sizable profit; as it was, after paying Amy back, she'd only come out with the down payment minus capital gains for her future, which they would be sure to point out. If she could sell at all. The bottom was falling out of the housing market; everyone could see that.

Donna knew that Lorna knew that Hams believed Curt was actually in touch with her, Donna, and was hiding because of some financial crime, but she put this belief down to their ancient sibling rivalry. He hadn't been in touch. But then, not too long after her lunch with Lorna, Donna's happiness and sense of good fortune were rudely blighted by an actual letter from Curt. To date there had only been a few postcards, but here was an envelope. She was hoping for a return address so she could let him know about their good fortune and Amy's generosity, and tore it open eagerly. It was handwritten in Curt's correct, rather prim script but seemed a bit incoherent:

Darling Donna,

All is going well, but I'm writing to say I'm going to
make my life here. It's nothing to do with you, I was perfectly
happy in San Francisco, you shouldn't blame yourself. There
are a lot of opportunities here.

The twins are so young, they won't miss me, I'm thankful
about that. You can have the house, that should cover what
you need. I thank God for your MBA, you'll know what
you're doing.

Of course you'll say it was my accident that brought on
this need for a life change, and that would be right. There's
nothing like looking into the face of God.

Just as a precaution, it's better for you if you don't have
my address, and anyhow I'm on the move. I'll figure out some
way to handle legal things that might come up.

Love,
Curt

Donna read this letter with bafflement, reread it, her heart con-
gealing with fear as she came to understand it. He seemed to be saying
he wasn't coming home. That he was cutting her loose with only her
MBA to face the future without him. Or was that it? "You can have
the house." That much was clear, though it didn't escape her that Curt
didn't yet know about the paid-off mortgage. He might not realize he
was leaving her with a multimillion-dollar asset. When he did, he'd be
sure to renege on his generous offer.

Why was she sure he was leaving her? He didn't actually say so. Her
legs felt weak and trembling, and she had to sit down. She had to think
what to do. He didn't say don't come to Thailand. During his coma, she
had so often reviewed what she would do if Curt were to die, but all her
ideas deserted her now.

When her blood began to run again, she slid into the first of the
stages she'd read about: denial, quickly dispatched with, since the words

were before her. But still, she might not be reading him right. He might mean he wasn't coming home yet.

Anger. Rage, more like. The words of a letter she'd write to Curt formed and re-formed in her mind, but it was time to pick up the twins from their nursery school; she banged the fender backing out of the garage and didn't bother to get out to review whether there were scratches or dents on his precious Beamer.

22

Some blithe spirits have perfected the art of laying their worries on you.

Because Gilda did not seem very interested in her own plight, Julie took on for them both the inner turmoil, the worry, the kaleidoscope of possible outcomes, measures for Gilda to take, and personal actions she, Julia Willover, ought to take. Julie knew she herself might, in the same fix at the same age, have been as vacuous and drifting as Gilda was.

They would start by repeating the pregnancy test in case Gilda had read it wrong. On the next Saturday, she steered Gilda into a Walgreens and they bought the cheapest one, one that claimed it could tell as early as six days after the event. She went with Gilda to the ladies' room in Macy's and read the directions herself, coaching Gilda through the door of the toilet stall. The enclosure said, "Because this test detects low levels of hCG, it is possible that this test may give positive results even if you are not pregnant. If you test positive, but think you may not be pregnant, you should check with your doctor."

"Did you ever hear that your diabetes medicine could, like, give a false positive on something like this?"

Gilda laughed. "Where would I hear that? We don't discuss pregnancy at Saint Waltraud's.

"Okay, I've peed on the stick," she said in a minute. She came out of the stall with her warm paper cup.

Julie studied the instructions, written in barely comprehensible English translated from an unknown tongue: "It is need to remove the hCG test strips from the conserved pouch and dip the strip in the urine through the arrow point to the urine. It is very important that do not let the urine level to go above the maximum line; otherwise the test will not do properly."

"Okay, I get that. Dip the strip in. This must have been written in Bangalore."

"People speak English in Bangalore," Gilda said.

" 'The hCG test strip is absorbed into a urine sample, capillary act carries the sample to transfer along the covering. When hCG in the taster makes the Test Zone area of the covering, it will appear a colored line. But not appear of this colored line recommend a negative result.'

"Now we wait, I guess," Julie went on. "I'm not sure what this is saying."

"I did all this," Gilda said. She dipped the paper strip into her cup and watched the capillary action. Soon it turned a vigorous pink.

"See?" said Gilda.

"Okay," said Julie, chilled at the horrid, emphatic dawning color and its significance. She felt she was reacting for the two of them, since Gilda seemed so unaffected. Once you got used to her pallor, she was beautiful, like the statues of saints in dim churches. Julie wondered about the mechanics behind Gilda's description of goo mostly on her thigh. Could sperm crawl as well as swim? Could that have been what happened to the Virgin Mary?

"I have to go. Carla should be here," Gilda said. "She's picking me up in front of Macy's."

Over the next few days, Gilda's plight continued to weigh on Julie, along with a sense of duty, which she tried to define: What was her duty here? She thought of the cute little baby Gilda could have with the handsome young man, she thought of Gilda's age and cluelessness, she thought of the reputed wealth of Gilda's parents—Julie's own grandfather—and of how easily Gilda could disappear to some comfortable Caribbean island for a few months on account of her health; no one would question it. Then Grandpa Ran and his wife could adopt the baby. She began to have a sense of her duty, and once she became convinced of the wisdom of this adoption plan, she became fearful that something would go wrong, Gilda would do the wrong thing, or miscarry. The girl had still not told her parents.

The handsome young man, Ian Aymes, for his part, had told his mother. Ursula's reaction was not at all what he expected. Far from fainting with dismay, she sighed a rather insincere sigh and said she supposed such things happened. Young people nowadays. Gilda was a pretty child, though it was wrong of him to forget her age. Of course she did look older, she thought in his defense. How were Amy and Ran reacting? Ian was astonished at her calm.

"She hasn't told them. She's pretty scared. We thought she could go, you know, to the doctor, without them having to know, but I would need some money."

"Is that a good idea?" Ursula mused and seemed to drop the subject, leaving Ian unsure what he ought to do or what she thought. He chalked it up to her being stunned. But he still needed money.

"I think my mother will help," he assured Gilda on the telephone, but he really had no reason to think so.

Ursula, for her part, was by no means appalled to think of having a biological connection, a family connection, to Amy Hawkins and her millions, or billions; no one knew how much, Silicon Valley numbers were ridiculous, perhaps unaffected by the ongoing grimness of whatever was happening to the American economy, disaster all around them, especially the real-estate market.

How unlucky that Gilda was only fifteen and probably would not be allowed to have a baby. The more Ursula thought about it, the more proprietary she began to feel about her incipient grandchild in the womb of the teenaged heiress. She and Ran and Amy needed to have a serious talk. Questions of posterity and sentimental visions of adorable babies in bassinets and recollections of Ian when a baby of greeting-card beauty stirred her heart to something almost akin to pain, to think of the difficulties ahead, the confusion of the paths that beckoned.

Ian, meantime, was taking a makeup class in Western civilization at the junior college in Mountain View, as was needed for the Thinking Matters core curriculum requirement at Stanford. He kept his mind on that, and was also involved in intramural soccer, which took up a lot of time. When he was not enjoying violent athletic activity, thoughts tormented him, about Gilda's age and about the possibility of her parents prosecuting him. Whenever he and Gilda spoke, he apologized, again and again, sincerely.

Gilda had read on the web that diabetic pregnancy had more complications and produced more congenital anomalies than normal, and you had to achieve better glycemic control, and that she should have gone to a diabetic control clinic before conceiving. There were personal testimonies: "My doctor told me to check my blood glucose every two hours, make sure I bolused 15 minutes before a meal, and I should exercise at least 30 minutes a day. I also tried to shoot for a premeal blood-sugar number of 60–90 mg/dL and 120 mg/dL two hours after eating."

Another diabetic woman had written: "I checked my blood sugars as the doctor instructed, every hour, and at 2 hours I would correct if I was above a 90 mg/dL blood sugar." Reading further, she found: "I also sent my blood-sugar log to my endocrinologist every Friday and, shortly after emailing, my doctor would call with new basal rates and carbohydrate ratios. The rates varied throughout the entire pregnancy. If I didn't send my logs on time, I got a phone call from her. Now if they only did that all of the time, I would never have a high A1C!" Gilda understood the arcane language of diabetes control better even than her parents.

Alone in her room, scaring herself with reading these things— "Check your blood sugar every hour!"—she was coming around to the idea she was going to have to tell her parents so her baby would turn out okay. She was pretty sure they would want the baby. She might need special doctors. She might have to check her sugar every hour!

Otherwise, in general, she figured out from all this, a diabetic person like her shouldn't have a baby, maybe she could never have one, pregnancy would mess her up or kill her. She didn't care that much; it was only one of the bad things she was always finding out about her illness, how she might lose her toes someday, or her sight, things talked about online all the time, horrors of mutilation and gangrene, which never had been mentioned by her doctors or parents.

23

Moral decisions are more comfortably shared than brooded over alone.

Julie had told her mother Peggy all about the gala, with Grandpa Ran's silvery fifteen-year-old maiden daughter (Peggy's own half sister!) in the ugly lace dress, and about the other dresses she had seen, and the flowers, and the radiance of Amy Hawkins Mott in black-and-rose Givenchy, or so it had been described in the *Chronicle* the next day. Peggy in turn said nothing about the gala to her mother Lorna, but she wondered if Lorna was reading the paper. Peggy had some residual scruple about being too friendly with Amy and Ran when Lorna was so bravely hard up, but she did talk to her father once a month or so.

Now, Julie decided to also tell Peggy about Gilda's catastrophe and get her advice about what she, Julie, ought to do to help Gilda or intervene or tell Grandpa Ran or what. Maybe some sisterly instinct might guide them. Gilda was her mother's half sister after all—weird as the chronology was.

She telephoned Peggy. They talked a little about this and that— they were friendly but not as close as some mothers and daughters; Julie didn't have much sense of what her mother did all day and vice versa. The subject they most had in common was Julie's own fate—her tuition, her student loans, her whereabouts, her weight, at least when Julie had been pudgy, at age fourteen, and the Circle of Faith, which Julie had tried to interest Peggy in. Now they talked of Julie's crusade for going to Greece, then eventually Julie brought up the subject of Gilda.

"It's hard to imagine, but your sister Gilda is in trouble."

"You mean 'in trouble'?" Peggy asked. "You mean, shoplifting or something like that? Pregnant?" She thought she was being funny.

"Pregnant, yes. She made it sound like a freak thing. A boy her family knows. She's afraid to tell Grandpa and Amy." She described the situation. Peggy expressed her astonishment. They laughed a bit, both feeling guilty for laughing at someone's plight.

"Are you telling me this so I'll tell Dad?" Peggy finally asked. "I don't even know Gilda—hardly know her. I saw her when she was about five. I have dinner with my father once in a while, but I've never even been to their house. Is she very upset?"

"Not as upset as you'd think. She's a strange kid, kind of spacey, nice and polite. She did tell me, though, so she seems to want some moral support."

"Well, sure." Peggy sympathized with any girl in that predicament. "I always wondered what we would do if anything like that happened to you."

Julie sniffed at the idea. Something like that would not happen to her; she was more competent than that. But she hadn't been sexually active at fifteen, either.

"Dad is a doctor, after all, he'll deal with it," Peggy said. "She has to tell him, though. Has she?"

Julie did not think so. She told Peggy some of her imaginary baroque, inventive solutions involving trips to the Bahamas or Greece, or maybe a semester in France working on French language skills; they could make up a history for an unexplained baby—an orphaned refugee; a pregnant housekeeper mown down in a mall incident, followed by emergency C-section, adoption by the Motts . . . None of these ideas would be of any use if the baby should turn out to be an albino freak like Gilda, but probably it wouldn't; her coloring was just a fluke.

When Peggy just laughed, it seemed to Julie that her mother wasn't focusing on all the real tragic possibilities, and the ruin of her little sister's life.

"I told her I'd go down to Woodside with her, be there when she tells them," Julie said.

"I wouldn't, Julie, they'll think you encouraged her or him, or something."

"I don't even know him," Julie protested. "I told her she could go with me to Greece. Grandpa Ran could help with the expenses."

"That's not a bad idea," Peggy agreed, wondering who would ever suggest it to him.

24

The world does not like a sponge.

Lorna had begun to feel the judgmental eyes of Pam's doormen calculating that she'd been overstaying Pam's hospitality. Their perhaps imaginary disapproval was the impetus, finally, to give up on most of her requirements and decide *faute de mieux* to take the next affordable apartment no matter how grim.

And Ursula had found one for her rather nearby as it turned out, on Larkin just off Union, in a modest frame duplex dating from the 1900s. There were horrible linoleum floors in some places, but she would get rugs and stylish furniture from Ikea, as all the young people did nowadays, enhanced by an artful antique or so; she could perhaps ask to take back one or two nice family pieces she'd given Peggy all those years ago when she left for France and Peggy had been getting married.

Despite having kept its original moldings, her new place was really pretty shabby—all the rooms painted hospital green—hence the rent only a little more than she'd planned to pay; but she could have it repainted, and the elderly Chinese couple renting the other apartment seemed quiet and perfectly friendly. They appeared to her to be almost identical, the man and the woman, with thinning gray hair cut the same and matching eyeglasses, the same slightly crouching stance, wearing the cotton vests you saw everywhere in North Beach, and you would not know they were there except for the drying and dead chrysanthe-mums in the garbage. There was an overgrown patch of garden in back, a good feature they did not appear to care about, where Lorna would have a few vegetables—French beans, she hoped. She found American green beans horrible, big and fibrous; why couldn't they think to grow the little French ones?

As a younger woman, she would have been in tears at a place like this; but your expectations evidently faded along with your shrinking life expectancy. Really her spirits were good. She could move in as soon as she wanted, which was lucky, as Pam Linden was reclaiming her apartment in a week, announcing her return so promptly after Lorna told her she was leaving that Lorna feared that Pam had been waiting bags packed for the merest sign that she was getting out.

She organized Hams for an Ikea run; she'd need sheets, lamps, a bed, right away. She got the phone and the electricity and gas put in her name the same afternoon she signed the lease, amazed at how quickly you could set up house in San Francisco. It would have taken a month in Pont-les-Puits, though doubtless faster in Paris. In Pont she'd have had to have a letter from the bank to have the lights put on.

It was nice to be in America. Looking back, she'd come to feel that some essentially American part of her had been stifled in France, but was now reawakening, some innate appreciation of local efficiency and traditions of welcome she'd forgotten about. Like Rip van Winkle, she told Hams, she had been in a long French fugue. Now, speaking of her time in France, she caught herself perpetuating certain American myths about French coldness, rudeness, in comparison with here, though in fact no one had ever been rude in Pont-les-Puits. Cold, maybe, but for other reasons—her American-accented French, her idiotic cookery.

Yes, she was happy to be back in America, she told herself, even if it was not as—not as nice, really. Life was harder in San Francisco. In France there were trains and medical care. Here the news featured people being evicted and living in containers. Her emotions churned in a confused, deracinated way; people (Pam, on the telephone) inevi-tably told her it would take time to put down new roots or find her old groove.

There was also the issue of invisibility. When she had left America to marry Armand-Loup, she was still a pretty young woman, and the world responded to her. Now, twenty years later, however good-looking she was for a person of her age, to the world she had entered the invisible phase you always heard about. Whether she talked to the butcher or the banker, she did not experience that animated twinkle from the man she was talking to, that special energy that was the product of, well, sex. More precisely, fertility. In France, though, men sustained the twinkle longer. Armand-Loup did for sure. In America it was extinguished early. American men evidently didn't have the same appreciation for women of a certain age. It was a cultural almost as much as a biological issue.

There was an electric stove already in the apartment, which she was sure she'd hate but would get used to. In Pont there was an old farmhouse stove, built to use either gas or wood. But she was charmed by her slick new cookware with its nonstick coating. She liked the old-house smell. The garage was hers, a valuable feature, though for the moment she had no car. "In this neighborhood you could rent it out—you can ask four hundred a month for it," Ursula told her. "People will kill for parking places."

It was fun settling in, finding joy in each item she added in the name of livability. She found a big glass vase at the secondhand store on Polk Street, thinking wistfully of the vases in her cupboard in Pont— Baccarat, Lalique, and the handsome local stoneware. But even in a Mason jar she would still have flowers, and books in the bookcase she would fashion from cinder blocks and a board, like a college student. Bunches of flowers took away the impression of sad austerity. She knew that books would accumulate soon enough, it was the way of books to proliferate, but meantime, when the bare booklessness of the living room bothered her, she bought an armload from the same thrift store, Athena's Shelf, and propped them on the windowsills. Art books nobody read, with reproductions of Verrocchio and Giorgione. And, as if owing to her acquisition of a fixed address, she was immediately invited to a dinner party by Nancy and Howard Fludd, people she'd known forever, museum people she'd kept up with over the years.

She subscribed to the *Chronicle* and the *New York Times* both, and read diligently, somewhat appalled by her growing sense of the tone, especially in the *Times,* of people's discontent with all aspects of life— their gender mostly, but qualities in their mates or coworkers, ethical questions people seemed no longer to know the answers to, where people of Lorna's age knew the answers perfectly well. "My coworker is having an affair. I am having lunch with his wife. If I accept her hospitality, is it moral to conceal what I know about her husband?" A layer of moral anxiety thickened the air now. Maybe it was just the people who wrote in to newspapers who felt it. Maybe it was good that people recognized the existence of a moral dimension, but there was a new level of self-involvement that seemed to Lorna not to have been there before, or at least not to have been "out." That was it, there was a new level of outness about everything, and it was aggressive. And all the new etiquette about roommates and one-night stands. There was so much to learn, not that a person of her age would be having one-night stands. She did begin to be solicited for e-dating services for people with silver hair—that is, her age group: the widowed, the late divorces.

For someone very experienced at dinner parties, she was more pleased and excited than she ought to have been about the Fludds' dinner, she knew, but couldn't keep down a tingle of anticipation. Going to a dinner party on your own felt different from the way you felt when the actual or merely virtual moral presence of a husband went with you. In her husbandless interregnum between Ran and Armand-Loup, she fitted into the raffish category of the husband-hunting divorcée; obviously, no one would think of her that way anymore, would not feel they had to invite an eligible man to make up the party, or be thoughtful about the seating. What a relief to be done with all that.

She was chagrined, though, to feel herself still worrying about what to wear. She really had nothing to wear, had come away from Pont-les-Puits with nothing, and, too, what people wore in San Francisco was slightly different, in what way she could not say, beyond that San Francisco was a city, not a village, and the seasons had changed. She could justify a new dress and would make a hair appointment on the day. The words of the old gay baron in Proust came to her: "Of course I'm no longer five-and-twenty, they won't choose me to be Queen of the May, but still one does like to feel that one's looking one's best."

She saw, arriving at the Fludds', that when reentering society after a long absence, you came in by the same door you had left it, both in the minds of your hosts and in your own; if your last party was when you were fourteen, your emotions now, at a certain age, were of a fourteen-year-old, as if no time had passed. When she'd first moved to France, her French had been at the level of junior high school, the age she had studied it, though she was by then a woman over forty, and so people seemed to think of her as mentally fourteen. Her life was like lace, or net, or laddered stockings, with many holes between the ruptured threads.

It was ruddy-jowled Howard Fludd who welcomed her in, gave her a kiss on each cheek, two—whether in deference to her recent return from France, where two kisses were required, or because two were meant to convey especial warmth, an escalation of the conventional American single air peck.

"We tried to call you and Armand last year when we were in the Luberon," he said. "Are you still there, in Pont-les-Thing?"

"Armand Loup is," she said, not clear whether Howard understood why she was back in San Francisco alone. At table, a man she didn't know, Ray someone, was to her right and asked about her children. Howard Fludd, to her left, mostly had to deal with the hostlike administrative duties of serving and passing. As a well-socialized female of her generation, she was meek about dinner conversation and was content to respond to questions and, above all, ask them of male dinner partners, although, after all those years in France, she had learned not to ask American-style personal queries like What do you do? but more general questions like What will happen to the mayor if the bridge inquiry goes further? or What do you think of the museum's new Monet? Or Don't you think we should spend our funds on Diebenkorns? assuming a collective interest in the art museum, local politics, or some new film. The financial crash seemed to be a touchy subject: What do we think about the bailout? Voices were raised, but rancor was avoided. One of the guests, Marina Box, she knew was the art museum director, so

Lorna could slyly insinuate into the conversation her opinion that the museum ought to spend its funds buying local painters like Diebenkorn and Thiebaud, not French Impressionists of another day.

Later, at the table, she had a success telling the story of the slipping graveyard in Pont-les-Puits, but it was her only moment of speaking up.

"It must be so dull for you, being back here," said Carol—Mrs. Ray. "After France. We always have such a nice time in Paris. Of course you're out in the country, aren't you?"

"Armand-Loup keeps a little pied-à-terre in Paris," Lorna said.

"We go every June," Carol said. "We have a restaurant list if you'd like me to pass it on. Out-of-the-way places, not Americanized."

"Thank you," Lorna meekly said. "I'd love that."

"France has seen its day," said Howard Fludd. "You've probably bailed out at the right time."

"Bailed out," Lorna heard her own voice uncertainly repeat. She suddenly saw it: she had bailed out and was now at a dinner party in San Francisco, having recently given a lecture in Bakersfield, hoping for Fresno, in a country experiencing a crash.

"That's a country that's over, but they don't know it," said Carol's husband—wasn't that Ray?

"Did you happen to know Russell Woods?" asked Marina Box suddenly, and a whole new topic blossomed for Lorna, her friendship with Russell, his death, his life. She felt she could add something to the evening after all. "In some fashion, I've become his executor," she said. This, she saw, got Marina Box's attention.

"You must come to lunch at the museum next week—we have so many new acquisitions, and you may not have seen the redo of the atrium," Marina said, and Lorna thought she saw a petal or two of her immediate future unfold.

Still, in a further week, she had not heard from any museum, university, or lecture agent to whom she'd reached out professionally. She did have a phone call from Carol, wife of Ray, the woman she'd met at the Fludds'.

"You know we have this group—it doesn't meet too often, no panic: Friends of Proust. We'd love it if you'd join us. You must have such a great sense of the social realities he's talking about—the whole background—and we need someone who's spent so much time in France. I know you'll enjoy it—we read a few pages aloud, and then someone gives a report. 'Menus at the Duchesse de Guermantes'—that was a recent one—or 'Proust and the Theater.'"

For a moment, Lorna was abashed—she was no Proustian. Still, she had always meant to go beyond *Swann's Way*, which is where she had stopped. Poor Russell had been so keen on the character of Elstir, the painter. Yes, she ought to carry on reading Proust. Still, how embarrassing: twenty years in France without going beyond *Swann's Way*. And she was a scholar! Would she be exposed? Did she have time to catch up? She thought of that party game Humiliation, in which you confessed the most shameful omission in your education.

25

Loyalty is a virtue everyone admires, especially the disloyal.

Julie ignored her mother's advice to stay out of Gilda's worries, and agreed to go down to Woodside for dinner and be there when Gilda revealed her plight to her parents, who, in their leafy paradise, had remained innocently unaware of everything that had happened. Gilda had pleaded with Julie to come, and promised that Carla would drive her down to them and back to the city afterward, or they could organize for her to take one of the tech buses that made the trip often. Gilda came along with Carla to fetch her, but they naturally couldn't discuss the pending matter in front of Carla. Carla was playing an old Santana CD too loud to talk anyhow.

Carla Alvarez had worked for Amy Hawkins since before Amy married Ran Mott, nearly sixteen years ago, certainly entitling her to be thought of as a loyal retainer, though she was not forty and was still planning to study to be a CPA when she got the money together, and to marry and have a family, and to travel. Carla looked like a college girl, but called herself a personal concierge, was unnaturally taciturn, and seldom spoke even to Gilda, but smiled pleasantly under all circumstances. She'd begun as an office helper for Amy, but evolved into a driver, occasional cook, confidante, and unofficial nanny; Gilda had

had an actual nanny, too, when she was younger, but not since she began school. "Call me Figaro," Carla had once startled them by saying.

She had a nice apartment over one of the garages, and since her family lived in Mountain View, she was just the right distance from them, not too far but not too close. She feared getting dragged back into their Beaner ways, as she thought of them—the basically high-fat, high-carb Hispanic cooking of her mom, their lack of interest in music; Carla had excelled at her music lessons at school, had received a violin, had even played for a while when younger in the junior orchestra of San Jose. Unlike her mom, she did not go to church. Mr. Alvarez, her father, had been doing the Mott yard for years, but lately had gone into making dry-rock walls and now had a fairly successful landscaping business, more in San Jose than Woodside.

When they got to Woodside, they pulled up to some high wooden gates painted black-green, concealing what lay beyond, and Carla pushed a button on the dashboard of her Chevy Tahoe to make them slowly open. Julie had been to Grandpa Ran's place here years before, she forgot why but supposed with her mother; she didn't really remember it and was unprepared for its comfortable grandeur, if these were not contradictory terms, the ivy growing over the garages, and a rose hedge, the doors dark green and shiny, the brass latches polished to gold. With a sidelong glance at Gilda, she saw the girl's lips tightly pressed together, as if so in dread of the coming scene she could barely force them open.

The evening started in an ordinary fashion. Gilda and Julie joined Ran in his study where he was watching the news. The economy was looking very bad; foreclosures were crashing the housing market; people were living in boxcars. "The bastards have to forgive the mortgages," Ran said. He was having a glass of white wine and asked Julie, but not Gilda, if she would join him. Gilda's mother was not around, but stuck her head in around seven o'clock to say *"À table."*

Julie noted the dining room furniture in pale woods, like the glamorous interiors in vintage films of the forties where the actresses wore feather-trimmed dressing gowns. Was it a real Picasso over the buffet? There was soup to start, served from an antique tureen, then chicken with artichokes and preserved lemons. At dessert, when Carla, who served the dinner, was not in the room, Gilda, dawdling with healthful orange sections dusted with coconut, brought up her situation. She falteringly announced that there was something she wanted to tell Ran and Amy.

"You aren't going to like it," she added. They looked a little alarmed at this warning, at the solemnity of Gilda's tone, not the usual tone at their dinners, and Julie felt them glance at herself, as if she ought to corroborate or was somehow behind Gilda's gravity. Or, horrors, had instigated it.

"I have a problem I think you should know about," Gilda said. "I'm pregnant." As she expected, she had their instant attention; they were the most attentive parents possible. She hastened to embroider: "Uh, it was an accident, I can explain . . ." The thunderstruck parents said nothing for what seemed to Julie an excruciating pause. Then Ran rose from his chair.

"Did someone hurt you?" he asked with menace building in his voice as he imagined violation by the gardener or some teacher at her school. No other explanation seemed very likely. She had never had a date, though there were school dances to which boys were invited en masse. After the ineffable silence, Amy rose, too, and came around the table to hug Gilda and say, "Oh, honey, are you all right?" her expression one of love and motherly concern. "Oh, honey, surely not?"

The parents continued to look stunned, though only for a moment more. Then there were questions: "What happened? How do you know?" Deeply embarrassed, Gilda described coming home with Ian the night of the gala and admitted to the brief tussle in the car behind the garages, and, without going into detail, since her own grasp of the details was extremely vague, explained about the heavy petting and then the pregnancy test, and that Julie had helped her confirm it. Julie felt their accusing gaze, as her mother had predicted.

Gilda's parents persisted in unexpectedly kindly tones with questions. Since her ideas of anger, ostracism, and disgrace had been taken from nineteenth-century novels, and she had built a solid edifice of mental preparation, she and Julie were both a little disappointed at their relative calm.

It also became quite clear to Julie as she followed the conversation that Gilda's parents were mainly stricken with guilt, feeling they hadn't given her adequate instruction in the ways of the world, hadn't talked about contraception, had not realized she was getting to the age . . . Gilda found herself reassuring them as to their excellence as parents, their total guiltlessness, her confidence in them.

"You guys have been wonderful parents, you should talk to my friends. You have no idea. I know how lucky I am . . ."

They heaped her with reassurance in turn. She was not to lose her self-esteem or feel that her future was changed in any way. "We'll get through this, darling girl, everyone has a bit of trouble of some kind at some age, no one comes out unscathed . . ."

Her father was concerned about her health. Had her blood sugar been normal, was she under control?

"I'm fine, everything is normal. Really."

As to what to do, "As a procedure, it's nothing," Ran said, "the work of an afternoon, a minor intervention." He became aware that both his daughter and wife were looking at him with astonishment. "Absolutely no implications for future childbearing, really very simple."

This sounded horrible to Gilda. How could he talk that way? It was a baby after all and, with such a beautiful father, bound to be a superior baby, if it didn't get diabetes.

"I think we ought to think about this," said Amy, with a meaningful glare at Ran intended to convey, We'll talk about this between ourselves, without Gilda.

It seemed to Julie that they glared at her, too, as if she'd done something horrid to Gilda to cause this—procured her for Ian, or pep-talked about sex. An ignominious wave of envy washed over Julie at the privilege that enveloped Gilda, the kindness and understanding that it seemed to convey. Lucky Gilda had everything; even her unfortunate pregnancy was not the doing of some grubby high-school hood but the dreamy Ian Aymes, a trophy boy.

As the discussion unfolded, it was clear to Julie that Ran and Amy were mostly concerned for Gilda's mental state, her health, and her morale, seeking to reassure her that everything would be all right and that they were in total support. This somewhat defied the conventions governing parental reactions to unplanned unwed teenaged pregnancy—like Gilda, Julie had read plenty of stories in magazines and books about scandalized parents, ostracism, disinheritance, even violence. She had seen a movie about Irish nuns who enslaved pregnant girls in laundries and buried the babies in the foundations. What luck to live in calm, affluent Woodside. Judged by the measured kindness of Gilda's parents, Gilda's plight seemed only a minor pickle. Julie wondered how her own mother and father would have reacted if it were she. She basked a little in the serenity of membership in such a civilized family, though she did wish it were clearer that Gilda's pickle had nothing to do with her. And she wished her grandfather would pay her college fees. Otherwise, Grandpa Ran and Amy were unbelievably nice!

Still, what was to happen next was not discussed, and was clearly not going to be discussed in front of Julie, or until they had slept on it, or whatever the explanation was for the light, solicitous tone, their suggestion that Gilda ought to go to bed early. Gilda, clearly relieved to end the discussion, said good night and fled. Thus did Julie find herself being driven home to San Francisco, the back way through dark hills, alone in the seat next to Carla with nothing to say to her. Julie presumed she knew nothing about Gilda's unwelcome state, or had she heard the whole thing?

26

Parenthood hath murdered sleep.

Ran Mott was no stranger to family anxieties, since he had already raised the three children with Lorna—his two sons, who had generated fears, eventually proven valid, about wheeled vehicles, and one girl, Peggy, who as a teenager had not seemed likely to blunder into an unwed pregnancy. But now here was little Gilda, and pregnancy was the last thing he had worried about in her case, at least not yet. Till now, it was always her serious diabetes that had preoccupied him; now her condition was doubly precarious. Some sort of inept coitus interruptus, he had concluded from Gilda's faltering description of what had happened. He reflected on how the specter of unwed pregnancy almost surreptitiously dictated the customs and decisions of all of Western society, maybe every society, his household included, and there was no point in getting worked up about the social aspects now, though he did have an impulse to go beat up the Aymes boy.

His real fear now was that Gilda's health could not support pregnancy, it would be a nightmare of metabolic crises and insulin shock. It was dangerous for young teens to have babies in the best of circumstances, and her diabetes was the worst of circumstances. Intervention would be needed immediately, but her psychic situation worried him, too. He hadn't been able to tell how she felt about this emergency. Amy would talk to her, but still, he hadn't been able to gather from her calm, almost pleased demeanor whether Gilda might not kind of want to have a baby.

Alone in their bedroom, after expressions of shock, Ran and Amy almost instantly found themselves disagreeing about what to do next. Ran was firm about the health risks of pregnancy for diabetics, and about another set of risks even for healthy adolescents, their immature bodies, the incidence of prematurity and low birth weight in their babies. There was no way Gilda, in both these categories, diabetic and teenaged, could be permitted to give birth. To say nothing of the social difficulties and school. Also, an innocent child, she was a victim of this older man and should not be made to suffer the lifelong consequences of his cynical exploitation.

To his surprise, his usually phlegmatically calm wife Amy began to sniffle and mop her eyes and murmur her reservations, her distress.

"I know, I know, it's so sad, there must be some way . . ." Could Amy pass the baby off as their own late baby? *Le petit dernier,* as they said in France. Could it be a niece's, an impulse adoption as a sibling for Gilda, or a Russian orphan, or . . . Julie?

"How can you be thinking this way?" Ran said. "Gilda's health is the issue."

"I know, I know . . ."

"And psychologically . . ."

"What about that? It's going to be horrible for her, whatever we do."

"There's no question about that."

"What if . . . I can't help thinking . . ." Amy, too, could research on the Internet. After untold more years of diabetic medication in her future, would Gilda ever again be able to conceive? Might this be the only chance she would have to be a mother? Would she blame them if, later, she couldn't have a baby and had missed this chance? Over hours into the night, Ran teased out his wife's deepest fear, unspoken, unsaid, the truly unsayable, an echo of his own: With the shortened life span of childhood diabetics, how long would they have Gilda herself?

After an hour of anguished argument, Amy's real feelings came out: her long-held fear that Gilda would not live. She had always been afraid

Gilda would not live to grow up. Now another unsayable thing that occurred to both of them was that if something happened to Gilda, a possibility that had tortured them often, they would at least have her baby.

They decided to sleep on the problem and talk to Gilda again in the morning, not, naturally, mentioning their unsayable real fears.

This was the morning, unfortunately for him, that Hammond Mott had chosen to visit his father in his San Francisco office to ask for help with a down payment if they could find a house in a better neighborhood. He couldn't erase the sight of the fainted Misty's ashen green color, her slightly swollen belly, the look of her puffy ankles, the dried tears on her cheeks.

Ran was himself in a trance of dismay, thinking over the words he and Amy had begun the day with, in disagreement even before breakfast, where they found Gilda serene and normal, ready for school as if nothing were different, finishing her cereal when they heard the crunch of school's ride-share van's tires in the driveway, and she ran off. Ran had left directly after, plunging into the morning's commute traffic heading toward San Francisco, which he usually waited to avoid. Counting traffic, he had already experienced two upsetting encounters before nine o'clock, and now here was his son Hams, whom he hadn't seen in—how long had it been?—and it usually meant saying no to something. Hams sat down; Ran indicated an array of coffee pods for the machine—espresso, Guatemalan, French roast. Hams shook his head no.

"How are you, Hams; how is your wife? Misty."

"It's sort of what I wanted to talk to you about, Dad. We're having a baby, I guess you knew that."

"Of course," Ran agreed. "When is it? Must be soon."

"Well, in February. Life is going to change."

"It certainly is," Ran said, regretting the note in his voice that revealed his real attitude about the threats or menaces of paternity in store for Hams.

"We really think we should move to a quieter neighborhood, but we may need some help swinging that. We want to stay within our price range, for sure, but quieter. But the down payment . . ."

"Whiter, you mean? Orinda or somewhere like that?"

"We'd like to stay in Oakland but maybe in the hills, somewhere with a yard? We don't have a yard to speak of, just a small one."

"You need the down payment?"

"A loan, just, you know. I'm working and all that, but I know I won't get far at the bank. We've got some money saved up. We'd get some back from our security deposit."

"Is Misty feeling all right? Healthy?" Ran couldn't stop thinking about pregnancy, "nine months of pathology"; he'd heard that saying in medical school. Nine months of pathology for Gilda, Ran thought. Misty probably healthy as a horse, but did she do drugs? She looked kind of druggy, that nose ring, probably pierced nipples. He'd seen babies born addicted. Spastic limbs, cry all the time.

"How much will you get back from the security deposit?"

"We haven't taken such good care of the yard," Hams admitted. "Neither of us has much of a green thumb."

"No, gardening is not a family trait," Ran said. "What price range? I don't know anything about property in Oakland. I know everything has gone up."

"Going down, Dad. It's a good time. There are a lot of foreclosures. Maybe something like a foreclosure would be cheaper."

"Well, Hams, I'd like to help. Can't you give me a specific proposal? You know I'm retired, my income isn't what it was when I was working. But my point of view is that since it comes out of your inheritance, you should have it when it will do the most good. I could probably come up with twenty thousand, that's what I gave Peggy and Dick when they were buying that little house in Ukiah."

"That was a while ago," Hams said. "Houses don't cost as much in Ukiah, either." He wondered if Peggy, who was always whining about being foreclosed, had come to talk to their father. Maybe he was feeling beleaguered. Twenty thousand wasn't much of a help. "You get more house for less in Ukiah."

"Yes, true," Ran said, "just let me know when you've got a specific property in mind. And keep me posted about the baby of course. I suppose you don't have health insurance."

"Well, no."

"I can help with those expenses."

"Right, Dad, thanks," Hams said, thinking of Curt's three million dollars. He was too abashed to mention it, or say that twenty thousand probably wouldn't get you the down payment on a shipping container these days. But at least his father had acceded to the general principle of a loan or even a gift and help with the baby. Yet, riding back on BART, he felt rising rage with his father, the sum of all the times he'd disappointed Ran, been reprimanded, been undervalued. He knew this was irrational; Ran had not said no to anything, yet he vowed again never to ask Ran for anything more. Ever.

27

W̶e all need guidance, whether earthly or preferably from above.
Though not at all metaphysically inclined, Ursula Aymes
was moved to consult a spiritual counselor, the Reverend Philip Train,
about her impending grandmotherhood and the moral dilemma it
posed for Ian. She made an appointment with Reverend Train at the
cathedral for the following Wednesday. She had never before sought
advice from such a figure; usually she asked her Jungian psychiatrist
to ask the *I Ching*. Now behind her need for Christian counsel was a
need—unconscious perhaps—to get the news out, if only to one trust-
worthy person, to nail down the connection between the Aymes and
Mott families. She didn't analyze her motives, she just experienced a stab
of unexamined spiritual anxiety. At some level she may have expected
that the Reverend Train, though an Episcopalian, might interdict abortion no matter the age of the girl; weren't they almost Catholics? She
was not a regular churchgoer, but thought she should have some frame
of moral reference when she talked to the Motts, and to her son Ian,
though Ian might be surprised to have her invoke anything so solemn.
Ursula had been raised a Catholic, and though she had given up the
Church long since, it shadowed her still in the realm of sexual morality;
in that of commerce too she was perfectly in tune.

The Reverend Philip Train was used to people he knew socially turning up in the role of parishioner to ask advice even if they never came to church. Here was Ursula Aymes, at whose wedding—which of her weddings?—Philip had officiated. Her aroma of violets was somehow familiar.

"It's a sad situation, though hardly unusual," he agreed when she had described the painful occurrence, adding, "I was in college with both Ran and also his first wife a hundred years ago. Lorna Morgan. I ran into her a few weeks ago. I gather there's a new wife, the mother of this girl. I'm not in a position to speak to them about this, though. Haven't seen them in years."

"Heavens no, and anyway, it's nothing to do with Lorna," Ursula agreed. "It's for myself. I don't know how to advise my son. Part of me feels he should do his duty by the girl, but that's old-fashioned, I suppose. Ian is a good boy, he's not a cad, but he hasn't finished college, and he hasn't a clue as to a profession. And the Mott girl is only fifteen years old."

"You can marry at fifteen in California if your parents okay it or with a court order."

"What an idea," Ursula said.

"It could be statutory rape, unless they married. He could be prosecuted," Train said. "It depends on the age difference. How much older is he?"

Ursula shuddered. "He's twenty. Almost five years."

"Yes, well, to answer your question, which you haven't asked, we—the Church—believe in abortion only for the life or health of the mother and in cases of severe birth defects. It is a sad situation and to be taken with utmost moral gravity."

"I understand," Ursula said with a sigh. "My view exactly."

"Have you seen Lorna, by any chance? She said she was staying somewhere near the cathedral, but I've forgotten who she said she was staying with."

Ursula told him, wondering why he wanted to know.

"I've forgotten her new last name, though she told me," said the Very Reverend Train.

A few days later, Ursula, taking a figurative deep breath, telephoned Gilda's parents. Amy's helper Carla answered and put Ursula through to

Amy with so few questions Ursula surmised that Amy must have been expecting her call.

"Ursula, what is your point of view on all this," Amy asked, startling Ursula with her directness. They hadn't even established what Ursula was calling about, and whether they agreed on details—for instance, that it was Ian responsible for Gilda's condition.

"It's tragic, of course," Ursula said. "Um, I'm very upset. Children these days—well, I am so upset with Ian, I hardly know what to do."

"Mmm," said Amy. "We don't, either."

"Is Gilda—well, she's just a child herself," said Ursula, feeling on safer ground with her sense that Amy and Ran were not including her in any escalating rancor. "Though she looks very mature."

"Mmm," Amy agreed. "Girls mature earlier now than when you and I were adolescents . . ."

"What to do?" said Ursula.

"Gilda wants to have the baby," Amy said.

Ursula could not have explained her feeling of relief, the quickening of her pulse. An adventure lay before them—at least if Gilda got her way. "Is that your view, too?"

"I don't know," Amy admitted. "Ran is against it, on account of her health—well, for all kinds of reasons. You know she's a serious diabetic?"

"I just want you to know Ian will do whatever is required of him, and I will, too," Ursula said.

Amy thanked her, somewhat stiffly, it seemed to Ursula, but you couldn't blame her, really, for the note of frostiness toward the mother of the miscreant. Ursula understood.

Amy did not go into the scene with Gilda which she and Ran had endured, the tears and hysteria when Gilda perceived that her parents were determined she not risk her health by having a baby. No more could Ran erase from his thoughts the scene with a child whose stoicism in her short life had always astounded them, who had never complained about the doctors, the hospital visits, the bruises, the streaks of blood beneath her skin after injections, the bottles of medicine, the

needles in her tiny seven-year-old arms. She had endured all the intervening years of torture in silence; she screamed and sobbed in a way
they had never heard her do: she had to have a baby now, she knew she
wasn't destined to live to grow up, and this was her only chance; she
could feel the baby, it would give her life, might even cure her.

"Honey, it just won't be wise for you to risk your health, you know
that pregnancy is nine months of pathology," Ran began.

"I don't care. I want a normal life, normal people have babies."

"When you're older, when you marry someday . . ."

"I'm never going to marry. Who would marry me anyhow with
all my needles and pouches? At least I'll have a baby. Let me do one
normal thing."

"But honey, Gilda, honey dear, you have so much to do—finish
school, college, you don't want a baby to weigh you down, and other
things—they wouldn't have you at Saint Waltraud's, you'd have to go
to, I don't know, some other school, or drop out . . ."

Useless their attempts to show her how dangerous, how in their love
for her they couldn't let her risk her life or the future that lay before her
with cures impending; how the collection of cells inside her was not yet
a baby, not a person yet for some weeks; how the cells might be being
damaged by her medicaments anyhow, how it could be deformed . . .
How Ran and Amy ached to save, to soothe, to do something for this
beloved being, without a clue as to what that would be.

"I know I'm going to die, at least let me leave a baby in the world."
Tears ran on her cheeks. If they killed her baby, it would kill her, it
would take with it the life force she had saved up, leaving her dead.
What shocked them was that death—the outcome and even the word,
which had always carefully been omitted from any discussions of her
future—had been in her mind all along.

She accused them of robbing her of her God-given and probably
only opportunity to experience motherhood. Of parsimony, not wanting to support another family member. Of indifference to her emotional well-being. Ran and Amy had never seen their self-contained
little girl rant in this manner and had retreated in shock.

Over a few days, Gilda began to sense correctly that their solid
parental stand was dictated mostly by her father, and that her mother

would always be on her side in her heart, however much she sided with Ran officially. Gilda understood that Amy would kind of like a baby. After dinner a few nights after the tormented scene, she knocked on their bedroom door and said, "Parents, I love you and I know you love me and want what's best. This time I know what's best."

Ran said, "No, you don't." Amy suddenly sobbed and pushed shut the bedroom door.

At his office the next day, Ran turned over various possibilities. Whatever they did about interrupting the pregnancy, which he would certainly insist on, Gilda should see her doctor immediately, and maybe he should talk to the doctor first. Definitely also her therapist, Mrs. Klein—she had had a therapist since her initial diagnosis with diabetes, to help her adjust, to hear her fears, to generally support her. Like many people in their demographic, white and Protestant, he and Amy had a certain indifference to psychotherapy; didn't disbelieve it, of course, but thought it was mostly for people who believed in it. Wouldn't have liked to spend all that money on themselves but had never begrudged spending it on Mrs. Klein for Gilda. This was their attitude to faith generally, that it was fine for others; also, they weren't in the right zip codes—New York or LA—where the shrinks were mostly to be found.

Gilda had never expressed much interest in seeing Mrs. Klein, but dutifully went once a month and discussed her classes and friends. Now Ran wondered if Amy would consider seeing someone, too—maybe even their minister, not that they had much contact with religion. He seemed to remember that his college friend Phil Train was now the dean at Grace Cathedral. Someone to reassure Amy, whatever they did.

"Why would I do that?" Amy asked.

"Just to help you get through this. Someone more sympathetic than I am."

"You aren't supporting me?"

"You know what I think. I'm concerned about Gilda's health uppermost."

"And I'm not?"

"No, of course you are, but you'd like a dear little baby, too."

"Okay," Amy said, which meant We Aren't Discussing This Anymore.

Eventually Amy had proposed they call Ran's granddaughter Julie to help talk to Gilda; she and Julie seemed to be friendly.

"I think Gilda looks up to her, she'll be able to talk to her," Amy said. "I couldn't be a co-grandmother with horrible Ursula Aymes, though," she added.

"Ursula isn't so bad," Ran said. "I have no idea about the child-molester son."

"Well, call Julie," Amy said. "Invite her to dinner. I suppose we should invite the Aymes boy, too," though they didn't.

And Ran had more than one thing to worry him. He continued to get communications—phone calls and emails—from Harvey Avon, the colleague of Curt's, the shakedown-artist colleague, who seemed to believe Ran would somehow cover his grown son's debts, or putative debts, or poorly advised investments, or whatever you wanted to call them. Ran had so far refused the temptation to sic the guy on Donna, who after all would be the one more responsible than he for Curt's financial obligations, and now, moreover, thanks to Amy, could afford to deal with them. She could sell the fancy house if she had to. He didn't mention Donna to Avon in part because he couldn't really believe the guy was on the level, such were the outrageous claims, the extremely bizarre investments, his descriptions of behavior he could not recognize as Curt's. He feared, though, that Donna would be intimidated and fall into some trap of Avon's, and he resolved to have a talk with her, and also to confront the guy again.

Another of his concerns was personal; he needed to understand what he himself wanted from the accursed young man who had abused and impregnated his daughter. He could be made to marry her; he could be jailed for statutory rape; he could be sued for—for what? Ran felt intensely that Ian Aymes should pay in some way, should face the consequences of his crime. In his ears the encouraging whispers of men down the ages who had been made to take responsibility, as he himself had been made to take responsibility, to pay through the nose for every bang, why not this twerp as well? Indignant fathers down the ages seconded Ran's motion, they carried him on their shoulders. Gilda's life had been ruined, or at any rate changed irreversibly, why not Ian Aymes's, too? It was only fair.

In the middle of all this, he was not entirely surprised to get a call from Amy's financial person Drake Titian, saying he'd been alerted by the people who monitored the web and print media on their behalf—the alert was set for "Hawkins"—about an article that detailed the crimes of Curt Mott, stepson of Silicon Valley figure Amy Hawkins, on the lam for nearly a year, funds missing from companies he co-owned, himself out of the reach of prosecution, probably in Shanghai. Ran typed in the web address and saw the headline "Former MacChester Star Mott Disappears—with the Money?" MacChester referred to a consulting firm Curt had worked for just out of business school, and risen quickly within, and then left for his own pursuits. The article that followed detailed Curt's crimes in spurious and vengeful detail, even linking them to his stepmother Amy and other family members, clearly the invention of a disgruntled enemy somewhere, perhaps even an enemy of his own, someone bent on slandering both his son and his wife—the disinformation included plenty of aspersions on Amy as a dishonest bankroller and the brains behind the scams. He knew it could not be true. It was one more thing in a day, a week, filled with nothing but vexation and worse.

Julie found a message from her grandfather on her phone: Could she meet him and Amy for dinner to discuss Gilda? Along with the little chill of fear—the feeling that she was to be somehow blamed in the Gilda situation—she felt pleased to be included in her grandfather's general consciousness and his specific thoughts when, she knew, that wouldn't have happened if she hadn't bearded him in his office that time. She texted a response, and also texted her roommates that she had to exchange her turn cooking that night with one of them, on account of an important summons.

28

I have it," cried Barbara Levier to the Pont-les-Puits council before they had settled in their chairs to discuss the mounting costs of the cemetery cleanup: "We have only to sell the *tableau* belonging to the *mairie*. It is ours to sell, Monsieur Woods donated it to us himself. With this, we pay for the cemetery cleanup and much else without having to claw back these tiny sums from each descendant, *quelle poisse* after all. It is valuable, I am told."

People advanced various objections—no art dealers in Pont-les-Puits, no familiarity with the art market, doubts about its value, logistical issues, general ignorance about sales procedures. But Monsieur Dumas, when he came in a bit late, agreed with the project. There might be export issues, to be sure, since their Woods had been painted in France and therefore belonged in France, but it probably would sell better in the U.S. where Woods was more of a name. He put minds at rest about the logistics of an important transaction in the art world by pointing out that Madame Dumas, despite their estrangement, could be trusted to conduct a sale; she was familiar with the art world and was conveniently in America.

"Export will be easier if my wife can take it as a personal effect," he mused, "along with some of her other things she'll be sending for. Her silver, some furniture, in connection with our divorce . . ."

Silence. No one liked to comment on the Dumas split, the rumors of which he was now confirming. "Never mind, I'll make inquiries," he said.

Now, in June, the season when the American food world began to stake its claims in various French villages and regions, well-known California chef Susan Warner-Ford brought the first of her cooking tours to Pont-les-Puits. She would have three such sessions over the summer. She had begun these tours mostly with women from San Francisco as clients, where her cooking show originated; but gradually participants were also drawn from Marin County or Napa and came to include men and couples. She accepted a group of eight for each session, they stayed at La Périchole—the one small hotel in Pont. They had classes in the mornings: Pastry/Knife Skills/Braising, or Bread/Hors d'Oeuvres/Le Rôti. In the afternoon, they absorbed the touristic wonders of the region, shopped at the open market for the local onions and mushrooms, toured the cheese makers, examined the churches, with a certain amount of free time for trying local restaurants on their own, and hiking or pursuing photography, which seemed to interest a high percentage of Susie's students, all passionate Francophiles.

The group was barely settled in at La Périchole when one of their number, Tory Hatcher, a brisk and competent blonde from Larkspur, went out with her camera to explore the village and wandered by the market hall where the ongoing forensic examinations were visible through the screened-in walls. Astounded when she thought she perceived long tables arrayed with packets topped by skulls! Astonished and revolted by the grisly apparition, without doubt the aftermath of some local massacre or sinister religious rite! She had lifted her camera—one of those assertive, protruding, black weapon-cameras—and opened the screen door to what was obviously a public space, planning to steal in for a close-up photo, when a deep male voice behind her said, "Madame?" She turned.

"Madame, *s'il vous plaît*, this is a sensitive area, a grave site, if you will, and I'm not sure it is correct to photograph here."

Tory, like the other members of her party, was extra concerned not to commit faux pas or offend the sensibilities of French people, or call attention to her own Americanness. She'd seen how badly her country-men sometimes behaved, not anyone of course among their group.

"I'm so sorry," she gasped. "What is . . . it, exactly?" Now she saw that the man who'd reproved her was a handsome though stout person, sixtyish, gracefully graying at the temples, unmistakably French but with perfect English, like a film actor playing a French diplomat. His expression was more amiable than outraged, which relieved her.

He explained the cemetery catastrophe, and as they fell into conver-sation, Tory discovered that the man had San Francisco connections—had been married to someone from there—and undoubtedly knew lots of people she knew. She accepted a coffee at La Fringale. He then invited the whole group for a drink at Fringale at the end of their day, with the promise of some local lore and info on the onion growers and potters of the area. This was a pleasant addition to the food adventure they were embarked upon. All was to be possible.

When they assembled at six o'clock, including their leader, Susie Warner-Ford, Armand-Loup bought her and the eight cookery acolytes a round of drinks. Tory lost out with the handsome though stout ex-museum director to Susie Warner-Ford herself, whom he invited to go up with him to his room over the bakery, ostensibly to plot out some promising local food experiences in nearby villages he knew about. He was called Monsieur Dumas, no relation to the writer. Later that eve-ning, Susie and Monsieur Dumas were seen eating at La Roulette and sampling *turban de sole au saumon, sauce à l'oseille,* an old-fashioned specialty of Monsieur Wake, the chef. They drank a Meursault, it was reported, and then a Montrachet.

Later, Tory googled Armand-Loup Dumas. In his working life as director of a museum, he had been influenced by the Frankfurt School and especially the work of Jürgen Habermas, with its whiff of Marx and Hegel, influences found in his published articles discussing the economics of the art market. What a wicked bunch, art dealers and such! It made her happy that their new friend was a well-known figure in the museum world. Part of the allure of these art-and-food trips was the off chance of a little fling.

29

L et winners run.

This was one of Dick Willover's favorite investment maxims.

He had had investments with Curt Mott, his erstwhile brother-in-law, and when Peggy and he divorced, he hadn't liquidated them; he'd left his money in Curt's enterprises—a promising hydroponics program with brick-and-mortar installations underway, other agricultural software, a motorcycle-insurance scheme, a biking video game, some iPhone apps, some computer peripherals being manufactured in China—all of which had sounded good to Dick, or good enough, assembled in his portfolio as Mott Development. As investments, they were never going to be Netflix or Apple, but all had been showing signs of vigor, and then when Curt was in a coma, it seemed insensitive to the Mott family for him to pull his money out. Above all, he hadn't wanted to irritate his former father-in-law, Ran Mott. He stayed on good terms with Ran at both the Bohemian Grove and the Cal Club—though Ran didn't play very often anymore—and Dick wanted to keep it that way. Family riffs often do but need not cause business ruptures. He satisfied himself that Harvey Avon was running the show with sufficient competence.

He and Peggy talked from time to time, Dick in the role of a kindly stranger, almost as if they'd seldom met, which Peggy understood was to avoid his getting drawn into the cost of Julie's college or any of her own financial troubles. She did tell him about Donna's windfall. This animated an unexpected wellspring of indignation from Dick on Peggy's behalf, that she should be passed over to the benefit of Curt's horrible wife. He had expressed this indignation to several people in the Cal Club locker room and bar, also at a Bohemian Club event. He regretted his resentful outbursts lest they get back to his former father-in-law Ran, but maybe it wouldn't be so bad if they did?

"So then Amy Hawkins came up with three million dollars in cash to pay off Curt Mott's—my brother-in-law's—mortgage, out of the kindness of her heart, but left the other kids out in the cold. My wife Peggy"—he often mentioned Peggy, as if to consolidate his former heterosexual creds—"gets nothing, her other siblings, either, just Curt. Of course there was no reason for her to help any of them, Hawkins is only their stepmother. Her and Ran's own kid, Gilda, will get all the money. Still . . ." He knew that several of his auditors, taking note of Donna Mott's windfall, would soon be getting in touch with her on behalf of the Sierra Club, Yosemite, Save the Bay, Marin Headlands Preservation, the San Francisco (no-kill) SPCA, Berkeley Humane, dolphins, whales, beavers, Marin County deer, and much else—if she wasn't already on their rolls.

The skinny at the Cal Club, when Dick wasn't around, and especially when Ran Mott wasn't around, was that Curt Mott, with a serious cocaine problem, had taken off to the source to avoid vengeful dealers he owed money to in the Bay Area. There was a certain ironic pleasure to hear of the stranded wife's windfall, out of his reach. Go, Donna, go. But certain of his creditors, too, had begun to feel anxious, and whereas they had been reluctant to call in their chips while he lay in a coma, they now felt resentment at the idea of him disporting himself in Southeast Asia, with its lurid opium dens and sexy dragon-lady bar girls. Harvey Avon was but the first of these to make appointments to see Ran Mott.

Lorna had just been thinking about Peggy when Peggy called, with the gossip about Gilda and other things: the loan shark lurking outside her house, the garbage disposal incurably blocked, and so on. Lorna was ashamed of the glint of Schadenfreude that flashed through her thoughts when she heard about Ran's troubles with his younger daughter; part of her felt, guiltily, a sort of glee that Ran would have trouble with his late child with the rich princess.

Her own daughter with him, Peggy, had been a model of trouble-free adolescence. All of their children had skated through that life phase, had not had many of the usual troubles of adolescents, were not even derailed by the divorce of their parents. Neither Peggy nor granddaughter Julie either had frightened them with unwed pregnancy scares.

"And apparently the boy, the responsible party, is the son of that real-estate lady friend of yours, Mama."

"Ursula?" Lorna laughed. "I wonder how she's taking it. I almost feel sorry for Ran."

Maybe it was Gilda's great expectations that had run her aground—rich kids got into trouble, disaster always lurked for them, though usually via drugs or motor vehicles. Since she didn't know Gilda, the situation was abstract to Lorna, and almost comic.

Lorna had understood for a long time that Ran had lost interest in the problems of their children together once these became the usual problems of adulthood, normal and predictable—money, cholesterol, the PTA. He had ponied up for large expenses—chiefly down payments on houses or medical crises—but was not really concerned or involved beyond perfunctory help. Not estranged, but detached, and it was Lorna who had taken on the responsibility of the worrying, and about Peggy especially. She noted as a passing thought that these concerns had become more intense now that she was back in California.

On the positive side, her French troubles with Armand and wifedom had faded to a bearable background hum, a kind of tinnitus. Her immediate problems were to do with her lecture life. She had received an invitation to Ann Arbor, Michigan, but only for September, and nothing before then. America was not proving as welcoming as she had hoped; what did she expect after twenty years away? She'd fooled herself.

Lorna had confided to Peggy her ambivalence about calling Philip

Train and reminding him of his offer to invite her to give her lecture to his Altar Forum. She didn't explain to Peggy the humiliation she felt about being pushy this way, not something she would expect Peggy to understand, Peggy being in such a, well, different line, wind chimes. Lorna had always been careful not to disparage any of her children's activities, even while trying to suggest to them that they were meant for great things. One of the hardest tasks of Motherhood, she had always found, was keeping this delicate balance between helping children maintain their self-esteem on the one hand, and giving them the requisite little pushes from time to time. But that had been mainly in the era before she had copped out and fled to France.

She did still feel that Peggy was capable of better than wind chimes, and thought Peggy should be mature enough by now to handle the realization that her mother thought she could do more with her talents. Lorna was brooding along these lines when the phone rang again. It was Armand-Loup, calling from France. Her heart quickened with dismay.

"*Allô*, Lorna, *chérie*."

"Armie?"

"*Oui.*" He explained why he was calling—the painting she was to sell in behalf of Pont-les-Puits. Lorna, relieved it wasn't something that she was expected to pay for, agreed, if they could get the painting to her. Afterward, she mulled over the drastically impersonal conversation, as if he were an art agent or a stranger, and she found his cold tone even worse than if they'd fallen into one of their fights; it provoked her into a tear or two, almost. Twenty years. She thought of their frolics in bed. Did he have a permanent someone else already, who had supplanted her, who had erased any note of intimacy in his voice? But what did she expect?

30

Pace Freud, does talking about a problem always make us feel better? Gilda had not been confined to her room, but that was the practical effect of the solemn, unnaturally solicitous, and kindly expressions worn by her parents over the next few days. They were always proposing eagerness to talk or, worse, asking to hear what she was thinking, feeling, remembering. She dreaded their questions about her health. And her mental health. She was fine, but she stayed in her room, reading.

Gilda's bedroom was vast, decorated in a handsome English chintz of yellow roses, with French doors opening into the garden, an altogether-pleasant place in which to hang out and avoid parents. Here were her bed, her desk, her books, her diary, TV, teddy bear, girlish stationery with a border of flowers and little birds, marked with her initials, GJM.

She had decided to write to Ian. To say what, she wasn't sure. She just had the impulse, the need to communicate about their scrape, and she felt funny calling him, and anyway didn't have his number. She didn't feel in any rush about anything—she figured she was only four weeks' pregnant, and after all, there were forty weeks altogether. Anything could happen.

Dear Ian,

I'm wondering what people are saying to you—I mean
your mother etc. My parents are concerned but my feeling is
that I'd sort of like to go ahead, not for any religious reason or
anything like that, but I do think things happen for a reason.

But I don't want you to feel any pressure or that you
have to take a role, I don't mean that at all. I just believe—
have actually been taught by my parents—that you have
to have a go at life even if it doesn't go as expected. They are
always talking about my disease—you know I have diabetes
and in the summer I go to diabetes camp, where they say the
same thing. So this is my personal deal, and luckily I know
my parents can afford to support my decision. I DON'T
CARE about what people say, or about scandal. If you want,
I won't ever mention you.

How to sign it gave her some hesitation. "Love, Gilda"? That
seemed too possessive in the circumstance. In the end she signed it:

Affectionately, Gilda

She would have to figure out where to send it. She didn't like it to
go to his mother's house, the only address she could find, though in
the end that was what she had to do. She didn't think it was time to
propose names for a baby, but she wondered what he would think of
Pomona for a girl. The goddess of abundance. She was taking Latin at
Saint Waltraud's, her favorite class.

Ian, a gentlemanly young man, well brought up according to the
notions of his European-born mother, would never do something like
reveal the name of a compromised woman, but did fall into general
discussions about the female sex with his male friends, discussions he
sometimes welcomed for the brotherly advice they offered and was
sometimes offended if someone was too gross about a girl someone
was dating, say, or about women in general. He accepted the level of

discourse common to his species—guys—but had little to contribute from his side, had not had serious girlfriends or problems before this.

Now, however, he was in a bad situation and needed to understand what a woman in Gilda's spot would be going through. Would he be a target of her anger, for instance? Of the long arm of her powerful parents? Was she obliged to be in love with him as the father of her baby? Should they go to Mexico or somewhere out of the light, to have an operation or get married? Was he a sex criminal? He was nearly paralyzed with contrition.

He was ashamed of certain unworthy thoughts that crept in, too, like getting a big payout from the Motts to drop a claim of paternity, or landing a great job at Gilda's mother's biotech firm.

Today he was in that bastion of male provenance, the weight room at Mountain View Community College, where he was enrolled for two makeup courses and played right midfielder on the intramural soccer team. The air of the weight room had the pleasant scent of rubber mat and sweat, comfortable and familiar, against which the female world, with its difficult realities, seemed distant and repulsive.

He brought the Subject up as casually as possible, in the vein of "a friend of mine has got a girl in trouble." No one was fooled by the "friend" thing. "Dude!" A problem of this magnitude deserved respect. He felt enveloped for a few moments in the intangible but warming regard of his friends, respect mixed with relief it hadn't happened to them. No one seemed surprised it was Ian in this fix; though he seemed unconscious of his unusual beauty, no one else could be, and his friends imagined mistakenly that women threw themselves at him right and left. There was commiseration about his fix. Many of his teammates contributed anecdotes and hearsay. She can get it taken care of, get it adopted—no biggie. But for a relationship it was a negative, the beginning of the end.

His mother also seemed to treat him with a measure of solicitude that both puzzled and pleased him. He began to dream idly, while driving up to San Francisco from his apartment in Mountain View to see her, of the respectable and adult state of paternity, maybe even wedlock, when he would have finished Stanford, say, and lived with Gilda in a little house in Woodside near her parents, with a squash court, say, or at least a pool, and playing soccer at the Menlo Circus Club nearby, and studying something interesting like astronomy, which he was taking an introductory course in for the core courses needed to transfer. And if he married Gilda, he wouldn't be a sex criminal, and also he could fuck her properly; he'd made kind of a mess of it, not a very nice first sexual experience for her.

Ran and Amy had agreed to disagree about Gilda's next step regarding her pregnancy, with Amy ambivalent about what to do, and Ran, convinced of the dangers to her health, believing they should end it. They had only a few weeks to decide, after which an intervention—the euphemism they used—favored by Ran, would be too late, at least by the pill method; they had a bit longer if by D&C.

He understood that something in women, even, evidently, girls as young as Gilda, and entrepreneurs as successful as Amy, predisposed them to adore infants, never mind how they treated them later; overall, he deplored the tendency of women to get pregnant at all. "Women just irrationally respond to the idea of babies. All women do," he accused Amy. He did remember feeling a similar emotion as he felt now of disapproval of Lorna, back when she had kept getting pregnant despite their efforts to the contrary. He recognized how essential it was that Gilda, and Amy, too, be comfortable with an intervention, so he saw no problem easing off the discussions, postponing them as long as they could. Physically, in the next couple of weeks, Gilda showed no signs at all of her condition—no changes in her appetite or thickening of her waistline—he even wondered about some sort of bizarre Munchausen syndrome or pseudocyesis. But of course it was much too soon for her to be showing. And this didn't make pregnancy less dangerous for a fifteen-year-old diabetic. They had found the right specialist in diabetic pregnancy; Gilda had gone to her appointments with uncomplaining docility.

They also had a talk with Mrs. Klein, Gilda's longtime therapist, and brought her into the picture. Gilda had been seeing Mrs. Klein for years, every month or so, ever since second grade. She seldom told her much—mostly stuff that happened at school. It was understood that

Mrs. Klein didn't disclose Gilda's secrets to her parents, and they didn't pry, but so far there had never been anything they couldn't know. Now Mrs. Klein was nonplussed at what she had failed to pick up.

"I hadn't even realized Gilda was sexually active," she said in dismay to Ran and Amy, who had implored her for advice. "She hasn't shared that."

"Nor with us," said Amy. "Well, she wouldn't, would she?" She told Mrs. Klein such details as she knew. Mrs. Klein definitely agreed that it was important that Gilda, once she understood all the ramifications of her plight, felt herself to be the one making the decision about what to do next.

"Gilda has a desperately negative body image, and so her feelings about this will be complicated. She may feel that pregnancy is very positive, a sign of health and power. Any intervention could be seen as failure. It would certainly be better for her not to have a baby, but the situation is delicate."

They thanked her; it was sort of as they'd feared and what they'd been seeing. Amy and Ran had always been in a sense afraid of Gilda, afraid of crossing her and somehow setting off a negative physiological effect, a diabetic crash or something. They knew their inability to assert themselves was a reflex of their feeling guilty for whatever bad genetic combination they had cursed her with, but knowing that didn't help.

"I'd like to see Gilda as soon as possible," Mrs. Klein said.

When Gilda came to her appointment, Mrs. Klein found her worryingly calm. The girl said very coherently that she welcomed the baby and had always been afraid she wouldn't be able to do the things normal girls could do—like having a baby—so she was reassured now, and, yes, she was aware of the awkwardness around having to skip a semester at school.

Mrs. Klein, who was trying to be neutral, said, "Gilda, you are a little unrealistic about the negative social consequences of unwed motherhood. You are a young teen with many years of education ahead, and bright prospects. You like school and are good at it. You don't want to spend your life bagging groceries."

"I would still go to school, Mrs. Klein."

"Some schools don't accept unmarried mothers. And who looks

after the baby? And you miss all the normal things for girls your age—the prom and so on. Editing the school paper."

"I don't care about all that."

Beyond reporting this to Amy, Mrs. Klein kept between herself and Gilda the details of the conversation, as Amy expected she would do. In fact, there had been very few details. Gilda might be a virgin for all she seemed to know about what had happened.

Amy and Ran went up to the city and took Julie to dinner at the Fairmont to discuss Gilda.

Julie had some ideas about how to handle the situation. "Grandpa Ran, I told you about my hope of studying in Greece in the fall? That's why I was working at the gala? I was thinking that if I could afford to go, I could take Gilda with me to Greece. It might be a good solution—she'd see all the things, Parthenon and so on, very educational, the Grand Tour. With her niece, only we'd say I'm her aunt, that she had this chance while her aunt was going to be there, she could clear it with her school very openly, and then when we were there, she'd take Greek and stuff. Come home knowing Greek."

"And just happen to come home with a baby, too?" But the solution to that was obvious: the baby would be Julie's, or a Greek orphan or something.

"The only trouble with Greece is I haven't saved enough money yet," Julie said, heart pounding at the temerity of this broad hint. Grandpa Ran seemed not to notice. No money was proffered. He thought it was not a bad idea, except for his view of Greece as a place full of men in sleeveless striped shirts and neck scarves, and dumpy women in black, where people gave birth in caves.

"No."

Or another idea, "The Circle of Faith sponsors adoptions sometimes," Julie said.

She had to explain about the Circle of Faith, which Ran and Amy of course thought sounded completely fraudulent, maybe sinister, even with the participation of an important British politician. Julie could hear as she was describing it how New Age and flaky it sounded, a bunch of comfortable San Franciscans who, to quote its literature, "help raise money and awareness about shelters for orphans in Africa, and teach them positivity and reading."

"We would take the baby!" Amy cried. Out of the question that strangers in a cult would take their baby. Carla? Could Carla be the designated mother? Or Amy herself, only a little too old, or maybe not even; these days people had babies up into their fifties. They could raise the baby. For one hallucinatory moment, Ran felt his life, which had already reset once when they had Gilda, more than twenty years after his first batch of children, now reembarking on child-rearing, trapped for eternity in a permanent time warp where he grew ever grayer and more bent of spine in a purgatory of vaccinations, aggrieved nannies, and diaper pong.

With uncanny accuracy, the gods, knowing the perfect moment to heap another torment upon their designated sufferer, had clearly noticed Ran; he had nothing but vexations. He was not successful at getting the evil website slandering Curt taken down, and it looked like he would have to go to some extreme measures—there were people who could do it for an enormous price. And to add to the situation of his adored child Gilda, and his troubles over Curt, came the return of another aggravation, the small lawsuit aimed at him by a woman who had in fact hit his car with her bicycle, not the other way around. She had hit him, scratched his passenger door, and claimed to have cracked a rib. Not looking where she was going, not noticing that Third Street curved gently to the right when crossing Market to enter Kearny, she had gone straight on and ridden smash into the right side of his car.

He'd ascertained she wasn't hurt and waited with her until an ambulance came to take her to her health-care facility to be checked over. Had suggested driving her there himself, but she'd preferred an ambulance—suspicious, in retrospect. Some care had been taken to downplay his identity as a doctor, or well-known name—that she not be aware of his general affluence, Amy's, that is; and the modesty of her claim had reassured them she wasn't a scammer. She was suing for one hundred and seventeen thousand dollars. This had happened a year— almost two years—ago and been confided to his insurance company and forgotten, and was suddenly back.

But he'd made a mistake, he saw now, in giving in to irritation. He'd directed the insurance company to counterclaim, or whatever they did, and not admit guilt: the accident was not his fault. The bitch had hit him, not the other way around, and he didn't want to be blamed or have his insurance rates go up, or his perfect driving record blemished. The insurance people had protested but sued her back, or so he'd thought. Yet, here, a subpoena and a deposition date. He was flabbergasted. Of course this was only a trifle compared with the Gilda situation, but just one more thing he didn't need.

He was required to turn up at a lawyer's office—he had the name somewhere—next Tuesday to be deposed. He drove himself to his office on the appointed day and, rather than struggle with the parking downtown, took a taxi to the offices of the enemy lawyers, Schwartz, Kaufman and Cinders, on Spear.

Ran and Amy's legal affairs were normally conducted by senior partners in Henson Bernstein Jaeger, but sitting in on the deposition insisted upon by the lawyers for the woman who had run into his car would be one of the junior partners, Casey Schwartz; he'd been advised of this by letter, but was still surprised at the apparent youth of Casey Schwartz, a tall young woman with glasses and a power suit who looked to him about twenty-five. Her youth mildly offended him. The enemy lawyer was also a woman, somewhat older, who projected a glitter of dislike for him when he came in. Ran was told to sit beside Casey, and the two women were arrayed across from each other at the table and armed with yellow legal pads and pencils. There was also some-one taking notes. Ran supposed this was okay, or else his side—Miss Schwartz—would have objected.

After answering some simple questions about his age, home address, and the make of his auto, the enemy lawyer asked, "Did you see Miss Powers before you hit her?"

Ran was irritated by this clumsy trick question, which seemed to indicate they thought they were dealing with an idiot or someone senile.

"I did not hit Miss Powers, she hit me," he said mildly.

"Before the impact, I should say," the opposing lawyer corrected herself.

"No, she came at me from the side, the passenger side. I could not have seen her." Casey Schwartz gave him an intense look that meant, probably, Don't elaborate. She had warned him to answer briefly and not embroider, though he hardly considered a plain statement of fact embroidery. She led him to disclose in grudging monosyllables the details of the accident, though Kaufman and Cinders plainly knew them; the enemy lawyer had a sheaf of photographs and testimonials.

When the ordeal was over, he went with Casey Schwartz into her office. "I think that went very well, you did well," she said. Ran also found this irritating. Why did he have to be here at all? He, a victim, grilled like a thief and patronized as a dotard. But instead of uttering this complaint, he expressed his unconscious preoccupations with a question about California laws on statutory rape and child endangerment. The disconcerted Casey Schwartz said, "I don't know anything much about that. I think the age of consent in California is sixteen."

"The son of one of our friends—in trouble—wondering . . ." Fifteen. Gilda was soon to be sixteen, but not yet, so her age did not rule out some sort of statutory rape charge for Ian Aymes, as Ran often indulged his dream of initiating. But another problem: Gilda's equanimity was such that he wasn't sure of her role in the sexual episode—not sure enough to contemplate ruining some boy's life when Gilda might well have cooperated or even initiated their congress. Still, the temptation tormented him; he wanted to turn Ian in.

"We have people here who specialize in felony defense work," said Casey helpfully. "Let me know if you want some names." This was enraging, too, that the system had no compunctions about defending criminals who preyed on girls under sixteen, his own lawyers had no qualms about unquestioningly defending rapists if you could pay. Could Ursula Aymes pay an expensive law firm like Henson Bernstein Jaeger to defend her criminal son? He firmly quashed this line of thought. Ursula was okay and, he was sure, just as worried as he and Amy were.

"I'll get the transcript to you as soon as possible," Casey said. "Don't worry about this, your umbrella more than covers this, it's only pain and suffering, she can't show any physical injury. They'll settle for sure."

"Sometimes latent injuries can show up years later," Ran the doctor said. "I once had a patient . . . well . . ." He didn't feel like recounting it. He remembered it too well.

"Years later will be too late anyhow," Casey said. Her expression was cheerful—he saw she meant, Too late for Miss Powers to collect, but he took her at first to mean, Too late for an old guy like you.

Leaving Miss Schwartz, going down in the elevator to look for a cab, he allowed himself the pleasure of lapsing back into his daydream, since childhood, the rowboat dream, where he had always left enemies and irritating people to drown. He now included in his rowboat fantasy Cecily Powers, the woman who ran into his car. Cecily and Ian Aymes both foundering in the water, Gilda and Ran in the rowboat. The scene now went: Gilda and Ran can't decide which one to save so opt to go get help for both, though they know that by the time they get back, it'll be too late, both would have drowned. No, Gilda shouldn't be in the rowboat. She isn't vengeful, and she would try to save Ian. Only he, Ran, in the rowboat, was responsible for the decision to let them both drown.

When the elevator doors opened to let him out on the ground floor, a small woman, vaguely familiar, stepped in and, seeing him, gasped and stopped. He was momentarily abashed to have such an effect, and nearly checked his fly. Looking again, he saw, but could hardly believe, that it was his ex-wife Lorna, Lorna whom he hadn't seen for more than twenty years. Twenty years during which their rancor, while it had not subsided, had more or less been put out of mind.

They stared for seconds before breaking into polite greetings. Automatically, Ran impeded the closing of the elevator doors and they both stepped into the lobby.

"Lorna! I—uh—what brings you here?" he asked. "I had no idea you were . . ."

"Well, yes, living here now."

"Well!" They both thought of the oddness of their children not telling him this. Or had Julie mentioned something . . .

"You're in touch with . . . ?"

"Of course."

"Well—you look very well. The years have been kind to you," he said. In her mind she remembered seeing the teeniest beginning of white roots along the parting of her hair, she had noticed them this morning, and he, taller, would notice them of course.

"You, too, Ran." He was fitter looking than Armand, with a tennis player's tan. They exchanged a sentence or two of banalities.

"This business with Curt," he said. "Have you got any news?"

"I suppose we should compare notes," Lorna said.

"I, yes, do I have your email? We should have lunch," Ran said. *"Lornamottdumas1@gmail.com."*

Shaken, they took their leave, planning to lunch.

31

How do we dismiss those movies that play in our minds in obsessive loops?

Lorna found she was able to put this meeting out of her mind, it had no hold on her except that she afterward found herself in a kind of continuing conversation with Ran in her head, reproaching him for this and that—for not doing things he could have done to help the children—or confiding some of her concerns about them. He was the one other person on earth who must have a parent's concern about these particular progeny. She and Ran could have satisfying chats, now that anger was officially gone. But they didn't, though they did make the lunch date.

She also had a bit of good luck that cheered her a lot; someone at the museum heard from Nancy Fludd that she was back in San Francisco. This museum person, a Mrs. Norma Coleman, in charge of publications, happened to have just ordered copies of Lorna's recently published art lectures for the museum shop, hence was aware of Lorna's name, was thrilled to hear she was in town, and got the idea of inviting her to fill a vacancy in the museum's monthly lecture series. Though they were a modern museum, Mrs. Coleman explained, they did discuss subjects related to the roots of modern art; and Lorna's presentation of

Meissonier, one of the last academic painters of the pre-Impressionist period, would interest them enormously.

Lorna responded with professional gravity and inner elation. It was to be the first week of September, giving her plenty of time to work up Meissonier a little more; in her excitement over the tapestries of Angers, she had let him begin to rust. Feeling lifted by the invitation, back on her horse, she finally called Phil Train and invited herself to lecture to his Altar Forum on the tapestries.

"You did mention . . . ," she diffidently began. Train accepted with enthusiasm, and they arranged that her talk there would be in three weeks, end of July, just as people were leaving for the summer; she mustn't expect an enormous audience. "But I know it'll be well attended. The Book of Revelation is so little understood."

Buoyed even higher by his enthusiasm, Lorna invited him to drinks on the following Friday. She had no idea if there was a Mrs. Train, but he'd bring her no doubt, or he could just stop in on his way home from the cathedral, which was so nearby.

"Small gathering—just a few friends," she said, and gave him the address, thinking now she'd have to dredge up a few other guests. Pam Linden, of course, and the Fludds, and maybe those people she'd met at the Fludds'. And maybe Peggy would drive down from Ukiah to help. She was glad that events had bestirred her to this effort to come out of her shell.

Working through the stages of grief over Curt's letter, Donna had arrived at bargaining. She had got over her angry stupefaction at Curt's not coming home, steadied by her natural inclination to believe the worst anyway, her knowing that good luck couldn't last, and that this was some sort of retribution for her windfall from Amy. Now she saw a hope that Curt might rethink his plan for a new life if she told him about how they owned their house free and clear.

Or maybe she wouldn't tell him. Had he fallen for one of those impossibly small, titless bar girls you saw on Thai Airways commercials? Who walked on your back and gave massage with their sidewise vaginas? Whatever the explanation for his behavior, she now had a house worth

some millions—she planned to discuss selling it with Ursula Aymes—
and she would just as soon go back to Delaware anyhow, where she
could get a job in finance and live on less. Curt was crazy and men were
crazy, and the East Coast was a better place to raise kids anyhow.

Or else she could take the reins of some of Curt's unfinished business, along with Harvey Avon. Did she not have an MBA and plenty
of smarts in the world of business, if anybody had ever cared? In many
ways, this was the option she favored.

She and Ursula sat in her still-somewhat-underfurnished living
room, air fragrant with the wax that had been applied to the beams just
before she and Curt had bought the house, a lavender scent reminding
of Aix or Grasse. They had splurged on an antique Provençal chest of
drawers and a love seat, both from France; otherwise they had only a
card table and some folding chairs, but everything takes time. Donna
had read a magazine on French style that said, "If you put even one
piece of French furniture or fabric—say a toile de Jouy—in any room,
even one loaded with other influences, the result is elegant and time-
less." She clung to this dictum.

"We'll bring in some furniture and plants," Ursula assured her.
"Some staging in the master bedroom is all we'd need, some sort of
imposing bed. The kitchen alone will sell the house.

"But with the market crashing, we'll be lucky to get what you
paid for it," Ursula added, a little worried that she ought to buy it
herself at a reduced price, if she could get financing. The market was
bound to pick up. However: the Asian buyer was eager and not to be
tossed lightly aside while Ursula sent out some feelers about loans in
an increasingly chaotic loan market. Banks had begun to throw a few
curves—something was happening there, but she didn't yet know what.
She finally decided she didn't need the headache, what with the Ian
situation and all.

Donna was disappointed in the realities Ursula sketched out. She
was good at math and saw that at the asking price, in the tanking market, after Ursula's commission and paying Amy back, minus the taxes
and Ursula's fee—Ursula had agreed on 4 percent, less than her standard 6—she personally might just break even. Clearly selling was not a
good idea, but she didn't say to Ursula she'd changed her mind.

"Curt will be devastated," she said. This thought was not without satisfaction but led her to remember with a chill that Curt's name was on all the house-related documents, and she wouldn't be able to take any action about the house without him signing them, unless she got him declared dead or herself legally deserted. She longed to ask Ursula about this but dared not.

"When do you expect him? I think we'll sell quickly here, and there'll be things for him to sign."

"I'm not sure. I may have his power of attorney," Donna said. She had begun to think she needed to tell Amy about the letter from Curt, but she was by no means sure it was she, Donna, who was the object of Amy's affection—it might be Curt Amy had wanted to help. By this light, she should conceal the letter and maintain that everything was fine. "Can we send documents to him?"

"Of course. That *petit canapé* is lovely, Donna, did you buy that here?" said Ursula, speaking of the splendid French Provincial sofa in striped blue-and-white linen.

"On Sacramento Street," Donna said. "For French antiques, LA is amazing, too. Better yet, Texas or New Orleans, they have shiploads, I've heard."

Why do Americans aspire so to France? Ursula had always wondered. She had always found the French a grouchy, vainglorious bunch. She stayed a little longer, hoping to figure out why Donna thought of selling, and whether Curt Mott was in accord, but was no wiser when she left.

Ursula had other things on her mind. She had the reputation of being an excellent, punctilious real-estate agent, very particular about the details, reliable and honest, qualities her rather fast, *poule de luxe* appearance belied, and she benefited from both images: successful businesswoman and expensive party girl. It was in her nature to be respectful of contracts and bottom lines, and she found herself wishing they—she and her son—had some kind of contractual connection to the unborn baby.

She still thought of Ian as her dependent child rather than as an independent being who had knocked up a teenaged girl and was going to be a father. And the young mother would probably inherit a dot-com fortune! If they got married, Ian would be legally connected to this potential fortune, unless they had a prenup, which probably Amy Hawkins would insist on. What should Ursula do?

Rationally, she knew perfectly well that there would likely not be a baby or any news of one, that all would be dealt with discreetly as if it had never happened, and that Gilda Mott would show up at her class at Saint Waltraud's in September without having missed a day of school; but this didn't seem right somehow, not only for the moral reasons the Very Reverend Philip Train had elaborated, but also because she, Ursula, would have to live with regret for such a wonderful opportunity missed; it would haunt her forever. What the opportunity was wasn't clear, besides the adorable baby itself, but something to do with money, leisure, the Mott world, connections for Ian, jets—she hardly knew, she didn't formulate it clearly. Also, didn't Ian have some rights? Didn't she herself as a grandparent have some rights? Such things had been adjudicated in courts, she was fairly sure, and grandparents had rights.

She encouraged Ian—she insisted—that he see Gilda and Gilda's parents, that he step up in some way. He knew he should and had proposed meeting Gilda somewhere or going over to her house. But Gilda hadn't seemed very enthusiastic. He explained to his mother that whenever he suggested a meeting, she would always say she had homework or had to go somewhere with her parents.

"I don't know what to say to you, dear," Ursula said. "I want to help, of course, but you have to think about your responsibility now. I'm not even sure I understand what you think about this."

Ian, far from knowing what he did think, shrugged. It all depended on what happened, what Gilda thought, what her parents thought, and no one had told him anything. One of his friends had remarked, "Once they get a kid, the guy can go back to the barn, he's just the stud."

"I think she'd kind of like to have the baby," Ian said to his mother.

"She's only a baby herself."

"Well, I know, but she does have some say in the matter."

"Of course, Ian, but so do you. That's what I'm driving at here. If there's going to be a baby, and I hope there will, you will have to have some part in it—in its life."

"It just seems kind of—theoretical," he said. "At this point. It was only a few weeks ago."

"For instance, child support."

"I suppose."

"Education. Have you any idea what that will cost? I know Gilda's parents have means, but you don't want to entirely sign over your rights to this baby to them."

The blankness and misery of Ian's expression suggested he was several paragraphs behind, still wondering about what he wanted to happen. Ursula would have suggested sending flowers or a present for Gilda, but nothing short of a pre-enrolled scholarship to some fancy nursery school or, eventually, Yale seemed quite equal to the grandeur of the baby's expectations; and as the days went on, neither of them was sure what Gilda was going to do about—the problem of whether there would be a baby at all. For all they knew, the Motts had dealt with it already. Ursula found ignorance unendurable but didn't feel she could call Amy again, and Ian found he could easily put the situation out of his mind.

Gilda agreed at last to have lunch with Ian, but she begged Julie to join them. "I'll just say I already had a date with you, could you join us? He doesn't really want to talk to me anyhow, I expect his mom made him call me."

"Not necessarily. He may be very concerned," Julie protested, certain that Ian was the best of young men, how could he not be, with his looks, not like the greasy handsome hero of old Errol Flynn movies but like someone playing Prince Valiant, or Prince Hal in *Henry IV, Part I,* or a football star in a film. She told herself it would be easier on Gilda, who didn't know what she was going to say, if she, Julie, was there to make conversation. As they waited in the St. Francis Oak Room ("Have a nice lunch," Carla, by now suspecting the situation, had instructed, handing over two hundred-dollar bills), it was Julie who had flutters of apprehension, Gilda not so much. Her mood of silent resignation was that of a child being made to do something distasteful. She'd insisted on wearing jeans.

Ian appeared in chinos and a polo shirt and the blue blazer he'd worn to the gala. For the first few moments, Julie's feeling, like the first time she saw him, was of speechless freeze-up, as if speaking to him was out of the question, as if he were an image on a movie screen.

"You know my niece Julie?" Gilda said. Ian shook her hand, as at dancing class or when meeting a bank manager. The stricken Julie couldn't help Gilda out of the awkward silence Gilda had feared, so the general speechlessness spread for a minute.

"Do you live in San Francisco?" Ian asked Julie.

"Out in the Avenues, but I go to Berkeley," finding her tongue.

"I went to Brown for two years, but I'm hoping to transfer to Stanford." They discussed colleges, transferring, Julie's hope to go to Greece for the fall semester. Gilda, who wouldn't begin college for three more years, pretended to look interested, happy to discuss anything but the Situation.

Eventually, with a little sigh of reluctance, Ian asked as required about how Gilda was feeling, and she replied she was feeling fine. In the daylight, her pallor struck him anew; she was like a swan. She might be gestating an ivory egg.

"Everyone asks me every ten minutes," she added.

"Are you going to, you know, have an operation?" There was no point in beating around the bush.

"I don't know. I don't really want to," Gilda said. "But my father worries about diabetes, and, you know, school."

"I suppose so," Ian agreed.

"Her parents are being really nice," Julie put in. "Grandpa Ran. Her father is my grandfather."

"Do you have an opinion?" Gilda asked Ian.

He didn't, really. His fantasies about the future made no sense out loud.

"I wish you were older," he said. "I'm so sorry, Gilda. This shouldn't have happened." He glanced at Julie and felt embarrassed that she was there. Julie, though, was lost in a tumult of desire. She couldn't help imagining him without a shirt, or aroused even. She felt her face getting red. When Gilda had to excuse herself to go to the ladies' room, which she had to do a lot, it seemed to her, Ian said to Julie, "Take my email in case you need me or anything," and wrote it on a scrap he found in his pocket.

When Ian had left them, and she and Julie were waiting for Carla, Gilda said, "If my parents make me have an operation, I'm going to run away, and I might need some help."

"They'll let you make that decision, I'm sure," Julie said, far from sure. She hoped not to be put in the position of defying her grandfather or else disappointing Gilda. Gilda was wondering at what age you were a moral agent who could make that sort of decision yourself. Could they force her? Whom could she rely on?

32

Enjoying the company of friends is a reliable human impulse.

With her apartment snug and presentable, Lorna began to build upon her invitation to the Reverend Train for a drinks party. She sent a little email to the Fludds, to Ursula, of course, to the Reverend Train to confirm, to her very presentable dentist Dr. Lamm and his wife, who happened to live nearby, to Marsha Fredericks, to Pam Linden, naturally—she stopped there till she heard back from these people:

> I'd be so pleased if you could join me for drinks on Friday next week, July 19, 1521 Larkin, just off Union. Call me for my parking strategies.

She could offer one spot in her garage and another behind it, sticking out over the sidewalk. She'd been struck with the difficulties of San Francisco parking—how did people bear it? When she'd lived here years ago, you just pulled up in front of your house.

She was pleased with her guest list, people she liked who might like each other. She'd chosen them with some care. Marsha Fredericks and Nancy Fludd were both involved with the museum—Nancy on the board—and Lorna had intrigued them with her story about the bones of Russell Woods. She would tell them more about her connection to his estate when she knew more. If it turned out to be in her power to steer one of his pictures toward SFMoMA, so much the better. Would that be insider trading? She thought of the absurd, sexist fate of the nice woman magazine editor who gave household advice, who got sent to prison for something men did all the time.

Lorna had no doubt that the Reverend Phil Train would enjoy her museum friends or anyone else she might know—would not be doctrinaire or anything but civil and conversable. Though she hadn't seen him for fifty years, except that once, she was familiar with his category: Stanford, Episcopalian obviously, played college—was it baseball or basketball? Other things followed from there—good works, especially among the homeless, familiarity with current novels. What she didn't know was whether he was bringing his wife, or if there was a wife, not that it mattered.

Lorna was aware of maybe another little concern when it came to Philip Train. Mindful of the details that had gone wrong—had not gone perfectly—at her lecture in Bakersfield, she needed to talk to him about her coming lecture to his parishioners, about the degree of interest in the Book of Revelation within an audience of San Francisco Episcopalians. She needed to learn whether or how they might differ from people in Bakersfield. Would they want the long version or the short one? She'd try to bring this up at the party, if there was a moment when it seemed natural, to get his advice on where to pitch her talk: How much did his parishioners know or care about the Book of Revelation?

Julie agreed to come help her grandmother, though it wasn't terribly convenient. The notable British sponsor of the Circle of Faith—they usually, discreetly, did not dare to mention his august name—would be at the Circle again, and she had been picked to assist at a reception for him there and sort of shepherd him; but she could come afterward until she had to show up for work; she had plans for earning some of the Greece tuition money by doing other jobs for the caterers who had worked Grandpa Ran's opera benefit, and she was supposed to check in with them later that same night in case they needed someone last minute at a big reception at city hall.

Lorna's drinks preparations occupied a part of several days, as she had to round up the ingredients by bus, organize cases of bottles to be delivered, and do a little baking herself. Her budget didn't stretch to champagne, so she settled for prosecco, but she'd decided there should be a French cast to her hors d'oeuvres, testimony to her twenty years in France. California since her departure seemed to have adopted French dishes almost without remembering their origins—*tarte à l'oignon,* for example, or *crème brûlée.* She'd been served these several times since coming back, dishes already solidly on American menus since America discovered Alain Ducasse and Joël Robuchon.

She had no radio but had learned to find stations on her computer; the trouble was she didn't understand the music in America anymore. Her ear was still tuned to French music, holding on to its twangy plaints in the Piaf mode, so unlike American pop. She settled for the classical station, itself locked into endless repeats of Vivaldi and Mozart and Brandenburg concerti, whose familiar strains she turned down to a subliminal level. She didn't like music to be too loud—a function of her age, no doubt.

She'd asked people for six o'clock and was startled when her doorbell rang at four-thirty; it could be Peggy early, or Julie. But it was Donna, wearing a long face, and no children with her, to Lorna's relief—what with the dishes laid out and the nut cups filled and the chafing dish in place, though not lit. Surely the last chafing dish in use in San Francisco—they abounded in the thrift shops from which Lorna had done her furnishing. The twins would reduce all this to rubble in ten minutes.

"I came because I want to show you this letter from Curt," Donna said, looking around fearfully, Lorna could see, taking in the party preparations or fearing to be overheard. Clearly shattered by something, and Lorna had a stab of fear for the twins. "I should have called."

"Sit down, Donna," Lorna said. "I'm having some friends in later. My first party! I hope you'll stay."

"Uh . . . I'd offer to help, but I have to pick up the boys—I just wanted you to see this. Hear what you think." Donna handed her the letter, and Lorna read it with dawning inquietude. She took in the salient phrases—"make my life here," "nothing to do with you," "the face of

God." Lorna understood Donna's tense and scared expression, a trace of tears in her dark eyes. She made her sit down and sat beside her. This would take a while.

"Out of the blue," Donna added. "I don't know how to respond."

Lorna had a firm policy of not seeming to intervene in the affairs of her children, however much she wanted to be helpful to them, but Curt's case was a special one. Being deserted was terrible for a young mother, no matter how unsympathetic one might find her. There was nothing wrong with Donna, it was just—Lorna could never find the word and put her own tiny antipathy down to some natural tendency of mothers-in-law not to like the wives of favored sons. Wasn't there a play about that?

"Clearly he's still suffering some kind of brain damage," Lorna said. "Someone has to go over there and try to find him. Tell me frankly— before the accident, were the two of you getting along? It's hard, I know, with small children . . ."

"Yes, I thought so. Yes, we were."

"Throwing away all he's built, it's not normal, he's never been religious. Do you think it's a religious thing? Something during his coma? Maybe it was then he saw the face of God? People talk about it, the tunnel and whatnot. Near-death experiences." They speculated for a few moments.

"What should I do, though?" Donna insisted. Lorna heard a note of hardness in her voice, a note of *sauve qui peut*, for which it was hard to blame her. Lorna had sounded that note herself, when she was divorcing Ran, knowing that people said, behind her back, "Three children, she ought to stick it out. She shouldn't think only of herself."

Lorna felt obliged to defend her son—injured, not himself—but she saw Donna's predicament. "Do nothing right now," Lorna said. "Wait awhile. At least you don't have worries about the mortgage. Let's make a date to think this through."

Donna suddenly saw she should not depend on Lorna and said nothing about her wish to sell the house. Nor did she mention her imagined adversary, the Thai beauty of tiny proportions and ancient Asian sexual expertise. They left it that Donna should do nothing for the moment, they would meet on the morrow, and agreed that Curt had lost his mind.

Almost as soon as Donna had left, Phil Train came in, the first of her cocktail guests. To her surprise, he kissed her on the cheek, brushing her lips unclerically on the way.

"It gave me a turn to see you in the 7-Eleven that day. I recognized you instantly," he said. "I would plausibly have been within my rights as an old friend to kiss you hello then—something I wanted to do back when we were in college. Life sends opportunity but not always when you need it."

"Me?" Lorna said lamely, dumbstruck at this flirtatious overture.

"Well, yes, but you had a boyfriend."

"Yes—back then Ran."

"What about these days?"

"Now that all that is behind us, my mind is on my lectures," she said firmly. "For one thing, I need to support myself and build my reputation again." He pursed his lips as if to say something but said nothing more. Of course she didn't believe that "all that" was behind them, didn't think that life—erotic, artistic, professional—was over for people of any age. Was it his being a clergyman that brought out her fit of prudery? Did he believe people should have ascended to the spiritual plane by now? Here she thought of Armand-Loup, so robustly sensual, so emphatically rooted in the mire of the physical: sex, cassoulet, a good Bordeaux. Not "mire," wrong word—but pleasure. Pleasure in the physical. Now with a packet of blue pills, but still with cheerful vigor, even joy. Joy seemed in short supply hereabouts. Was there more joy in France than in America? She'd be as joyful as she could muster with her guests.

People trailed decorously in. About a dozen, she'd figured, could fit in the small living room and make a satisfying buzz, with enough places to sit and things to set their drinks down upon. It was working out exactly as planned, even without Julie's help. Peggy put hors d'oeuvres on trays in the kitchen and pitched in with the greetings. If only she'd worn something more becoming, not navy blue. Maybe Peggy should ask Ursula's advice, they were the same physical type. Here was Ursula looking ravishing in a dark green cocktail dress with a low neckline, and very good pearls, enveloped in fragrance—what was it? Good old No. 5?

Her friends were glad to see one another and Lorna herself. Where was Julie? With the thought, here came Julie and a familiar-looking person whom it took some seconds to identify, so improbable was it: the telegenic English politician who served as patron of the Circle of Faith. This seasoned official accepted a scotch and soda and effortlessly conquered the room. Americans always swooned before a good English accent. He talked up the Circle as his reason for being in town, to be sure, and implied that he and Julie and Lorna were practically family. In the faces of her guests, Lorna read that her social reputation was now invincible, though that was the last thing she cared about. She felt a wave of estrangement, of longing for her house, her village, French harmony, walking to the butcher, the fragrant boulangerie.

"He was determined to come, Mom," Julie whispered to Peggy in the kitchen about the sponsor of the Circle of Faith. "He has a couple of hours to kill before his plane. When I said I was needed at my grandmother's drinks party, he was eager to come. He's a people person, I guess. He's nice," she acknowledged, lowering her voice, "but he's almost—um—too friendly."

The great man was just leaving for his plane when the company became conscious of a thumping noise against the ceiling of the living room, loud enough to stop the conversation. Thump, thump, thump, thump, it came so insistently, Lorna at first thought it must be the Chins complaining about her guests—the noise—though there had not been untoward noise.

The thumping certainly came from the Chins' apartment. Stepping close to her wall, she listened for something to explain the repetitive blows against it, and from inches away she thought she could make out muffled squeaks and "oofs," sounds of effort, maybe even cries from the other side. Some of her guests came closer, leaning in to hear, and people began to agree that something was throwing something against the wall to attract their attention.

The British politician couldn't stay, he had the excuse of his airplane, but nonetheless exuded the aura of authority in any circumstance. "Call them if you have their phone," he advised as Julie saw him out, "or call the police directly." In leaving he wore the relieved expression of the student lucky to not be called upon, or the man who is able to jump aboard the train at the last second or receives the biopsy report of negative.

The other authority figure present, Philip Train, had already called the police on his cell phone, then strode across Lorna's porch to the door of the Chin apartment, Lorna and others following. Like many other San Francisco Victorian houses, Lorna's consisted of her apartment on the ground floor, with another above, the two doors side by side to the street. The Chins' apartment was the upper one, and, peering through the glass of their door, the rescuers could see only the stairs leading up to the second floor. When the Reverend Train tried the Chins' door, it opened easily, as if the latch was broken.

Lorna's guests, led by Reverend Train, crowded en masse up the stairs. In the room at the top of the stairs, they found the Chins themselves, bound to chairs and gagged, reduced to groans and gasps to show their relief at being found. The room was in immense disorder. Mr. Chin was tipped over and had pounded with his feet against the wall, the sound they'd heard. Before anyone could untie the two victims, police bounded up the stairs, guns drawn, and told everybody to freeze.

Events followed: explanations demanded, names and addresses collected, an ambulance called, though it appeared that the Chins were not hurt. Ursula, who had rented them the apartment, was all over them with dismay. Men had been waiting in their closet and attacked them. Lorna did not hear why the burglars had waited for the Chins to be at home before ransacking the place, or what they were looking for, or whether they had found it. She and the other onlookers were shooed back to her apartment; a police sergeant took all their names.

"Lorna, this is so upsetting, I never would have put any of you into these units if I'd known," cried Ursula Aymes. "Normally the Chinese keep these things among themselves," she muttered when they were back at Lorna's.

Later Lorna looked up crime statistics for Larkin Street. Until then she hadn't been concerned about crime or burglars. Now she learned that San Francisco had a safety rating of 2, which reassured her until she understood what that meant: it was safer than 2 percent of America.

Or, 98 percent of America was safer than it. Larkin Street was practically the most dangerous place in California. Surely there was some mistake in these statistics?

Never mind, she was not going to become one of those timorous, fearful elderly people. She could hardly bear to frame the thought. But she would have to be more careful about locking the doors. Did she need a can of mace or a whistle? She had worried about Hams and Misty in Oakland, but here was crime in her own building.

She had turned the second bedroom of her new apartment into her study, but had put a futon in it for anyone staying over, specifically now, Peggy after the party. Lorna hoped to go to bed promptly after the tiring day, but Peggy wanted to talk about the Chin burglary, and her mortgage, as usual, and Lorna heard herself say about that, crossly, "Peggy, you should talk to your father, I'm sure he'd help out, at least he ought to. But you have to tell him about it."

"I know, but he has a lot on his plate—the thing with Gilda, for example."

Lorna had always found unfair the way people took care to spare those with the fewest worries, like Ran, more worries—people protected them instead—while the same people, their children, heaped their cares on her, who had no power to help. She kept this cynical observation to herself and kissed Peggy good night. As she was falling asleep, though, it wasn't the party, or Curt's letter, or Peggy's mortgage she found herself thinking about but what Phil Train had said about having wanted to kiss her in college. How durable some memories, how fugitive others. Why had she said romantic feeling was in the past for people of their age, when she didn't feel that way at all? She knew it wasn't true; she was the same person she had always been. Well, that had been his point, they were the same, just less trim and energetic.

Was she attracted to Phil Train? She didn't think so. And there was also the matter of faith. She didn't deride faith—after all, the mighty works in Angers were among its greatest testaments. She just didn't happen to have it herself. She firmly brought her thoughts around to Donna, and how to help her, but couldn't think how.

. . .

Leaving Grandma Lorna's party before the excitement at the Chins', Julie saw the British politician into his taxi. He pressed her hand and said, "Julie, my dear, I'm so pleased you take an interest in the Circle. May I get in touch if there's any special concerns I have? I'll be back in a month. We could have dinner. Do I have your email?"

Julie's cheeks, normally rosy, blazed like a sunrise. To be spoken to kindly and personally by an English statesman seemed to symbolize the future, the possibilities in the world, the way a winning ticket might, or finding a fifty-dollar bill in the street. He appreciated her competence and enthusiasm. She thought of Ian Aymes and was immediately stabbed by the pain of knowing he was stuck with Gilda, and then stabbed again by the selfish way her thoughts had framed it. She should send Ian an email pledging her friendship to them both.

Peggy, drifting off to sleep in Lorna's living room, felt a little cross with her mother, the way everyone fawned over her—the minister kissing her, an important Englishman turning up. The way she constantly asked her poor daughter to do the drive from Ukiah, such a drag. But she was happy to see Julie. What was Julie doing with that English guy anyhow? What on earth was the Circle of Faith? It suddenly came to her it was almost the end of the window she had for returning something to RealSteal, an expensive Céline handbag she thought she could resell well but changed her ideas about. She'd have to drive back to Ukiah tomorrow morning to get it into the mail.

Lorna lay awake, too, still thinking about Donna and the letter she'd got from Curt. In some sense, she wasn't surprised, had always felt Curt's coma would mark his transition onto another plane. His mother did not entirely rule out legal or financial or sexual transgression, but never suspected a religious conversion. How little one knew one's own children really, especially their spiritual lives. How could she help him, or help Donna, who was bound to be desperate?

Dick Willover had the idea, which had always in his case proven correct, that if you found a puny, failing investment and fed it, it bulked up and thrived. In vain did his broker assure him this was not a reliable principle, but Dick always had the example of his last success, when a stock had split, or when a company had sold itself just after he bought some shares. He was an investor on a modest scale, but his proportionate gain was a satisfying confirmation of his ability to navigate the fiscal labyrinth and fortified him in his financial squabbles with his erstwhile partner Tommy, who was after him for what they used to call palimony. It was a hell of a lot easier to get divorced from a woman—there were guidelines for that.

He checked with Ran Mott about Curt, made inquiries, and found himself in contact with Curt's colleague Harvey Avon, who was warmly confidential about the finances of Mott Development, in the spirit of misery loving company. They met at the Cal Club and sat in the lounge bar.

"I've tried every way of finding Curt," Avon said. "Private detectives, want ads. Nothing. My lawyer is looking at contractual default clauses, things that would free me up to take over. But it would land me with the debt, too. He's got a chunk of Mott Development wealth offshore somewhere, but the good news is he doesn't have a chunk of the recent appreciation. Some of the decisions I've had to make myself have paid off; I'm not feeling so burned, though I'm not giving up on finding him, either. Our hydroponics is hot. Emplacements all around Watsonville. Big Ag! Love it! It still amazes me I'd get involved in something like Big Ag."

Dick had the fugitive thought of putting a few thousand more with Harvey Avon, in Big Ag or whatever you wanted to call it. He liked the man's resilience, his acerbic brilliance, the fact that Curt had relied on him in developing amazing software, hardware, brick-and-mortar facilities—real salable things in the real world. He put some tentative questions, they ordered another drink and talked for some time, and settled that Dick would invest some more money in Mott Development, what a paradox, just the opposite of what he'd been intending to do. They also agreed that Avon had better talk to Donna Mott, to rule out interference from her, or seek her cooperation in dealing with Curt, wherever he was.

33

After the fainting episode, Misty had never come back to feeling well, and Hams was concerned about it to the extent of keeping an eye on her and asking about how she was feeling more often than she liked, but, she noticed, not doing extra chores or the dishes, oh no. She herself wasn't worried, because she had not felt "well" for weeks now and was facing months; she was crazy to get it over with. Delphine, next door, had brought a strange little apparatus she said her son had liked, which looked like a chair on springs on which was attached a pair of little underpants with some sort of tray in front. The eventual baby was to bounce up and down in it, his little legs through the pant holes. This bouncy chair symbolized for Misty the forthcoming change in her life, which she dreaded more and more.

Ian was not surprised to get an email from Julie Willover; there was something preordained about them getting together given their mutual friendship with Gilda, and the Situation. The meeting of Ian and Julie had been prompted by Gilda: she had asked Julie to try to find out what Ian really felt about the baby. "When I ask him, he only says he'd support anything I want to do. Just talk to him like a friend—even if he doesn't say specifically, you can get an idea."

Probably that was why he had given her his address, unconsciously wanting to see her again. "Hi Ian," she wrote, "would you like to have coffee one day? I know you're concerned about my aunt Gilda? Her parents suggested I should talk to you about it; and of course it would be nice to see you anyhow."

Ian accepted promptly. It turned into more of a date, in that they had lunch and Ian paid. They went to Cafe Bronson near Ursula's, where there was parking. Julie was a beautiful girl, Ian thought as she came in; Julie next to Gilda was like a painting next to an etching. Together, the strange coloring of Gilda always drew the eye, but apart, Julie bloomed with color and sexy ripeness.

They ate pasta and eventually got around to the assigned topic: "My grandfather and Amy aren't on the same side about Gilda, about what she should do," she told him, "and everybody wonders what side you're on."

"Having or not having the baby?"

"Yes."

"I try not to think about it, I guess. If I had to say, I wouldn't want to say get rid of it, so I'd rather Gilda decide, or her parents or whoever. Of course I'll step up, as my mother puts it." Whatever that meant. He then had a burger, so did Julie, to prolong the meal.

Julie shivered with jealousy of Gilda to have had Ian inside her. That's what she herself wanted more than anything. Over ice cream, when their eyes met, she thought she could read his similar desire. An idea came to her. She still had money Carla gave her for her Gilda lunches. While Ian paid the bill, Julie said, nearly choking on her temerity, "Would you want to go to a motel with me right now?"

Amazed to hear this bold suggestion from this beautiful girl, Ian said, "Definitely. We should get better acquainted." In his car, they kissed and discussed the whereabouts of motels. Lombard Street seemed like a good bet. In their state of almost unbearable suspended excitement, they had little to say except "That looks okay there," "No, it says NO VACANCY," "Try over there," trying to look calm, ignoring the studiedly nonjudgmental demeanor of the desk clerk who showed them up the outside stairs. The door once closed, they fell upon each other without discussion. Each step brought happy surprises—her unexpectedly full breasts, his well-developed pecs and other splendid natural endowments, their mutual energy and enthusiasm. They happily passed the rest of the afternoon and stayed until nearly seven, when Julie, sticky and sated, had to be at work.

Things progressed very rapidly between them after that. Their affair was more or less biologically inevitable, Darwinian, the lovely Julie very stuck on Ian, the handsome young man, the superabundance of hormones, the family connection of his mother as longtime friend and adviser to the Mott-Willovers, Julie's admirably adventurous outlook on life—planning to go to Greece—his prowess at all things physical. They right away began having a great time in bed whenever they could organize it—when Julie's roommates were at school or Ursula wasn't home, or once or twice in Menlo Park when Ian's roommate was away for the weekend. Ian, who had never had much sex, and never a steady ongoing affair, now gained in technique to match his talent. Julie, who hadn't really seen the point of sex when she tried it in high school—had thought of it more or less as something boys liked and you put up with—suddenly got it with enthusiasm. Her body throbbed and moistened at the merest thought of Ian, and embarrassingly explicit thoughts continuously intruded on her study of the Mediterranean market economy, or the legacy of the Peloponnesian War on contemporary Greek social attitudes.

In both their minds, little Gilda began to recover a sort of virginal innocence, becoming, except for the inconvenience of her pregnancy, the incarnation of chastity, the remonstration of their own carnal preoccupations; she was their nice little teenaged friend. Even in bed they didn't feel they were betraying her; they talked of her affectionately, admiring her good nature and her calm acceptance of the tough things fate had thrown at her, and her uncomplaining determination to brave the world—especially when it came to her health and facing down her parents. They wanted to help her.

As their love grew, there occurred to Ian and Julie separately, but they did not discuss, the idea that if the two of them got married, they could disappear for a few months and come back with a baby that people would assume was theirs. Or even without getting married, either way helping Gilda and maybe getting some financial help from her parents, given Ian's part in the affair. No one must know they were screwing their brains out; Gilda, Ursula, Ran, Amy—everyone would freak out at the very idea.

It was his mother who kept urging on Ian some sense of his financial responsibility for the baby. They all knew he was a penniless college student and the Motts were loaded, but Ursula felt that fathers, in order to keep a say in a child's upbringing, needed to come up with some support, at least from time to time. Specifically, she was afraid the Motts would buy the baby and edit Ian out.

Ursula was a practical and ambitious woman, not in a bad sense, as she put it to herself; it was actually a maternal duty to scheme a little for the future of your children, and as she had only the one, the precious Ian, it was doubly incumbent upon her to understand his deficiencies— mostly youth—and supply the remedies, the assurances, the steering of him upon a right course. At the moment, his future seemed a bit bleak: twenty years old, an unimpressive college record, no discernible interests apart from soccer—she would not have included sex among his pursuits until belied by this development—a baby coming, the mother a fifteen-year-old child.

She rallied: on the plus side, his good looks, amiable and compliant nature, sterling character—truthful and thoughtful—and intelligence visible in occasional flashes though usually hidden under his jock façade. She could in good conscience quite apart from maternal pride hope to see him placed within, say, the Mott family with its millions or billions and its jobs to dispose in software development; they wouldn't be disappointed in him.

But Gilda—her age! There was no solution. A child of fifteen could not marry and set up house. A boy of twenty, either. There was no scenario of the future involving that. Should she herself offer to adopt the baby? She should reassure Amy and Ran again that she would do half, or her part, or whatever was required—financially, that is; she didn't see herself doing child care. That was the course she resolved upon, offering to help, without knowing what it would be.

It was now mid-July. Gilda must be more than a month along—the baby would be born mid-March. That meant when school started next September, she could be showing a bit, so Amy and Ran had better let it be known now she'd be starting a new school in the fall, maybe in Switzerland or at an unnamed school in the East. What if her parents were required to be on the East Coast for some months and took her along? Or were planning a season on, say, the Riviera, or were putting her into a Swiss school for the term? Many things that would seem implausible for regular people seemed easier for the rich, a truth beyond question. What more normal than for the Motts to go to San Tropez, say, or Rome for a season? Ursula's practical planning skills came powerfully to the fore.

Ursula lived in a stylish Victorian on Washington Street in Lower Pacific Heights amid handsome furniture made from whitewashed tree trunks, imposed by a fashionable decorator she had briefly dated. She was pleased, of course, when her son started coming home weekends, which he never used to do, though his sports gear and bags of washing seemed out of place with the serious white upholstery and expensive drapes. He normally stayed at college down the peninsula, doing weekend soccer and whatnot with his friends; now, oddly, he appeared at her house most Friday nights and midweek sometimes twice, but never ate at home and was slightly taciturn about his plans. Ursula could divine that they didn't involve Gilda, and she was determined that little Gilda not get her heart broken. She tried to talk to Ian about his moral duty, not only to the baby, if there was to be one, but to Gilda, a duty of normal civility and concern. She got no argument about that, but it still didn't seem to her that he spoke to Gilda very often, and he never went to see her. She did surmise that he was terrified of her parents, who had made no effort to invite him over or get to know him. She was right about his terror of Amy and Ran. She had no sense of Julie in the picture.

Ran Mott had initially accepted Ian's role in Gilda's plight as almost accidental, incorporeal, almost as if an airborne seedpod had drifted by her and was merely inhaled; but as time went by he had begun to focus on the young man's responsibility, and his iniquity. Though by no means a vindictive person, Ran found himself hoping for bad things to happen to Ian. In idle moments, Ran's well-honed drowning fantasy obsessively flitted across the screen of his imagination: now Ran and Gilda are in the rowboat on some lake, Ian in the water. Father and daughter laugh as they row off. How long can Ian tread water?

Another scenario, to be taken seriously, involved informing himself about statutory rape, age of consent, accusations involving jail. But what—something short of incarceration—would punish him and at the same time oblige him to spend all the weekends of his foreseeable future taking the toddler to the park? That was punishment for sure. Yes, Ian needed to be legally required to spend enormous amounts of time with his child. Supervised, of course, in case he was an abuser.

Thus his somewhat-obsessive ruminations, possible to forget only by playing tennis, or in conversations with Amy on other topics, or in medical reading. He came to dread his drive to his office, when the Ian hate thoughts could not be dismissed, but kept creeping in among the weaving lanes of traffic on 280.

Now Ran's thoughts wandered to how they could use Carla in some way in the Gilda situation. Ran and Amy had decided to consult her on the new family drama—she often had insights into Gilda's phases that had escaped Ran and Amy. Also, Gilda's condition would soon be obvious to her anyhow. Carla's devotion to Amy and Ran was reliable, especially to Amy, and to Gilda it was practically fanatic, that of a mother or, better, a grandmother, meaning she never disciplined, only indulged and advised when asked. It was a problem for her that Gilda didn't ask her things very often; she seemed to understand Carla's rank in the family as someone who could be overridden, or at best was another adult, therefore aligned with her parents were divisions ever to appear. But she depended on Carla for rides, errands, and, occasionally, advice: How does this look? Should I wear the blue one?

In his mail, the usual collection of ads, invitations, and bills, was an ad/invitation to the opening of Tory Hatcher's latest photographs at a gallery whose mailing list he was on. He and Amy were vaguely acquainted with Hatcher's photos, though didn't have any of her work in their collection. According to the little history in the catalog, when in Pont-les-Puits, France, Tory Hatcher had managed to elude an irate gentleman who had tried to prevent her from going into the market hall and got to photograph a local event, a picturesque but macabre spectacle of bones and skulls laid out on pillows of muddy rags. She thanked the PhotoArt Gallery on Geary that the show could be put up quickly when the gallery had had to cancel another show, of prewar Appalachian mining towns, when the photographer encountered framing delays. Ran idly thought of going to the Hatcher exhibition, out of mild curiosity to see the French village where his children had been going to visit Lorna all those years.

34

We all value edification, if only for the self-satisfaction it gives.

The audience gathered at the Altar Forum that afternoon for Lorna's lecture was seated in the small conference room off the vestry, about thirty women and a couple of men, all smiling in welcome. The women of the Altar Forum were nice-looking Californians, mostly between forty and fifty, wearing pants and blazers, the women with shoulder-length hair and good handbags. The French-influenced Lorna couldn't help but notice people's handbags. She'd been amazed at Donna's beautiful one, apparently new, seen when Donna stopped in with Curt's letter: red, stamped crocodile—surely not real crocodile?

A screen had been set up in the back, and Lorna had brought her laptop containing her PowerPoint presentation. A youngish man in overalls organized the cords and plugs. The Very Reverend Phil Train was talking to a group of the women parishioners to one side but waved to her. When people had settled into their chairs, he addressed them.

"We didn't dream back at Stanford—I hate to say how many years ago—that my classmate, the sweet, frivolous little Lorna Mott, Morgan then, would morph into one of the world's leading authorities on the tapestries of Angers. It's such a privilege to have her here today to tell us something about these wonderful, holy works. I've been shown some of the photos, but we'll see them in much more detail on the projection screen.

"First, though, we'd like to hear—Lorna, what path took you from coed at Stanford to authority on French tapestry?"

Frivolous coed? Astonished and embarrassed at this peculiar description, Lorna felt blood rise to her cheeks. And what had been her path? She had lectured at the Doria Pamphili and the Louvre. Sweet, frivolous, little. The inexplicable knot of irritation did not subside. But why should she care?

"My field is really academic French painting of the nineteenth century, rather an orphan category. You might have heard of the *art pompier*—I'm especially interested in the painter Meissonier, one of the *pompiers,* whose work was so reviled, after being the most celebrated painter in France, that a statue of him in the Louvre was thrown out. But Meissonier is another subject. Today I want to tell you about the tapestries of Angers, in France.

"I happened on the Angers tapestries almost by mistake," she began somewhat crisply. "They are conserved in a dungeon in Angers, quite far from where I live—lived—in France, so I went to see them. I found them overwhelming, and then discovered the scholarship was directed mostly at conservation issues rather than the artistic traditions of their composition . . ." The audience shifted and settled back, sensing the autobiographical introduction about Lorna to have finished and the lecture to have begun.

"I say 'dungeon' advisedly," Lorna said, initiating her first slide with a touch to her computer keyboard. Miraculously, a photograph blazed onto the screen, a big relief to Lorna when the photo appeared clear and in focus; she was quite used to technical glitches with the first few images, the pauses, fiddling and apologizing, a volunteer from the audience, usually male, bounding up to help. But here were the perfect images of the dank and mossy stone ramparts of a forbidding, window-less castle, in French, *donjon.*

"This is the Donjon d'Angers, built by Duke Louis I, partly dating from the thirteenth century, now refurbished as a safe repository for these precious fourteenth-century tapestries. The dungeon is dedicated to preserving the seventy-one surviving pieces, which are extremely delicate. It has been retrofitted with climate control and lighting—you see them in near darkness. Bear in mind that these tapestries are immense—each about ten feet high and fifteen feet wide. Here is the first of them." A broad-winged angel bearing a scroll fluttered over the morose figure of Jesus on a donkey, with Saint John diffidently shuffling behind.

"It was a miraculous concept and a tremendous tour de force to achieve—each segment would have taken months to weave, probably in the Flemish provinces. They were commissioned by the local duke for his cathedral, for ceremonial occasions, but lost over the centuries, and in obscurity they fell to being used as rugs or for lining sheds and stables, or as horse blankets—anything you need a heavy cloth for." She had not spared the conscientious learners at her Altar Forum lecture the technicalities of tapestry preservation or the minutiae of medieval iconography or the controversies in biblical interpretations of the Book of Revelation.

She thought it over back at her apartment later, making herself a cup of tea. It had all gone very well, but had one astonishing aftermath. When it was finished, the Reverend Train—Phil—had insisted on walking her home, since the cathedral was not far from her house, and they'd had a drink in a cute little bar, the Nob, on the way. At a back table, inconspicuous, and anyway no one was there, it was only about four in the afternoon, he had taken her hand and squeezed it affectionately and said how much he enjoyed the lecture, how much he had learned, and so on. Then he had asked her if she'd thought of remarrying.

She had laughed. "I'm not exactly divorced yet."

"No, but eventually."

"I have a bad record, after all," she said.

"You and I have known each other a long time. I'm a widower, you knew that?"

"I wondered what your status was," she admitted.

"I thought we should explore that," he said.

"Oh, Phil, what a funny idea," she had said, not dismissively but caught off guard.

"Not a picnic being the wife of a clergyman, a lot of work, actually. I know you'd want to continue your career . . ."

"I can imagine that the dean of a cathedral needs a wife," she said, not meaning it to sound like an accusation. An attractive man was making a marriage proposition to someone her age! Well, his own age.

"I didn't mean this to sound like a job interview," he said. "I've admired—loved—you for forty years. More."

"Thank you, Phil. I'll think about it. I really will." She really would, she told herself. "I can see how we'd suit."

She did think about it, all evening. The compliment, how much sense it made, how it would solve a lot of problems. The negatives were, did she love Phil Train, and would she love life as a minister's wife, something out of an English novel, tea and jumble sales, parish visits?

And would she like living forever in the U.S.? This thought was unbidden. Hadn't she come back with the idea of returning forever to her native land, as Americans were fated to do? Why did this prospect now strike her as bleak? She had remembered America differently, without people lying in the street, neighbors being tied up and robbed, junk food, obesity, cars everywhere.

How nice of Phil. Yet she couldn't bask in satisfaction, because she also couldn't stop thinking things about how little a lecture meant when a life was beginning—for instance, Hams's baby or Gilda's—and would need help and love. The uneasiness didn't leave her, about the triviality of lectures on tapestries beside the wish to devote her life somehow to something larger. And there was the idea of remarriage. Usually she was an impulsive person, not given to rumination, just kind of knowing in her heart what to do; but neither instinct nor impulse was of help now in thinking about marriage.

A few weeks passed. She had an email from Armand saying to expect one of Russell's paintings. She had dinner a few times with Phil, went to a few dinner parties. She was aware that she had achieved a modest local celebrity in San Francisco, and had not been unhappy with the glamour lent her by being someone who had lived in France for a long time, and knew both Russell Woods the painter and a former English shadow secretary—attested to by those who had seen him at her party—and was also a recognized expert on an art subject or two. But she felt fraudulent about claiming the politician and was piqued that her serious scholarship seemed to count for little alongside her social achievement, though this did not surprise her. The upside was that as a result she had been invited to several very nice dinner parties, among art people and Episcopal laymen both, and began to feel more like a San Franciscan again.

She had projects—had resolved to read some serious works from the past she had not read, like Spengler and Nietzsche and Max Weber—she had a list. After dinner with Phil Train one night, he stayed over. They had quite a nice time, despite some senior complications, but overall so much less complicated than in the days of fertility; and life as a single, older woman began to seem not so bad, though she was never sure how much she owed her social success to Julie's stopping in with the British politician.

She had not forgotten the day of the promised counseling session with Donna, who came back at the appointed lunchtime, for which Lorna had made sandwiches. The weather was fine and they could sit outside in the somewhat-mangy garden, where Lorna had put in tomatoes that weren't thriving, and some daisies.

"You have to put in Early Girl," Donna said of the tomatoes. "Nothing else works in San Francisco. There isn't enough sun."

Together they parsed Curt's letter again. "The face of God." Was God a metaphor? For what? The part about coming home was clear enough. They discussed the practicalities. What was Donna's income? What were her expenses? What did she herself want to do professionally if obliged to go back to work? Shouldn't she go to Thailand to look for her husband? Lorna was impressed with her own businesslike competence on Donna's behalf; too bad she never applied it to her own life.

"I can't go to Thailand, the children . . . ," said Donna.

"Peggy then. She and Curt have always been close and she needs some variety in her life, some adventure. Plus she knows how Curt thinks, she always has." Lorna thought for the millionth time that she needed to help Peggy if only she could think of what Peggy needed most, and maybe this was it, a trip to Thailand.

"For sure I don't," said Donna. Lorna was prepared to be irritated by Donna's passivity, but discovered that she did have some initiative, some spark; she was already involved in Curt's business ventures and directing them herself, or at least in tandem with Curt's partner Harvey Avon, whom she seemed to know slightly, though Curt had always kept home and start-up separate. Since Lorna could see certain parallels between Donna's situation and her own—Donna's so much more serious, of course—on the whole, she was disposed to be admiring of her abandoned daughter-in-law.

Later that same afternoon, while toiling away at Derrida, she became aware that someone was ringing at her door. After the burglary at the Chins', Lorna had formed the habit of peering from a certain spot in her living room where she couldn't be seen, to check out who was on the steps. If they were standing in just the right place, she had a view of the whole figure, but now she could only partially make out someone in dark pants, probably a man, vaguely familiar and not menacing, pressing the bell. She crossed her living room, bringing the person into view. Armand-Loup. Though she had expected the painting, she hadn't thought it would be he bringing it. Armand-Loup here in San Francisco! Carrying a large parcel, probably the Woods, or maybe her silver, and peering into her hall. It was too late to pretend not to be home, he could see her, the disadvantage of the glass-paned front doors common here. Despite herself, she felt a hostesslike, welcoming smile stretch across her face.

"Well, hello, Armand."

"Chérie." He bent to embrace her, shifting the parcel between them.

"Well, how amazing, come in. You didn't say when you were coming."

He looked around. *"Un peu triste, ta nouvelle maison, non?"*

"Un peu," she agreed. "I've just moved in.

"What are you doing here?" she added in a less friendly tone. He looked significantly at a chair; she waved him to sit and sat down herself. He'd lost weight. She had remembered him stouter, less the picture of a suave senior dignitary. She caught the familiar scent of his after-shave cologne, was it called Mariner? Corsair?

"I emailed you about this, didn't you get it? I've brought you one of Russell's pictures, the one owned by the *mairie,* the one for you to sell. And"—here he brought a little parcel from his pocket—"a bone, presumably a pinkie, presumably but not certainly Russell's."

"Good God, why on earth?"

"Relic. *Porte bonheur.* It could also be Saint Brigitte's."

"Good God."

"San Francisco has changed, I find. Many more tall buildings *depuis* the five years since I've been here. More traffic. More people lying in the gutters."

"You came all this way to deliver a human bone?"

"Well, *non,* I came with a friend for a short visit and to bring the painting, naturally."

"Oh, Armie," she said, not recovered from this surprise, not happy but not unhappy to see him. She supposed, while she had him and thinking of Phil Train, she ought to ask about the status, from his point of view, of their separation. He said vaguely that the necessary papers had all been filed, all was well.

"Except with the house. The Anglais who bought it, at the signature they forfeited their deposit. They didn't 'perform.' Curious word, only used in English for the theater and the bedroom, I gather. And for real-estate transactions. Couldn't get up the money. I don't know but what I might not move back in for the nonce. How are all your children?" He once might have said "the" children, or even "our" children.

Lorna heard herself launch into a too-voluble response to this question: "Hams's expecting a baby, and they live in a rathole. Peggy, too, no boyfriend, getting fatter, Curt whereabouts unknown. He's found God, apparently, his wife came by a couple of days ago to tell me this. Or he's on the lam, no one knows which, or both. Ran has so much money, his wife, that is, but he does nothing for them—the children—and then his wife gave Donna, hence Curt, three million dollars for their mortgage, the others nothing, how can there not be hard feelings, though they don't express them? So well brought up . . . Donna never hears from Curt, not that I like her that much, either, and then she got this letter . . ."

Much more came tumbling out. How comforting to talk to someone who knew what she was talking about, knew the names and characters of the children, had always taken an interest, always been a good listener—the reason for his success with women probably, one of the reasons . . . her thoughts flew. She took a breath.

"Some coffee, Armie? Whom are you visiting?"

"A photographer friend. She is having a success with her photographs of the bones in the market hall in Pont, her show is here at the—PhotoArt Gallery, I think is the name. The spectacular bones of Pont-les-Puits." With a familiar stab of rage, Lorna couldn't resist asking "She?" about the photographer.

"Called Tory Hatcher. Tory? I suppose that must stand for something. Victoria? Seems like a nice woman."

"Doesn't ring a bell," Lorna said. Was this a new girlfriend? Armand-Loup extracted his phone and showed her the images, the skulls laid out on their cushions of rags on the long wooden tables where apples and fish were usually displayed for sale. She had the startled idea that the upheaval in the cemetery in Pont-les-Puits had been predicted in the Book of Revelation, and that a morsel of the prophecy had been borne out. She knew the book by heart from the tapestries:

12 . . . 1. he had opened the sixth seal, and, lo, there was a great earthquake; and the sun became black as sackcloth of hair, and the moon became as blood;
13 And the stars of heaven fell unto the earth, even as a fig tree casteth her untimely figs, when she is shaken of a mighty wind.
14 And the heaven departed as a scroll when it is rolled together; and every mountain and island were moved out of their places.

Despite the creepiness of the photos of skulls and tibiae, Lorna had a pang, not the first, of missing the village where she'd spent, after all, eighteen years. Maybe she was even missing Armand-Loup, his cheerful hedonism and real erudition.

She had a few practical questions about the painting—in whose name would she sell it, where did he think would be best: Sotheby's or Christie's? Privately? Was the ownership clear? What was the insurance status? Was he comfortable with her keeping it here, or should they put it in the bank? When these issues were settled, he rose to leave. How little their twenty years together appeared to weigh on him, how like that of business associates their conversation. At least this was amiable, even affectionate, in tone.

At the door he said, almost an afterthought, "*Est-ce que tu es heureuse ici,* Lo—are you happy here?" Lorna had no answer to this; it struck her with the force of a paralyzing dilemma, like the lady or the tiger. Was she happy here? Was "happy" an operative term in her life anymore? Here were all the things she hated—the automobile, her dingy apartment, traffic, the immediacy of family cares, crime, a new hairdresser, the mystery of her finances, the lack of response to her professional queries, and the absence of trains. Deciding how to answer was like teetering in an open window ten stories above a sea of cement pylons, drawn to jump.

Anyway, happiness was not a commodity one ought to covet, or even think about. Evanescent, it would dissolve in your grasp like foam. It had to exist in an oblique peripheral field of vision where you might be conscious of it but shouldn't seek or define it. It was a thing you just were. Or weren't.

"It's all right," she said. "There are advantages an—"

"—and disadvantages," he pronounced with her in chorus. "Well, when are there not?" He kissed her on both cheeks, like a stranger. She thought of how much she loved him—had loved him. She could not resist watching out the window as he rejoined the woman in the boots, presumably Tory Hatcher, and got into her car.

The same afternoon, about twenty minutes later, her doorbell rang again. She could see it was a woman she didn't know, probably selling something, or a religious proselyte, though the Jehovah's Witnesses and Mormons always came in pairs. This person was in jeans, expensive shoes, and a suede jacket. Lorna went to the door.

"Excuse me, but was Tory Hatcher here by any chance?"

"I don't know Tory Hatcher, sorry," said Lorna warily, having just heard of this person from Armie.

"Oh? Well—sorry to bother you."

"That's okay."

"Okay, um, goodbye." Peering at the card over Lorna's bell, MOTT DUMAS. The unfulfilled quality of this encounter prompted Lorna to add, despite herself, "I think she may know my husband, Monsieur Dumas."

"Ah—it was really him I was looking for."

"He was here, but I don't know where they went."

"Oh." They looked at each other with commiseration about the futility of quests to know where people went. As the newcomer took her leave, she turned to ask, redundantly, if Lorna was Mrs. Dumas.

"Yes," Lorna said, without further explanation, and got no hint from the woman's expression what this was about.

"I'm Susan Warner-Ford. The cook? You may have seen my book on the cookery of the Pont-les-Puits region? Emphasizing the *Allium tanisium* and the *puitières*. I give recipes using the *deux-sauce* capabilities of the *puitières,* and a lot of onion recipes, of course. The quiche recipe from the Fringale restaurant, and so on."

The Fringale! Lorna liked this reminder that the world is small, and she liked this woman for having been to Pont, and she remembered the quiche but had never ordered it. She asked Susan Warner-Ford if she would like some tea, regretting that she only had Earl Grey, nothing more exotic. They talked about food, and France, and Susan's plans for new explorations in the Dordogne. They had quite a nice chat. Only when Susan Warner-Ford had left did Lorna realize she hadn't heard what she wanted with Armie.

Later, Lorna wondered about the strange visit, and had the paranoid thought, bearing in mind what had happened to the Chins, that she was being watched, maybe cased. Two strange women in one afternoon. She had a valuable painting in the house. Without unwrapping it, she put it carefully in the back of her closet and draped clothes over it.

She didn't know where to put the pinkie bone; you couldn't just throw out someone's bone. Maybe she should bury it in the garden. For the moment she put it in a nest of cotton wool in her sock drawer. It was rather pretty, had a sheen.

At about seven o'clock she had a third visitor, Mrs. Chin, at her door with a little tray of something—ribs, as it proved, steaming deliciously.

"We have so much of this, many of these, we thought you might accept some," she said. At first Lorna was startled, but why was it any odder for Mrs. Chin to bring her food than for her to have taken them some, if only she had? It marked a new stage in their neighborliness. Lorna thanked her profusely and, when she'd gone, poured herself a glass of wine and tucked into the hot, spicy morsels, thinking agreeable, neighborly thoughts.

35

Who was it who said, "If you can't fight them, join them?" Ran was starting to explore this strategy.

"You're going up to San Francisco? No need to drive myself then, Carla can drop me," Ran said, observing Amy and Gilda in preparations for a trip to the city. This was a rare venture for Amy, who tended to do her shopping in Paris or Palo Alto.

"We need to get Gilda some clothes," she said.

"To fit her expanding figure." Ran's tone made plain that he saw any concession to Gilda's condition as defiance of himself. Not that he ruled Amy, but he had tried to explain—and just couldn't make her understand—the health issues for Gilda and the high incidence of birth defects, the danger of eclampsia and other life-threatening results for diabetics, which, added to the social implications of a fifteen-year-old having a baby, made it imperative to terminate Gilda's pregnancy, and the clock was ticking. Gilda was now by his calculation about six weeks' pregnant, and in a week or so, an ultrasound would show the beating of a fetal heart. This was bound to enrapture the two women, and harden Gilda's determination. Right-to-lifers counted on this reaction; in some states there were laws forcing pregnant women to look on a screen at the little throbbing cells.

About pregnancy termination, he had been peculiarly paralyzed, unwilling to drag Gilda to the hospital kicking and screaming, which is what she threatened, hoping she'd come to her senses, hoping she'd miscarry, hoping for some event that would convince her to think of her own health and demonstrate to her how unwise childbirth would be for her. Mrs. Klein had no influence; evidently he himself had no influence. Amy was officially on his side, but her ambivalence was clear to Gilda, and he felt she had come to act a little coldly to him, distant and preoccupied, he knew because of this situation, as if he could change the facts of biology. He was also aware in himself of a paradoxical sense of wonder that their lives could take such a strange turn, his especially, in late middle age, or was it early old age?

"It's another deposition today," Ran said. "It shouldn't take above an hour."

"We can go together. Gilda has invited her friend Bookney, they have a meeting they want to go to. I'll go to Macy's. You and I could have lunch afterward," Amy said.

Gilda's school, Saint Waltraud's, was mostly a day school, but had several boarders, one of whom, Bookney Ravanel from Virginia, was one of Gilda's best friends, and the two girls had planned to go to San Francisco for a day in the city and to attend a lecture at the Circle of Faith, a group, Gilda explained, that her sort-of-cousin-actually-niece Julie was mixed up with, where they had very interesting programs. She couldn't explain its slightly mysterious aura of virtue. She told Bookney about the slave.

CF meetings took place in an apartment with mostly glass walls and a fabulous view over San Francisco and the bridges and bays. Gilda hadn't thought of it before, but of course this location must belong to a very rich person. Members of the Circle welcomed the two girls, who were the youngest people in the room, and gave them brochures. The opulence of the surroundings was reassuring, but the absence of people in their age group was a little alarming, as if they had blundered into something X-rated, all these well-dressed adults looking clammed up, as if they would not begin their activity till Gilda and Bookney were not there.

Gilda actually enjoyed the Circle of Faith more without Julie, who had a sort of proprietary manner when it came to the meetings. Here with her friend Bookney, people came up to them in the friendliest way and did not seem to find them young. There were always a few African and Indian people at the meetings, in their saffron tunics and sea-green saris, as well as well-dressed San Francisco women and students from Berkeley and SF State. Gilda had heard that a former British prime minister or something like that was sometimes there, but she had never seen him. Gilda didn't know if Julie would be there—Julie hadn't been down to Woodside in a couple of weeks, with the explanation that she was starting a summer-school session at Berkeley.

The program today was going to feature a woman who had walked with her baby from Afghanistan to Munich, running away from unfair punishment after being made to marry someone whom her society said she had to marry. Now she went around lecturing on the condition of women in Afghanistan, victims without money or jobs, beaten by their husbands or worse. Also, if you were a girl in Afghanistan, you couldn't go to school, and they had a custom of mutilating you Down There; your own mother would take you in to have it done. Gilda couldn't help but reflect that if something was to be done to end her baby, it would be her own father who would take her to have it done. She of course didn't mention all this to Bookney.

When the speaker came in—a dramatic black-haired woman wearing a headscarf and shawls over an attractive pantsuit—they were reassured that the event was as scheduled, and that they had come on the right day. The audience settled down; plates of cookies and coffee urns waited on the sideboard. Louise and Roger Brody, whose apartment it was, welcomed everybody, and Louise introduced the intrepid walker, Marga someone, a name hard to catch, or even nonexistent.

"In some categories, Afghanistan is the most dangerous place in the world for women," the speaker Marga began. "The dangers are rape, feticide, honor killing, genital mutilation, economic powerlessness, and absence of health care. The most dangerous thing a woman can do, or have done to her, more often, is pregnancy. Then her chances of survival are only fifty percent. There are no doctors, no post- or prenatal care, no pediatrics.

"The second-most-dangerous thing she can do is think for herself. If it should strike her that she doesn't want to marry the ugly old goatherd, or that she'd like to become a doctor, or hear a musical concert, she is also in danger of her life." In the slideshow, Gilda and Bookney saw the faces of the women in Marga's village, lovely, some of them, but veiled and not smiling, just staring hopelessly out. Gilda began to feel a little odd, maybe just with empathy. Things women had to bear that she hadn't thought of. She herself was transgressing two of the things that could mean her death in Afghanistan—pregnancy and thinking for herself. There was something thrilling to think of her situation that way.

What if the baby was a girl and had to live in some country like Afghanistan? By what slim accident had she herself been born in Woodside, not Kabul? She had always been aware of her privileged life—Amy and Ran had drummed it into her about good manners and noblesse oblige, though they didn't put it like that. Awareness and gratitude were what they emphasized. She saw that she had more than most people, but believed she paid for it with her diabetes, that there was a sort of karmic equivalence. Now Marga made her see that there was not; there was just the fact that some people were luckier than others, without there being any reason.

Gilda didn't know why these thoughts were extra strong today; she'd had them before, the feeling of being undeserving and at the mercy of capricious fortune. Whenever Gilda thought of the baby growing inside herself, she began to feel woozy, thinking of the things in store for it, it not having asked to be born, maybe marked for unhappiness or illness. She knew the woozy feeling was probably morning sickness, as the books predicted; she was often on the cusp of wooziness these days. At school she just said she had eaten something, and they were used to her health issues anyhow. Now she felt faint. She looked at Bookney and saw that tears were standing in Bookney's eyes, too, at the things Marga was saying.

Marga and her baby crossed from Afghanistan to Iran on foot. Then they had to travel across Iran to Turkey, and got some sort of ride in a cart to Istanbul. Smugglers took them to Lesbos, in Greece. She paid the smuggler twelve hundred dollars, but the baby went along for free. They almost drowned when the raft to Greece leaked, but they were near to the Greek shore, and she, unlike many, could swim the short distance, even with the baby, even with her robes weighing her down.

But then after they fell into exhausted sleep on the Greek island, someone took her baby. He was nowhere, just gone from his blankets. Why? No one had seen him. Gilda saw that Marga's escape would have then been easier without the baby, but she accepted that Marga probably wouldn't feel that way. She thought of the story they read in English class by Joseph Conrad where someone says, "The horror! The horror!" which pretty much described Marga's conclusion: the heart of darkness exists, and not only in Africa. The more Gilda read about the world, the clearer it became that the heart of darkness was everywhere.

Gilda and Bookney stayed for the tea or juice and cookies. A cookie helped with the wooziness. Gilda hoped Julie might show up, but she didn't. Instead they fell into conversation with a nice older woman who told them some things about the Circle of Faith, including about the Retreat Facility in the Alexander Valley where you could go to meditate and get your head together for a low weekly fee. Gilda tucked this information away, as she was wont to do these days with information that could serve in her situation in case she needed to escape or hide.

36

D ivine intervention can't be counted on.

After a few more weeks, Ran abandoned his hope that Gilda's pregnancy would end spontaneously and stepped up his vigilance about her day-to-day health. She had always been responsible and careful with her blood sugar and other numbers, and she claimed to be in good control of her diabetes as usual, and to be checking her numbers more often than before. "Before" was ideally three times a day. He couldn't quite bring himself to sit her down and hear him out about the importance of even better control for her fetus and herself; to do that would be too much like approval or acceptance of her condition, and he wasn't there yet.

"I've made an appointment for Gilda with Frank Gill, a gynecologist with a specialty in diabetes," Ran remarked to Amy at breakfast. "I'll take her, because I want to talk to the guy about the general subject of diabetic pregnancy."

Amy was plagued by the suspicion that Ran intended to do . . . something. Maybe something to make Gilda miscarry, though it was officially too late for the abortion pill. It would be like him to take the matter into his own hands, and to get his own way, despite Gilda's wishes. This mistrust made her miserable; Ran was her best friend as well as the only person she could turn to in this crisis, and here she was mistrusting him.

"Shouldn't I go with you?" Amy said to Ran. "In case he says things we both should hear? Can't you talk to Dr. Thing without taking Gilda? She has her regular doctor. She likes him."

"She should be with someone who specializes in diabetes."

And whom in this situation could they trust to help and advise about the practical question of what to do about the incipient scandal? Carla had a lot of practical common sense, but she seemed strangely hostile to the whole subject of Gilda's plight. She had the Catholic view against abortion, and she also had the Catholic view about marriage, its sanctity and being required for being pregnant, though she wouldn't admit to attitudes so square. What Carla was hoping for, and Amy understood this, was a beautiful wedding, white dress and orange blossoms, soon, before Gilda was showing. Amy had naturally ruled this out, but Carla, thinking it would be making the best of a bad situation, was in favor of the marriage of Ian and Gilda, Gilda in white lace, maybe in the garden, Gilda's age notwithstanding.

Gilda's delight in her pregnancy was evident to both Ran and Amy, and it added to their dismay. She was excited and elated. They reproached themselves that they'd never given her a sense of the realities of adult life, about money, or social disapproval, or the hardships of child-rearing, or the need for an education. She'd been too sheltered, a maiden in a bower. They could keep sheltering her now, and the baby, too, but they also had a sense this would in the long run be a disservice, cutting her off from . . . from what they couldn't say. From having a good character formed from understanding others, and partaking of their struggles. Whatever people meant when they told someone "Grow up!" they felt now about their own child. Somewhere along the line you had to understand the solemnity and importance of life. You had to feel its pain.

Ran remembered asking his own father why he, nine-year-old Randall, had to go to Sunday school when his parents didn't go to church like other parents, and his father had said, "We had to go when we were your age, it's part of your education." Education was what Gilda needed, and a little pain, which she was not feeling at all. The school of hard knocks. They earnestly asked themselves whether their wish to hasten her interface with reality now didn't contain a little envy, too, of her blithe nature and confidence in the world.

"We should have them to dinner," Amy said one night.

"Who?"

"Ian and Ursula," Amy said.

"I would like to know your reasoning around that," Ran said, his usual way of signaling resistance, no matter what her proposition was to be.

"We'll always have this connection to them, no matter how it turns out, we might as well get to know them. Reach out."

"No, Gilda will go back to Saint Waltraud's slender and normal; Ian will do whatever he does, we'll see Ursula occasionally as we always have, and it will never be spoken of."

"Did you sleep with Ursula, back when you dated her?"

"I don't think so. There wasn't so much of that then. We only had a couple of dates, to people's parties."

"I think there was plenty of that in Ursula's life—all those husbands." He probably did, Amy thought, but she didn't continue her inquiry.

It was Ran who pressed on: "We do not have any connection to Ursula and Ian and we don't need to have them to dinner."

"Ursula will be our co-grandparent," Amy reminded him, hastily adding, "if Gilda were to . . ."

"Forget it, Amy, she is not going to have that baby." This brought them to their usual impasse, which was understood to mean that, while officially Amy and Ran agreed against Gilda's wish for a baby, unofficially Amy leaned to Gilda's side and was even willing to care for the baby herself. Ran understood this very well, but couldn't resist from time to time making Amy restate her solidarity with him, even at the price of her increasing frostiness.

"I thought next week, midweek; Wednesday is what I proposed to Ursula." They would come, no doubt. Ran didn't take his objections any further, but looked ahead with dread to a confrontation with the criminal young man who had violated Gilda. What had Amy been thinking to ask him here?

"Can you think of a couple more people?" Amy asked.

"Since it's a family affair, maybe Julie, she knows the sordid details." They asked Gilda to invite Julie, but when she did, Julie said she couldn't come, which was unlike her: "Want to come to dinner with Ian and his mom?" Shocked expression. "Uh—ah—I can't." Formerly she had seemed always free, and always delighted to come. Amy had sometimes even thought Julie might be grateful for a good dinner, so available had she always been; girls that age ate so badly and didn't look after themselves. Maybe Julie didn't like Ian, she thought. On feminist grounds. What he'd done to Gilda.

Ursula looked forward to the dinner, which she hoped would clarify the future. Were they family now? Or had they been summoned to hear bad news? She interpreted the invitation as familial, a sign of a new relationship with the Motts, and also a sign that Gilda was planning to go through with the pregnancy. She told Ian that was her interpretation. Ian had no response. He longed to be in the arms of Julie; after their lovemaking, they usually discussed together new developments as they arose but had no views. They couldn't ill-wish an unborn baby or Gilda, either.

He had accepted his mother's view that he was now in for the long haul of fatherhood. When he thought of the reality, he felt light-headed, but could dismiss any apprehensions by focusing on the Stanford fall semester and his new academic chances, which in the long term would help him be a responsible parent.

There had been joy when Ian's application to transfer to Stanford in the fall was accepted, pending good grades in his summer courses, and this was a positive development sure to endear him to the Motts. He himself was excited and surprised, and looked forward to announcing it at the dinner with the Motts. But Ursula found herself otherwise exasperated at Ian's lack of affect about his impending fatherhood. He went out nights, but not to see Gilda; she wasn't sure whom he did see. She found herself saying more than once, a sort of shock tactic, "I think you should do the right thing and marry the girl," even though it was certainly not what a young man ought to do, saddle himself with wife and baby, let alone a wife barely into her teens. Ian's response was to laugh that the Motts wouldn't dream of letting Gilda get married. "She's only just starting tenth grade."

"I don't understand what the Motts do think, frankly." Ursula sighed. "What they plan to do. I wish I knew."

"I could ask Gilda," said Ian, infuriating his mother with his off-hand lack of personal involvement in the unfolding drama of decisions about life and death.

". . . I don't think they have a cook," Ursula was musing. "I think their person does a lot of the cooking, and Amy does some . . ." Ian realized with a start he had tuned his mother out.

The Wednesday of the awkward dinner arrived in due course. Gilda seemed pleased but not excited, seemed to think it was perfectly normal that Ursula and Ian would be coming to dinner at her parents'— weren't they now all connected in this surprising way? She asked what she should wear, an interest Amy noted was very uncharacteristic. "My same clothes? I haven't changed sizes at all," Gilda said.

Ian drove his mother in her car—her respectable Mercedes—down the leafy lanes of Woodside; Ursula was bringing some chocolates, regretting the banality of this offering but couldn't think of anything else for people who had everything. She instructed Ian to hand them to Amy. When they pulled in, Carla came out of the kitchen back door to wave them to where they should park, making them wonder if this was to be a dinner party with more people. Then she led them around to the front door and inside—at least not through the garage entrance. She took their jackets and the chocolates.

Amy, Ran, and Gilda were in the living room, whose understated opulence—custom sofas, low glass tables, an important Jawlensky over the fireplace—Ursula had seen before but now noted with more interest. The living room opened into a garden room—they called it a lanai, in Hawaiian fashion—which in turn opened onto the garden. This was at a peak of bloom, a mass of hydrangeas and late poppies, roses, scents of basil and lavender reaching them in waves on the light breeze. Gilda was actually lovely, Ursula decided, like an illustration in a book of fairy tales. She had radiance—women often did when pregnant; that was it. Pregnancy could explain the faint chubbiness, or was it the normal chubbiness early teens often had? The late-afternoon sun behind her strange silver hair lit a corona around her head.

"Come outside," Amy invited. "We have peonies, they're incredible this year." Amy was proud of her peonies, which were not meant to do well in climate zone 9; the gardener, Mr. Nakamura, was a genius.

"What will you drink?" Ran asked. Though it was a habit of Amy's, learned from her French sojourn, to serve champagne before dinner, Ran had nixed it as too celebratory. Ian asked for a beer, and Ursula a scotch and soda. Carla went off to make the drinks.

He is a wonderful-looking boy, Amy admitted to herself. Ran shuddered at the young man's athletic body and pretty face, blond, with a shadow of gold whisker over his chin. The party trod a garden path or two, admiring the peonies, with Gilda hanging back to bring up the drinks Carla was concocting at the bamboo-bar affair in the lanai. Ian tried to catch Gilda's eye, to give her a smile of sympathy and fellowship. She avoided his gaze. She didn't look any fatter; she just looked the same.

The Motts' round dining table was a little too large for just five people. Ursula wondered how the family sat when just the three of them were eating together. As it was, five people seemed far from one another, increasing the Waspy, distant tone of the occasion: Ian and Gilda sat on one side, Ursula around next, Ran and Amy yet farther around, so that Amy and Ian were in a sense next to each other but still separated by a vast stretch of the table's perimeter. There was a hot starter of scallops and grapes in hollandaise in individual shells, brought in by Carla, and a platter of chicken and a bowl of salad waiting on the sideboard. No extraordinary effort had gone into this, Ursula judged: a family meal. Was that good or bad?

"One of Carla's specialities," Amy said of the scallops.

"Wonderful," Ursula said. In fact, eating the delicious substance, her mouth had begun to feel puckery. Was there something wrong with it? She reached for bread from the basket on the table; maybe some bread would stop the strange, warm tingling that coursed through her lips and tongue.

"Do you follow the Forty-Niners? Stanford?" Ran was asking Ian, searching for something apart from saying, So you fucked my underage daughter.

Ian, relieved by the fraternal tone, said, "I'll be transferring to Stanford in the fall, so I guess I'll be a Stanford fan—I'm basically a soccer player, but . . ." Exclamations of commendation greeted his Stanford news.

"Amy and I went to Stanford," Ran said, and was about to say, "We hope Gilda will be going there," before he remembered how unlikely that would be now. But at least Ian was going to Stanford. In a stretch of silence, Ian looked at his mother for some conversational cue, but now noticed that her lips had swollen up to a bizarre and unfamiliar Ubangi dimension. "Mother?"

Ursula was speaking but continued to feel an odd tingling. "Isn't it wonderful? We're so pleased. It's still a matter of him taking a few makeup courses, things he hadn't taken at Brown, but still a relief to hear he got in." Ursula continued to feel the odd sensations but had no sense of anything exterior. Though she could hear that her words were coming out oddly damped down, as if she were speaking through the screen of a confessional, and her tongue was clumsy.

"Mother, are you all right?"

Now Ran also noticed the very pronounced swelling of Ursula's lips and half rose from his chair to lean closer. "Ursula? Are you allergic to something? We keep some epinephrine in case the bees—with all the fucking flowers, we have bees . . ."

Ursula touched her lips and felt their unfamiliar size. She did feel somewhat short of breath, too. Her throat—something was wrong. Ran was on his feet and left the dining room, coming back in a minute to ask Gilda if she knew where the EpiPen was. Gilda went to find it in the kitchen drawer where they kept it, close to the garden.

Ursula felt the increasing constriction of her throat. The Motts were all cool in medical emergencies, apparently, but Ursula began to panic, and Ian was trying to urge her out of her chair toward the other room. As she sagged against the sofa, Ran bounded in, pulled up her skirt, and jabbed her thigh through her stocking with the EpiPen. Almost immediately her throat began to feel more open and she could breathe. She tried to smile at the anxious company through her hugely swollen lips.

Ran thought, randomly, what were the odds somebody would have an EpiPen? Did Amy know how many people were allergic to shellfish? What would have happened if they hadn't had epinephrine? Could he even do a tracheostomy anymore if he had to? They needed to take her to an ER.

"We'll use the one in Redwood City," Ran said, "there'll be less traffic."

"There's roadwork on Alameda de las Pulgas," Gilda said, looking at her iPhone. "Stanford would be faster." They half carried Ursula out to the driveway and into her own car, which was parked nearer than Ran's. Ian got behind the wheel. Ran went to get his car. Ursula began to protest that she was fine, and that she hardly knew what had come over her. As they drove off, leaving Gilda and Amy in the driveway, Gilda took a picture with her cell phone of Ian's mother's strange countenance.

"Seafood allergies can come on at any time," said Amy to Gilda. They both had noticed when her skirt was pulled up that Ursula was wearing stockings instead of tights, and a garter belt of blue lace and little ribbons where it attached to her stockings. Such an apparatus was familiar to Amy from French shopwindows, but Gilda had never seen a garter, let alone those suspender things, on a living person, only in comic books to denote bad women. Why didn't Mrs. Aymes wear pantyhose like normal women?

"Will she die?" Gilda asked, assuming not, but it was good the way Ian acted fast, her father, too. She admired Ian more and more. What with her girls' school and lack of neighborhood playmates, she didn't know that many men and boys, actually, just her father and one or two teachers.

As she lay across the backseat of her car, Ursula's mind accelerated as from a shot of speed, maybe from the infusion of shellfish toxins. It whirred with the energy of an idea that had been floating up to her conscious mind each morning upon waking for a couple of weeks, but which then dissipated with the concerns of the day. Now it was almost as solid as a conch; it had the thick plasticity of a living starfish, with motile tentacles that could reach out in several directions at once: her idea was that Ian and Gilda must marry.

With marriage, all the problems would be surmounted and it needn't be forever, and it needn't ruin the lives of the young people or deter their education, but it had to be. An amicable bond would unite her and Ian with the Motts: their mutual grandchild would be named Aymes. Make a note to inform Pud Aymes, wherever he was, that Ian was going to be a father. It was all clear to her. No sense in beating around the bush among the parents, she would put it to Ran and Amy directly. She and the Motts, mostly the Motts, she hoped, would support the young couple while necessary. The child would live with the Motts, but Ursula would be there a lot, an active grandmother.

She felt better and tried to sit up a little. She touched her lips, which had begun to subside with prickly tingles, as when you sat on your foot too long. The certitude of the recent moments subsided, too, though she retained the sense of what had seemed so clear to her moments ago and realized there would be a better time to bring up marriage. She may have fainted a little; she had no sense of how long they had been in the car.

Looking around, she now saw that she was at a hospital, or the annex of some clinic, people in cots around the walls but no medical personnel in sight, no paper sheet under her. No, here was a paper sheet, bunched up under her bottom. A few feet away, there were Ran Mott and her son, Ian. Had she been close to death or something? She remembered the ride, the sense of speed and emergency, and her brilliant solution to the problem facing them all.

"Thank you," she said. "It happened so fast."

"Scallops," Ran said. "You've eaten your last seafood salad, for sure. Have you been allergic before? It only gets worse with time, you have to be clear about that." His voice had assumed a doctorly neutrality. "Once you're sensitized, you have to stay away from them like the plague. No oysters. Stay away from shellfish generally." The relief of seeing Ursula's color return, and that she was sentient, made him suddenly remember his night with her.

37

The past has lessons for us, though we may not like to dredge them up.

Ran's lunch with his former wife Lorna had been fixed for a Tuesday, kind of a nuisance as it was a day he had a dinner later at the Bohemian Club, and he liked to keep social engagements down to one a day. Also, he dreaded it. Lorna had not impacted his life in the twenty years they'd been divorced, why now when he had so much else to worry about? He suggested they lunch at Greens, an upscale vegetarian restaurant on the Bay, run by Buddhists; they had liked it back when they were married. Lorna was touched by this sentimental gesture. Or the choice might reflect his belief that she was still kind of a vegetarian hippie—her tendency during their marriage—though she had long since graduated to *boeuf en daube* and *magret de canard.*

They were both prompt people and came in on the dot of one, thereby running into each other by the giant tree in the foyer, and were shown together to a table near the window, which looked out on sailing boats at the pier, glamorous tall masts like birches rocking against the yellow mist. Refracted in the sunshine, everything inside glowed providentially.

"You look well," Ran said. "The years have been kind to you." He made an apologetic patting gesture toward his practically nonexistent paunch. "How is—uh—Armand?"

"Fine," Lorna said, noticing that he had repeated the line about the years being kind—maybe his usual compliment to people getting older? "Much stouter now." They quickly moved on to a safe topic, the children. Lorna asked if Ran ever saw their former son-in-law Dick Willover.

"At the Grove."

"I always liked him. I'd love to see him, but the feeling isn't mutual, and Peggy would be upset if I called him, I suppose."

"He sees Peggy from time to time. His love affair with the man is over, I gather," Ran said. She noted his equable, nonjudgmental tone, probably the influence of his younger wife. Back when she and he were married, he would have said something about pansies.

Lorna sometimes found herself reflecting on subjects like the transience of human love—things you'd rather not think about. Such thoughts came to her now, to think of Dick Willover no longer loving poor Tommy, of Armand-Loup, and of the empty astonishment she'd felt on seeing Ran today; to think of how in love she had been with both of them, them with her, too, perhaps, and how hard her heart had become, thinking only of lecture dates or the children's mortgages. When she tried experimentally to think of being in love, however ridiculous at this time of life, only the image of Reverend Train floated before her, in his college incarnation, his handsome legs in hiking shorts. Now not Ran and certainly not Armand, but, alas, not Phil Train, either.

They continued with the subject of their children. Curt of course. The problem of Peggy's life. Hams's expected baby. Misty not doing too well.

"Naturally they have no insurance," Ran said.

Lorna thought of the costs of a baby. Up to Ran, no doubt, or his wife. In France it would all be paid for.

"How are they going to afford the maternity costs?"

"Oh, I've paid," Ran said. "You have to pay up front. Unless you show up on the day, in labor, I suppose then . . ."

"Oh, good, Ran, thank heavens for you." She'd always known he responded better to praise than to the idea of duty.

Ran realized he found it satisfying to be with someone as interested as he in their mutual children and grandchildren, not the case with Amy, though she tried to be.

"The person who could use some help is Donna. You could help there. She'd like to go to Thailand and look for Curt. I have a lot of time for Donna. How she sat there day after day after day by Curt's bedside," Ran said. "For instance if you stayed at her place and freed her up to go to Asia? She'd accept a grandmother staying with the twins a week or two. I'd ask Carla to give you a hand."

"Your wife gave them a huge sum of money! They could spring for a babysitter!" She heard how inappropriate this was as she said it. "Peggy is free. She should do it."

"Peggy isn't close to Donna, no one is, actually. Grandmotherly moral support would do wonders. Just for a couple of weeks."

Lorna stared. A second of familiar rage stirred, to do with Ran, their marriage, all those years in the past, when he failed always to see that her work was important, that she couldn't just drop it and move into someone's house and look after small children, even grandchildren. She was giving a lecture in Ann Arbor in two weeks; he had never understood that.

There was no point in mentioning it. "I'm afraid I have commitments," she said. She thought of Phil Train, of how he understood her professionalism. "Send Peggy."

Evidently some of Ran's memories covered the same territory. "Ah yes, you always have your work, so much more important." She felt he was going to add "than the family." That's what he would have said when they were married. How easy, from here, to slide into the fight; they could still enact their basic fight by rote; you never forget your lines. Here she says he thinks women's work is not important; he says she is a self-centered person. Repeat several times, with small paraphrases each time. He's a bully, she is vain and—always—both are egotistic monsters.

Today his accusation of self-centeredness had a fresh edge, like a newly sharpened knife she would test against her thumb at leisure and always draw blood. This time, instead of rejecting the accusation of self-centeredness—if only because it wasn't said explicitly this time—she was afraid he might be right. So what? She held her defenses in reserve. The time was over when women had to be weaned away from too much self-sacrifice, which in turn had given them chronic head-aches and unknown ailments, a time when "self-centeredness" was a term of reproach, to now when people talked about "me time" and encouraged people to look into their own hearts. Not that she believed in doing that, or in "me time"; she was too old for that.

Now, instead of righteous indignation, she had an unfamiliar stab of ambivalence. Maybe she was a self-centered person, like you had to be to get anywhere; but where was she? Was her work really more important than helping out a poor abandoned young woman and her lively twins? Or spending some time with poor Misty? Was she giving herself airs? No and yes. What was the boundary between healthy ego and monstrous self-centeredness?

Ran continued his attack, as if he too had a few things bottled up. "What are you doing back here anyway; career, whatever, at your age, is it sensible or even safe? You've obviously left the husband. Do you have any security? At your age, what are you expecting to happen? This is just plain silly."

Speechless, she reflected that he said "your age," not "our age." He, of course, had no worries. And men did not age. She held her tongue.

The dangerous moment passed. "Peggy is the one who should go to Thailand," she repeated finally, ignoring his diatribe. "She has nothing to do, so to speak, and she's devoted to Curt. It would be good for her. She needs a cause, some new thing in her life."

"Mention it to her, I'd help with it, Peggy is good at that kind of practical project," he agreed, seeing too clearly that their grown chil-dren were still a kind of moral connection drawing them together but not necessarily harmoniously.

"She has the problem with the thing she signed for a loan. Did she talk to you about that?"

"She doesn't talk to me much," Ran said. "She thinks I've always been on Dick's side, since I see him from time to time. I was sort of on Dick's side, never thought of him as gay, though."

"She signed with a loan shark, now she has to pay a larcenous amount of interest. She was trying to prepay her mortgage or something."

"Oh, Peggy. Well, tell her to send me the papers, I'll get my lawyer to look at them. My life is run by lawyers cleaning up life's gaffes these days."

He's a fat cat now, she thought; she couldn't hire a bank of lawyers to clean up her gaffes. "Yes. You still have your lordly, domineering way, you know." It slipped out before she knew it, but he didn't rise to it. They skirted contention again and continued their careful discussion, two people who were still rancorous.

"He might find some kind of clause," she agreed.

"About Curt, I was on the point of asking a Thai guy I know. Peggy should sell that damn silly little house," he added. "It's not going to appreciate. I'm going to talk to her about that."

"We had too many children too fast," Lorna said, suddenly. "We didn't enjoy them enough. It's nice you're getting a second chance with your new daughter."

He didn't know if she knew about Gilda's situation. Was she needling him in some way?

"People generally agree that grandparenthood is the chance you get to repair your sins of omission," Ran said.

"That's the cliché, but I don't believe it," said Lorna. "You have the one chance with your own children."

Ran, thinking of Gilda's pregnancy, would have liked to tell Lorna about it, but didn't.

Ran offered to drive her home, but she refused, said she'd walk, but she took the bus. Her thoughts were darker than her usually optimistic temperament permitted or the note of friendliness at the end of the reunion warranted. As she talked to Ran, a reality had clarified, and it was unwelcome: a woman alone, without a job or money, can barely manage her own autonomy, and can't help her children very much. So much of her life had always been predicated on her having a support system—male, in general, given the way society was presently constituted. Ran had at one time been her support, enabling the school and tuition and new shoes and things the children had needed.

In reality survival meant sellout, a tangle of dependence, as fragile as a spiderweb, or as strong as a spiderweb. She'd been so unwise, her whole life, and foolish now to think that because she'd written a book and given some lectures she had the power to help her kids or even keep herself in a halfway decent fashion. Silly.

These broody ruminations wouldn't go away but instead darkened to encompass sickness and death: life was wonderful, and then it was over. No one ever got around the sadness of that. She remembered Hams when he must have just figured out about death—he was about four, saying You're going to die, Mommy, and how she didn't say the unthinkable: And so are you, but not for a long, long time. But he knew, though only four years old.

How short the bliss of feeling immortal. Did Phil Train still have it, believing as he did in the life of the world to come? Presumably. She thought of the new babies—the baby Hams and the other one little Gilda would be having. Ran had stayed away from the subject of his other family and Gilda, and she shouldn't have mentioned her; probably she wasn't supposed to know anything about her.

Amid these thoughts, something happened getting off the Union Street bus; one of her legs, something, failed her as she stepped off the last step, and crumpled, landing her on her face, skinning both her knees and the palms of her hands, smashing them painfully against the pavement as she slid forward with the momentum of her fall. The woman who had got off the bus just ahead of her turned back to help her up and brush her off.

"Are you all right, dear?"

"Shaken," Lorna was able to say. "Shaken" barely described it. Her knees and the palms of her hands stung, and there was something wrong with her ankle, not a sprain, just a weak lameness. Had she tripped? Had she fainted? She felt the stares of the bus passengers behind the windows as it pulled off: Look, an old woman fell off the bus.

"Are you okay? Can you walk?"

"Yes, yes, thank you. I don't know what happened."

"I heard you crash. Let me help. Do you live near here?"

"A couple of blocks." Lorna looked up the daunting hill that led from Van Ness to Larkin. She couldn't walk; there was something wrong with her ankle.

"Look, you need to get those scrapes cleaned up," the woman went on, with an air of authority vaguely nurse- or doctorlike. She waved at a passing taxi and put Lorna into it before Lorna could collect her wits. Her rescuer climbed in, too, and directed the driver to take them to Saint Francis Hospital, only a few blocks away. There was no point in protesting the kindly but patronizing offer of help, reflecting the bene-factor's perception of Lorna's age; she could resent it later.

"I can't stay, but they'll look you over," the woman said, nodding to the taxi to wait for her. "Do you have insurance?"

"Oh yes," Lorna said, though of course she did not, her health insurance was in France.

The woman deposited her on a chair inside the emergency room and apologized for abandoning her there. After she left, Lorna weighed getting up and just leaving, too, but her one leg was strangely weak, though it didn't hurt, and it was true she didn't want the scrapes on her knees to get infected. Eventually a young intern saw to her: X-ray— she had torn, but not severed, an Achilles tendon. It could happen at any age, the intern reassured her. Tendon pulled, hence the fall. The sting of her knees being painted with antiseptic brought back the spe-cial nostalgia of childhood skinned knees. Why had the intern men-tioned age?

The worst of it was humiliation. Sprawling off the bus before the world, an old lady, Are you all right, dear? Your confidence in your own two legs is shaken; in your ability to keep upright, even; in the whole orientation of your body. And when she was discharged, them asking if she was okay to go home alone, was there someone there to care for her? Yes, yes, she had said, but of course there wasn't. The Chins. Or she could call Hams, but she wouldn't.

The ER desk summoned a taxi from the rank lurking across the street, and an orderly put her into it. "Keep your heel up," he said in a strong Russian accent; he was probably a doctor in his native land.

"Keep off it but keep the heel elevated, wear a shoe with a heel," he said, and handed her the paper on which this instruction was written.

"You don't bandage it? Something?"

"Nothing to do. Just keep the heel up."

Later she saw that the bill they pressed into her hand was six hundred dollars. "We can take something off that if you pay right now up front," the person at the desk told her.

"Six hundred? But—" She'd only been there forty minutes and had her knees daubed with Mercurochrome. In France they wouldn't have charged for it. Well, the X-ray. Had she needed it really?

"How much would you take off?" This was more curiosity than it was a plan.

"Thirty percent." Lorna realized that since she had no insurance, she'd better take the deal. She fished for her credit cards.

Once home, she hobbled into her apartment and to the sofa and propped her leg up. Only then did a worse pain set in. She sat there and tried to read the stuff she'd grabbed out of her mailbox, but the episode had shaken her, as she'd said when she fell off the bus. Her tendon had torn, but why had it torn? What sinister condition did this portend? What if she died alone in her mean little apartment? It wasn't impossible; people died. Found in their rooms after days, after people noticed something, or rang many times on the phone. It was more than humiliation, she didn't care about that, it was the sudden snap or twist, having your body betray you without warning. Where she had been high-stepping with life, she now felt the plunge, the crash, into reality.

As she sat there, Armand-Loup telephoned to discuss an idea he had about Russell, but didn't persist with once he heard her wan voice.

"Lo, *est-ce ça va?* You don't sound yourself."

Somehow the idea that there was someone who knew how she should sound brought tears, but she bravely said she was fine.

38

Nearly meeting death at their hands seemed to entitle Ursula to greater familiarity than before with the Motts, or it was clear she thought so; and her pronouncements did seem to them to carry a certain extra weight they couldn't explain. She became comfortable calling Amy to chat about Gilda and the Situation, or with dropping in to ask their advice about something. She thought her ideas for the baby's future would be better discussed in person, so about a week after her allergic reaction, she came to see them without Ian. She wafted in, enveloped as always in a certain scent both woodsy and floral—was it Calèche?

It was five o'clock. They had drinks in the garden, to the hum of bees, which reminded them all of the EpiPen incident. "Are we okay out here?" Ran asked. Ursula assured him she did not fear bees and now stayed far away from all shellfish. Gilda was staying late at school, which was just as well.

"I thought Gilda looked lovely the other night," Ursula said. "She's obviously feeling well. You would never know that she is . . ." She suddenly realized, with a chill, that perhaps Gilda wasn't, anymore.

But Amy nodded enthusiastically. "She seems thriving. Her diabetes is under good control. Ran is watching her meds carefully, and she's careful herself. We've found a doctor who specializes in diabetic pregnancy."

Ursula had known vaguely about Gilda's diabetes but not realized it bore mentioning and surveying, had not understood its seriousness. Her famously large and smoky eyes widened with expression—was it horror, earnest hope, concern? "I gather she's—going through with it?"

"No" and "Yes" the Motts said in chorus, and Ursula saw how it was.

"I'm against it for reasons of Gilda's health," Ran said, "but Amy and Gilda seem willing to run the risks." Which meant, Ursula saw, with relief, that Gilda was going through with it.

"Of course Ian and I want what is best, whatever is best. I hope Ian has told you he plans to step up, whatever is needed." It was awkward but true. "Play a role. Accept a role, I mean." The Motts looked reflective. Did they even want Ian to be involved? Ursula felt the chill again.

"Ian's starting at Stanford in August?" Ran asked. "Good. That's good. Amy and I both went to Stanford." He remembered too late that he had said this before.

"He'll be a junior," Ursula said, conscious that Stanford did not mean as much to her as to those who had attended it; in them it produced an emotion she could detect but not share. "They accepted almost all his credits, but there are core courses he'll still have to take."

"What's his major?" Amy asked.

"I'm not sure he has to declare one till he makes up the requirements," Ursula said evasively, not knowing the answer. Political science, was it? Psychology? Phys ed?

"I wanted to discuss with you my idea that it wouldn't be a bad thing for Gilda and Ian to get married. I know it's hardly ever done anymore, but I'm an old-fashioned person, I guess. A strong footing for the child. The young people would carry on with their schooling, of course, and eventually, well, who knows. Maybe a marriage wouldn't last forever, but it would be an adult way to start. Responsible and mature."

Shock registered on the faces of Amy and Ran. The idea of their child of fifteen being tied down to marriage was unthinkable. But of course she was going to be tied down to a child, unless some other solution presented itself. Their thinking had never progressed beyond the basic dilemma, nor had they chosen among the possible solutions—

adoption, someone else claiming to be its mother, the Motts acting as parents themselves, Julie . . . Ursula watched them carefully in hopes of divining their feelings, but they were inscrutable, and divided.

"Gilda will be sixteen next March," Amy said.

"Sixteen seems less drastic than fifteen," Ursula agreed, "but then it will be too late."

"No, it's unthinkable," said Ran. "We aren't hillbillies. You don't get married at sixteen, either."

"Quietly. I'm not talking about a big fancy wedding," Ursula said. The very idea of a big wedding seemed to upset them even more. Ran stood, paced around the room. Amy stared, pale.

"Out of the question. Gilda has her whole life ahead of her. Ian, too—he's how old?" Ran said.

"He'll be twenty-one next February."

"Demented," said Ran.

"Then what are you thinking, about the baby?" Ursula asked.

"We just don't know," Amy cried. "It could live here, there's Carla to help, or I thought Gilda could go somewhere with Ran's granddaughter Julie. She would miss a semester and then just be back—we'd say illness, maybe. We haven't discussed it with her, really, until we could have a coherent proposition."

"What are Ian's thoughts?" Ran asked, in a voice Ursula thought a little menacing.

"I'm not sure he's grasped the realities," Ursula admitted. Collectively, they despaired, but agreed that it was good that Ursula had come to talk it over, ice broken, subject become more comfortable.

As she left, Ursula asked, "Do we know if it's a boy or a girl?"

"She hasn't yet had the first ultrasound," Amy said. "Not till the beginning of the third month."

"I'll discuss marriage with the lawyers," Ran said. "It's either a bad idea or a good idea, they'll know." Though he had no intention to do any such thing.

"Of course only a technicality," Amy said. "It wouldn't have to last."

When Ursula had left, Ran and Amy discussed Gilda getting married. "I can somewhat see the point," Amy said. "The baby has a name, so to speak, no iffy episode for it to find out about later, respectably married parents, romantically young, like Romeo and Juliet. But Gilda goes on with her schooling, marriage would just be a technicality."

"And they live with us? No."

"No, no, they aren't a couple, nothing changes. I don't think they even know each other."

"That boy is not living with us. Or with Gilda, God knows."

"No, of course not, nothing changes."

Ran realized that he had ceased to argue the case for interrupting Gilda's pregnancy, and that Amy had dropped her token solidarity with him in favor of the unborn child, whose future reactions she was imagining, its satisfaction to find its parents were respectably wed. But there was still some hope of miscarriage, even a likelihood. Otherwise, he dreaded the sight he could imagine too well of his adored child swelling like a seedpod, her waddling gait as her pelvic ligaments loosened, her biochemistry off the charts . . .

Ran had dragged his feet about an ultrasound, despite the suggestions of Dr. Gill, Gilda's ob-gyn, who thought it should be done immediately. Ran feared that Amy and Gilda would be sentimental about the humanoid fetal outline, but now he accepted the inevitability and took Gilda himself to the facility in Palo Alto. His fears were realized: Gilda was delighted with the little printout of a smeary blob and declared herself scrupulously unwilling to know its sex, the way people in the olden days didn't know until the surprise at its birth. Accordingly, he suggested to Dr. Gill that he and Amy not be told, either, lest they betray it some way. Ursula was rather cross about this failure, and was hoping it would be a boy.

After endless discussions, weighing pros and cons, Ran and Amy reluctantly acceded to the idea of a city hall wedding some morning, the minimum just to get it recorded, with themselves and Ursula as witnesses, and maybe a passerby, just to emphasize the absence of significance and sentiment, just a nod to the requirements of society when it came to recording a new citizen. Amy's lawyers hastily prepared a prenup designed to disenfranchise Ian and especially Ursula as far as could be done from any share in Amy's money.

The form of her marriage didn't seem to matter to Gilda—she

had never been a girl who leafed through *Brides* magazine dreaming of her someday wedding or wrote down lists of children's names. "I don't want to marry Ian," she said when they brought up the idea. "I mean, nothing against Ian, I'm too young to get married. No." Since her parents agreed with her, they dropped the subject; but Ursula was not letting it go and came up with ever-more-inventive reasons why it was indispensable, or beneficial, or wise. She never told the Motts, even when they asked, what Ian thought about marriage. She had not asked him.

Ian was basically unaware of his mother's contrivances and thought the subject had propitiously gone away. He was too wrapped up in the lurid carnality of his affair with Julie—plus his studies and soccer—to wonder very often how Gilda was doing. What he did wonder was: Theoretically, how many times a day could a person have sex, given the luck of a long day alone with Julie in some private place? When Ursula finally told him he probably would be getting married to Gilda, he had no reaction but shock.

"Not for life, probably, but for the sake of the baby," Ursula said. "Gilda is an agreeable, pretty girl, after all."

"This is the most cynical and medieval thing I've ever heard of," Ian said. "You can't be serious."

"Think about it," said his mother. "It's in everyone's interest, Gilda included, I hope I don't have to spell out all the reasons why." Ian had a perverse wish to make her spell them out, make her confront the venal and empty foundation of the whole idea. Instead he pleaded a date and got away. He had seen from his studies that the history of the world attests to the number of bad ideas that nonetheless prevail, from inertia, from the absence of good counterarguments, from fanaticism or wrong convictions, from connivance and self-interest.

Thence the idea that Gilda and Ian should marry, fortified by centuries of tradition, prevailed over the common sense and financial puissance of Ran and Amy; they knew perfectly well that it was unwise to entangle Gilda legally, but they were also intimidated by Ursula's resolve, and by the absence of any good arguments against marriage they could admit to, and by the unconscious vestiges of their own belief in society's oldest conventions. After all, weren't they married themselves?

Just a quickie—city hall, a nice dinner, followed shortly by annulment, just to get something on the books. They all agreed on the formula, even, eventually, Gilda, when it was explained to her that she wouldn't actually have to live with Ian or perform any of the duties of a wife. At school they were reading the *Odyssey* in translation, and were starting Caesar in Latin, and she had decided to become a classicist; she was all wrapped up in that.

Soon there were modifications to the city hall plan, so that it wouldn't be a sordid or bad experience for the young people. Say have it in the Mott garden, early in August, family only, and they'd ask the Very Reverend Phil Train, who was aware of the situation, to officiate. Neither Ian nor Gilda paid attention, but neither raised a fuss, either, which worried Amy and Ran. The only one who was horrified by it all was Julie, when Ian told her what was in store for him. It fell on her like a curse of God. In her heart she had imagined she herself would marry Ian someday.

"Ian, you can't do it, you don't love her, you're still in college, what about us?" She had millions of arguments, millions of words like this, and inexhaustible tears.

"Not really a marriage. More like a legal arrangement. We won't be living together or anything like that."

Julie felt her misery deepen to an omnipresent bass note in her life, like the low note of the baroque continuo. Her life was in chaos already. With some help from Ran, she had finally got the money for a place in the Peace and Conflict Studies program in Athens, but had just about decided not to accept it, because she couldn't give up the biological compulsions that now defined her whole being—Ian. Her biggest problem until now was how to tell Grandpa Ran she didn't need the tuition he had handsomely agreed to pay. Luckily she hadn't yet officially resigned from Peace and Conflict and could still go drown herself in the Aegean or jump into a crater. Her misery, she knew, was shared by Ian, but his sense of duty was ingrained, too.

"How can I not? The facts are there. It would just be, you know, on paper . . ."

Julie had her ideas about men and what they would expect to do when alone with their wives, however ill sorted a couple they were. She didn't mention this to Ian, didn't want to put ideas in his head.

"You have to tell them you won't."

"But, Julie, it's my fault. I can't not." These sentiments were repeated over and over, the scenes escalated, then ended in tears, and then sex, and then, alone at night, more tears as Julie foresaw the end for all time of her happiness. She made Ian promise they would still make love at their present rate. She tried not to hate Gilda, but she did, hated her privilege, her beautiful house, her silver hair, her unconsidered sense of entitlement.

"Where will they live?" Ursula asked the Motts one day, assuming the young couple would live at the Mott house in Woodside. The Motts had not thought this through, either. Amy and Ran didn't even have to discuss the unthinkable idea of Ian and Gilda living together, and all that implied. Fifteen years old! Ran at last said that Gilda would continue living at home, of course. He didn't say he didn't give a fuck what happened to Ian, but he wasn't living with Gilda or them. He didn't have to say this; it was clear.

"A young married couple not living together?" Ursula said. "That would be odd." Seeing their expressions, Ursula's mind whirled. Was the marriage not to be consummated? Was it that the young couple wouldn't . . . didn't a baby constitute proof of consummation already? The whole plan seemed so—so unnatural, and yet did she really want to think of Ian condemned to live in a student apartment with a spoiled, indifferent young teen he barely knew? She had a vision of the student apartment in South Palo Alto or Menlo Park, the bride cooking really terrible meals, she herself invited to eat with them, lending a hand so that poor Ian wouldn't starve.

"After all, they aren't a couple," Amy said, agreeing with Ran. "We think Gilda could stay in school and finish the fall quarter at least. If she transferred to a school on the quarter system she could finish the September-to-Christmas term; we just haven't found the school. We're thinking abroad."

. . .

Realistic concerns reasserted themselves and Julie had changed her mind about refusing Greece; she would go after all, and when she had thanked her grandfather for his help with the tuition, it prompted in him the idea that abroad might be the answer for Gilda, too. Greece might do. Julie would be there, it was an advanced nation but without the shared cultural assumptions of, say, England, where people could all too easily read the stigmatizing implications of a young pregnant woman, seemingly single and far from home. For all the Greeks knew, it might be quite normal for Anglo-Saxon females to await motherhood familiarizing themselves with the Acropolis and reading the *Iliad* in translation with some cultivated Greek.

"We're in the process of consulting a woman in Palo Alto who specializes in placing students in foreign schools—sabbatical families and so on. She thinks she can find something appropriate," Amy said.

So—they were planning to send Gilda discreetly away. With this, Ursula saw her hopes fade of getting any help from Ran and Amy with Ian's Stanford nightmare extortionate tuition of fifty thousand dollars. She renewed her mental resolve to track down Pud Aymes and put pressure on him to help with his son's education. Why should she pay it all? Pud had been good about money when Ian was at Brown, but then one of his ventures—a silver mine?—had gone wrong. She had heard he had stayed in Argentina.

Mrs. Thurber, the educational adviser, made inquiries in several directions, describing the special conditions under which a nice California girl from an affluent family would be needing a semester or quarter of high school in the tenth grade with the possibility of returning after a hiatus in the winter term. There was one complication that ought to be mentioned . . .

Finally, Greece was not to be. In the end, Mrs. Thurber found a reassuring-sounding school in France, outside of Paris, in Saint-Cloud: Saint Ann's British School. "Students will wear the uniform and follow the standard British curriculum and will sit the IGCSE examinations as a prequalification for British university and excellent academic preparation for the International Baccalaureate (IB) programme."

The idea of France was more reassuring than Greece to Ran; he knew several doctors there and after medical school had taken a *stage* in Paris on psoriasis with the famous *dermatologue* Rene Dubuque; and he had few worries about French obstetrics if something happened prematurely. If all went well, she would be coming home for the delivery, but if not, after all, France's medicine was superior to that of the United States. If WHO statistics were to be believed, the U.S. had the worst maternal mortality in the industrialized world.

Saint Ann's British School had had to be convinced and paid extra to accept a pregnant girl and made clear it would never have done so had Gilda not been married, though it was also against their policy to accept married women, the legacy of a time when schoolteachers had presumably been virgins, when marriage implied knowledge of certain intimate things and conveyed a certain stain their students would feel clung to their teacher.

But this was the modern era, and in today's world, as married Mrs. Aymes she could not cause dismay. Curiosity maybe: If she was a wife, why wasn't she at home somewhere being a wife? Was she a widow? A tragic scenario involving a military conflict? In some cultures, her age would not surprise; also the girl was American; and also, money talks.

Ursula, who had never had a daughter, indulged her wish for one by projecting onto Gilda some of her idea of the fun of dressing a girl; and a wedding dress was the summit of maternal thrill. Of course she knew Gilda wouldn't be wearing white or a veil—the ceremony would be low-key in the Motts' garden with no one there—but Gilda should have a pretty dress at least. Ursula wasn't sure about Amy Mott's degree of interest in clothes or even whether she was really in her heart behind their collective decision about the marriage, but she included Amy in the invitation to go dress shopping and, to her surprise, Amy accepted.

Amy and Gilda drove up to the city and met Ursula at the appointed hour in the designer dress department of Saks. There was a bridal department, too, but they didn't want anything overtly brideish. Ursula found a little irritating Amy's condescending air of being too fine for shopping, of never having been in Saks before, of always buying her clothes in Paris, or—judging from her clothes—not being interested in fashion at all. Which of these things accounted for her withdrawn silence, Ursula couldn't decide. Maybe it was just her dismay at the circumstances, but Amy was saying very little, forcing Ursula into a real-estate saleswoman mode of bright encouragement as they rifled the racks and Ursula tried to divine what both Gilda and Amy were feeling, about the wedding, the baby, Ian, herself. Ursula found it hard to imagine that Gilda wasn't delighted to be marrying her handsome son, but she was beginning to see the truth.

At least Gilda was interested in the dresses like a normal girl, though her choices—the ones she chose to call to the attention of her mother and Ursula—were a bit *jeune fille;* of course she was a *jeune fille.*

"Blue? That's not a bit too bridesmaidy?" said Ursula. They had spurned the advances of the saleswoman, but when the woman kept hovering, Ursula brought her into the situation, explaining Gilda would be attending "a summer wedding in a garden," not mentioning, of course, that this child was the bride.

"What colors do you like, Gilda? You probably could wear any color," the saleswoman agreed. "Your own—um—neutral coloring . . ."

"I think I look good in black, but I guess that wouldn't be appropriate." Gilda said. Amy and Ursula exchanged an anguished glance to think of how close to the surface Gilda's feelings were.

"This is a mostly cotton dimity." The saleswoman brought out a floating, longish dress in a shade between gray and lavender, sprigged with little green flowers. "Cool and pretty. It has a little polyester to keep it crisp."

"Okay, that's great," Gilda said. "Thanks."

"Try it on!" said the saleswoman, and tyrannically led Gilda to the dressing room, scandalized that the girl hadn't meant even to see how it looked on her. Aura of shotgun here. Gilda came out to show her mother and Ursula; it did fit and suited her well enough, a little frilly but adequately bridal. Amy paid for it; but both Ursula and, apparently, Amy too felt the anticlimax of Gilda accepting the first dress she was shown. Gilda was thinking of the child brides of Africa, being decked out and painted red by bangled relatives in turbans who led them to their sacrifice.

Amy didn't keep her next appointment, one she had made with Adoption Services of San Francisco. One detail had not been addressed, the most difficult of all: What was to become of the baby? Ursula, it was clear, believed/hoped that the Motts would raise it, while she, one of its grandmothers, would pitch in with birthday parties and movie days. Ran would not hear of Amy's similar plan; the baby was not coming to live with them. It would be a constant reproach to Gilda, and a subject of curiosity and gossip with all who knew them. The possibility of Carla claiming to be its mother, or even Amy herself, came up again and again, but Carla let it be known she was unwilling to shock and horrify her Catholic parents, let alone look after it. They discussed Julie, but didn't ask her directly. Of course they could just face it down, let people talk.

Gilda seemed indifferent to where the baby would live, and the more Amy thought about it, in fairness to the innocent newborn, it seemed imperative that they would take pains to find it a more attentive home. Amy broached the matter with Phil Train and with Gilda's doctors. Ministers and doctors heard of cases, situations, opportunities— somebody's baby dies, they need another to fill the empty cradle and mend the broken heart. Virtuous childless couples, too old to qualify at adoption agencies but loving and solvent. For the moment, neither Phil nor the doctors had any prospects.

Amy, surreptitiously to avoid upsetting Ran and, for different reasons, Gilda, had begun discreet inquiries about adoption agencies. Amy quickly understood that public—civic or state—services were constrained by rules outlawing things like race or income.

She read the websites of adoption agencies, looking for ones that maybe had a minimum income requirement and a high education stipulation. This she did not find. She did find that fathers had rights of custody above all if they were married to the mother, or if they had put their paternity in writing, and if they hadn't abused the child or committed any of the revolting felonies detailed in the statutes. Did they have to fear that Ian Aymes would exercise his rights to take, or at least see the baby? What about Ursula?

The websites did let you see videos about potential parents; you could sort by religion, race, job, region. Would she like the baby's parents to be like her and Ran or unlike them in some adventurous way? She looked at one or two families, the ones who emerged when she put down her and Ran's own characteristics: white Episcopalians who worked in IT (her) or biotech (Ran). Smiling younger faces came up, characterizing themselves as liking to do all the things she and Ran liked to do: ski, read, concerts, travel. Fawn and Rick. Davia and Matt. Were she and Ran issued from the same cookie cutter in the sky as these people?

Would not a biracial couple, testimony to a certain amount of free-spirited independence, be better? Artists? Circus performers? None of the videos discussed people's reading habits.

She dropped the California and Episcopalian requirements, ran the program again, this time found more possibilities—fatter, sweeter people—a wrestling coach in Kansas and his choir director wife; Merry and Tom in Florida. Tom was Chinese. All the couples said the same things, about how much they loved kids, struggled with fertility, longed for a baby, all the fun they'd have. "Though we are not religious, per se, we value the ethical principles of Western civilization and the Golden Rule," wrote Jeffrey and Karen.

There were different ways of handing over the baby—at the hospital without the mother ever seeing it, letting her have it for a few days to adjust her milk; there was a time period she had during which she could change her mind. Adoption agents would be present at every meeting, by law.

Amy saw that official adoption was not for them, not for her, and not for Gilda, at least not via bureaucracy and websites. That still left the question: What to do with the baby? But they still had months for something to suggest itself.

39

A course of action once decided, the sooner the better.

The coming Saturday was chosen for the wedding, accommodating Phil Train's need to be at a church convocation in Denver the following week. Amy couldn't bring herself to think about a lunch or drinks for the dozen or so people who would have to be invited, counting Gilda's half siblings Peggy and Hams and Misty; Donna; Ian's aunt Renny—Pud Aymes's sister—who lived in Wyoming; Phil Train, of course, and Carla. Would it be cute to have Marcus and Manuel as ring bearers?

For Amy and Ran, the whole thing was terrible, the ruin of their hopes for Gilda—hopes until now not even consciously formed. They had always had the expectation of an unusual destiny for her, the reward of her physical calvary; and she had so far seemed not to disappoint. Her intelligence and poise had always testified to her promise. But what would happen to her now? This marriage was a denouement, not a beginning. Not a happy ending, a tragedy. Why were they doing it to her? They couldn't explain the vestigial docility that was making them make her conform to the world's belief in marriage.

On the Friday, the day before the wedding, Ursula showed up with a box of white cloth napkins from Gump's—as if Amy didn't have napkins—some silver saltshakers, and a wrapped present, also from

Gump's. This jarred Amy into a discussion with Carla about what they ought to be serving; she'd given it no thought. Champagne for sure, Carla objected, and some fancy sandwiches, not a real lunch. Or should they sit down to a real lunch? Ran, intruding, thought certainly sit down to something nice for lunch; as long as they were at it, nothing should be halfway. Important that they look back on it with pleasure, or at least not shame. There should be nothing bad to remember; that was the main consideration. He imagined the baby in later years looking at its parents' wedding pictures, and it was important that the photographs be free of that retrospective *tristesse* that patinates old images in hindsight. He realized he'd fallen into Amy's way of thinking.

Photographs? That required a photographer. Normally at family events, Carla skulked around with an iPhone, but tomorrow she'd be too busy. Maybe they should skip the photos, which could be thought of as endorsements. The same with music, but maybe a few notes of *Lohengrin* all the same?

"Out of the question," Amy snarled.

The day was fine; no one had worried about the California weather or made alternate plans for rain, though there were uncharacteristic clouds. The brief ceremony would be at 11:00 a.m., and Phil Train came at about ten to have coffee with Ran and Amy and try to cheer them a little with the idea that society's (and God's) designated forms preserved those aspects of human existence worth preserving, and by acceding to them, even with whatever reservations, they were helping civilization along.

Gilda stayed in her room until it was time. She would have liked one or two of her friends to be there, but everyone had firmly nixed it. Julie was invited but said she was down with the flu. Only Carla was cheery. She did Gilda's hair into a fat, shining braid and zipped up the dress and seemed over the moon about the whole thing.

Gilda understood her parents' general air of false cheer and felt it herself; she certainly didn't want to get married but would be polite about it. She knew she didn't have to go off anywhere alone with Ian afterward, and that was a relief, but she also felt slightly sick to her stomach. She heard the tires on the gravel of the parking area, probably the Aymeses.

She still stayed in her room. At a little before eleven Carla came in and hugged her. "Your dad's out there—there'll be a ten-yard wedding march from the lanai to the gazebo, what do you think of a few strains of Mozart?"

Gilda wondered where Amy was. She could hear Ursula, Ian, and another voice, perhaps Ian's aunt, greeting the Reverend Train. She could hear Carla taking them through the garden to the little gazebo where Ian and the Reverend Train were to stand. Finally Amy came in and hugged her. Gilda noticed that her mother's eyes were red and swollen.

Outside, standing in the garden with Ian, Ursula thought the Motts were getting on with things a little precipitately; they were not in the right spirit. She looked around for Amy, who soon came out of the house with Gilda. This also didn't seem quite in the spirit; Gilda ought to be concealed somewhere, then emerge on Ran's arm to the strains of a wedding march.

Gilda and Ian nodded to each other in a cousinly fashion. The dress looked pretty on her, Ursula thought, but in the sunlight its ambiguous color was maybe a little too gray, not flattering with her pallor. The girl had a determined look, and a polite, self-conscious smile. Ursula kissed her. Amy led them the few steps through the lanai to the garden, and Carla put on some music. It all seemed lacking in some sense of occasion, seemed peremptory, nothing you could put your finger on, but sort of atheist intellectual and Soviet. Carla led Ian off to stand by the Reverend Train, and Amy went to find Ran, without any of them knowing why these ceremonial forms were prevailing over their inner reluctances and general dislike for what they were up to.

Ran could hardly dissemble. His eyes were filled with tears; but he took Gilda's arm and they moved from the lanai into the garden to the strains of the overture to *Figaro,* a walk of a minute or two toward the gazebo through the blooming roses and peonies and new hydrangeas and an unexpected efflorescence of blue dahlias, hard to grow in Woodside, that seemed just to have appeared to line the path like courtiers or police officials. Something blue. Ran and Gilda did not keep time to the music but plunged along the few paces toward Gilda's fate.

Ian's personal beauty, new blue blazer, and serious mien reassured Amy and Ran, as did the gentle, understanding smile of Phil Train, standing next to Ian, welcoming them and mentioning Holy Matrimony, as his role obliged. Ursula had written out a simple, formulaic vow which no one had objected to, now to be recited by Ian and Gilda.

"I, Ian Geoffrey Pearson Aymes, do take you, Gilda Jennifer Honor Mott, as my wedded wife to have and to hold till death do us part."

"I, Gilda Jennifer Honor Mott, do take you, Ian Geoffrey Pearson Aymes, as my wedded husband to have and to hold till death do us part."

No lightning came down to strike them. Phil Train pronounced them husband and wife with the authority vested in him; there was an exchange of gold bands, Ian gave Gilda a brief, correct kiss, and that was it. A low sob came from someone; people often cry at weddings.

Afflicted by a strange paralysis of will, Amy had had recourse to caterers for the dozen people for lunch. Carla had a lot to do as it was, so they just ordered in the cold salmon, salad, asparagus, and cake, leaving a happier impression of hospitality than had the tense faces at the brief ceremony. Gilda, from long experience of being the sprightly child at her parents' gatherings, reverted to that mode and seemed to forget that she was the bride. Ian didn't lose his solemnity but did talk to Amy and Ran about general subjects and soccer. He called Ran "sir." Seated next to her new husband at the lunch, Gilda told him briefly about the school her parents had found for her in Saint-Cloud, France, where she'd be going in a few weeks. This momentarily stunned Ian, who was dismayed enough about Julie's planned absence, but relieved him when he thought about it.

"It should be great," he agreed.

After lunch, and coffee in the garden, Ian left with his mother and aunt, with handshakes and smiles all around and a chaste kiss for Gilda, and Gilda went to her room to change out of her dress and take off the ring. When she was gone, Amy broke down a little and cried for a few seconds into Ran's lapels.

40

Harvey Avon had been impressed with Curt's wife; she seemed nice and also smart, understanding what he was talking about when he clarified a few of Curt's ideas for her. Since she was the nominal owner of Curt's stake in Mott Development, her grasp and cooperation were propitious. She seemed to have heard about some of their holdings from Curt, who was apparently not one of those husbands who kept his work at the office, and she had expressed an interest in keeping a finger in the pie, not merely accepting the income but involving herself in the management decisions. This could have been a pain in the ass, but Avon, who might have simplified his presentation for most women, saw she could understand the full complexity of their situation. She seemed especially knowledgeable about the hydroponic software they had developed, and was interested in Avon's plans to expand it to the brick-and-mortar phase, specifically installing a small test facility somewhere near Colma, where he had bought land.

"Tell me more about what Curt owes and the value of his shares now," she asked. Believing in Curt's vision, she figured that if only she had some money, she could follow it up. His ventures would repay further investment. She was captivated by Curt's—and Avon's—imaginative range. She was impressed by Avon, and also had her own good ideas about applications for the plant material Curt's hydroponic unit would produce in shimmering vertical strings of saladlike leaves.

"I'll get the financial statements to you," Avon said, wondering why he hadn't approached her before. "Curt's father doesn't seem that willing to get involved."

"I don't know that he controls the purse strings at his house," Donna said. "Who else do you have on board?" He gave her the several names, including her former brother-in-law Dick Willover. Only after he'd gone did Donna think of one way of getting some capital, taking out a second mortgage on her free and clear house. She'd talk to the bank about it, and then ask for some of Avon's practical smarts for getting her ideas about plant protein into production.

Later she also consulted Amy, who understood investment and banking issues, and who seemed almost maternally pleased with Donna's grasp of her business situation, though not surprised, since Donna did have an MBA. But in the end, Donna was unable to get a loan on the house, now deemed dangerously overvalued—an ominous indicator of the problems that seemed to be looming in the economy in general.

Despite this, Mott Development thrived. Donna was almost unprepared for the speed with which money began to pour in, jolted forward by a remarkable event, a huge investment by a firm in Bahrain that had learned about Mott Development innovations at an agro-tech fair in Singapore. That location, Singapore, when they learned of it, gave them hope that it had been Curt himself at the agro-tech fair, and it revived their notion of beginning there to look for him, picking up the trail from the fair, Singapore hotels, and airline records.

The money came from start-up investors—Willover, Donna, Harvey Avon, Amy, and a few others, but within months also from the profitability of the product, this gooey plant protein extracted and distilled from ropes of sparkling green leaves dangling above the hydroponic vats in Colma. Donna drove down to look at them twice a week like a responsible entrepreneur, and more than once dusted or dabbed with her hankie at specks that had fallen on the spotless stainless-steel tanks. She interviewed, or was interviewed by, manufacturers of food products, plastics, toys, and vending machines, all exploring uses for her nourishing protoplasmic blobs of green stuff. Simple as it was to produce, she and Harvey Avon, and their maintenance guy, Juan, couldn't even meet the demand. She and Harvey began talking it over at dinners and, later, in bed.

The summer did not bring much change to Gilda's silhouette, slightly disappointing and slightly relieving her. She insisted on going to diabetes camp as usual in the middle of August, against the strenuous objections of her father, and no one but the director even knew her condition. "I'm not going to let this ruin my life," she insisted. She hung out with her friends in Woodside and read *War and Peace* and the orations of Demosthenes, and some Greek plays in line with her plan to do classics someday. She and Ian never spoke, not for any special reason, they just had nothing to say, but exchanged some laconic emails.

Ian tried not to think about his basic life situation, facing a new, notoriously demanding educational institution in the fall, hoping to continue with soccer there (time consuming), and with two women—one an actual wife, though in name only, the other hot and in need of a lot of sexual attention—three women if you counted his mother, who required phone calls and dinner at least once a week, and he had no money. How quickly things had evolved from just the beginning of the summer, when he lived peaceably in Mountain View and took classes and played soccer with other guys.

August drew on. In the cemetery of Pont-les-Puits the work of the forensic analysts was nearly done, and preparations began for a reburial celebration to be held early in the New Year, which left time to get in touch with all the descendants, find donors for the cost of processing the bones still unclaimed, and organize the wine and food, which was to be elaborate and revive or maintain the culinary reputation of the town. Famous chefs had been recruited from America and England as well as France.

Armand-Loup consulted again the Woods papers in the *mairie*, studying the artist's words about selling his works, and especially the role assigned to Lorna. He went over the passage a number of times and came to a new conclusion, that not only was Lorna to get a fee for selling the village's Woods painting, she was to become in effect Woods's agent for future dealings, the actual transactions to be conducted by the guy in Chicago, but with a cut for Lorna if she found buyers. He was glad about this, some income for Lorna, not only because it took the heat off of himself, but from genuine goodwill. His thoughts warmed tenderly at the recollection of his visit to her drab San Francisco apartment, her looking so distracted, and her hair so different; she could use some money. He missed her. He brought his discovery about the legalities to Mayor Barbara Levier, who promised to investigate. Madame Dumas, *très bien*! It would come as a relief to them all if someone took charge of the pictures still stored at the hotel and dealt with the encroaching PR demands of Woods's posthumous career.

In Woodside, Julie, Gilda, and Carla prepared for the fall semester in France, in a suburb of Paris where it was unlikely Gilda would meet anyone they knew. Ran and Amy had convinced Julie to shift focus, giving up Greece and Peace and Conflict, and she was now enrolled, at their expense, in Global Cities, Urban Realities, also a UC Berkeley program, but in Paris, which they assured her was more useful and prestigious in the long run, and situated conveniently in the Parisian seventh arrondissement, where she along with Carla would be able to keep an eye on Gilda.

The young women were intensely excited at their prospective adventure, though Julie's feelings were mixed: she expected to miss Ian, but she had positive memories of France from childhood visits to Grandma Lorna when Lorna lived in the big house in the French village and they had had amazing roast-pig feasts and a man came in and cooked for them all—pie was what she remembered best. Carla had never been abroad, and she was apprehensive, foreseeing her inability to speak French, getting lost, and catching giardia and other untreatable stomach bugs from the undrinkable water.

. . .

On the website ParisChezVous, Amy had found an apartment in Neuilly for Carla and Gilda, and large enough for three now that Julie could commute from the seventh. Amy flew with them to Paris to settle them in. They allowed a few days before school began to enjoy the Louvre, the Musée d'Orsay, the Bateaux Mouches gliding around the islands in the Seine. The apartment was more than acceptable, a roomy Haussmannian place with carved mahogany furniture and an iron-grilled elevator, and lumpy beds with thin mattresses. Gilda had to buy school uniforms, which she got prudently overlarge at Carla's suggestion. Carla was to cook dinners and was enrolled in a language course at the Alliance Française during the day. They bought a blackboard and put it up in the kitchen to keep everyone's schedules straight, and conjugate French verbs on.

Ran's old friend the French physician Xavier Karas—they were in medical school together—had been contacted to oversee Gilda's health while she was in France. In Paris, she had agreed to a weekly visit to Dr. Karas, who wasn't an obstetrician but could monitor her situation, with his colleague the ob-gyn guy Olivier de Panapieu standing by in case something went wrong. Amy, usually comfortable with foreign travel, was beset by images of dreaded European germs menacing Gilda and the fetus, though she gallantly controlled her anxieties and didn't mention them to the travelers.

Gilda's new school, Saint Ann's British School, was in Saint-Cloud, twenty minutes to the west of central Paris. As an American and pregnant, Gilda was conscious of her outsider status at Saint Ann's and didn't expect to make friends. Her schoolmates, mostly daughters of English businessmen in Paris for a year or two, some French girls perfecting their English, and some random Greeks and Lithuanians, were friendly nonetheless, as far as it went, and her teachers seemed to like her even if she was behind in a few subjects. The school allowed for Americans always being behind. Yet it was odd and disagreeable to be called Mrs. Aymes in class where the rest of the girls were called by their names: Vèronique or Hélène or Marigold. Gilda wondered, if she had been permitted to go on at Saint Waltraud's, would they have stopped calling her Gilda and switched to Mrs. Aymes?

But apart from that, Gilda had never been so happy, so enraptured with the romance of history. Everything Parisian thrilled her—the statues in the Louvre, the old-timey carpets in the halls of her building, the buckled sidewalks where the roots of ancient trees pushed up. She had discovered there were concerts and paintings in churches, no matter which one, though they were all Catholic; she took to going into any old church to see what she would find. She loved a composer named Pergolesi whom she and Carla heard at Saint-François de Marie-Rose. Above all, she was amazed to see how many churches there were, and how old, and how beautiful. She got interested in the tombs within them, their half-effaced inscriptions hard to read, sometimes topped with carven effigies—sometimes in armor! Sometimes the effigies were naked, to symbolize how you came into the world and left it. She began to feel that her parents, though loving and intelligent, were not especially tuned in to all this, and neither was Saint Waltraud's. Californians were not as cultivated as Europeans were.

For her whole life, she had had to allow for her physical condition, so pregnancy was just one more pathology she could cope with by ignoring it as much as possible. Sometimes it rushed in on her that this Paris idyll would end, she would have to go back to America and be a mother, whatever they decided to do with the baby. Whereas the idea of a baby had pleased her at first, she had begun to regret it and put it out of her mind as much as she could. By the end of September, she still didn't show too much; she just looked thicker. She loved it here. Maybe she could come back after—afterward.

Carla, too, was in heaven, entranced by the foreignness, all the people blithely, guiltlessly smoking, the lovely wine, above all not having to get in a car and tool endlessly back and forth on Highway 280 between Woodside and San Francisco. She felt dumb at French but didn't care—it was pretty close to Spanish—table, *tabla, table,* no big deal. *Je* instead of *yo.* Easy. Some French words were better—*je suis désolée,* for example, was a wonderful phrase, more expressive than *lo siento.* Desolate.

Julie hated Paris; she was on hold; this was a break from real life. She didn't like not being able to speak the language and thought knowing about the many kings all called Louis didn't seem useful to her future life. She hated the smoking, hated cheese, missed Ian and lovemaking—the latter not something she could discuss with Gilda and Carla, who had no idea she had seen Ian more often than meeting a time or two for casual lunch. And now the love of her life was three thousand miles away. She and Ian had long, passionate conversations on FaceTime about when they could be reunited. They never discussed that he was married now, and Julie tried not to think about that. "I love you, I love you," she sobbed at night into her pillow as silently as possible, so the others couldn't hear.

41

Lorna's lecture at the San Francisco Museum of Modern Art on the painter Meissonier was to be September 15. She gave herself a lot of trouble over it, found herself nervous, fussed over what to wear, and reviewed her projection images more times than usual. Her talk was in a way radical. In the late nineteenth century amid the newfound admiration for Impressionism, the painstaking realism of Meissonier's renditions, say of the tiniest details of the bridles of Napoleonic soldiers' horses, had been savagely taken against; realism was out, and he had been thrust from the ranks of artists whom it was acceptable to admire. His statue was dragged out of the Louvre. She couldn't find out what happened to it. From being the painter whose canvases had commanded the highest price per square inch the world had ever heard of, he was cast away as rubbish, though if you had a Meissonier you of course held on to it. Lorna had perfected her account of him, where he might be put back in place, and updated her theories about the transition to Impressionism generally. In Lorna's view, his moving little canvas in the Louvre, of bodies on the barricades during the 1870 Commune, showed signs of Impressionism creeping into his work.

At the reception after her lecture, Lorna had occasion to ask the director, Marina Box, if she would like to see Pont-les-Puits's Woods, in case the museum might be interested in acquiring it, and Mrs. Box eagerly said yes.

Lorna had learned from simple Internet research that the village of Pont's Woods would be worth around seven hundred thousand dollars, and she had also been told, though she discounted it, that she herself, according to the terms of Woods's instructions, would have a small fee for her trouble finding a buyer. Real art galleries would take as much as half of a painting's value, but Russell had frugally designated ten percent as a reasonable sweetener for his old friend's efforts, and to Lorna even that was an amazing windfall. She was not above some commercial calculation, but she also knew that the museum would pay what it was correct to pay. Beside the older grandes dames it had a canny board of yuppie MBAs and McKinsey alumni who might not know much about art but knew about prices.

Though the lecture had on the whole been a success, with the reservations she had felt in Bakersfield, she mistrusted her own understanding of the audience, or what interested people now. Looking out at the polite, attentive faces, she had seen, or rather, felt, their provisional commitment, their basic indifference to nineteenth-century painting, to France maybe, even to art itself—was that possible, given that they were all patrons of this art museum?

Even more clearly than at the lecture to the Altar Forum, she saw that all was over: she was over, and so was the lecture, or at least her own powers of animating this nineteenth-century genre of performance in the twenty-first century, was over. She felt empty with shock but didn't resist this revelation. She would have to adapt, soldier on, but how, in what direction in a country she no longer understood.

Ran and Lorna had run into each other downtown twice, so that it got to seem almost normal to see each other, even to feel a kind of comfort in their shared concerns. Today Ran was arriving and Lorna was just leaving Hams's after one of her visits. Ran politely stood with her a minute as she waited for her taxi.

"During Curt's coma I always made sure to avoid you," Lorna said, meaning long-divorced people running into each other in family crises. "It's nice that we can talk now." Each thought of Curt—how he had survived his coma but was lost, apparently, to them.

"We have a lot of hostages to fortune, don't we?" he said. Meaning she and he together? Mankind in general? Lorna had always worried by herself, but of course Ran must worry, too, and there was collegial comfort in them worrying together. It was hard to remember them being in bed together, though.

"Maybe you knew about my other daughter, with Amy," Ran suddenly went on. "You must have heard about her from Peggy or Julie?"

"Yes, of course. How old is she now? Your daughter. Fifteen, sixteen?"

"Sixteen in March. She's in school in France. Julie's over there, too, of course."

Lorna didn't know if she was supposed to know about Gilda's pregnancy, so she changed the subject without learning what Ran meant to bring up: "According to Peggy, she—Julie—is very brokenhearted over someone she left behind here."

"I don't know about Julie's affairs of the heart," Ran said. "I expect she'll meet some nice Frenchman."

They recognized simultaneously that this remark could also have described Lorna, who had met some nice Frenchman all those years ago, although well after she and Ran were definitively on the rocks.

"I wish Peggy would meet someone," Lorna said. She had a flurry of thoughts: she would have liked to see a photo of Gilda (what a name!) but hesitated to ask. Was Gilda smarter or as pretty as their granddaughter Julie? Or as Peggy had been?

Her thoughts flew to Peggy: Peggy might meet someone if she dressed better. Maybe she could pay Ursula to diagnose Peggy's wardrobe, Ursula always looked magnificent. Not that meeting someone was the be-all and end-all. Women had to forget that formula; Peggy needed a more interesting life. How clear things became when one reached a certain age.

·   ·   ·

In Woodside, Ran and Amy began preparations even before Thanksgiving for Gilda's return at Christmas and the baby's birth in March. The baby would be born; it by now existed, unnamed, but a person, unthinkable to dislodge. Amy especially now thought of little else. They would put the bassinet in Gilda's room with her, but it could be rolled into the adjacent room and be with the baby nurse when Gilda needed sleep—the nurse would sleep in the nanny's old room, which they repainted. Was there something punitive about planning to insist that Gilda take care of her baby through the night? Maybe, but examining their feelings, they didn't think so; it was more a concern for the well-being of the baby. In China the baby slept in bed with its parents for months. When Gilda was born, she slept in a basket at the foot of Ran and Amy's bed. Amy had not been parted from her for a second.

Amy had flown to and from Paris three times since the girls had been there, and thus had been monitoring Gilda's increasing size, keeping her in smart loose-fitting fashions when not at school; Saint Ann's cooperated to the extent of permitting her to wear her uniform blouses untucked. Gilda had insisted on playing field hockey until early November when she became conscious she was getting slow and becoming a liability to her side. Now when the baby moved inside her, she felt scared and invaded, and hated it.

About Gilda's pregnancy, Ran had researched the incidence of birth defects in babies of diabetic mothers: even in those like Gilda with good glycemic control and folic acid supplementation, malformations were three to twelve times more frequent than in normal pregnancies. There was also an increased frequency in very young mothers. With these statistics, it was almost a certainty that something would go wrong. He kept tight watch on any changes in Gilda's physiology in case it did. Her numbers were faithfully reported to him by Dr. Karas and by Gilda herself. And they began to worry him. He and Amy decided to go to Paris during Gilda's end-of-term break, maybe take the girls for a few days somewhere nice in the South of France.

42

Lorna was to take the Woods canvas to the museum for study by the board members, their experts, conservators, and financial people. This she did, wrapping it up in a scarf, putting it in a paper shopping bag, and taking a taxi, which seemed kind of unceremonious, but what was the alternative? She was glad to get it out of the house, and she knew a museum had lots of insurance. The director reproached her for not using one of the bonded and expert art-delivery specialists in San Francisco, who would have crated it for the short distance to Third Street from Russian Hill at great expense. "My God, don't tell anyone you transported it like that." Lorna began to understand the new concerns of high-end art conservation: condition, provenance, intrinsic interest, and the fame of the artist.

She unwrapped it in the director's office, with people standing around to admire. They planned, if Lorna consented, to put it or a facsimile in a vitrine in the lobby, to solicit comment by the public about the projected purchase. "That's the church in his village?" people asked of the subject. "Charming."

Seeing it in this new setting, Lorna could newly understand the picture's intense charm, the inspired management of the light, and the genius of the brushwork, the something distinctive about Russ's way of seeing, his particular shade of blue; it was like a new painting for her. Probably she hadn't been supportive enough of poor Russ's obsessive paintings of version after version of the church in Pont seen at various times of day.

"The church was his sole subject," she explained to the committee, seeing in Russell's obsession the lineaments of a new lecture. "He found it inexhaustibly interesting, above all the play of shadow on the façade, but also the details of the carving . . ." So apparently did the viewers, and it was plain that the museum would be enriched by owning the painting.

After leaving the painting, she had a conversation with Marina Box and a young woman lawyer as they walked her out through the cavernous entrance hall; Lorna, who considered herself rather slow at grasping business matters, thinking over their conversation on the way home, came to see they were suggesting a discount for the museum on whatever the appraised valuation turned out to be, with a small rebate for Lorna herself, on top of her commission, if the discount was meaningful. Something about institutional versus market prices, things like that. There would of course be legalities, authentications, title searches, verifications of the provenance . . .

Lorna tormented herself for a few days with ambivalence about whether to go see, and then went to see, Tory Hatcher's photographs of Pont-les-Puits. No one had yet asked her what she as a person who had lived in the village thought of them, but they might. She couldn't account for her dread of seeing the exhibition; was it that it might be too grisly, or was it that it might awake a longing for the little place where she had lived for eighteen years?

Neither of these responses turned out to be hers—the scene of unearthed bones and tipped tombstones was grisly, but the emotional distance afforded by the black-and-white medium privileged the art with which the rows of skulls, the architecture of the market hall, the symmetry of its arches, the picturesque castles of mud created by the digging machine repairing the terrain, blanched away emotion. It was very interesting, she found, and there was the pleasure of recognition, an almost proprietary feeling about the village and its impromptu ossuary, so she felt no pangs. Or maybe a pang, was it of nostalgia? Or was it something else?

Seeing it made her think of a conversation she'd had with Donna a week or so ago. "Could you move back to France if you wanted to?" Donna had asked. "Legally, all that."

"I guess so, I'm a French citizen by marriage. I don't think they take it away. I have a French passport. An American one, too, of course."

"Would you, though? Why did you come back here anyway?"

Lorna wasn't sure anymore. "I'm an American, this is my native land. I'd always be a stranger over there." It was a pat answer, but she didn't know the real one. Why do people who leave usually come home? Why did others find that so peculiar?

"Stranger, so what?" Donna said. "I'll always be a stranger in California. Isn't it nicer in France?"

"It is, I guess. Cleaner, safer. Prettier." She felt irritated at Donna for forcing her to confront these comparisons, and at her native land for not dealing with, even neglecting, such quality-of-life issues in favor, supposedly, of its superior "energy" or for fear of offending someone whose culture might include throwing gum wrappers on the street, or some other offense you dared not reprimand.

Then, when looking at Tory Hatcher's photographs of skulls and mud and tombstones, she had felt proprietary, of knowing that just down that road in the photo lay her home for eighteen years. Maybe you could have two homes in your heart. Heart's homes. If just one, which one was really hers?

In her mailbox was an actual paper-and-envelope letter from Armand-Loup with a handwritten list of twelve Woodses still in the possession of the *mairie* of Pont-les-Puits, and suggesting she ought to come back to Pont to look at these valuable *oeuvres* with a view to selling them for her usual fee, incidentally evading customs coming back to the U.S. by checking them through in her luggage, one or two at a time if necessary. His letter explained that shipping valuable artworks was out of the question because of the massive duty, but it was legal to bring in personal property more or less legal. *"Je t'aime,"* the letter added.

For once, this suggestion of going back to Pont-les-Puits didn't horrify her, though at first she had no plans to do it. The idea of the village was rosier now in hindsight, and in photographs wonderful—wonderful Pont-les-Puits. After a couple of days, softened by Tory's photographs, she began to find his suggestion of going back to Pont-les-Puits tenable. Dear Pont-les-Puits. Soon after this, Armand-Loup telephoned to follow up his suggestion, and she said she'd see.

Among her accumulating responsibilities, Lorna had taken on the task of telling Peggy the good news that she'd been designated to make a journey to Singapore or Thailand or both, to perform the vaguely defined task of finding her lost brother. Ran and Lorna had pursued this idea during one of their infrequent phone conversations.

"Mother, how would I even start finding someone in Thailand?" Peggy had protested. "Private detective?" This was sarcastic, but it was in fact how they proceeded. Ran made Internet forays; a Bangkok detective agency was hired. It was odd they hadn't done this before. Peggy had about ten days to get her affairs in order and pack. Ran would deal with her mortgage and getting someone to water her lawn. In Bangkok, the detective found Curt immediately, and Curt had consented to be found but encouraged the visit from Peggy all the same. Ran decided not to tell Peggy Curt's whereabouts were known, because with her slightly masochistic tendencies, she would cancel her trip, saying, Now that I'm not needed.

Lorna had her own travel apprehensions. She came to agree with Armand-Loup that if she was to have an official role in Russell's estate, she would need to return to Pont-les-Puits to look at his pictures and whatever other stuff he'd left behind; she'd have to know what was there. On the other hand, she dreaded going back to the memories both bad and good—mostly good, admit it—and dreaded the unkind way memory had of forcing you to compare your present state with the past, back when she'd been the happy citizen of a charming and enviable foodie destination in France, even if it had gone downhill a bit since the days of James Beard and M. F. K. Fisher.

Despite her annual visits to America during her marriage to Armand-Loup, when she left France for good, she hadn't had a realistic picture of her native land in her mind; she hadn't yet tried to find *magrets de canard* or attempted to deal with an American bank or parking meters you operated with your cell phone, or tried to go somewhere on a train; hadn't read about all the shootings, home invasions, homeless people, crashing economy, or heard the stupefying cost of turning your ankle or, for Donna, of sending the twins to nursery school. All the bad things had been unwelcome surprises.

Just as in France she had always kept a mental list of things that were better in America, the whole time she'd been back in San Francisco, she'd unavoidably been keeping a mental list of things that were better back in France, as her recent brush with an American hospital confirmed. In some perverse way, France's strong points now seemed all the more reason not to go back to Pont-les-Puits and risk sinking again into French safety and ease; the list of things that were better and easier in France was long. Now she saw that the secret message of all American folklore—Frankie and Johnny and Bonnie and Clyde and all Western films and songs about logger lovers like Paul Bunyan who stirred coffee with their thumbs—was: you have to be tough to live in America.

"Come for a week," Armand-Loup said on the phone. "Not long enough to get jet lag. I'll pick you up in Lyon or Grenoble—whatever is the best connection from San Francisco."

She continued to feel a little dread of seeing the places she'd lived in for so long and loved, for fear her resolve would break down. Yet it would be nice to see some of the people she'd loved in Pont—Mademoiselle Sylva at La Périchole, Vincent at the Friandise, Daisy Magnum who ran the one bookshop, Veuve Duval—always called that—Monsieur Vlad the gardener, on and on, so many. How many people did she know in San Francisco?

Only her children and one or two old friends from college days—Pam Linden, Phil Train. The Chins. The museum women. Mostly things were changed. The doctor who had delivered her children was long retired; she had to find a new dentist. You don't make new friends so easily after a certain age. You don't actually want to. An image of a quilt came to her, like the AIDS quilt from the eighties, with the names of people who had died sewn in. Despite her apprehensions, she booked a ticket to France for just before Christmas in defiance of the increased fares; it was the professionally responsible thing to do now that she was Russell's agent. She'd fly to Grenoble and take a train to Valence, and then Armand would fetch her from there—"No problem, *chérie*,"—or she could rent a car.

43

In Woodside, Ran was mostly worrying about Gilda, and about the email he got from Dr. Karas in Paris one morning in early December, reporting that Gilda was having headaches—headaches a well-known symptom of preeclampsia, her diabetes a well-known predictor of it, and her teen age practically a guarantee of it. Gilda was almost bound to develop this menacing condition, and Ran had unconsciously been waiting for the call.

In Paris, Gilda's Olympian indifference to her pregnancy continued to puzzle Carla, and puzzled Julie, too, when she thought about it; Julie tried not to think about Gilda's pregnancy, or rather the circumstances of its happening, and was confused by Gilda's lack of connection to Ian, her lack of interest in him, almost as if they didn't know each other, instead of being married. How could anyone be indifferent to Ian?

"Have you talked to Ian?" Julie asked a time or two, but got the same answer, "No, we send the odd email." The girl often spoke on the phone to her California friends and her parents, but never Ian, and yet there was nothing suspect about her indifference, no sense that she protested too much: it was true indifference. Both Julie and Carla agreed, out of Gilda's earshot, that if it were they pregnant, they would be counting the days and watching their diets and making sure the responsible male got every detail; but Gilda made no concession to her condition. Just as the baby had been put inside her almost unnoticeably, so she imagined it would exit; she hadn't focused on the travails of childbirth and the scary stories of pain, it would just slip out, like a quail's egg.

"In denial," was Carla's confident diagnosis.

"I think she genuinely forgets," Julie said.

Gilda was having a romance instead with Virgil's *Aeneid,* which they were reading in her Advanced Latin class; she loved Juno, so feminist, and Deiopea the Beautiful, which they tried different ways of pronouncing, and even pious Aeneas despite her suspicion of piety. "O Muse, inspire me, hear my song," she would declaim, walking rapturously through the Bois de Boulogne in the glorious fall weather. Californians, none of them had experienced a real autumn before. Even Carla, in her dignified thirties, waded into piles of leaves and joyously kicked them.

Gilda's headaches had begun in late November, before the start of the December break but before they were set to return to California anyway. They came on in the late afternoons at first, and then after a week, they lasted all day. They weren't terrible, but they were there, and she finally mentioned them on her weekly visit to Dr. Karas. That was the visit where he found her blood pressure had spiked up, too, and called her father. The two doctors agreed these were symptoms of mild preeclampsia.

"She should fly home right now," Amy argued, but Ran had more confidence in French medicine than Amy had.

"Let her finish the semester, that's mid-December. She loves her school. We don't want her to get a negative sense or be resentful of the baby." They had always been careful to let her do everything, even if it might hurt her, up to a point, so that she would not feel handicapped. Differently abled.

Gilda's own feelings decided the matter; she didn't want to come home—she refused to come home. She knew the thing kicking in her belly must be addressed, but she was reassured when her dad said her headaches were probably a condition that was treatable. She would gladly continue seeing Dr. Karas and Dr. de Panapieu, who seemed super competent; she'd be fine. She didn't want to leave Paris, especially before the end-of-term exams.

In her heart she wanted to stay always, away from Woodside, social awkwardness, Saint Waltraud's, Ian Aymes, his mother, the baby, Carla—everyone but her parents, they could come visit. They could all move to France; why did you have to be the nationality you started out as; lots of Americans had changed into American from Lithuanian or Polish, couldn't you change the other way, become Mexican or Pakistani—or French? In France she could go on to study Greek and read Homer, eventually, and Sappho and Theocritus. And Russian; once you were good at transliteration in general, why not Russian, too?

She preferred to think about Latin declensions, but once in a while, when the creature inside her kicked insistently, she did think about it. Whereas she'd been charmed by the idea of maternity at the beginning, the longer it took, and the larger her belly grew, the more she saw it— him? her?—as an impediment, and the sooner it got born the better. Then other people could help her and take it off her hands. She had no image of herself bending over its basket, or—super revolting—suckling it.

She didn't wish it ill—on the contrary, she wished it would start its successful life soon, just without her. She knew that all the lore predicted that she would feel differently eventually, the process known as bonding, as soon as she saw it. It was a biological fact. She thought of Marga, the Afghani woman swimming ashore with her baby on her head, or however she did it. Gilda supposed she could swim with a baby, she'd try to save any baby, the normal human response, but that didn't make you motherly. Or maybe it did. Just the fact of being responsible for it made you motherly. If that were true, anyone—Julie?—could become its mother. Would Julie like a baby?

Julie and Carla, charged with keeping an eye on Gilda, differed with each other about going home to California in view of Gilda's worsening condition, pre-whatever. Julie, guarding her secret love of Ian, was tremendously in favor of California and didn't mind leaving her course before the finals. "We were planning to go home soon anyway," she argued, "and if we went now, it would save your parents the trip— you know they'll be over here tomorrow morning otherwise." No one could say to Gilda, We need to go because you and the baby could die if something went wrong and we were here instead of there. Such a thing hadn't occurred to them until Julie googled Gilda's symptoms.

Now it also drifted through Julie's mind that if the baby wasn't born at all—or, rather, if there were no baby—there would be nothing to tie Gilda and Ian together. Then she was so appalled at the things that could occur to her unbidden that she said a prayer, not a religious prayer, more a Circle of Faith hope that such ideas not come to her again.

Except for the looming threats of premature birth and/or returning to California, and Julie hating France generally, the three young women were otherwise happy in their little French ménage à trois and felt keenly the inconvenience if Gilda's unfortunate pregnancy went wrong. Carla was still reveling in freedom from her California servitude, and therefore was on Gilda's side in favor of staying and, besides, had met a nice Slovenian man in her Speak French class. They had taken to going together after class on Thursdays to hear a jazz trio at the Deux Magots.

It was two weeks before the Christmas holidays would begin. Little Christmas market huts seemed to install themselves overnight along the Champs-Élysées and in Saint-Germain to sell woolen caps, bottle openers with horn handles, Russian amber, and ornaments made of straw. Tonight, in their apartment, Carla was making *coq au vin jaune*, a variation in *Jean, Maître de Cuisine*, a book they were cooking from now. She called Julie and Gilda to the table. They talked over their day. "I know it's stupid, but I want to take my exams next week. It's a matter of national honor," Gilda said. "I'm the top in Latin, above this English girl Marigold Butler. Bottom in French, though."

"You aren't the bottom," Carla protested.

"Nearly, but I don't care."

Gilda had come home more than once to find Carla and Julie watching videos about maternity hospitals. "Why are you watching that?"

"Look at this one, so cute." On the screen a nurse whispers to a newborn as she dunks him in water the temperature of amniotic fluid.

"They give the baby a spa treatment. He's only ten minutes old, or half hour tops. You have to go to this place. All kinds of stars give birth there, it's supposed to be the best."

"Oh, stop it. I'm going to give birth in the street," Gilda said. "On my way to school, and I'll leave it in the bushes." This startled Carla and Julie—it was the first note of discontent Gilda had sounded aloud, though her indifference had been obvious.

Once someone rang the interphone in the late afternoon. Carla asked into the interphone who it was, but the others couldn't hear the response. Carla shrugged and went to the door and waited for whoever it was to come up. It was a woman with a briefcase.

"Bonjour, madame, mesdames," said the newcomer. *"Je suis venue d'AME. De la part de la ville . . ."* They didn't quite understand this puzzling declaration, heard as if she were from "Om." Gilda, the one with the best French, the one the group expected to do the work of understanding here, said, "Pardon?"

"L'Aide Médicale de l'État." The newcomer struggled to accept that she was going to have to trot out her English.

"Aide?"

"De la ville de Neuilly-sur-Seine. Mon enquête concerne une jeune fille," indicating Gilda. "I have come about the young lady. *Puis-je*— may I sit down?"

"Please!" Carla jumped forward to indicate a chair.

With difficulty they began to understand that some civic agency was inquiring into Gilda's health and was offering, or maybe requiring, medical supervision.

"There is l'EPDSAE, *par* example. L'Établissement Public Départemental pour Soutenir, Accompagner, Eduquer—to sustain, accompany, and educate this underage girl, unmarried, in state of difficulty. La France wishes to be sure she has what is needed. Has she seen doctors?" The woman looked intently at Gilda as she spoke.

"Certainly," Carla answered, feeling irritated that la France would think they would not get a doctor—or whatever it thought. "How did you happen to find us?"

"The name, please," the woman said, waving her pencil over a form on her clipboard.

"You must have it, you found us."

"The name of zee *médecin*."

"Um, Karas. Really, this is not necessary."

"Le prénom?"

They drew a blank. "Cyrille, I think," said Carla.

"The clinic where she will give birth?"

To them, "clinic" conjured a grim charity ward, long waits. "She has a private doctor and will go to the hospital for difficult births, I've forgotten . . . Xavier. Xavier Karas is his name. The doctor."

"Maternité Port Royal," said Gilda. She read that in the seventeenth century it was a hospital for *allaitement*. Lactation to feed abandoned babies. The idea had scared her, made her think maybe it was better to be back in California when the time came. "It's a Monument Historique."

"She's going to the Clinique de la Rossignol," Carla corrected. She and Julie had cased hospitals and decided it looked like the best one, with its luxurious baby spa, and massages for the mothers. "Or else the American Hospital."

They were given to understand by the stern newcomer, evidently taking them for improvident runaways, that citizens were not born unnoticed in France, however widely they were ignored in the U.S. La France would be watching, concerned for the welfare of the coming baby. Though they were almost sure there wouldn't be a problem, Gilda suddenly glimpsed the hope there could be some rule requiring her as its mother to stay in France. This was a new thought. She could imagine one of those international custody battles where France intervened on behalf of the mother of one of its citizens (herself) to keep her from being sent back to America against her will.

When the woman had gone, Julie and Carla railed with Western gusto against state meddling, but Gilda said, "I almost forgot! Yay! The baby will be French! Will they even let it leave the country?" To anchor its Frenchness, she would give the baby a wildly French name, Antoinette-Clotilde or Marie-Louise-Camille instead of Pomona Deiopea as she had intended.

"What if it's a boy?" Carla said.

44

The Stanford fall term was well underway before enrollment for intramural soccer in November, and Ian was comfortable enough with his courses by then to estimate that he could fit sports into his schedule. A talented right midfielder, he was welcomed onto the intramural scene, which operated at a high, though not varsity, level. He was happy, a man with everything. He did think of Gilda, mostly when talking to his mother, but with affection, defined as mild interest and, when reflecting more deeply, panic. Julie was often in his thoughts.

Ursula Aymes was driven frantic by Gilda's absence abroad, and the likely departure to France of Ran and Amy, which would leave her without news of her grandchild-in-utero, and not knowing whether Ian was even in touch with Gilda. She renewed her efforts to cajole him into at least calling the mother of his child once in a while, or at a minimum emailing.

"You need to show some interest," she insisted. Ian protested that he was interested and concerned, of course, but didn't like to intrude. He disciplined himself to send encouraging emails from time to time and always got a polite and friendly reply, but no real news about Gilda's state and that of the fetus.

"She's reading in Latin at her school," he told his mother. "The classics, the *Aeneid*." Though Ian admired that, Ursula was crazed by it, accepting that Gilda might read anything she wanted, but finding Virgil so unsuitably far from the preoccupations she thought natural for someone expecting a child, so ditzy, even if Gilda was only in, what was it, the tenth grade! What could you expect? What was really going to happen to that baby when it was born? Would anyone notice?

She could talk matters over with Ran Mott if he were around; she could expect straight talk from him, but she assumed he and Amy were on their way to Europe, presumably to see Gilda, and of course they wouldn't think of sending her and Ian a word; she and Ian were supposed to just fester in ignorance as if paternal grandmothers had no interest and no rights. Fathers, either, though she avoided mentioning paternity to Ian, since it seemed to upset him and he would direct his irritation at her; and certainly she wouldn't mention Ian's part to Ran.

"Don't you even wonder?" she had once asked Ian. He knew the right answer, but she wasn't convinced. He had said, "Of course I do," but she doubted it.

Because of Gilda's preeclampsia, instead of Gilda running the risk of travel, Ran and Amy decided to spend the Christmas holidays in Europe. When Peggy told her mother about their plans, Lorna took the chance to do Armand-Loup a favor by suggesting to Peggy that Ran and Amy rent his farmhouse for the holidays; they didn't have to know it had been hers; it was on VRBO now.

Over the years, Julie and Gilda and even Carla had heard enough about the place in Pont from Peggy and Curt and Hams, and now that it was on VRBO, they could check it out themselves. Julie had memories of being taken there by her mother when she was a tot, and she talked up the beauties of this remarkably bleak, unvisited region.

Peggy, wondering why she hadn't thought of this before, suggested it to her father and Amy. In this big house, all of Ran's progeny could be with him for the holidays.

Thus it was organized that Gilda, Carla, and Julie would join Ran and Amy for Christmas in Pont. The girls could go there as soon as their classes were over, and Ran and Amy would join them when they could. If Ran and Amy were aware they were renting Lorna's former home, they didn't say. Never mind the tainted provenance of the house, with its checkered memories of Lorna. Though they suspected that Amy might not like being in Ran's former wife's former house, the young women looked forward to seeing a new part of France.

Carla especially had weighed in with Ran about whether it would be safe for Gilda to get away from Paris. At first, Ran said no, definitely not safe; the longer the pregnancy endured, the better chance the fetus had of a trouble-free start in life, and any disruption that threatened to bring on early delivery shouldn't be thought of. But he knew Gilda was determined to go with the others, and he didn't want to impose any interdictions that would affect her positive attitude. With Gilda feeling fine and not at all near term, and with no warning signs of premature labor or anything ominous except the headaches, as long as her blood pressure was controlled and there were available hospitals in the French countryside, it would be okay. Anyway, at more than thirty weeks along, a fetus could survive, Ran had said to himself, although it would require enormous luck and high-tech effort if a baby did come early.

Carla was not enthusiastic—didn't want to leave Paris and her new boyfriend, and foresaw her role with the family if they did go: cooking and dishwashing. Gilda earnestly wanted to go. She had heard tales from her older half-siblings about the happy times spent in Pont-les-Puits on their school vacations, when Grandma Lorna was married to someone called Armand the Wolf—something the others tended not to discuss around Ran. Julie had reservations of her own.

Julie wasn't thriving. Sometimes, getting ready for dinner, she was attacked by a stab of free-floating sexual desire—she was so prone to this now. Her thoughts fastened on Ian, but she almost felt that anyone would do, men were so essential; what happiness that the world was full of men, what promise for being alive! Even if there were nothing to be done about it at the moment. Maybe if Gilda had her baby, Ian would come to see it and they could take up where they left off.

Then, as Christmas neared, there was a change in Julie's emotional and sexual life. Gilda had not thought to tell her that the British politician had visited Saint Ann's British School, looking it over for one of his children, and that at the reception held for him, she had said, for something to say, "My sister—niece—Julie from San Francisco, would want to be remembered to you, from the Circle of Faith," and he had politely agreed that he remembered the nice girl in San Francisco at the Circle of Faith who had dragged him to her grandmother's cocktail party. That was the extent of Gilda's conversation with him as she passed along the reception line, so how amazing that Julie should get a telephone call from him, asking her if she could by any chance assist him with some Circle of Faith–related events through the holiday season, in Paris, Geneva, and Lisbon: meetings and celebrations, organizing his plane tickets, schedule, and so on. His usual assistant had children and needed to stay in England through the holidays. Julie seized on this as the perfect salvation, a job! With pay! And it would be over with in time for her to be with her grandfather in Pont-les-Puits at least by New Year's Eve.

"Our trip should be productive for the Circle. Lisbon in particular has a very active chapter."

They started almost immediately after Julie's exams by flying to Portugal and checking into a super-smart little hotel, with a roof garden that looked out over the city; and there was sunshine after the winter gloom of Paris. Away from the tension around Gilda, away from her own dreaded urbanism class in which she was not excelling despite being used to getting good grades, Julie was suffused with happiness. In the hotel bar, the British politician ordered her a Manhattan and said, "We should just get this issue out of the way at the outset: this is where I hit on you, Julie. The loveliest young woman I know. We might have a delightful few weeks together."

Julie was startled at this directness but not altogether surprised, since men almost always hit on her. Not that she approved of distinguished Englishmen using American teen slang like "hit on."

"Can you envisage a relationship with an old man like me?" He rephrased the question.

"I don't think of you as old," she said, which was perfectly true; she thought of him as powerful, a powerful politician, the most attractive attribute imaginable. Probably only in his fifties. Younger than Grandpa Ran. He could yet come back into office. She also liked his aftershave, something really English about it.

"That sounds great to me," Julie said, with a lot of curiosity about the future and only a little regret about not seeing Ian for a while longer and, most important, a vengeful feeling connected to his marriage. Why shouldn't she have some fun? This would show him.

She maybe wouldn't mention her new job to her mother. Without formulating to herself in words the details of her revenge fantasy, she was satisfied that married Ian Aymes would be chagrined to hear she'd gone off with a world leader.

Later, Julie was also delighted to discover that male enthusiasm in bed overrode age, and that art compensated for stamina, up to a point. There were now some things she could teach Ian someday, and in all, she was enjoying her temp job with the British politician. They were received in a number of cities, distinguished statesman and beautiful young secretary, a familiar conjunction, like stocks and dividends.

Before her flight from San Francisco to France to look at the Woodses, Lorna had had an SMS from Armand-Loup that he'd be waiting at the Grenoble airport. She remembered their many instances of misunderstood directions for missed rendezvous, so her heart lifted with relief to see him standing there in Grenoble, cordoned behind a rope with other greeters right outside the arrival door, rather grandly dressed in a suit and open-collared shirt, and carrying an umbrella: a handsome, substantial older man. He gave her a brief husbandly peck and commandeered her rolling bag. They walked outside. In the distance, a frieze of white snowy peaks dazzled and thrilled her with the impending change in her circumstance—the Alps, Europe, a different language, a different climate zone, air crisp already with winter.

Armand-Loup was parked in the short-term lot only a few steps away—he always managed to avail himself of desirable perks. "How was the flight, *chérie*? How do you manage to step off a plane looking so rested and pretty?" She recognized his typical gallantry, and it was always pleasant. On the short drive to Pont-les-Puits, he caught her up on village doings, especially the planned celebrations for the *re-enterrement* of the cemetery bones.

"That will be any day now. Needless to say, Hôtel La Périchole is complete and neither can you stay in my—our—house for a reason that may surprise you: some of your relatives are coming. Or maybe they told you? They rented it from me some time ago—your granddaughter Julie and some others, I guess Julie would be your granddaughter—she is one I don't know—with two other girls, and the parents of one of them are expected: the father of your children and his wife, if I have it right."

Lorna could not express her irritation; she gaped dumbly. Of all the times to have come, and for her not to have been told: Ran and Amy and their child the pregnant teen in her own house? And it was she herself who'd brought this on by mentioning that Armand might be renting the house out to foreigners and strangers. Since it was Lorna who had suggested to Peggy that Armand's house was empty and that Armand could use the rent, and Peggy had passed this news along to Ran as the perfect place for the Parisian schoolgirls to spend the holidays, it was her own fault.

"Where am I staying?"

"With me, since you are my wife. I promise we won't quarrel or anything dismaying. My rooms are perfectly comfortable, it's only a few days. If you like, no need even to admit you're here, we can skulk around without your family seeing you. We'll concentrate on the Woods paintings, and you can see your granddaughter later, back in California."

"Oh, Armand." Lorna knew there was no way out. "Where are you living?"

"Still over the bakery. Still very pleasant. Lovely smells of baking bread."

45

Though they had paid the rent, Ran didn't think he and Amy would stay in Lorna's former house in Pont-les-Puits, no, that would be a little weird for Amy, but the girls could, and there must be a hotel for him and Amy. Ran called Dr. Karas to tell him his travel plans.

Karas caught Ran up on Gilda's condition, though Ran had been talking to him almost daily. "She's very cooperative," said Dr. Karas. "So mature for fifteen, she understands all." Ran doubted that but was glad to hear it. The same great unspoken questions hung behind Ran's conversations with the French doctor as they had with American doctors, a sort of collegial reproach: How could this happen? Why did you permit this dangerous pregnancy to continue in an underage diabetic? If these questions had been spoken, Ran wouldn't have had an answer. How was it events slid by you? He was a sentient and even controlling guy, yet things slid by. He had respected the natalist views of Amy and Gilda.

Ran and Dr. Karas had discussed which measures of surveillance to institute in the face of preeclampsia, mostly frequent blood-pressure checks and medication to lower it. They agreed that the preeclampsia was probably not harmful to the fetus at this late stage, almost seven months, but if or when hospitalization was required, proper facilities must be had in mind, both in the vacation village and in Paris. Ran needed some input from French medical colleagues about where would be best. In Paris "not the American Hospital," Ran specified, "the best crisis pregnancy place," which as far as they could find out was called Maternité Port Royal and was centuries old though in a new building. They also discussed her return to California for early delivery if signs warranted it.

On their last visit, Amy and Ran both had been braced to see a change in Gilda, who was just entering her last trimester. Even so, they had been shocked to find how much she had thickened with a definite baby bump; and she was generally fatter, more like she herself had looked as a baby, with a little angel's double chin and round cheeks. This prompted especially tormenting reflections about how Gilda was still a child herself. Their precious daughter, the victim of unfair biology since her birth, was now trapped for the indefinite future. Biology was destiny, even though they'd tried to protect her, a futile effort.

The victim, as always, had been joyful to see them and was evidently having a wonderful time with her studies and with Julie and Carla, though on that last visit, Julie was for some reason not there. "She has a temp job," Gilda explained. "She's in Portugal. She's helping someone she knows from her cult. He was almost the prime minister of England or something. She'll be back before New Year's." Her absence peeved Ran a little, since he was paying for her to follow a course of studies, not to go off on dirty weekends with men.

Amy and Ran didn't know of any cult, let alone likely prime ministers. "Prime minister? Come on," they said, wary of men with far-fetched claims, to say nothing of cults. Gilda laughed. "The Circle of Faith. It meets across from Grandma Lorna's, where Grandma was living when she got to San Francisco, Julie showed me."

"You don't even know Lorna," Amy pointed out. "She's not in any sense your grandmother."

"Julie showed me Lorna's house when we went to a meeting. The man she's helping is one of the sponsors. It's not a cult, it does good works—educational—and food packages. Not really religious in the bad sense. Bookney Ravanel and I went to a couple of meetings on our own and no harm came to us."

· · ·

Amy had planned to book their tickets to Paris for the week between Christmas and New Year's and the first week in January, but they had a complication that kept them in California through Christmas: the deteriorating American economy. Finance people drew together like refugees. Though Amy was assured by her financial people that her positions were sound, the market was crashing and she was entirely in the market, mostly in tech futures. The talk was of nothing but bailouts and safe havens, and what the government might do to save people. She herself didn't expect to be rescued; she thought that the new president should use money set aside for the so-called bailout of failing banks and crooked brokers to bail out individual homeowners instead of letting families lose their homes and sink into renting and poverty. They heard from Hams that the slum rental he and Misty were living in was itself being foreclosed on the landlord who was underwater with his empire of tottering Oakland rentals. The crisis was national, but Amy felt somehow personally involved, as if, by staying in California, she could influence a conversation about what measures would be taken.

Earlier, Ran and Amy had had other rationalizations for staying away from France; they didn't want to hover, wanted to encourage Gilda to take responsibility for her own health as she always had. And they had confidence in Carla; after all, preeclampsia notwithstanding, Gilda's pregnancy still had more than two months to go, and Carla reported that Gilda spent the designated time lying down with appropriate docility. Until he himself could travel, Ran spent a lot of time with Gilda on the phone. "What's your blood pressure today?" When they had nothing else to say, he and Gilda had always had her numbers to discuss. Today her numbers were too high.

"You know, honey, we may have to think about bed rest for a few weeks, or early delivery," he said.

"Delivery, yay," Gilda said.

Ran explained about preeclampsia, and how it was important to control, and again felt her resistance to pregnancy, this runaway process that was dictating the terms of her life. Her spirit was already wary, and honed by her lifelong diabetes to a state just short of bitterness, and though they had done their best to make her illness as easy as they could—diabetes camp, Mrs. Klein—here was another ultimatum, another imposition of fate, the liabilities of being female.

"Born today, the baby could survive, with a lot of support, but in a couple of weeks its chances would be better, so there's some thinking that your just taking it easy, lying down pretty much of the day . . ."

"Exams are next Thursday and Friday."

"Could you somehow take them at home?"

"No, Papa, I'll take them at school like everybody else."

"I'm sure they'd understand."

"No."

"You'll be taking some medicine to lower your blood pressure, and it may make you feel a little . . . less sharp . . ."

"Okay, okay." Gilda never wanted to talk about her health. He took "okay" to mean don't talk about it anymore, not that she was giving in.

They negotiated. Gilda could go to school but come right home afterward and lie in horizontal boredom till dinnertime and had to go to bed at eight. Okay, she could lie on the sofa and watch TV or listen to the radio with her earphones till ten. Carla would enforce this. The idea of this stringent regime didn't seem to bother Gilda. It wasn't as if she had made friends who were likely to ask her out, though she, Carla, and Julie had gone to a lot of movies until Julie had split. Now Amy sent them a DVD player.

Gilda took her exams and remained top in Latin and middling in French, which she didn't care about; she was delighted to outrank the snooty British girl and show the other girls who might have thought a pathetic, knocked-up American girl was probably stupid. She overheard her principal British rival also say, "Money talks," but she ignored it and wore the aura of her dominance with becoming modesty, as someone else remarked. What made Gilda happiest was the commendation from Mrs. Whistle, the head of the school, who said, "I have heard of your fine results, Mrs. Aymes, and I do hope you plan to continue your education." She seemed to glance at Gilda's swollen belly.

"Yes, Mrs. Whistle, I do," Gilda said.

46

In California, Ran and Amy had taken a few other things in hand: someone must go look for Curt and drag him home, now that they were sure he was alive and in Singapore or Thailand. Peggy, as having the least to do, though they didn't put it like that, had been designated to travel, and Ran would cover her house payments and, as he said to himself, confront Dick Willover about his duty in that quarter. Donna, beside her lively twins, now had her business interests to oversee, while Peggy was—well—dispensable, as she herself recognized, with no job and no pressing concerns. They had a quick picture of large, blondish Peggy wandering lost among the dainty Thai. Lorna bought her some tropical clothes.

Thus Peggy found herself in Bangkok with a new light cotton wardrobe from Lands' End and L.L Bean, looking very American. She was in a trance of deracinated happiness, delighted at the way invisibility and anonymity set you free. It was strange to be in a place, warm, exotic, beautiful, that took no notice of Thanksgiving or Christmas. Why live forever in Ukiah? Why knock yourself out about Christmas, all those damn presents to wrap?

She was on a little barge thing taking her across the river from her hotel to the main part of Bangkok. She didn't know the name of the river. The hotel was superbly fancy, paid for by her father or, frankly, her father's wife. Her twentieth-floor room had a balcony for gazing across the river and down upon the smoggy city. There was a television sunk into the marble wall above the bath taps so you could watch TV while in the tub, and lounge chairs for reading—she'd bought several paperbacks in the San Francisco airport before she left, in case they had no books in English; but you could get everything here. If she could live here, how would she make her living?

She was crossing to the main business district. Other tourists, and businessmen with briefcases, stood near the far edge of the ferry, ready to leap off when they bumped up to the dock. Orange peels and palm fronds swirled in the draw of the water. No Easter and no Christmas here. As she stepped off into the busy lane leading away from the ferry, she felt her name fade away, too, wafted off on an odorous breeze of lemongrass and the toxic exhaust fumes of the tuk-tuks. She was anonymous and free.

Her rendezvous with the detective hired by Dad and Amy was to be at Jim Thompson, a famous tearoom attached to Jim Thompson's house-turned-museum, chosen as easy to find and symbolically appropriate, Thompson a figure who in the 1960s had wandered into the jungle and vanished the way Curt had vanished. Peggy had printed out the baroque, inscrutable address—6 Rama 1 Road, Khwaeng Wang Mai, Khet Pathum Wan, Krung Thep Maha Nakhon 10330—to show when asking people the way, but each passerby she stopped waved her confidently toward this well-known establishment.

Suddenly some peculiar impulse made her slow her steps. What was the rush? Maybe she should call the guy and postpone the meeting until tomorrow or the day after. There was so much to see in the fragrant boutiques selling carved Buddhas and strings of mirrored beads and painted fans and other crafts she should learn about. She could feel out whether her decorated dog collars would sell in Thailand; it looked like they would, there were lots of posh little dogs everywhere. The shop interiors were dim; at the backs were promising teak armoires filled with T-shirts and carved rosewood combs. Next to the tiny proprietors, Peggy felt like a big ox woman invading them. People came and went along the street on scooters or pushing carts of merchandise; a breeze stirred the T-shirts festooning the doorways of the cubicle boutiques.

A vague smell of cooking oil carried scents of shrimp and lemongrass while skyscrapers swayed overhead.

On the veranda of the tearoom, it was Curt himself sitting at a little round table, and he slightly rose when Peggy approached. Postponing the recriminations, they joyfully embraced. Peggy sat down, looked at the English menu, babbled of the amazing thing, them both being in Thailand. His shoulders felt solid, not those of the thin invalid who had left; he'd gained weight, back to his normal self preaccident, muscular and fit. He smelled of sandalwood.

"This is so weird," Peggy said.

"Sister mine."

"You were perfectly easy to find, why haven't you been answering everybody?"

"I'd taken a kind of oath of silence for a while," Curt said. "Now I can talk about it."

"It better be good, as Mom and Dad used to say." In her relief, she almost didn't care about explanations. Curt had always had plausible explanations.

"What would you like? I'm having a beer. Thai beer is excellent."

"Okay. It is very nice here," Peggy agreed.

"Nicer than Ukiah, you'll admit."

"It's very crowded, though." Peggy knew they would get to Curt's story when he was ready. "Is it true what you wrote Donna about seeing the face of God?" she asked after a while.

"In a manner of speaking. Speaking metaphorically."

"You were never religious at all," Peggy said.

"In a coma, you still have your brain process. Something goes on in there. It was then I underwent some changes."

"That was your medical condition, the drugs they pumped into you."

"Who knows? Here I am."

She sat back to hear his story. The only part of it that surprised her, when it came out, was the part about finding God. The rest had a familiar, literary feel: arriving lost and sick, getting into drugs and wandering, then a guru, reading, a monastery—the lot.

"Well—what is God telling you to do?" Peggy tried to ask this in a straightforward, nonironic way.

"It's a path, it's a path. The book says 'Buddhism in its multiple forms acknowledges the radical insufficiency of this shifting world.'"

"I suppose it must," Peggy agreed.

"It teaches that men—women and men—'in a devout and confident spirit, can either reach a state of absolute freedom or attain supreme enlightenment.' It's a path."

"Path back to California, I hope. Your wife and kids—the twins are so cute, by the way—and now that Amy has paid off your mortgage . . ."

That got his attention. He demanded an account of how this windfall had occurred, had not got Donna's letters telling him about it. If she had written them. It crossed Peggy's mind that Donna may not have told him everything. She described the dinner where Donna had announced her windfall, the surprise.

"Amy did that because she was worried about Donna losing the house. If I went back, I'd have to reimburse her," Curt said.

"I don't think so. Just someday when you sell."

"Where are you staying?" Curt asked. "How long?"

"The Peninsula. Staying long enough to convince you to come home," Peggy said.

Curt laughed. "Settle in. It's good you're comfortable there."

"What do you do all day?" Peggy asked. "Hang out in bars? Chase bar girls? Do you have a job?"

"In a way," Curt agreed. "Tell me how everyone is. What about you? Didn't Amy give you anything?"

"How did you know? Nothing for me, nothing for Hams. Just perfect you and perfect Donna."

"Donna and Amy always got along. I hear Donna is amassing a nice little packet herself."

"It did cross my mind that Donna could share a bit with the rest of us, but silly me. There's lots more news," Peggy warned. "Mother and Armand-Loup are separated. Mother is back living in California. Gilda is pregnant. They're afraid Misty is in a clinical depression."

"What went wrong with Mother and Armand?" He ordered them

each another beer and sandwiches and settled in to hear the family doings. Peggy noted that apparently he spoke Thai and could read the strange curly script that looked like wood shavings. She brought him up to date.

"Is Mother happy being back in the U.S.?" Curt wondered.

"I guess so." She hadn't thought about it. "I don't think of Mother as happy so much as busy. She's busy, she's sort of an art dealer now, and she goes out with the dean of the cathedral. And gives her lectures."

"Good God. Hams?"

"Hams seems happy, except for the Misty situation and being so poor. He's started working full-time, as a chef; hash cook would be more like it." She also told him what she knew about Gilda, which wasn't much.

"Wait, wait, back up!" Curt pleaded. "Gilda? How old is Gilda anyhow?"

"Fifteen. Dad and Amy are in France seeing to her, I think planning to take her back to the U.S."

"The Princess. What happened there?" The First Three, as they thought of themselves, never had known much about Gilda except that she would come into Amy's money someday.

"Teenage slipup, according to Julie. Julie spends—did spend—a lot of time with Dad and Amy and Gilda, and she says Gilda is not the spoiled brat you'd expect."

"How's Julie? Is she a junior now?"

"I guess, but she's in Europe, kind of junior year abroad. I think there's a man in her life, but I don't know."

"Did you imagine when we were little we'd be so scattered around the world?"

"When we lived on Lake Street, that was the world. No, I never imagined anything—French stepfather, zillionaire Silicon Valley step-mother, weird expatriate brother, that's you . . ."

"It's how we live now," Curt said.

47

Success does a lot to encourage revenge.

In San Francisco, upon hearing that Curt had been found, Donna made up her mind: until now she had been able to keep her wounded vanity and fury at Curt at manageable levels, but the idea of him actually coming home made more urgent her need to do something irrevocable, burn his bridges. Curt had been swanning around Southeast Asia without telling them, allowing everyone to suffer; he had deserted them and she had not forgiven it.

Selling the house was the best thing she could think of to retaliate, and then she would take the kids and go back to Delaware as she had long wanted to do. It was a better place to raise kids anyway. She called Ursula to say that she had decided to sell their house.

Her sense of virtue and entitlement carried all before it. Donna knew she was behaving rashly, but she was done with Curt, with the Motts, with San Francisco. Yes, finished with Curt—it was what he deserved—and without her, he wouldn't be needing this big house. Selling had to be done, or underway, before he got home. She had not even realized, until she brought herself to say a few things out loud, that she had been this resentful of Curt, this furious at his desertion, this angry at—some of the things he'd done. If she didn't protect her situation, Curt would come home, take it over, and tear it down. In the meantime, she had built a future for herself. She had prepared a solid ground—had built up vegetal protein to a state Curt had only imagined, and started a relationship with Harvey Avon.

She remembered that Ursula had mentioned a buyer who was eager, who particularly admired the house. Did her deal still stand, with Ursula reducing her fee to 4 percent, and had there been changes in the market that would affect the price, six million five, they'd discussed?

"The market is not great," Ursula said. "Dropping, in fact." This was true, and had made her decide against her former idea of buying Donna's house herself. She didn't need such a big place, and the uncertainties of the economy had brought her to her senses.

"Time is of the essence, though," Donna said. "I've decided to go back East, where I'm from. Family reasons. I'd like to be at least in escrow before I go—for peace of mind."

"Escrow is not necessarily peace of mind," Ursula reminded her. "Things fall apart. Often. Banks renege, people drop out." Just to correct Donna's misapprehensions about the real-estate business.

"It can take some time to sell these high-end properties," she went on to remind Donna. "I'll go back to my Hong Kong buyers, but I can't promise they're still interested or ready to pay a premium." Ursula's suggested asking price was on the low side, priced to sell, and beneficial for herself, too, in case she changed her mind about buying it, as she admitted to Donna; she was in no way deceptive. "Say five million five." Donna did the math and agreed with it. Okay.

Ursula's clients were the Chins, the couple to whom Ursula had rented the apartment next to Lorna while they undertook their real-estate searches. Ursula had shown the house to them when it was first on the market, and they had lost their hearts to it, but then Donna and Curt had bought it first. Now they were delighted that Donna's house had come back on the market. They were cash buyers, but luckily not so stupid as to have left the cash around the apartment, as the burglars had apparently believed. The cash was in the Sunshine Happiness Bank on Columbus Avenue and could be safely, electronically, transferred into escrow at a moment's notice.

Donna decided to say nothing about the sale to the Mott family, who would only want to deter her impulsive course.

48

It had been planned that Ran and Amy would spend the holidays in the rented house in Pont-les-Puits, but first they intended for Christmas itself to be in Paris with Gilda and Carla and, they had thought, Julie. But other matters in California impeded their Paris visit—the first Christmas of Gilda's fifteen years not spent with her parents. To add to this, Julie had vanished, represented by cheerful emails sent from Portugal. There were other shadows. Poor Hams and Misty were obliged by Misty's feelings about her pregnancy to stay in California, though Ran handsomely offered to pay their airfare. Julie's absence annoyed Ran when he heard about it—he was paying for her studies, and they had had an understanding that she would be keeping an eye on things with Gilda and Carla, not taking up with some man. Nonetheless, he said nothing, for fear Gilda would feel herself too surveyed and spied upon if he mentioned Julie's real role.

Paris wore its usual Christmas finery, colored lights strung on the trees, across the boulevards, and along the Champs-Élysées, and store windows decked with holiday wares. After some shopping and Christmas matinees and one three-star restaurant, Carla and Gilda hired a car and, the day after Boxing Day, with Carla driving, spent three days touring in the Camargue to see the wild horses, bulls, and flamingos, a great success with both of them. They bought leather hats and objects bearing the strange half-Christian, half-pagan symbol of the region and ate the local pastry, *aigues-mortes*.

At the end of the third day in the Camargue, they followed their GPS the couple of hours to Pont. Julie had just arrived there and had picked up the keys to the house—Julie's grandmother's former home—which Ran had rented on VRBO. Julie, even more healthy looking than usual, said she'd had a great time with her holiday temp job, and something about her, a certain smugness, confirmed this.

"Well, where were you, anyhow?" Gilda wondered. "Was it interesting?"

"Sure, yes. Lisbon. It was totally interesting. Beautiful tiled walls." She would say no more than that.

Julie remembered the house, her grandmother's former house, from when she was a tot, when she and her parents had spent a couple of vacations there. Through its association with pleasant times, Peggy had always spoken fondly of it to Julie. Had her father Dick ever mentioned it? She couldn't remember.

In Paris, Julie had shown Gilda and Carla her old room on the website and recounted what faint memories she had. Now Julie had saved what they imagined had been the master bedroom for Amy and Ran, and then she, Carla, and Gilda each chose a bedroom; it was like having a whole hotel of choices. "You should take the one closest to that bathroom, since you have to pee so much," Carla told Gilda. Gilda took everything in a genial light and was grateful for this nice room, where she'd be obliged to lie down for what seemed hours every day according to Dr. Karas's instructions.

Julie, Carla, and Gilda planned some expeditions to neighboring villages. Poor Gilda appeared to shock the locals with her big belly, almost like a clown belly with a stuffed-in pillow, so ill did it fit with the rest of her childish features and dramatic pallor.

On New Year's Eve they all decided to go out instead of firing up the imposing solid-fuel range and darkening the beautiful copper pots before Ran and Amy had seen them. It was at dinner that they heard from the waiter Luigi, who was perfectly informed of the connection of the newcomers to Monsieur Dumas, that Madame Dumas herself was back in town for the upcoming ceremonies in the graveyard, a measure of how festive a funeral it would be.

"Grandma Lorna here? How weird. Where is she staying?" Julie asked. "Not at her house, because that's where we are."

"Monsieur Dumas lives above the Pâtisserie Friandise—*il y a un appartement.*" But Julie found it hard to believe that her grandmother would bunk in with someone she was divorcing.

They were eating at La Roulette, with its lace curtains, menu on a blackboard *(rognons de veau, choux farci),* the sideboard showing off giant magnums of *poire* and brandy. They were on dessert when a party of eight men and one woman came in for dinner. They could see their minivan parked in front of the restaurant but couldn't read the writing on its door. The newcomers took the long table on Carla's side, and one of them chatted up the girls in English, explaining their presence in this friendly village establishment.

"We're the Subcommission on Cretaceous Stratigraphy." He explained that the *département* meant to make a geopark here in Pont-les-Puits and was investigating promising sites.

"What is a geopark exactly?" said the young women cooperatively.

It was a pedagogical park, an enterprise sponsored by the minister of the interior to showcase sites where geological features, with edifying labels, could be demonstrated to schoolchildren and amateur geologists. Little by little, they learned the details of what the party meant to find by discovering "the biostratigraphy, sedimentology, paleoenvironmental interpretations, and outcrop accessibility for candidate sections for the bases of the Valanginian, Upper Valanginian, and Hauterivian Stages or substages in the Pont-les-Puits area."

"My word!" Thinking of the bones they would dig.

"I think myself that the topography is a little steep right around here for a park, but it's very much a candidate. The fossils indicate it is Cretaceous, and there's a perfect overhang for viewing," the man went on.

The girls also speculated about the news that the house's owner, Monsieur Dumas, and Julie's grandmother were somewhere around. Could they be back together? They lingered, they ordered coffee, but no Lorna or Armand-Loup. These two were late getting up after an afternoon romp for old times' sake and were having a nip of *porto* in Armand's rooms, only coming in to eat at quarter to ten, looking very cheerful and clearly had already had their *apéritifs.*

Above the bakery, Lorna had done her best at getting presentable, for there wasn't a long mirror in Armand's rooms, only a shaving mirror over the washbasin in the bathroom, okay for putting on lipstick and combing your hair. Armand was wearing an old green shooting jacket and chinos and looked dashing, she thought. For people of their age, they were a handsome couple, showing that life had treated them well and they had not affronted the world, either. An intimation of felicity must have struck Armand-Loup at the same moment it had struck Lorna. He said, "Seems right to have you back here, Lo."

"Mm. *Moi aussi,*" she said. This sentiment just came out in French. She did feel very comfortable.

"After you left, I came to realize how I miss you," he said. Lorna was startled; he was doubtless referring to their last angry argument, her very well-founded accusations. "I'm sorry you left."

"No more reproaches from me. I came to realize people are how they are," Lorna said. She hoped he wouldn't take that to mean that she had come to accept his demeaning, unseemly chasing of women. But anyway, this was not a negotiation, their marriage was over.

"I have come to realize many things," Armand-Loup said, but they left it there. By the time they got to the restaurant, Julie and the others had gone, but had left a note in case Grandma came in.

Back in Armand's room again after dinner, Lorna put in a call to Hams, midafternoon in California, but Misty was asleep. "We miss you, darling," said Lorna. "Courage."

Lorna reflected as she snuggled under the covers that it had been easy to fall into bed with Armand that afternoon—making such things easy had always been his specialty. And kind of nice, with the ease of long practice together, love amid the fecund aromas of rising yeast and warm baking from Pâtisserie Friandise below. Really, late middle age was not so bad. She had never thought of it with dread, but now she appreciated its true comforts.

Earlier she had been to see the village's Woodses at the *mairie*—a serious holding requiring delicate and protracted management, if only for one reason, as Armand pointed out, to avoid flooding the market. Russell's remaining dozen works—a couple of them less finished, and ten very fine ones—were stacked in Barbara Levier's office at the *mairie* with newspapers between the canvases to prevent damage. She'd have to look up whether newsprint came off. The smaller paintings, each about two feet wide, could certainly be carried on an airplane without a problem. She could probably take two at a time as personal luggage. She didn't want to know too much about the legality of that. "It's probably okay," Armand said.

Lorna looked at the pictures a long time, thinking of Van Gogh's crows, trying to see if something in them predicted Russ's darkening mood before his death; had he felt a premonition, an approaching void? Russell had died suddenly of pneumonia, it was said. It had seemed such an old-fashioned way to die. She shivered a little. What was the new way? What better way? She saw that the last two pictures did use more black; the blacks were deeper and more enveloping, so that the gargoyles were almost hidden in shadow, glaring out ready to pounce.

What tremendous good fortune that the task of seeing to them had fallen to Lorna. How strange that Julie and Ran's daughter Gilda were here in Pont, in Armand's house—the big house that had been hers, too; maybe she'd see the family and the house tomorrow before the ceremony for poor Russell. Her head was almost too full of dislocated and jet-lagged thoughts to sleep, but she slept well.

Ran and Amy talked to Gilda every day, often more than once, and they hadn't been alarmed by her daily symptoms until New Year's morning, when she had told them about a trace of pink mucous coming out of her vagina.

"It isn't pee," she said. "It's some kind of discharge." Ran took the phone and asked a few terse questions. Did she have back pain or cramps? Headache?

"None of that, just a sort of a menstrual feeling from time to time. About an hour ago, but now I'm fine. It's not that bad," Gilda assured them, "it's like a period, but no real blood, it's more pink traces." Yet again, her lifelong acquaintance with health emergencies had given her considerable calm and dispassionate frankness.

After a few more questions, Ran had learned everything he dreaded: Gilda a million miles away, almost three months too early, in danger of a miscarriage, or, in the best case, of giving birth to a premature infant, and they needed to line up somewhere with the proper neonatal equipment.

He told her to lie down immediately and call him back if she experienced any cramps. "Take it easy," Ran insisted, knowing that Gilda would do as she pleased. He felt his own breathing grow shortened with anxiety, a wake-up call to calm down about Gilda, Curt, Harvey Avon, Peggy, the financial crash—all the things that were constricting his arteries with panic and plaque. It'll be better on the plane, he told himself.

49

The ceremony for reburying Saint Brigitte, Russell Woods, and the other accidentally unearthed dead of the village would be at eleven on January 2. The weather was not raining so far. The young Americans had been interested to see the preparations the day before: the ground bare and newly turned, like a turnip field in winter. The polished, shining tombstones, with the air of having been set up all at the same time, resembled a new game of dominoes. Small family sarcophagi sprouted among the graves, looking almost livable, like marble pup tents. "You might think the tombs had been moved from somewhere else, or that the place was recovering from some disastrous flood," Carla said. They were rapt at the smell of the loamy, newly dug earth, at the menacing gaping open graves, with the tombstones already labeled; it might be the day of the Resurrection with the people already raptured away. This, too, had occurred to Carla, who had had more religious education than Gilda or Julie: the dead people had left their tombs and had ascended to paradise.

Gilda had called her parents again, to ask if they would get there in time for this event. "When are you coming? There'll be ceremonies tomorrow, where they are reburying the bones that got washed out of the cemetery, or something like that," she said.

. . .

The order of the ceremony had been planned for months. Le Père François would say prayers over the bones of Saint Brigitte but had hesitated
about what to say about the case of Russell Woods in case he was Jewish. He had consulted a list of Jewish surnames and found it there with
two spellings, "Woods" and "Wood." Lorna Mott didn't know Russ's
religion but didn't think he was Jewish—she only knew he came from
Iowa; Russ had preferred not to speak of his earlier life. His fascination
with painting churches, he had said, was purely aesthetic. Nonetheless
Father François did not wish to compromise the spiritual destiny of a
person of another faith or impinge on the prerogatives of another pas-
tor, and so had asked a rabbi he knew to come down from Lyon for the
event; and together they devised a few nondenominational words of
remembrance.

Just to be sure, they had also invited a woman they knew who
also lived in La Charce, who conducted pagan festivals and alternative religious rites for the numerous Protestants in the area, she having
been ordained in the Universal Light Church of—something, no one
was quite sure about its name. And other uncertainties remained. For
one thing, the bones of Pont-les-Puits, having been buried once before,
wouldn't the appended souls have long since flown to wherever they
were going? Father François could find no theological rules about the
reburial of bones of people whose souls had already moved on. The best
they could do was obey the dictates of humane good taste and renew
their good wishes for smooth sailing in the afterlife.

The headstones had been cleaned and put to right, and holes had
been dug, but a ceremonious simultaneous burial of dozens of new
or rebuilt coffins was out of the question because of the manpower
required, so it was left to each family to cope with the practicalities of
filling in the graves in the days to come; Saint Brigitte's reburial would
symbolize the others, too. Armand-Loup had successfully argued
for Russell Woods's bones to be dealt with at the same time as Saint
Brigitte's—the saint and Russell the two leading stars of the forthcoming *obsèques*.

On the day itself, Gilda, Carla, and Julie were among the first attendees standing on the damp slopes of the cemetery. The weather was not terribly propitious. There was the smell of damp in the air, but the form in which it would declare itself was unclear. The geologists and the contingent of the new visitors from the Dumas house added to the general excitement of the occasion. The locals remembered Julie as a tot, Mademoiselle Peggy's daughter—if you remembered Mademoiselle Peggy, Madame Dumas's daughter. Her old neighbors were especially delighted to see Madame Dumas after her half a year's absence, and apparently she was still perfectly friendly with Monsieur Dumas despite rumors of their divorce. They all agreed that little Julie was now grown into a very beautiful young woman in her own right, plus now there was a young woman who did the marketing and errands and a very young, pale, very pregnant adolescent. The village also enjoyed some new, especially titillating gossip: up at Monsieur Dumas's house— though he himself was still living over the bakery—Madame Dumas's first husband, the father of Mademoiselle Peggy, was soon expected with his second wife as tenants.

At about eleven, Lorna and Armand-Loup approached the cemetery from the top of the hill. A small crowd had gathered in random clusters at various distances from the central graves. A little procession of seven or eight townspeople approached the cemetery, which lay on the downhill slope below the road at the southern end of the town. Two villagers bore between them a small stretcher upon which sat a large black cube, evidently a funerary box. On top of the box lay an artist's palette and brushes, painted gold.

"Put the Woods bones next to his *fosse* for now," instructed Mayor Barbara Levier to Monsieur Flores, coming along from the *mairie* with his shovel. "Bonjour, Armand; bonjour, Lorna."

Another small coffin-shaped box was lowered into the grave marked with an imposing stone cross; the artist's smaller box went into another hole nearby, as yet unmarked by a monument. A couple of people dropped clods into the saint's grave, but otherwise the troughs were not filled in.

Since they were a distance away and everyone wore dark coats and hats or headscarves and shivered in the drizzle, Armand and Lorna didn't see whether the tenants of their house, among them her grandchild Julie, were there, though surely they'd make an effort to attend this big civic event?

Down below them, standing next to Father François, a tall woman in a long white robe, whose voice carried up to them, began to speak: "We know that these bones are still suffused with the energy of the living, these bones contain life. Similarly these tombs, besides being reliquaries for the bones of our loved departed, are passages between the material world and the spiritual world. The rites we observe today were conducted by our ancestors in this very glen, preparing us all for the passage between the two worlds, which our beloved friends have already trod and are now retracing their steps."

Almost without willing it, Gilda, Carla, and Julie had drawn closer to the procession and fallen in among the mourners. Ahead of the procession, a small grave had been dug at the foot of an imposing marble plinth, a spire perhaps ten feet high. In her newbie French, Carla asked another of the mourners who it was being buried: *"C'est qui?"*

"These are the bones of Monsieur Woods, and there are Saint Brigitte's bones. *Attendez,* the box will be lowered and there will be speeches."

> *Deep peace of the rising wave to you*
> *Deep peace of the sweet air to you*
> *Deep peace of the slumbering earth to you,*
> *Deep peace of the night stars to you*
> *Infinite peace to you . . . ,*

intoned the priestess. Armand and Lorna continued to watch for a few minutes before concluding that similar words were going to be spoken over every newly dug grave. They decided to head back to the bakery but instead found themselves watching to the end.

"Deep peace, Lorna *chérie,*" said Armand.

"Sweetheart," Lorna agreed.

.   .   .

It suddenly began to rain, which lent to the scene a bleakness suitable to the burial of whatever poor creatures were leaving the light of the world for darkness and mud. People stirred and put up umbrellas or the hoods of their anoraks. The priestess began to speak more quickly. As she spoke, she appeared distracted by the sight of a strange being gracing this ceremony, and sure to vanish: a young—very young—pregnant virgin wearing a raincoat, with a halo around her head, an effect created by the feeble sun shining behind Gilda's crown of silver braids.

The priestess gave in to the temptation to wind up her speech and get out her cell-phone camera, dissembling her objective—Gilda—with a show of photographing the whole assembly, a growing crowd of celebrants, or mourners, whoever they were. She captured a significant image.

Julie said to Gilda and Carla, "Look, there's my grandmother." Turning, Gilda slipped and fell. Her fall was minor enough: on the slippery grass of the slope above the diggings; on account of her unfamiliar center of gravity she lost her footing, tipped over like a teapot, and slid a little distance toward the graves, unhurt but getting muddy and feeling humiliated.

The sight of a pregnant female sustaining a fall, even that mere slip, had brought people rushing to her side, and this was what enraged her—her new category of fragile, dependent female valued only for her role in perpetuating the human race. In a furious voice, as they walked back to the house, she protested that she was fine, but she was not. The injustice of it all had finally seized her.

Back at the house, Gilda went to take off her muddy clothes, unsure about whether to lie down as she ought to do before lunch, call her parents as usual at this time, or go back outside to try to get a closer look at her father's first wife, a person of immense interest. Gilda had never seen Lorna, mother of her half siblings and Julie's grandmother, but she had spotted the person she thought Julie was pointing out, the woman standing with their landlord, Monsieur Dumas. But they had been too far away to tell much.

She took off her muddy pants and shoes, wondering whether her mother would approve of her meeting Dad's other wife, a situation which had never come up in Gilda's experience, which had always been that Lorna was hardly to be spoken of.

The mud was clingy, slimy, all over her shins and forearms; she had to have a bath, and noticed more of the funny viscous substance in the bathwater, a trail of rose pigment, as if she'd floated a length of pink thread in the tub. She decided it must have been something already there from a frayed cleaning rag or something. She got dressed and walked over to the inn with Carla, who was waiting for her. But she felt a little funny, probably from the fall.

The discharge came back during the night, and another pinkish trail stained her pajamas. In the morning, she thought she better tell Carla. "I rinsed it out," she said. "Kind of a slithery red thing." Carla called Ran and Amy straightaway and left a message.

Amy and Ran had been flying to Paris to see Gilda at intervals throughout the fall, but it had been almost eight weeks since they had been there, delayed by the ongoing national financial troubles that affected Amy's business affairs. Gilda had called her parents from Pont-les-Puits on New Year's Day about headaches and mounting blood pressure, and other strange symptoms, and as a result they were already preparing to leave for France when they connected with Gilda about the slithery red string.

From Paris they would take the train to Valence, and rent a car for the drive to the village, to the house they had taken at Peggy's recommendation, a house large enough for a big family New Year's vacation. Ran and Amy had been unable to find the village of Pont on maps, but they counted on GPS when they got there, and they knew Carla and Gilda had reliably found it.

They had been a little worried by the Google Earth views of this region of France, the Drôme—nothing but the tiniest medieval villages and slow, stony roads; if Gilda should go into labor, say, or have some other medical emergency, it would be at least an hour to any town of size. Luckily, though the area was mountainous, there were enough flat fields to land a helicopter.

Ran had figured that the only responsible adult in Pont-les-Puits to see to Gilda was Carla, but he had also heard from Ursula, who had heard from Ian, who had heard from Julie via email, that Lorna was in Pont-les-Puits; he speculated that it had to do with her marital situation. Ran didn't know whether he could rely on her. Though he and Lorna had spoken from time to time in California since their lunch, they had recently spiked some new irritation over an issue relating to Hams and had sunk back into their official long-term estrangement. But she would know the region.

On the phone, he asked Carla to find Lorna, and Carla had already learned enough about the sociology of Pont-les-Puits to go directly to the bar at Hôtel La Périchole, known for its finger on the pulse of village activities as well as for its little cocktail meatballs, to ask where Madame Dumas was apt to be.

Thus Lorna got a surprising phone call as she was getting out of Armand's bathtub—Ran, very agitated: "Lorna, I'm sorry to—it sounds like my daughter Gilda might need some help, at least from what she tells us. We're on our way there, we're in the airport. She's there, in that village where you are, with her cousin Julie and others.

"She's only seven months along," he went on, upset, slightly incoherent. "Did you know she was pregnant? It's a—well— She's there in the village—what's it called? Seven months—a premature infant could live if there's a hospital with adequate neonatal facilities, and we thought you probably can find that out, if they have them, or your husband would know, or you would, from living there, and could get her to a hospital if it looks like . . ."

Of course she would help. "Is she at the house?" Lorna asked, seeing the problems: Was there a hospital in Valence that could deal with a teen having a baby? Would Armand-Loup know? What if they had to deliver a baby on the way to find a hospital? There was a kind of familiar joy—being of use and trusted.

"Don't worry, I'll go see her—Gilda?—right away," Lorna reassured him.

"We've got a flight in an hour, thank you so much, Lorna, just worried to death. Here's our phone number—you have my cell . . . ?"

"Yes, yes, what is it?" Lorna assured him, scrabbling in Armand's drawer for a pencil.

"I'll call you when we know what's going on. Don't worry," she said as heartily and reassuringly as she could, while wondering what on earth to do. Should she really interfere in her former husband's life-and-death situation? No, but of course she had to. Despite a feeling of being drawn backward, she went to find Armand-Loup, who would know better than she about suitable hospitals. She knew there was none in Pont.

At his side by the phone, Amy reached for Ran's hand and pressed it against the side of her right breast.

"Do you feel that? Is that a lump?" Ran pushed a little against the soft tissue.

"Not really. I'll see later." He was used to Amy's anxieties taking the form of breast lumps or sometimes leukemia. "I don't feel anything," he added. He heard her little intake of breath, reassured.

50

To see the right thing to do and not to do it is cowardice.

In Pont, Lorna and Armand-Loup hurried up to their former house, where they found things in perfect order. There were their sofa cushions of blue velvet arranged as before, their Quimper plates on the kitchen wall. Lorna introduced herself to Gilda and Carla as Julie's grandmother.

"The mama of Peggy, Julie's mother. I just talked to Gilda's father. He asked me to look in on you, to make sure all is well."

"Thank you, Madame Dumas," said Gilda in her best Saint Waltraud's manner. "I'm fine, really."

Lorna thought Gilda a pretty child, though in her view not as pretty as her half sister, Peggy, had been at that age; but you could see a family resemblance. Gilda had a strange pallor. Lorna felt a motherly surge of concern for her, a child far too young to be having a baby, and so far from her parents. Lorna had heard most of the story from Peggy. Poor Ran. She was ashamed to have laughed maliciously to think his late-born child, with another woman, was having an unwed pregnancy at fifteen.

After a short conversation, Lorna was reassured that all was well. "I did slip and fall down at the ceremony, but no harm done," Gilda said.

Lorna left them with her phone number and instructions to call if they needed her. She sent Ran a reassuring text.

Only an hour later, though, Carla came rushing into the pâtisserie seeking Lorna, who had gone out for a late lunch with Armand and was just strolling up.

"Mrs. Dumas, would you please come now? We think Gilda might be going into labor."

Lorna's worst fear. The poor girl could not have fallen into more incompetent hands. Lorna and Armand followed Carla up to the house, where Julie was hovering excitedly over the frightened Gilda, belly swollen like a pack animal's, sitting in a chair in the salon with a miserable though alert expression, as if expecting armed men to come in the door. She explained that she had had a bad pain, right after Lorna left, and was worried that she was going to have another one soon.

"We probably should get you to a hospital," Lorna agreed in what she hoped was a reassuring tone.

"I'll go look for Charlotte Bakewell, the Protestant from La Charce who was at the graveyard earlier today," Armand-Loup said. "She had lunch—I think she's still around. Maybe she would come along with us as a safety measure. She said she was going to wait for dark, to see the glowing of the saint's grave."

"It glows?" Lorna wondered.

"Yes, yes, they say. But she's some kind of midwife. I don't know certified by whom. The English have midwives because they can't afford hospitals, I'm told. She was at La Roulette having lunch," he said. "I'll go get her and I'll get my car."

Carla said, "I can drive, we have a big SUV."

"Armand can lead us," Lorna said. "Can you walk out to the car?"

"Sure, yes," Gilda said, looking relieved to have something to do. She got up, then doubled over slightly with a pain which seemed to Lorna to have come rather soon; had she not been having a contraction an hour ago when Lorna came in? Was something imminent?

"Maybe we should start?" said Carla. "Our car is right in front." As they got into it, Armand drew up in his small Peugeot with the priestess, or whatever she was, who clambered out and looked at Gilda with an informed eye. "I'm not sure those are real contractions," she said. "Yet."

Before Gilda's next pain, Lorna and the midwife had piled into Carla's rented SUV with Gilda. "I'll come along with her," the midwife said, in an authoritative voice, indicating Gilda, who was getting into the front seat with Carla. "Better get in back, dear." Charlotte Bakewell was English, like many residents of the Drôme region, with a reassuring upper-class accent and an air of competence.

With everyone studiously preserving calm and optimism, they set off. Armand-Loup drove behind them with Julie in the Peugeot, then pulled around them and led the way. No one mentioned prematurity or danger. Gilda herself did not seem to be suffering horribly, just uttering syllables of "er" and "uff" from time to time. The midwife, Charlotte Bakewell, sitting in back with Gilda, was highly pleased by the adventure, excited that her skills might suddenly be needed by the side of the road.

Lorna, too, had a moment of amazed, inappropriate happiness at finding herself back in France, hurtling through the stony, morainic landscape, albeit with a groaning pregnant teen and an English midwife, with Armand rattling along before on an errand of mercy. It was an epiphany she'd have to think about later, if it survived: the impression that she belonged here, helping with life as it happened, and not in California brooding about some trivial lecture no one cared about. She belonged with her family—parts of it, Julie, even Ran's family, even Gilda—for they were all enmeshed, and that was wonderful, living out her days in dear Pont-les-Puits giving her lectures to the visiting foodies if to anyone and letting her hair turn its natural color, whatever that turned out to be by now. Of course she knew this feeling of fulfillment would probably pass.

The drive seemed endless through the bleak landscape of rocks and gnarled brush, and the general air of desolation oppressed them further with a sense of impending catastrophe. Gilda writhed in increasing discomfort. "Errr, ufff," she moaned. Charlotte Bakewell coached her: "Breathe, deep breath, try to relax . . ." Between "ers" and "uffs," Gilda called her parents again, but there was no connection. She began to pant in a new register, faster.

"How far is it?" the midwife asked. "With very young women, labor can be short. It can be sudden." Only a little after this, Gilda screamed and thrashed with especial anguish. The midwife slipped off the seat, knelt on the floor of the SUV, and pressed Gilda into a more or less horizontal position on the seat.

The baby will be born dead, Lorna thought, foreseeing that the birth was going to happen right then and there, and the baby would probably be too premature to live; but she had no idea what to do. "Carla, pull over." Carla pulled over on a wide shoulder.

"She's precipitating. It's common with teens," said the midwife. "Here, let's get you out of your jeans," undoing Gilda's zipper and tugging at the pants legs of baggy jeans Gilda had bought big enough to fit over her belly. The awkward business of peeling them off Gilda's ivory legs was accomplished between the contractions, which came closer and closer together. They could see, on Gilda's inner thigh, a discreetly small tattoo that read VINCIT in cursive.

"Oh my God," said Carla, "when did she get that? Her parents will freak out."

Soon the poor child made a new sound, animal-like and agonized, and the midwife pushed her naked legs apart. This spasm over, Gilda struggled to sit up to stare at the lower half of her own body. The others at first looked politely away from her silver-furred crotch with something bulging partway out of her vagina. Then Gilda's new moan started and just as quickly turned to a scream, and suddenly the midwife was dealing with the slippery object that emerged from between Gilda's legs. They heard Gilda utter a huge exhalation of relief as the awkward, distending object left the birth canal with a whoosh.

Lorna and Carla from the front seat had twisted around to look, Lorna feeling faint. The birth process had only taken a couple of minutes. As Lorna remembered giving birth, it had taken hours of deep breathing and groaning. Had this appalling experience been what she herself had gone through three times? And every woman on earth? Carla looked shaken, too. Would this put her off motherhood? Thank heavens Julie was in the other car.

"Is it alive?" Carla asked in a fearful whisper. They were afraid to hear the answer, but Charlotte Bakewell said, "Wait," and made little slapping sounds against the creature's tiny back. A small bleat emerged. Lorna handed over her scarf, which the woman used to dab at the baby—living, apparently, though infinitely minuscule; it could have been a ferret or the fetus of a seal. They saw the tiny limbs twitch. Gilda, still scooted up to a sitting position, watched in amazement. Lorna's ears rang with terror that the little thing would die before they got to Valence, would just start and then run down, like a battery toy when the batteries go.

"Yes, breathing, but we should drive on, we should get her to whatever facilities they'll have in Valence," said Charlotte, swaddling the baby in Lorna's Hermès scarf. "She's definitely low birth weight, she can't be three pounds. She may have trouble breathing."

"Babies can live at that weight," said Gilda. "Usually babies of diabetic mothers are large." That was the extent of what she'd looked up.

The midwife carefully put the wrapped baby into her own blouse and inside her bra, to free her hands to press for a minute on Gilda's stomach. "What's this?" she asked, encountering the insulin pump stuck to Gilda's side.

"Gilda, honey, are you all right?" Lorna said, seeing that the girl was even paler than before, if possible, and her face was wet with sweat.

"Lie back," said Charlotte, "there's the placenta to come." Carla had already started the car and waved out of the window to Armand-Loup, who was just getting out of his Peugeot, signaling him to get back in and drive. He and Julie had not even had time to comprehend the significance of the last few moments by the side of the road.

"She's not bleeding, that's good," said Charlotte Bakewell. "You'll have another cramp now, but it won't be too bad." Gilda said nothing, just sagged against the seat, damp and inert.

They were only ten minutes from Valence, following Armand-Loup, who knew where the hospital was, wending down unfamiliar streets lined by trees pruned to knuckles for winter. The hospital was several stories high, in need of paint, its name written in cursive neon on a small registration building. They drove up to the emergency entrance. By the time they piled out of the car, Gilda had struggled back into her jeans and was trying to walk in with the others, but an orderly appeared with a wheelchair. Lorna took her arm, but it seemed to her that Gilda walked more steadily than she to the chair and sank into it. The seat of her jeans was wet and stained.

"Not quite ready to go back to the cotton fields," Gilda apologized.

Inside the hospital, the Englishwoman, Charlotte, rushed with the baby into the inner spaces of the emergency room, and a nurse stepped over to push the wheelchair. Carla dabbed anxiously at Gilda's sweaty forehead. Julie and Armand-Loup stood by the desk, Armand attempting to explain. "This young girl has just given birth, she needs care. There is a baby. It is small and it needs a specialist." Armand had to say it several times with increasing volume.

"Oui, monsieur, sit over there. Calmez-vous."

"Let me have my telephone, I need to call my parents," Gilda said. "It was a girl?"

"Yes," Lorna said. "Very tiny. Miss—Charlotte—has gone to see what they are doing with her." The Englishwoman had disappeared somewhere with the impossibly small baby. What if they didn't have an incubator here, or special equipment?

"She looked very sturdy, though, I thought," said Lorna trying to radiate assurance and comfort, feeling dismay.

"I still think Pomona. I'm not sure about Deiopea. All those vowels," Gilda said in a weak voice.

"Just wait, sweet," said Carla. "First things first."

"She needs a name, though," Gilda said. She was poking at her cell phone. "This works now." She started to say, "Mommy, the baby is here," to Amy's voice mail, but thought better of it until they knew what would happen. Why get them upset? "Just checking in," she said to the phone. "Everything is fine." To Lorna she said, "May I see her?"

"Wait," said Lorna. A pall of incertitude and fear about the baby overrode her worry for Gilda, who, although said to have delicate health, was seeming improbably stalwart. She was taken away, presumably to a room. Lorna and Armand waited with Julie and Carla on the uncomfortable benches of the waiting room wondering if they should follow. Carla had begun to sob lightly into a Kleenex.

The nurse pushed Gilda's wheelchair into a dim, bare room, where the window shades were pulled down and an incubator stood glowing in the middle like a television set. There was a chair or two against the wall, and a hard-looking metal bed on wheels next to the incubator. Gilda peered into the incubator.

Oh, please don't let me bond, Gilda prayed, looking at the small animal in the incubator; it—she—was wearing a little undershirt. It—she, Pomona—wasn't cute; she was like some other mammal altogether, rat or chipmunk, she was so small. Gilda thought she fended off the bonding feeling pretty well—she felt curiosity and concern, but not more. It would be interesting to see how she grew. Gilda's breasts stung a little, but she fended that off as well. She couldn't seem to develop thoughts, just an empty, ringing in her head.

Someone came and spoke to her in French, too fast for her to understand, and then, improbably, took the baby out of the incubator, pulled off its little undershirt, and stuffed the naked creature down the front of Gilda's shirt, a warm, wettish thing against her skin. She understood some words about contact with the *peau*. Something about a kangaroo, evidently the same word in both languages. Gestures made it clear Gilda was to sit quietly on the chair next to the incubator. She sat obediently, but did try her cell again and again to try to reach her parents but failed to. She felt the baby breathe, could see the barest rhythmic rising of its little back. She was terrified, and she felt weak now, and dizzy. She had given birth less than an hour ago; she had lost track. She wanted to sleep.

She tried to remember the giving birth part but couldn't.

In the waiting room, Lorna and Armand were confined to their chairs by their sense of proper hospital conduct, too daunted by the sanctity of hospital precincts to breach them by blustering behind the nurses' station unasked. Finally, a nurse came in and suggested they go get Gilda some dry clothes. *"Nous allons la retenir ce soir."*

"How can we leave her?" Lorna protested.

"I'm staying with her," Carla said.

"She's in a hospital. They will look after her," Armand said, planning to take Lorna and go. "We'll come tomorrow with clean clothes."

Lorna declined. "I have to see if all is well. The poor child gave birth a half hour ago and she was walking around. Maybe she's fainted or is bleeding," Lorna protested.

"Was it a girl?" Armand asked to no one in particular.

"I'll be right back. I'm going to check on her. She shouldn't be alone back there." She mustered an air of entitlement and walked around the nurses' station, which no one objected to, and found herself in a corridor with one open door, where Gilda was to be seen sitting up in a hospital bed, clutching her useless cell phone. She brightened at seeing Lorna.

"I guess I just have to sit like this. Is there any word from my parents?"

Lorna now saw the tip of the baby's head nestled under the top of Gilda's shirt and the bulge of a little body against her chest. She pulled up another of the chairs and sat with the terrified girl and the baby, who was tethered to bottles on stands.

"How do you feel, Gilda? Shouldn't you have something—some juice or a sandwich? I'll try to get something for you. You will have amazing stories to tell, someday, about this surreal experience," she said, not really expecting Gilda to understand this but trying for a positive tone. She understood that these remarks hardly rose to the enormity of what had happened to the girl.

"I'm sorry, I don't know where my insulin kit is. Is it in the car we came in? It's in my backpack."

"What do you need?" Lorna had been thinking she would want a comb or lipstick, and that she might be hungry.

"Some test strips, I guess, and I have some glucose tablets. And maybe I need an insulin cartridge. Maybe a cannula." Now Lorna saw that Gilda had to deal with some other problem. Had Peggy once mentioned diabetes?

"I'll get it. Your parents are on their way." She would just as soon not encounter Ran and Amy, but felt guilty about feeling relieved that she'd miss them. "I'll go look for your backpack, and bring it back if it's in the car. Otherwise we'll go get you some food."

Gilda agreed stoically with everything, but Lorna couldn't forget her look of abandonment and despair. She was about to say she'd stay with the child, when a man, perhaps a doctor, came in and gruffly told her to leave, looking at his watch. He made broom-sweeping gestures to rid the room of her.

Gilda said, "It's okay, Mrs. Dumas, I'll ask them here for test strips and some orange juice. *Jus d'orange?*" But Lorna could see she was frightened.

Lorna and Armand walked to his car, planning to get some food for Gilda; who knew when the hospital would feed her? She'd mentioned orange juice. "They must think the baby is strong enough to be out of the incubator. She wasn't attached to anything."

"No, she was," Armand said. "There was a tiny tube in her nostril. The machine was next to the bed."

"I didn't see the tube. Do you think that hospital has the necessary— the special things needed?" She had read about essential compounds to clear the lungs, of vitamins injected at birth, silver nitrate, advanced machines that saved the lives of ever-more-premature fetuses.

"I doubt it," Armand said. "Well, I don't know. It looks modern enough."

In the metal bed with its thin blanket, the dazed Gilda saw more clearly than before that the world is ruthless: when you have a baby, it is all your problem. If you are female. Never mind if it wasn't even your fault. Never mind if you were tired or going to have a hypoglycemic crash. Her bottom was still soaked, maybe something was leaking out of her, but she didn't dare shift her position. It could be blood.

The baby plastered to her chest was breathing steadily, softly; it was the incubator machine that made the whimpering noise audible. All Gilda could see looking down was the top of its head, with dark fuzz on it, at least it wasn't silver. She didn't dare move. No one came. No one had ever not come before, and it was a new feeling, not entirely horrible. It gave her a fortified, adult sense. She passed into a tense, exhausted sleep.

When she waked, there were noises of clanking carts, and food smells. Had she slept? What was the time? She knew she needed some orange juice, but she was exhausted, too, and felt herself nod off a little again, thinking about how life could change with you having no say about it, you just drifting along in a helpless panic like a stick in a stream.

She thought about how Virgil's Deiopea the Beautiful seemed not allowed to have personal feelings, she was just shuffled off to Aeolus, god of the wind, without anyone asking her, her job was just to make him the parent of fine offspring, she had no choice . . . Or was it that Virgil was too sexist to care about what Deiopea felt? Anyway, it was good not to have named Pomona "Deiopea," who had no personal volition. She thought about reading book 2 in the eleventh grade.

She had a terrible headache beginning, really needed food or her glucose tablets, but she was afraid to move with the baby attached; she was frozen there. Nurses and people looked in, and she finally called, *"Aidez-moi."* Her French was pretty awful, but when they heard, they came right away, and a nurse said in English that her grandmother was there. How much time had passed? The nurse carefully put the baby back in the incubator. *"Une heure à la fois,"* she explained. *"Une robe,"* and helped Gilda change into a new gown in the curtained booth in the corner of the room. Through the curtains Gilda saw that Carla was there, too.

"They said I could come in. There's the baby!" She peered into the incubator, her face contorted into something between tears and joy.

"I'm supposed to wear her like a kangaroo."

"I've heard about that, it helps them. Babies." Carla then remembered what she wanted to ask Gilda. "Gilda, sweetie, the tattoo. When did you get that?"

"Bookney and I got them after a Circle of Faith meeting once."

"Your parents will not like it."

"I guess they have bigger things to worry about now," Gilda said, coming out from behind the curtain wearing the awkward purple hospital gown, and the nurse helped her back into the bed. Just then Lorna rushed in with Gilda's backpack. Gilda wondered if Mrs. Dumas had described herself as her grandmother, which she wasn't really.

Think what the girl had been through. Lorna admired this valiant child, and was certainly relieved to see the tiny lump of baby sleeping quietly in the incubator, attached reassuringly to monitors and breathing devices, which would surely sound an alarm if all was not well? The room was dark and cell-like, monasterial but noisy, mops clanging, cleaning apparatuses and carts wheeling up and down the corridors and, in the adjacent rooms, bells going off. "Here's your backpack," she told Gilda. "What do you need? I'll tell them."

Gilda opened her backpack and fished stuff out of it—a vial, a plastic box, some tubing. She opened the box and popped a lozenge into her mouth. "Thanks so much, Mrs. Dumas, I didn't know how to ask for anything," she said. "I don't know the word for diabetes."

"Diabète," Lorna said. She'd given up trying to call Ran and Amy, who seemed to exist permanently in a zone not covered by a signal, though she'd been able to leave one message when she seemed to be connected to their voice mail.

It was true they'd been in a series of dead zones.

When Amy and Ran finally got on the Air France morning flight, SFO–Paris CDG, they knew only that Gilda might be in labor. When they landed in Paris Saturday around nine, they couldn't get her on her cell phone. They went directly to the Gare de Lyon for a train to Valence and planned to drive from there to Pont-les-Puits.

It seemed hard to believe that there would be places in civilized modern France where you couldn't reach someone on a cell phone, but they could get neither Julie nor Carla on their phones and had no idea where they were.

"It's the same in, I don't know, Idaho, probably," Ran said.

"Montana."

"Puglia, remember that time in Italy?"

On the train to Valence, they still had had no luck reaching anybody, and continued in tortured ignorance, knowing only from one hurried text message that the baby had been born.

51

Once in Valance, they rented a Citroën SUV in the Valence station and instructed the GPS, which spoke to them in French. They didn't know how to change her language but *à droit, à gauche,* it was simple enough. Amy drove and Ran manned the cell phone, trying at ten-minute intervals to reach Gilda or Carla. "Why is there GPS but no cell-phone service?" he fretted.

According to the GPS, it was fewer than a hundred kilometers to Pont-les-Puits, but would take almost two hours on the small roads. They decided to check the Valence hospitals before heading for Pont. There were several, so they started with the biggest. The phone in Valence worked fine; their French well enough: "Was there a young woman admitted, having a baby? Do you have a new patient in the OB ward? *Service obstétrique?*"

"*Attendez, je vais demander.*"

At the first hospital they called, apparently the main hospital, they learned with joy that a young American had been admitted on the maternity ward lately. Perhaps still there but being readied for transfer. They typed in the address and started on the route GPS directed them. "They didn't mention about the baby," Amy said. "Why would they transfer her?" That could mean out of danger or needing special treatment. The ambiguity was chilling. Was the baby born, was it okay, was it even Gilda?

"They wouldn't transfer someone really sick," Ran said.

In the waiting room, there were no magazines, just an old auction catalog from Paris, which Lorna appropriated and read fitfully; the auction sale was of amateurish watercolors with one or two more accomplished painters sweetening the others, all to be sold, or had been sold. Someone had penciled in some prices in the margins. Nothing on Woods's level; still, Lorna studied the suggested opening bids; she needed to be conversant with the art market. She was alone; Carla was sitting with Gilda, and Armand had gone for Gilda's clothes and personal items for her transfer to a hospital in Lyon, where the baby would receive specialized neonatal care.

She became aware of excited voices in the hall, and then heard the double doors to the hallway and then the door behind her opening, American voices, one familiar—the man. She turned and saw it was Ran. Well, Gilda's father. She felt thankful he was there—he had always made her and other people feel taken care of, a physician's skill. Even if they couldn't get along, he made her feel safe. The young woman—youngish—must be Amy, Gilda's mother. Despite herself, Lorna felt a little flutter of some emotion she couldn't characterize. She got up; they rushed toward her.

"Is she here?" Ran asked.

"Yes, in a room, and the baby, but they're being flown to Lyon very soon."

"Amy, this is Lorna," he said to his wife.

To Lorna's surprise, the woman seized her in a hug, saying, "Thank you, thank you." Amy was thin as a model and had shoulder-length dark hair, like a girl, but up close, she looked her age, in her fifties, with the beginnings of crow's-feet and fine lines above her lip. Why was Lorna even thinking about Amy's age?

"Show us where to go," Ran said. No one impeded them passing the nurses' station and heading down the neon-lit corridor beyond.

Gilda's was the first room. There was Gilda, in her hospital gown, sitting stuck on a chair, apparently tethered to the incubator, her chin sunk on her chest, asleep, her strange silver hair in oily strings. They were stricken into silence. Tiptoeing in, Lorna, Ran, and Amy gathered to stare into the incubator, where a little being in its undershirt lay breathing. The incubator made a low thunking and wheezing sound, as if it were magnifying its own heartbeat and breath. A sharp whiff of hospital antiseptic scented the room.

"Oh God," Amy whispered, voice tremulous, overcome by the sights of baby and Gilda. The nurse, standing in the door behind them, beckoned to them to come out, and she stepped in to do something to the machine.

Gilda stirred and opened her eyes. Lorna's own eyes shot with tears to see the girl's joy when she realized her parents were there. When she lifted her hands, they saw one was pasted with needles and a tube. Ran and Amy embraced her carefully so as not to dislodge them. *"Je suis la mère,"* Amy said piteously to the nurse, who was trying to stop them from staying.

"Did you see her?" Gilda said. "She's three pounds."

"I need to talk to the doctor," Ran said. "Have you seen the doctor, Gilda?"

"No. Yes, I guess there was a man in here, who worked the machine. I need some more glucose, though." Ran nodded and left the room. In the hall, he found a man, not a doctor, someone he'd not met but who was somehow familiar, carrying some clothes. This guy was his own height, substantial, with curly, graying hair and a cherubic, handsome, merry face. They nodded at each other and, as the man started toward Gilda's room, Ran realized he was probably Armand the Frenchman, the person Lorna had married. He caught his arm. "Ran Mott," he said. "Is that Gilda's stuff?"

"Ah, *oui,* yes," Armand said, smiling. *"Le papa de Gilda?* Armand Dumas." They shook hands perfunctorily, Armand handed Ran the clothing, and Ran rushed to give it to Gilda. It was not her dress, it was her diabetes that worried him. In a hospital, they normally would have cut back her insulin during the birth, but if her insulin pump had continued to work throughout the childbirth process, she would have received too much of it. But he found her alert, luckily not going into insulin shock.

"Honey, did you ask them for glucose?" Ran asked as he rummaged in her backpack for her glucose.

"Mrs. Dumas brought me my tablets. I wasn't sure how to ask in French," Gilda said. "Just now, dreaming, I guess, I dreamed that I was a doctor. I must have been dreaming about you, some sort of ESP."

The pediatrician from Paris had recommended that Pomona and Gilda be transferred to a neonatal unit in Lyon, and it was scheduled by helicopter around noon the following day. "I will feel better," the pediatrician assured them, "when the child has breathing apparatus at hand." Though this delay condemned them, in turn, to a night of panicked vigilance, they were relieved to do something.

Ran was a little shaken by Gilda's detachment about the baby. He was also shaken on account of what he had seen when Amy looked at Pomona, this little blob in an incubator. It was a change in her expression, some combination of tenderness and ferocious focus he remembered her having when Gilda was born, the look of Madonnas in certain paintings, haloed by the intensity of love for the baby, bonding. He saw even more clearly his own future of diaper pong and preschools and worry about teenaged driving and college applications—phases Gilda hadn't even got to yet, now to be prolonged by this new person that Amy would never give up.

52

L ife more often than not defies our wishes.

In San Francisco, an unfamiliar voice answered the telephone at Amy and Ran's Woodside house, and to Ursula's fury and anxiety explained that the Motts were abroad. The voice, some maid or gardener, refused to disclose anything more; for Ursula, the Motts had disappeared; there was no trace of them or news of Gilda and the precious grandchild she was carrying, or of anyone who could tell her anything. Ian knew not much more than she, though he got emails from Gilda from time to time and could reassure his mother that all was well with the mother of his child at least as of the week before Christmas. He volunteered to email Gilda immediately for an update on her condition.

"She has a couple more months, remember," he said.

"How can they let her bat around the world like this?" Ursula stormed. "They must be over there with her. Maybe there's a problem. No, they'd bring her back, I'm sure. What does she say?"

"I just now sent the email," Ian said.

"If she has that baby over there, we have to go over there," Ursula said.

"Mother, it's not till March." In fact, Ian was not entirely sure that when the baby came anyone would tell them. How would they even find out? Maybe Gilda would toss them an email. He'd see what she responded to the friendly inquiry he'd just sent. Ursula, unable to resist some adorable baby clothes she'd seen at Saks, had already laid in four pairs of tiny white kidskin shoes and a little cap-and-sweater set hand-knitted in Portugal on teeny needles in soft gender-neutral green.

So much to look forward to! And recently she had begun dating the Very Reverend Phil Train, who found her a very nice, principled woman, as well as good-looking. He respected and appreciated her inquiry into the attitudes of the Church about abortion, and her concern for the baby expected by the Motts. He took her to the symphony and they had started having dinner at least once a week, and who knew what might develop? He planned to see how she would fit into, and if she would enjoy, some of the social functions at the cathedral.

Peggy, sitting on the balcony of her room at the Peninsula Hotel, looking out over the polluted air of Bangkok, was remembering some words of Curt's. "It's how we live now," he had said, meaning Americans scattered around the world, and Peggy'd thought that didn't really apply to her, someone stuck in Ukiah—but why shouldn't it apply to her? Julie was grown now, Julie her initial reason for staying put for the reliable school system. Now she, Peggy, could stay in Thailand like Curt if she pleased, or any other place, as long as she could swing it. Sell dog collars to the Thai or, for that matter, sell something Thai to Americans. Curt could advise her. Say the charming jackets in Thai silk she had particularly liked in that strong teal color, though the magenta was good, too. She indulged a transient fantasy of living in a suite at the Peninsula, or in some lovely cottage on stilts like you saw here, running an import-export business; though if it were easy, why wouldn't everyone do it?

Visions of possibilities, newly released from the prison of Uki-ahan reality, floated through her mind in different forms—silk jackets, dog collars, studying Thai dance, no, she was too tall, studying it in the scholarly sense, then; making a film about Thai dance. Curt had taken her to a performance of dancers and shadow puppets with mean faces and the ability to turn their hands completely around on their wrists. She'd find some craft based on the iconography of Thai dance. She could write a book about it. To live, she could import the beautiful, amazingly inexpensive silk jackets. Well, she'd be here, so she'd be exporting them. It wouldn't hurt to talk to the people at the place that sold silk, Jim Thompson; maybe they'd need a representative. She might have to modify the design of the Thai jackets to fit Californians, who were bustier and broader in the shoulders. Misty could handle the California end, now that she was feeling better.

She'd felt for a while that her Internet purse-resale business was a little too hands-on, too small-scale, too mumsy. Her mind happily whirred on. Could she get her father to put up some money for a start-up? She was thinking about whether she could live permanently at the Peninsula by renting out her Ukiah house, but the economics didn't work. Who would want to live in Ukiah, even in her tidy, pretty little house?

For lunch, she ordered a couple of items from room service—sweetened tofu flower with ginkgo and water chestnuts, and double-boiled sea conch and morel in chicken broth. She was working her way through the alluring dishes in the several restaurants of the hotel—Thai, Chinese, and European—and today was on to the Chinese menu. Curt was joining her tonight for Thai, bringing his "new friend," Samar. She couldn't tell from the name what gender Samar would turn out to be—the language so difficult. She had to write down the names of the Thai dishes to remember if she had already had them: *tom yum goong mae-nam* or *poo-nim thod ka-prao grob*.

Lorna, at the Pâtisserie Friandise, felt strangely happy. The successful delivery of Pomona. The family. Maybe there was something aphrodisiac about the aroma of bread, cookies, cake, but it was fun being there with Armand-Loup. Lorna had always liked men categorically, their large bodies and deep voices fascinated her, just as biology intended. She admired their intellects, their application to professions and skills, and the gullible but brave docility with which they accepted being sent to war. She admired philosophers. She had not had any really bad experiences with men, nothing she couldn't deal with.

Well, two failed relationships; but that was a reflection on her, she thought, on her judgment, not on an entire species. Did she like

Armand particularly or as a member of the larger category "husband"? She liked him particularly, especially when she was with him. Her reasons for leaving him seemed less urgent after them laughing a lot through a satisfying dinner of quiche, *ris de veau, salade,* and a good Bordeaux. She'd been silly and impulsive.

At the hospital that afternoon, Lorna had had another epiphany. It was to do with the way the nurses smiled at Armand. She suddenly saw that women could not resist smiling at him, no matter if he smiled back, though he usually did. Women smiled first! Was it his somewhat-cherubic, boyish face, even at this age rosy and dimpled like a cherub on a painted ceiling? Was it just some pheromone he exuded? She thought of the photographer woman showing him around San Francisco. She thought of some other episodes. Maybe it was not all his fault; he was, after all, just naturally amiable; it was his nature to oblige with the things women suggested for him.

It was at dinner at La Roulette last night that she had floated her idea: she'd decided not to go back to California, or rather only for a while from time to time, and to spend more time in Pont with him, and she hoped he would get their house back. They'd been so happy there. She watched in suspense for his reaction.

He wasn't surprised at her giving up California, as if he'd expected it all the time. "We were happy here, Lo. I don't imagine you there in San Francisco." He didn't mention a divorce-in-process. She finally asked whether he had actually filed the papers.

"I did, but I always hoped we would not need them. About renting out the house, though, I need the money, alas," he said. "My retirement pension doesn't cover keeping it, heating it—but maybe you will get some lecture fees." They lapsed into a familiar discussion of their shaky but possible finances, and what other measures they might take: bed-and-breakfast, scenic tours. Things they had never been able to agree on had come to seem like the start of an adventure.

"Well, but the Woodses!" Lorna had almost forgotten; her potential agent fees hadn't yet penetrated her sense of her situation, hadn't conferred the deep feeling of security they should.

"Voilà," said Armand-Loup. "*Dix* percent?"

"Armand, that'll be thousands right there. The last Woods I looked up, the asking price was a million five, that is, the starting price; it was at auction. I don't know what the final selling price was."

"*Formidable,*" Armand said.

"One picture sold would keep us very nicely for quite a while."

"*Toi et moi, comme avant.*"

"Yes," said Lorna.

"I had a great blow to my *amour-propre* today," he said after a bit. "I was chatting with one of the pretty nurses at the hospital, and as I stepped away, I heard her say to another girl, in English, 'He considers himself quite the swain.' She might as well have said, How ridiculous he is, that old fat guy."

Lorna understood that this confidence must indeed have cost him something, and also that it was meant to reassure her about the future. Armand was superior to most men in understanding himself, she thought. She laughed. "I find you very attractive," she said.

" 'Swain.' I looked it up, not a common English word, a little note of mockery in it."

"Yes," Lorna agreed.

53

In the hospital cafeteria, Julie and Carla, Amy and Ran, were having dinner. The *canard à l'orange* was excellent, for institutional food, also the *choux de Bruxelles*. For the holidays the hospital had found some kitschy American Santas for the tables and put a tree in one corner, with *"Mon Beau Sapin, Roi de Forêts"* and "Adeste Fideles" playing on a loop. Otherwise, it would have been easy to forget that it was the holidays.

"So, Julie, what are your plans?" Julie's grandfather Ran asked her, after they had talked over the astonishing events of the last two days. Julie had had a fearful sense, from the scrutiny her grandfather was giving her, that she was going to be drafted to look after Pomona, or even asked to claim her as her own child. Either she or Carla was to be the designated mother; it was obvious.

"I could have a job with this English member of Parliament, if I decide to do that. And I plan to finish my UC–Sciences Po course on urbanism in Paris, which doesn't finish until July," she answered.

"Does this give you your BA?" Ran asked.

"I'll have to do at least one more semester in Berkeley, maybe two," Julie said, "but I don't know if I want to do it right now. Wouldn't it be better to get the European experience now that I'm here?"

Carla apparently had the same fear for herself of being co-opted for Pomona's care and broke in, "I plan to stay, too. I'm moving in with Slobodin and I'll finish my French course." Since Slobodin, whoever that was, hadn't penetrated their consciousness, they were startled before remembering he was her companion from French class.

"Then I'll do accounting, which can't be much different in French. Account, *compte.* They have a business school in Fontainebleau directed to international practices. You're supposed to already have an MBA to be accepted, but Bodi has connections there and can fix it so that my experience at Mott and Company will count."

Amy and Ran gaped, stunned, unable to grasp the idea of losing Carla, who had never been absent if she was needed, especially when it was Gilda who needed her, for the last fifteen years. Ran saw the moral problem with asking any more of Carla, but he wasn't sure Amy did, and shook his head in warning when she started to plead.

Later, in her room back at the house in Pont-les-Puits, Julie was writing an email to Ian, the first in a few weeks. She had before her mind's eye a vivid image of naked Ian, looking like *Apollo Sauroktonos,* a favorite Praxiteles statue newly familiar from her visits to the Louvre. With a shiver of desire, she told herself some things are hard to give up—for instance making love with Ian—but at last she knew where her priorities were: finishing her degree, getting on in international relations. She wanted to stay in Europe. She was surprised that Carla did, too.

Dear Ian,

I thought you'd want to know that Gilda's baby arrived early but seems to be doing well. Weighed just under three pounds and there's some talk that because a common condition might develop that so far hasn't, they'll airlift her tomorrow to a bigger center in Lyon. She's in an incubator. She's called Pomona, like the California city, which seems odd to me, but who am I . . . ? Right now, she's in Valence, France, at the Centre Hospitalier de Valence, if you want to call. I should be back in Paris soon.

I probably won't be coming back to California for the spring semester as I have a temp job here and also want to finish my course that I'm taking here in the Berkeley extension, so it will count toward my degree. I don't know when the Motts plan to come home.

I think of you often and hope you will always be my friend.

Love,
Julie

Would he think that tone somewhat cold? She did wonder if he had met anyone new at Stanford, and if they were doing it, but she could hardly object. Her tears ran as she was writing, and by the end she was sobbing frankly and gave herself over to the sad beauty of life.

"Mother," said Ian on the telephone to Ursula. "Let me read you this." He read her Julie's email.

"You must go there immediately," Ursula said. "It would be unnatural not to do so. What if something goes wrong and you haven't seen the little thing, your own—what? What was it? Pomona?"

Ian reread Julie's letter for pronouns. "A girl named Pomona." He liked the name. He had a friend who went to Pomona College, in Claremont.

"Oh, God," said Ursula. "The darling. Would they send us a photo? I'll see to the plane tickets. You'll miss a week of classes but never mind that, this is a unique lifetime experience. Your child needs to see you, like a little duckling, needs to bond with you."

"I know," Ian said. "But where are they, actually? I know they're in Valence, France. We should probably fly to Lyon," looking at a map on his phone. "That's where they'll be."

54

Sometimes, though rarely, things sort themselves out.

Ran and Lorna were sitting in the waiting room on the pediatric floor of the Centre Hospitalier de Valence while Pomona was being readied for an airlift by helicopter to Lyon, where they had more specialized facilities in the case of complications common for very low-birth-weight babies. Amy had gone to the roof to help, and she was expecting to fly with the baby and Gilda. It struck Lorna all at once that it was funny—both funny ha-ha and funny peculiar—and she laughed out loud.

"What?" Ran asked.

"Well, the two of us here, in really a pretty godforsaken part of France, waiting for a helicopter. Three of us, counting Amy—both of your wives—and also our progeny; you're quite the patriarch. Things unforeseen."

"Four of us with Armand-Loup," Ran said.

"Certainly. Four of us. The new extended family. It feels good, France. It feels like home to me, I lived here a long time."

"What about San Francisco? You lived there a long time, too."

"I'm not sure I fit back in; but I do feel like I can say a couple of things to you."

"Shoot."

"Now you're going to go crazy about this baby—we all will—but really both Hams and Peggy need . . . you could do more for them. I would if only I could."

"I've talked to Hams. They're buying their house."

"Then Peggy. I don't know. Her life needs a jolt. She's liking Thailand."

"I know that, I'm paying for her trip, and I must say, she's living it up."

"Really? Good. How?"

"Luxury hotel and a lot of room service. And spa service. The hotel bills come directly to us."

"I hope she isn't taking advantage of you," Lorna said. They had certainly taught Peggy not to spend other people's money self-indulgently. Then they both laughed to think of puritan Peggy, who had sometimes as a child refused to have new shoes if she thought she didn't need them, now going mad with extravagance in Bangkok.

"I was thinking of you getting behind some business venture of hers, something to spring her out of Ukiah. Silk jackets—has she written you?"

"Not about jackets, but I suppose she will."

Lorna dared to ask another thing that was uppermost in her heart: "Is the baby going to make it?"

"Probably. Yes, certainly. French medicine is very sophisticated."

"What does the father of this wonder baby say? Who *is* the father?" Lorna wondered, changing the subject.

"Ursula Aymes's boy. I suppose he should know the baby is here. I don't know that he and Gilda are in touch. Gilda's mind is on Tacitus and Cicero."

"I can write Ursula," Lorna offered. "We're friendly. She'll be thrilled."

"Ursula is one more complication," Ran said. On his telephone a text message he had barely had time to absorb, from Ursula: "Arriving Lyon tomorrow, please instruct."

"Where is Pomona going to live?"

"Where do you think?" Ran said. "Did you see Amy look at the baby, her expression?" Lorna had seen Amy's gaze of love. Seeing this was a sensitive topic, Lorna suggested, "Shouldn't we go see them off on the helicopter?"

"No, I couldn't stand watching, I'm afraid of helicopters," Ran said. "I'd rather not. Amy knows. I'm taking the train to Lyon tomorrow— it's only forty-five minutes."

How unlike a man to admit a fear, Lorna thought.

Falling asleep alone that night in the Hôtel La Périchole, having heard that his loved ones were safe in Lyon, Ran nonetheless had the rowboat anxiety dream: He is in the rowboat, but now it's a motorboat, with just him, no, he and Amy and Gilda and now, um, Pomona. An immense ocean liner, looming like a huge white orca, has almost hit them. A collision is averted, but the liner has disabled them some way, swamped them, and disabled their motor. Ran and Amy wave desperately for help, but the liner pulls away, braying arrogantly from its huge steam stacks, and strands them helpless in the endless sea. Ran has to stand on tiptoe and hold the baby's basket high above his head to keep it out of the water, hold it till his arms ache. He has to hold it forever. He sees Lorna waving at him from the deck of the liner, but he cannot read her expression, whether gloating or friendly?

Acknowledgments

Thanks, as at other times, to John Beebe, Robert Gottlieb, Lynn Nesbit, Victoria Wilson, and the patient friends who read sections or all of a work in progress. And to my late husband, John Murray, who had lots of good suggestions and laughed in the right places; and to my friend the late Alison Lurie, who felt that the people were a bit too preoccupied with money. The mistakes are mine alone—in French, in geography, in obstetrical expertise, and more.